THE ANGELS OF HELLAS

THE
ANGELS
OF
HELLAS

by

CURTIS "T" CHRISTIAN IV

ISBN: 978-1-07954-698-9 (Paperback)
Library of Congress Control Number: 2019909585

Publisher's Cataloging-in-Publication Data

Names: Christian, Curtis T., IV., author.
Title: The Angels of Hellas / by Curtis "T" Christian IV.
Description: Richmond, KY: Curtis "T" Christian IV, 2019.
Identifiers: LCCN 2019909585 | ISBN 978-1-07954-698-9
Subjects: LCSH Extraterrestrial beings--Fiction. | Extinction (Biology)--Fiction. |
    Voyages and travels--Fiction. | Science fiction. | Adventure fiction. | BISAC
    FICTION / Science Fiction / Action & Adventure | FICTION / Science Fiction /
    Alien Contact | FICTION / Science Fiction / Time Travel
Classification: LCC PS3603.H74566 A64 2019 | DDC 813.6--dc23

Editing by Amanda S. Adams
Proofreading by Dana Kearns Miller
Cover design by Lisa M. Dove
Front cover illustration by Nick Kaloterakis (licensed permission)
Back cover background photo of Gasa Crater by:
        NASA / JPL / University of Arizona / USGS / Kevin M. Gill (by permission)

Printed and bound in the United States of America
First printing October 2019

Copies of this book are available through Amazon.com

I write this book for the love of God
and for the awe of God's cosmos.

When I look at Your heavens, the work of Your fingers,
the moon and the stars that You have established;
what are human beings that You are mindful of them,
mortals that You care for them?
Yet you have made them a little lower than God,
and crowned them with glory and honor.
— Psalm 8:3-5

I dedicate this book to my wife,
Wendy Lynn Campbell Christian:

She is my vision of the heavens; she is the hand of God in my life.
She is my moon and my stars; she is the light of God in my life.
Who am I that she is mindful of me?
Who am I that she cares for me?
Yet she has made me more than I am alone,
for she has crowned me with God's compassion and grace.

Thallerian:

Sanskrit:

नास्ति दियां ऋते प्रेमन् ।
नास्ति यिज्ञं ऋते दया ॥

Arabic:

لا يوجد حب بدون تعاطف.

لا يوجد تعاطف بدون تضحية.

Hebrew:

אין אהבה בלי חמלה.
אין חמלה ללא הקרבה.

Greek:

Οὐκ ἀγάπη ἐστὶ χωρὶς σπλάγχνου·
οὐ σπλάγχνον ἐστὶ χωρὶς θυσίας.

English:

There is no love without compassion;
There is no compassion without sacrifice.

—Thallerian Proverb

TABLE OF CONTENTS

ACKNOWLEDGEMENTS

Although I have written this book as a science fiction, it is foremost a human drama; and, thus it is inextricably a theological drama. Nonetheless, it is still a science fiction, and as such, I have tried diligently to keep the "science" in this science fiction. I am grateful to the scientists who graciously assisted me in making sure that my mathematical calculations are accurate and that my scientific assertions are sound. Specifically, I thank the following from Eastern Kentucky University: Mark A. Pitts, Ph.D., Senior Lecturer of Physics and Astronomy; and C. E. Laird, Ph.D., Emeritus Foundation Professor and Professor of Physics. For their help with the medical sciences, I express my sincere gratitude to William H. Mitchell, MD, FACS, Medical Director, University of Kentucky HealthCare, and to Linda Adams, BSN, RN, CCRN.

Because much of this science fiction relies appreciably on ancient religious manuscripts and their languages, am grateful for the counsel of two scholars of eastern religions: Dr. Aleix Ruiz-Falqués, Pali Lecturer, Head of the Department of Pali and Languages, Shan State Buddhist University, Phaya Phyu, Taunggyi, Myanmar; and Dr. J. Abraham Velez de Cea, Professor, Department of History, Philosophy, and Religious Studies, Eastern Kentucky University, Richmond, Kentucky.

I am also grateful to Captain Louis Johnson, civilian flight instructor, and Randel Gray, Colonel, US Army Retired, for their counsel on matters pertaining to aviation and aeronautics. Their guidance has helped to add a greater sense of realism to all flight narratives.

For advising me on military protocol and marksman tactics, I express my thanks to Gunnery Sergeant Michael Leaverton, USMC, and Corporal Bret Lawrenz, USMC.

With gratitude, I also acknowledge Madeline Lee for her help with information about broadcast news, and Ellen H. Mitchell for checking my French dialogue.

Of course, I am most grateful for the ideas and insights of Betty Walden, Elizabeth Baker, and Lisa M. Dove. Their coveted suggestions served to make my narrative a better story.

Indeed, Lisa Dove merits special appreciation; for, she brought her incredible talents to bear as she came up with an amazing cover design for this book. Were it possible to judge a book by its cover, her design alone would make the narrative on these pages a great story.

I would certainly be remiss if I forget here to acknowledge the specific game of chess that is played by the main characters (Catherine Hewst and Níyol Kiiswood) in chapter seventeen. This game, Paul Morphy versus Duke Karl II of Brunswick and Count Comte Isouard, is traditionally known to many chess players as the "Opera Game." It is so named because it was played in the Paris Opera on November 2, 1858.

THE ANGELS OF HELLAS

Chapter 1 – Inverness University

Inverness University, Cape Breton Island, Nova Scotia, Earth

(Geographic Co-ordinates: N 46.358, W 61.038)

Friday, 03 April 2420 CE

Time: 2235 Zulu

Good Friday would otherwise be a sacred, somber observance for Christians, as they commemorate the crucifixion of Jesus of Nazareth. But the solemn mood of this holy day was eclipsed by the jubilations of the long-awaited war's end. The Martian Alliance had surrendered five days ago; still the celebrations persisted throughout the worlds of the Terrestrial Assembly—Luna, Venus, Mercury, and of course Earth. Likewise, the celebrations persisted among the faculty, staff, and student body of Inverness University of Arts and Sciences.

But Dr. Francis Hewst, professor of astrobiology, was not in a mood to celebrate. Instead, he sat behind his desk in his office reading the story about the massacre of the innocents in the Bible. He was pondering his faith in God—pondering the nature and destiny of the universe and of humankind. Does the human race exist for some divine purpose? Is it worth saving for that purpose? Christian theology maintains that none are righteous enough to be saved, but that humankind is being saved nonetheless—for no reason other than divine love. Is that reason enough? Francis had been alive for many centuries, if indeed his artificial anatomy could be considered alive. And in all those years of living and exploring the sum of human wisdom, he had not discovered any satisfactory answers to such existential questions. But he had faith. He believed that humankind must exist for some grand purpose.

Whatever that purpose might be, Francis was well aware that his part in humanity's grand drama was now coming to an end. He knew what was soon to happen because he remembered what had already happened. His history was now his future, as well as the future of Nova Scotia and of the solar system.

1

"Good Lord, Frank," said Dr. Rachel Levinson, associate professor of chemistry. He looked up from his scriptures to see his colleague standing in the doorway of his office. "Why are you still here working?" She pointed toward the right side of her head—to the c-nex, a thin disc-shaped telecommunication device that she was wearing on her temple. "I've been trying to call you," she said.

"Hey, Rachel," he greeted. "I'm sorry about that. I usually remove my c-nex when I'm reading."

"It's Friday evening," she commented. "Classes have been cancelled all this week. You should be out celebrating, not sitting here working."

"I'm not working," he replied. "With most of the students away, I thought I'd take advantage of the calm for some meditation. After all, it is Good Friday."

"I'm sorry to interrupt," she apologized.

"Oh, that's okay." Francis smiled; he actually welcomed the distraction. "I'm glad you're here. Perhaps you can lend your thoughts to a moral quandary." He looked back at the open Bible on his desk. "Have you ever read the story about the massacre of the innocents?"

"We don't do much reading from the New Testament in synagogue," Rachel replied, "but I'm familiar with the story. King Herod feared that the infant Jesus threatened his reign as king of the Jews, so he ordered the execution of all the children born in Bethlehem."

"That's it," acknowledged Francis. "According to the story, Jesus escaped the massacre because an angel alerted his father in advance. But there's nothing in the story about any of the other fathers being warned to get out of Bethlehem." He paused, then asked, "Do you think that Jesus' father had a moral obligation to tell the others?"

Rachel thought about his question for a moment. "Perhaps he did tell the others but they didn't take him seriously." She asked rhetorically, "Would you believe someone who claims to be counselled by angels?"

"Perhaps not," he said with a somewhat cryptic grin.

Rachel was so preoccupied with her own exuberant spirit that she failed to notice her friend's apparent melancholy. "The municipal council is celebrating the Alliance's surrender with a big fireworks display out at Cape Breton Park. A few of us from the chemistry department are heading out there for the festivities. Why don't you come join us when you finish your meditations?"

Francis glanced out his office window to confirm that the sun had just set. Being mindful of his colleague's religious traditions, he asked, "Isn't it the seventh day of Passover?"

Rachel laughed. "I don't think God will mind a little revelry."

"I appreciate the invitation; I may catch up with you at the park," he replied politely, even though he knew that they would not be getting together later—or ever again.

"Later then," she said and left on her way.

Francis closed his Bible and turned his attention to the framed photograph on his desk, one of his daughter in her Defense Force uniform. His heart overflowed with love and pride. She was his purpose for the past twenty-three years, but soon she would be called upon to realize her life's purpose. His synthetic eyes would never again see her. He felt like tearing up; alas, he could not. His artificial anatomy simulated most biological functions of a normal human body, but crying was not among them.

Now that his part in this world was drawing to a close, he wanted to speak with his daughter one last time. So he opened the top left drawer of his desk, retrieved his c-nex from its charger, and placed it on his right temple. His c-nex was now ready to provide him access to various communication networks, data suites, and utility applications around the world. Using a process called *thought-actuation*, or interfacing with the specific neural patterns of the cerebral cortex, the device was designed to interact with users' thoughts and accomplish tasks on command.

In this case, Francis concentrated on calling the Defense Force Communications Station at Wharton Basin, Indian Ocean; within seconds, the c-nex was relaying a call directly through his auditory cortex. "Shore-to-Ship

Communications. This is Petty Officer Gail," said a voice heard only in Francis' temporal lobe.

"Yes, Petty Officer Gail, my name is Frank Hewst. I'm trying to contact my daughter about an urgent family matter. Her name is Lieutenant Commander Veronica Catherine Hewst. She's stationed aboard the TAS *Orion.*"

"I'll be glad to assist you, Mr. Hewst," said Gail. "For family-related issues, I'm required to contact your daughter through the chaplain's office aboard the *Orion.*"

"Thank you for your help." Francis continued, "My daughter *is* the chaplain aboard the *Orion.*"

"Aye, sir. Please stand by." Francis sat in silence for several minutes, contemplating what to say to his daughter. Upon returning, Gail asked, "Mr. Hewst, are you still on line?"

"Yes, I'm still here."

"The ship's communications officer is putting your call through momentarily. Be advised, all video feeds are in use, so this call will be audio only. And there's currently an eleven-second delay between Earth and the *Orion.* Expect a twenty-two-second response time. Stand by."

After another brief moment of silence, the voice of his daughter came on line. "Hello, dad, are you there?"

His heart filled with pure delight. "Cathy, dear." His voice wavered ever so slightly. "I know that I'm not calling during our regular comm-allocation, but I really needed to hear your voice again."

The twenty-two seconds that lapsed seemed much longer. "I love hearing your voice too, Dad. I can't wait to see you again, now that the war's over. Are you okay?"

"I don't have much time. I'm calling because I need to tell you something." He wanted to pause, but he knew that it would invite another long response time. So he immediately continued, "Your life has been my divine purpose and my sacred joy; your part in God's plan is just beginning and my part is now complete. It has been my joy and honor to be your father, but now my joy has been fulfilled. You must increase, and I must decrease."

After another long pause, his daughter replied, "Dad, I don't understand what you're telling me. Is something wrong?"

"I am so proud of you, Cathy, and I love you more than life itself." He added, "Please pray for all souls of Atlantic Canada." He knew that his words would leave his daughter bewildered, even dismayed. But he hoped that someday his commendations of love would be heard and remembered beyond his woeful tones.

Francis terminated his c-nex connection before the response time elapsed—before she could ask the questions that he would rather not answer.

The sun had well set and the sky grew steadily darker. As the stars emerged, one by one, he decided to enjoy the beauty of the nearly cloudless night, not through his office window but outside. So he removed his c-nex, returned it to its drawer, and for the last time, left his office building.

Francis strolled along the campus quadrangle, trying to catch a glimpse of the stars in between the sidewalk's lampposts. He found a bench that afforded him the best view of the moonless night away from the diffusing brightness of the campus lights. There he sat down and enjoyed the simple pleasures of the cool evening. He entertained himself by connecting the starry dots of the springtime constellations while listening to the chirps of the evening crickets. There he sat, and there he waited.

Suddenly, a sphere of resplendent light engulfed Francis. He realized that he was not alone; he found himself immersed within a presence—a consciousness—a soul. And this presence was thoroughly immersed within him. "This is a surprise," Francis said. "I wasn't expecting you. Are you here to keep me company at the end?"

"You have never been alone," answered the voiceless presence within and around him.

"I know," he conceded. "You've been so gracious to fashion a life for me in this time and place, and to give me all the visages of aging. And you've been a faithful and attentive friend. But I assumed that my part is concluded."

5

"Yes, it is. You have given humankind a choice. But now that your part is accomplished, I come to be with you in your moment of choice."

"Haven't I already made a choice, to live and die a mortal life? Haven't I sacrificed for the hope of the human race?"

"Yes, you have. And soon, to the worlds of this star, you will have lived and died a mortal life. But in this moment, you have a choice. You may return to the life from whence you came—from whence you will come. You may return to a life among the worlds of other stars—a life among other children of the One."

Francis realized that his unseen friend was offering him a chance to escape his mortal lot, a chance that he could have taken so many times before now, for he long knew what was about to happen. His friend was offering him a choice. "What do you think God would have me do?" Francis solicited.

"I do not presume to speak for the One," said the presence. "Your faith is yours; you, and you alone, must answer that question."

Francis spoke in a slightly slower tempo as he deliberated. "I just want to make the right choice."

His incorporeal companion responded in an inspiring tenor, "Choices are not about righteousness; choices are about sacrifice."

"It's an appealing option not to die," confessed Francis. "But my friends and colleagues here on Earth are about to suffer yet another ruin of human war. So, as attractive as it may be to serve my fellow siblings of other stars, I believe that my final vocation is here and now: to share the fate of those whom I have loved and whose burdens I've gladly borne. I've chosen to live like a human; I should also die like a human."

"You are human, Frank. Even after all your centuries, you still struggle to embrace your humanity."

"In all my centuries, that might be one of the most profound truths I've discovered. All human beings, in one way or another, struggle to embrace their humanity."

"Perhaps it is that struggle that makes one human," the presence mused.

"Of course, I probably have more of a reason to struggle than most." Francis elaborated, "I'm artificial."

"Your humanity is your communion with the One, Frank; it is your compassion *as* the One. Your humanity is not artificial."

"Thank you for being with me at the end, my friend."

"This is but one end. You are never alone."

Suddenly, the skies over Nova Scotia were on fire, and the night seared brighter than daylight. Dr. Francis Hewst, the bench on which he sat, the campus quadrangle, and the university itself were instantly obliterated, as were hundreds of thousands of human lives across Nova Scotia, New Brunswick, and Prince Edward Island.

Chapter 2 – The Academy

Terrestrial Assembly Defense Force Academy, Waimea, Hawaii, Earth

(Geographic Co-ordinates: N 19.998, W 155.671)

Friday, 16 November 2429 CE

Time: 1946 Zulu

The auditorium classroom was filled to its capacity. All thirty-five seats were occupied by sharply-uniformed midshipswains, students of the Terrestrial Assembly Defense Force Academy. While most of the midshipswains sat at attention, clearly captivated by the professor's lecture, three of them in the back of the room were visibly distracted, perhaps contemplating their weekend plans. Undeterred by these few inattentive students, Dr. Veronica Catherine Hewst, professor of religious studies, remained focused on her lecture for the day. At both the right and left of the lectern, a series of large, colorful holographic images cascaded before the midshipswains, illustrating elements of Hewst's lecture. She pulled up holographic displays of an ancient Greek manuscript and, beside it, an English translation. With a spydre—a thin, sensor-laced glove on her right hand—she manipulated the holographic projections with each subtle move of her wrist and fingers. She would have otherwise used her c-nex to access the projection system, but because all telecommunication devices were normally prohibited in the classroom during lectures, Hewst had to rely on her spydre.

"Now here is an image of an ancient manuscript from the New Testament, a text that Christians refer to as 'First John.'" Dr. Hewst directed the midshipswains' attention to the pertinent holograms as she lectured. "Contextual analysis suggests that a schism had occurred in the author's community, which prompted this anonymous author to call the schismatics liars and antichrists. Those who broke away from the community allegedly denied that Jesus existed as a flesh-and-blood human being. In effect, the author of First John was accusing these schismatics—these separatists—of adhering to Docetism. But the author gives us another clue as to who these so-called liars and antichrists were; he accuses them of not knowing God because they don't

8

love their fellow members of the religious community. So from the contextual evidence, most biblical scholars believe that these separatists were a group of ancient Christians whom we know today as Gnostics."

Anticipating questions, Hewst paused momentarily. As several midshipswains indicated that they had questions, she called on the one whom she believed was the first to raise a hand. "Yes, Cadet Mauer."

"Professor Hewst," asked Mauer, "what's Docetism?"

Hewst posted a new hologram displaying a pronunciation guide and detailed definition of the word. "*Docetism* is the doctrine that Jesus, the Messiah of Christianity, was not really a human being; he merely appeared to be human. Some ancient Christians adhered to this doctrine, believing that Jesus was a wholly divine, incorporeal spirit, and as a divine spirit, he couldn't possibly exist within the physical confines of a human body."

She called upon the next student, Cadet Fakhouri, who asked, "You said in an earlier lecture that the Marcionites didn't believe in Jesus' physical existence. Why do scholars claim that First John is referring to Gnostics and not Marcionites?"

"That's a good question," Hewst commented. She then pulled up a display of the word *Gnosticism.* "Both groups believed that spiritual reality was inherently good and that material reality was inherently evil; thus, the goodness of Jesus could not take on bodily form without becoming tainted by its evil. By accusing the separatists of not loving others, this author is implying that they didn't care for the physical welfare of others, just as they disavowed the physical reality of Jesus. But what distinguished the Gnostics from the Marcionites was their belief in salvation through divinely revealed knowledge. Because the author connects loving others with knowing God, he was probably disparaging a group of Gnostics by assaulting their pride in divine knowledge."

Dr. Hewst's response had addressed many of the questions that the remaining midshipswains would have asked; almost all of the hands came down. But one midshipswain, Cadet Toma, suddenly interjected, "Excuse me, Professor. That hologram of First John—is that an image of a real manuscript?"

Hewst grinned. "Yes, it is," she replied. "The manuscript is very real; I've personally seen it. It's a vellum text, part of a collection called *Codex Vaticanus*—so named because it's conserved in the Vatican Library in Rome."

"How old is it?" asked Toma.

"It dates back to the fourth century of the common era," Hewst answered, "so it's over two thousand years old."

Cadet Toma shook her head in astonishment. "I just think it's amazing that something written down two thousand years ago could still be around today," she remarked.

"Yes," Hewst acknowledged, "it does seem amazing." She digressed, "We tend to think that we have more advanced systems for storing data with our modern technology than our ancestors who wrote on parchment or carved in stone. I know that all of you here can remember that the Martian Alliance assailed a 'holy war' against the Terrestrial Assembly nine years ago. But none of us in this auditorium are old enough to remember the worlds-wide data-crash of 2395. I remember my father telling me about it, how Martian terrorists unleashed a data-virus that wiped out every quantum information suite in the solar system. So much data has been forever lost. Banking records; property records; birth, marriage, and death certificates; college transcripts; medical and DNA records—all lost. And yet, to this day, the coronations of ancient pharaohs are still preserved in four-thousand-year-old obelisks. So before we sing the praises of modern technology, we would do well to remember the resilience of an antiquated, stone-carved, Egyptian data system. Perhaps we shouldn't be so amazed that a two-thousand-year-old copy of First John would still be around today." Hewst then added, "Forgive me; I digress. Are there other questions?"

Cadet Proyce promptly asked, "Professor Hewst, is the author of First John saying that Christians are supposed to act in a loving manner?"

"Well, yes, I think that's obvious," she replied with a slight grin.

"So," Proyce continued, "if Christians instigate a war against others, then how do they remain sincere to their scriptures? How are they being faithful to their God?"

"I'm assuming that your question is more practical than hypothetical." With a wave of her spydre, Hewst turned off the projector and brightened the overhead lighting, a gesture that the midshipswains recognized as an invitation to engage in discussion. Even the students nodding off in the back perked up. "I'm assuming that you're referring to the Martian Alliance's holy war."

"Well, yes ma'am," acknowledged Proyce. "The Alliance called itself a Christian Commonwealth—a 'Christocracy'; they even renamed themselves 'the New Jerusalem,' right out of the New Testament. Then, claiming to be doing God's will, they attacked the Terrestrial Assembly and our allies, the Jovian Confederation, without provocation—killing billions of people. Hundreds of millions of their victims were even Christians. It seems to me that they're like the separatists described in First John. Maybe the Martians aren't Christians at all. Maybe they're liars and antichrists like the ancient Gnostics."

"No! They're most definitely Christians," Fakhouri interrupted. "History is filled with stories of devout believers committing massacres and other atrocities in the name of their religious ideology. Christianity is no different than any other religion; they're all fanatics. If you don't believe in God the way they do, at best, they brand you a heretic, a blasphemer, or an infidel; at worst, they persecute, torture, or kill you. I think belief in God is a form of collective insanity. It's a blight on society. I just pray someday humanity will evolve beyond this primitive superstition."

"Really?" asked Cadet Osei. "Who are you praying to?" The auditorium filled with laughter. Even Fakhouri found the question humorous.

"It's a figure of speech," he responded while grinning.

Osei then asked Fakhouri, "Well, if you don't believe in God, why are you taking a course in religion?"

"Because I'm a candidate for Defense Intelligence," Fakhouri answered proudly. "You can't defend the Assembly from the enemy unless you understand the enemy."

"Religion wasn't the enemy nine years ago," Mauer protested, "the Martian Alliance was. And trust me, they didn't represent the Christianity I practice. I believe that my faith in God has made me a better human being. My faith teaches me to love others just as Christ loved them."

"My religion teaches much the same," added Cadet Toma. "According to the Prophet Mohammad (peace be upon him), 'No one truly believes until one loves for brother what one loves for self.'"

"So which is it, Professor Hewst?" Proyce asked. "Is religion a good thing or a bad thing?"

"There's nothing inherently evil about religion that corrupts a human being," she answered, "and there's nothing intrinsically good about it that sanctifies. Both good and evil reside in the human soul—every human soul. Religion gives the human consciousness a means of transcendence, a way to exist in relationship to a consciousness beyond itself. Most religions acknowledge a transcendent consciousness—a god through whom we can stand outside ourselves to see the evil and the good within us—the evil that we might be tempted to do and the good we ought to do."

Osei asked Dr. Hewst, "Do you believe in God?" Most of the midshipswains seemed a little more attentive as she paused before answering.

"Yes, I do."

"Why?"

As she opened her mouth to begin forming an answer, the carillons started to chime, sounding the end of the period. The midshipswains all jumped suddenly to their feet and snapped to attention. Hewst charged them, "Finish reading chapter twenty-four for Monday. I'll be in my office this afternoon if any of you need to meet with me. You're dismissed."

As the midshipswains were making their way out of the auditorium, Hewst removed the spydre from her hand and put it away in a compartment under the lectern. Then, from that same compartment, she picked up her c-nex from its charger and affixed it on her temple. As the last midshipswain was exiting, Hewst heard one of them out in the passageway shout, "Officer on deck!"

"Carry on," an authoritative voice ordered. Hewst glanced up to see Captain Sigrid Ellström, commandant of Faculty and Academic Affairs, entering the auditorium. Ellström donned a crisply pressed, summer white service uniform (the uniform of the day) and held her cover (that is, her hat) in her left hand. This was most unusual, Hewst thought; she had never seen the

12

commandant making a personal visit to a faculty member in a classroom. "Dr. Hewst," said the captain.

"Yes, ma'am."

"The superintendent wants to see you in his office immediately," Ellström said politely, yet assertively.

"The superintendent? Why such urgency?"

The captain did not answer Hewst's question. "I've been ordered to escort you there directly, Doctor."

Hewst picked up her lecture notes, and together, she and Ellström exited the classroom and then the building. The two of them made their way smartly across the Yard (that is, what everyone called the campus of the Defense Academy). The mid-morning sun shone brightly, and the Yard was alive with activity: companies of midshipswains running in formation, several aero-fighters flying in formation overhead, even a couple of orbital long-shuttles in the distance practicing launching and landing. Hewst was a civilian, so her movements about the Yard usually did not warrant much of a response from the midshipswains. But now every midshipswain whom they passed snapped to attention as they saluted the captain. As they walked, Hewst checked for a message that the superintendent might have transmitted to her c-nex, but she found none.

A few minutes later, Hewst and Ellström entered Apperson Hall, the main administrative building on the Yard. After passing through at least three outer compartments, and passing several yeoswains, administrators, and line officers, all dressed in summer whites, they arrived just outside the superintendent's office. Lieutenant DePaul stood up from behind his desk and came to attention.

"As you were," ordered Ellström.

"Aye aye, ma'am. He's expecting you," said the lieutenant. He reached up, touched his c-nex, and said, "Excuse me, Admiral, the commandant is here." He paused. "Aye aye, sir." DePaul stepped from his desk and opened a large African mahogany door to the superintendent's office. The lieutenant signaled Ellström and Hewst to enter. "This way ma'am, Doctor."

The superintendent's office was spacious, generously decked with leather and teakwood furnishings and trimmed with polished brass. Its bulkheads were adorned with copious photographs framed in teakwood—photographs of spacefaring frigates, destroyers, heavy cruisers, and spacecraft carriers from the past few centuries.

"Admiral Trendle," said Ellström, "I have with me Dr. Hewst."

Behind the large desk at the far end of the office sat Vice Admiral Robertson Jonas Trendle, a well-groomed officer whose tall stature was obvious even while sitting in his leather chair. Standing at his right was Chief Petty Officer Liko Tian, the admiral's personal yeoswain, whom Hewst had met on two previous occasions. She could also see two people she did not know, but she knew immediately that they were government officials. Both courteously stood from their seats as she entered the office.

"Catherine, come in, come in," Trendle implored as he stepped out from behind his desk. "Thank you, Captain," he said, addressing Ellström, "that'll be all."

"Aye, sir." Captain Ellström returned to her office and her duties.

The admiral greeted Hewst with a handshake and signaled her to have a seat. The two officials took their seats in turn as Trendle sat against the front edge of his desk. "Would you like some coffee?" he inquired of Hewst.

"Yes, thank you—with a little amaretto, please."

Trendle nodded to his yeoswain, but the chief, having anticipated the admiral's direction, was presently handing Hewst her coffee. As she took a sip, Trendle said, "Catherine, I'm sorry for summoning you so abruptly, but our guests are in a pressing need of your professional skills. This is Captain Anna Petrenko from the Federal Aerospace Intelligence Agency and Dr. Michael Takahashi, director of the Bureau of Archives and Antiquities."

"Certainly," Hewst said with an accommodating tone. She took another sip of her coffee. "How can I help you?"

"Dr. Hewst, it's a sincere pleasure to meet you," said Takahashi. "My staff has reviewed some of your research and publications. They're quite impressed with your scholarship of religious paleography."

"Thank you very much."

"I'd like your opinion on something," Takahashi continued. On the coffee table before her, he placed a pegmatech (peg for short), which housed specific data from the bureau's library. Dr. Takahashi waved his index finger over the peg's biometric sensor to unlock the device and to activate a preset holographic projection. The image of an ancient manuscript hovered just above the peg. "What do you make of this?" he asked.

Hewst stared at the hovering image intently, then asked, "Can you enlarge it, please?"

Pinching his right thumb and index finger and pointing at the hologram, Takahashi drew his fingers apart, and the image expanded in size.

"Thank you." Hewst set her cup of coffee on the table as she studied the hologram for a moment. "Well, it's ancient Koine Greek, and it appears to be written on papyrus. Is this an image of an actual manuscript?"

"Yes, it is," he answered. "Currently, it's being analyzed in Geneva at the Federal Archives Library. Our research team tells me that it's excerpts from the Christian Bible, from either the Gospel of Matthew or the Gospel of Luke."

Hewst was excited by this information and focused her attention on the holographic image with even more scrutiny. After a closer examination, the expression on her face changed from amusing curiosity to mild shock. She pensively inquired, "What date have you assigned to this manuscript?"

Takahashi's team of researchers had indeed dated the manuscript, but he was curious to test Hewst's scholarship. "You're the expert; you tell me."

Hewst pointed to the text in the hologram. "The orthographic style looks like first or second century of the Common Era, and the Greek syntax suggests this date as well." Hewst's eyes were keenly fixed on the hologram. "And, it may not be from the gospels either. The Gospels of Matthew and Luke are both narrative documents, but note that there's no narrative in this manuscript. It's a collection of Jesus' sayings—sayings that just happen to appear in the gospels. You're presuming that these are excerpts. But what if it's a copy of an independent document—a document that predates Matthew and Luke—a source document that the two employed to compose their

15

gospels?" She looked at Dr. Takahashi and said optimistically, "This might be a copy of the Q document."

"The what?"

"It's a hypothetical document that most scholars believe was a source for those two gospels. There's no surviving copy of such a source, but its existence was first proposed in the nineteenth century CE by German scholars, who called it *Quelle*, meaning 'source'—*Q* for short." Hewst turned her focus back to the hologram. "If this is indeed a copy of *Q*, and not a clever forgery, then I can't overstate the significance of this discovery."

"And why would you suspect a forgery?" he asked.

"It looks to be in immaculate condition," she observed. "Have you carbon-dated it?"

"We ran a radiocarbon analysis of the papyrus, and we date it to about the first century of the Common Era." Takahashi then asked, "Is its unusually pristine condition the only reason you suspect a forgery?"

His question made Hewst more suspicious. "Why do you ask?"

Takahashi pointed again at the hologram and made a circular motion with his index finger. The hologram flipped along its upright axis, revealing a mirror image of the previous projection. "What you were examining before was an inverted image of the manuscript. This is what it actually looks like." He continued, "Have you ever seen anything like this?"

Hewst sat silent for a moment as she tried to process this revelation. "I can say emphatically that I've never seen anything like this in a first-century manuscript. Where did you find this?"

Takahashi looked to Captain Petrenko as though he were seeking her permission to answer. "I'm sorry, Dr. Hewst," said Petrenko, "that information's classified, and I can't discuss it in this setting. But your security clearance will be concomitant with your recommission, so you should receive an extensive briefing while you're underway."

A sober silence suddenly displaced the conversation.

"Wait. While I'm what?" asked Hewst.

Petrenko was about to explain, but Trendle interrupted, "Captain, let me have a word with Dr. Hewst—privately?"

Realizing that Trendle intended to apply some diplomacy to a potentially stressful situation, Petrenko gave an affirmative nod. "Chief Tian," the admiral ordered, "please escort our guests to the anteroom and see to their requisites."

"Aye aye, sir," acknowledged the chief petty officer. Dr. Takahashi picked up his peg and turned it off. Chief Tian ushered the two officials from the admiral's office and closed the door, leaving Hewst and Trendle to their conversation.

Hewst's comportment betrayed both confusion and frustration. "What in heaven's name is going on here, Rob?" she asked. "What does she mean, 'while I'm underway'?"

Trendle took a seat in an adjacent chair and confessed, "Catherine, I honestly don't know why FAIA is interested in you."

"How's that possible? You're the superintendent of the Defense Academy. You must know what FAIA wants with one of your own faculty members."

"How long have we known each other?"

She thought for a moment. "Eleven years, give or take. Ever since we served together during the Martian War, when you commanded the TAS *Denali*."

"Eleven years." In a rare moment of sentiment, Trendle continued, "In that time, we've been through more together than most others would ever experience in ten lifetimes. I remember when the hull integrity was compromised during the attack at Vesta. The ship was dead in space, adrift in the asteroid belt—no communications, very little life support, almost no rations, and hardly any potable water that wasn't frozen. I lost nearly a third of my crew instantly from explosive decompression in the forward compartments. I lost another third much more slowly over the next twelve days. I watched as one crew member after another succumbed to their injuries, and I couldn't do a damned thing to save them. I never felt so helpless. With each death, my soul was rent asunder with grief; yet, with each death, I was also surreptitiously

17

grateful—grateful for having a little more air to breathe. Everyone was losing hope of being rescued. Hell, I seriously thought we'd lose all hands; I just wouldn't admit it to the crew. But then, there you were: Lieutenant Hewst, chaplain of the *Denali*, just three months out of officer training. I felt sorry for you, so naïve with your sanguine attitude and your tenacious faith. You were so certain that God would deliver a miracle, and I was so certain that our plight would surely crush your spirit. But, you surprised me. Your faith never faltered, and you never stopped praying. At mortal risk, you single-handedly pulled three wounded crewswains from a breaching compartment. You became a symbol of hope for an otherwise terrified crew; you held up their spirits long enough for the *Elysium* to find and rescue us. You made the crew believe in a miracle."

"So you believe that our rescue was an act of God?" Hewst asked.

"No, I believe *you* were an act of God." Trendle confided, "I was fortunate to have you as my chaplain. And after the war, when you left military service for the civilian world, I was fortunate to have you as my friend. When I became superintendent and the academy needed a new professor of religious studies, I regarded it as providence that you were available and that you came on board. When your father died, I grieved with you. When you renounced your ecclesiastical ordination, I grieved for you. I actually prayed for you. It was a strained and awkward prayer; you know I'm not the praying type. It certainly wasn't eloquent, not like your prayers."

"Rob, I don't pray anymore. God and I aren't on speaking-terms."

"You know that I've never been a very religious person, Catherine, so I'm certainly not one to judge. But since you lost God, since you lost your faith, you lost something of yourself."

"Oh, I still believe in God. Let's just say that we're not really friends anymore."

"Be that as it may, *I'm* your friend. And as your friend, I'll always be up-front with you. I don't know what Aerospace Intelligence wants with you. I received orders from the defense minister to relieve you indefinitely of your academic responsibilities with immediate effect. The orders came early this morning, just an hour and a half before Captain Petrenko arrived. I called a couple of my contacts on the Defense Committee of the Upper Legislature, but they weren't very forthcoming. The only thing they'd tell me is that the government has need of your talents off-world. I reminded them that you were no longer clergy, so you would no longer be eligible for defense chaplaincy, but apparently they want you for your scholarship and your military experience, not your spiritual ministrations."

"Well, I'm a civilian now. The Defense Ministry might be able to terminate my teaching contract with the academy, but it doesn't have the authority to dispatch me anywhere."

"I'm afraid they can. Check your military discharge agreement. If the government deems you critical to federal security, it can reinstate your military commission."

"What are you saying, that I'm being press-ganged into service?"

"That's an indelicate way to put it. But, yes, you're effectively being drafted." Although well-intentioned, Trendle made a vain attempt at consolation. "I was able to secure a promotion co-requisite with your recommission. You were a lieutenant commander when you were discharged, but you're being reinstated as a full commander."

She raised a few other points of protest, but these were more affective grievances than reasoned objections. The two then sat in silence for a moment as she eventually settled into her circumstances. "'Off-world,'" Hewst said with some antipathy. "Why can't the Assembly need my talents somewhere 'on-world'? Somewhere more scenic, like the Champs-Élysées?"

Chapter 3 – The Whitaker Institute

The Whitaker Institute, Polis La Hire, Mare Imbrium, Luna (The Moon)

(Selenographic Co-ordinates: N 27.792, W 25.514)

Monday, 19 November 2429 CE

Time: 1019 Zulu

Earnan M. Cobisson awoke. He could hear the voices of several people in the room, but the conversations were indistinct. He opened his eyes to discover himself lying on his back and staring into bright ceiling lights. Despite their intensity, he was able to focus quite effortlessly and without any discomfort; his vision was remarkably sharp and clear. His mouth seemed dry, yet he didn't feel thirsty, nor did he sense a real need to moisten his lips or tongue with saliva. Perhaps he was still recovering from the effects of the anesthesia, he thought.

Cobisson could see three people in the examination cleanroom, all wearing white scrubs, gloves, head-covers, and masks. With meticulous scrutiny and cautious enthusiasm, they analyzed the incoming data on monitors around the room. Two of them soon stood over him and hovered close to his face, while the laboratory technician continued to monitor the telemetry. Dr. Desta Negasi, a quantum neuro-engineer, illuminated Cobisson's eyes with a rather low-tech halogen penlight, while Dr. Sarito Madina, a neuro-cartographer, carefully studied Cobisson's pupil constriction.

"Look at that," Negasi said with some excitement, "pupillary light reflex is excellent—perfect myosis simulation."

"Yes, it is," Madina confirmed. "But that's just a simple photo-sensory reaction. I'm more concerned about the signal decohesion between the wetwear neurons. Did you notice the telemetry? The signal strength is abating in a matter of pico-seconds?"

"True," answered Negasi. "But the input strength doesn't have to hold forever, just long enough to reach threshold potential. The neural network is quantum-entangled—we engineered it that way—so the action potential is instantaneous." He set his penlight on an adjacent instrument tray and then activated his c-nex. By thought-actuation, he turned on the holographic projection system. A small, spherical green light was suddenly hovering about 35 centimeters above Cobisson's face. "Follow the light with your eyes only," Negasi instructed Cobisson. "Don't move your head." The ball of light began to jump randomly about—to and fro, back and forth, up and down. Cobisson easily tracked its dance while Negasi watched for symmetry and synchronicity of eye movement. "Excellent," he assessed with approval. "Excellent!"

Cobisson found their curiosity a bit excessive, even a little unsettling. The neurocartography scan was supposedly a noninvasive and safe procedure. Dr. Madina had assured him that the scan would produce a neural template, with no detrimental effects, from which a number of artificial neural networks would be replicated. Nonetheless, their meticulous attention to his welfare began to trouble Cobisson. "Is everything alright?" he asked. As he spoke, his voice sounded strange to his ears. "Did the procedure go well?"

Captivated by Cobisson's ability to articulate questions, Madina observed, "Remarkable!" with an almost giddy laugh. "Interrogative heuristics! Simply remarkable!"

Dr. Madina's response did nothing to settle Cobisson's concerns. In frustration, he pleaded, "Desta, please tell me what's going on."

The two stood momentarily speechless. Negasi broke the silence when he asked, "Do you know who we are?"

"Well, of course I do," replied Cobisson. "You're Desta Negasi, and this is Sarito Madina." While trying to point to her, he said, "And the lab tech over there, that's Madison Georgie." At that moment, he realized that he could not raise his hand; he was bound to the bed by his wrists and ankles. He lifted his head to examine his restraints and discovered that he was wearing a black, form-fitting bodysuit, not the hospital frock he had on before the procedure. Cobisson then noticed that he was not lying in a hospital bed but on a neurotelemetry platform, a scanning platform used for monitoring the activity of artificial neural networks.

A new person suddenly entered the cleanroom—someone who had apparently donned his scrubs rather hastily. Although a mask concealed most of his face, Cobisson recognized him as soon as he stepped into view. He knew those eyes—the same eyes he saw staring back at him every time he looked into a mirror.

"Desta, we've got a big problem!" the newcomer announced.

Cobisson was seized by horror at what he was seeing. He shouted, "What the . . . !" Dr. Negasi signaled to Georgie to shut down power to the artificial neural net, and Cobisson lapsed into unconsciousness.

"Yes, it seems we do," acknowledged Madina. "We may have replicated your neural template a little too precisely. It apparently believes it's you."

"It's a machine. It's not capable of believing anything," replied Earnan Cobisson—the human Cobisson. This was the Cobisson whose own cerebral cortex had been scanned earlier, whose own neural network had been meticulously retraced and uploaded to the meta-droid strapped to the platform. "But the android's programing is not the problem."

Before Cobisson could utter another word, Negasi's c-nex began to signal an incoming call from the director of the institute. He answered the call, and the c-nex, in typical fashion, accessed his auditory cortex. "This is Negasi," he answered.

"Desta," said the voice of Dr. Daphne Stathos, the director of the Whitaker Institute. "Shut down whatever you and Sarito are working on at the moment. I need you and Earnan to meet me in Conference Room Four immediately."

"But we're right in the middle of a critical boot-up!" protested Negasi. "What the hell is so important that you want us to shut down?"

"I understand your frustration, but I can't discuss it in an unsecured transmission. Just shut it down right now."

"It took us three and a half hours to prep for this initial boot-up of the network."

Negasi then heard three beeps abruptly interrupting the call, followed by the anonymous voice of a government official. "All incoming and outgoing calls on this wave are currently being monitored for matters of federal security. This transmission is terminated."

With an Amharic expletive, Negasi cursed, "*Merigeml!*" He broke protocol by pulling off his head-cover and mask before he had fully exited the cleanroom. Cobisson followed him into the adjacent prep room. There, Negasi discovered what Cobisson was trying to tell him; the prep room was congested with several cybernetics techswains suiting up in cleanroom garb over their military uniforms. Negasi and Cobisson were met by two masters-at-arms MAs), armed security personnel who were under orders to take them to the conference room. Of course, Negasi had no intention of going anywhere but Conference Room Four; he was so irate at what was an obvious militarizing of his beloved research endeavor that he was ready to vent his indignation to the institute's director. He threw his head-cover and mask at the MAs' feet and stormed out of the room and down the corridor. Cobisson and the MAs followed close behind, exerting some effort to keep Negasi's pace. Sensing their approach, the conference room door slid open. Negasi and Cobisson entered, while the MAs assumed posts in the corridor.

Conference Room Four was the largest and most handsomely furnished of the institute's conference rooms, and the only one with a large oriel—a window that afforded a spectacular, southern view of the desolate plain of the Sea of Rains. The desert-like vista was painted with a lifeless, yet stunning palette of gray regolith and black firmament. The room's ceiling lights seemed redundant as bright sunlight angled into the room from the western lunar sky. The citizens of Polis La Hire were seldom afforded such a view of the surrounding lunar landscape; much of the city was subterranean, or, more accurately, sub-lunar. The surface of the moon was indeed an infrequent sight for Negasi and Cobisson, but they clearly had no interest in admiring the beautiful scenery.

"I hope to hell you have a good reason for shutting us down!" Negasi shouted at Dr. Stathos, who sat on the opposite side of the conference table. He gave her no chance to respond as he noticed the three Terrestrial Assembly officers, uniformed in their service dress blues, seated next to her, and immediately asked, "Are you responsible for this? Are those your minions suiting up down the hall?"

The senior officer stood and courteously extended his right hand. "Dr. Negasi, my name is Lieutenant Commander Stefán Riddari. I've heard much about you. Your reputation is legendary." Negasi did not meet him with the same courtesy; rather, he stood with his fists firmly planted on the conference table and his ire firmly focused on the lieutenant commander. "Apparently, the legend is true," Riddari continued. "Please, gentlemen, have a seat."

Cobisson took a seat, while Negasi remained defiant. But after a moment of very tense silence, he acquiesced; he too sat down. "Commander, we've been working on this project for seven years," Negasi said with resounding indignation. "All of the test results so far indicate that we've accomplished something cutting-edge in android technology. And now you come in here, flexing your military muscles, disrupting our work right as we're about to confirm our breakthrough."

"Cutting-edge?" Riddari probed. "Tech companies have been building androids for generations. What makes your work so cutting-edge?"

"For centuries, humankind has been able to manufacture androids that are virtual humanoids—almost indistinguishable from human beings physiologically. During that time, android animatronics has improved, making android movements kinesiologically flawless. Artificial Intelligence has evolved to mimic inductive reasoning and cognitive aptitude. Android and human 'intelligences' are now clinically identical. As of late, the only obvious distinction between androids and humans has been sentience; androids simply lacked the ability to display psycho-social intuition when interacting with human beings. In effect, androids haven't yet been able to simulate empathy or self-awareness—until now."

"Until now?" Riddari asked dubiously. "Are you saying that what you're building here are self-conscious androids?"

"Of course not," Cobisson interjected. "Androids are just machines; they're just high-tech marionettes without the strings. They're no more self-aware than an antique grandfather clock. What Dr. Negasi is saying is that android technology has never been able to *simulate* self-awareness, until now.

Dr. Negasi's proprietary work is so innovative—he's pioneering what's arguably the next generation of androids. That meta-droid down the hall will not only mimic a human being, it will mimic *personhood*. It's one of 125 proprietary meta-droids that the Whitaker Institute is producing. Each meta-droid is programmed with its own particular personality and scientific specialty."

"I'm sorry, you are . . . ?" inquired Riddari.

Dr. Stathos made the introduction. "This is Dr. Earnan Cobisson, professor of astrobiology at the University of Aristarchus. He's the network donor. It's his cerebral patterns that were uploaded to the meta-droid of interest."

"Ah, Dr. Cobisson," acknowledged Riddari, having recognized the name. "You are, in part, the reason my team is here."

There was a sudden pause in the conversation as expressions of bewilderment settled upon both Negasi and Cobisson. Negasi broke the silence, asking, "So if you're here for Dr. Cobisson, why are your techs down the hall prepping to take one of our meta-droids?"

Flaunting a somewhat pompous grin, Riddari answered, "Be assured, we're not here to 'militarize' your project. The Ministry of Defense already has its fair share of government contracts with other tech companies; we have an ample store of weaponized androids. Candidly speaking, empathy and self-awareness would most likely impede weapon effectiveness, so we have no military interest in your meta-droid." He continued, "No, I'm a Defense Force liaison to the Federal Aerospace Intelligence Agency, and I'm here to borrow your android."

Dr. Negasi sarcastically snickered. "I don't see how 'borrowing' isn't the same as 'taking' my work."

"Aerospace Intelligence isn't interested in personified mechanisms, Dr. Negasi. But it is interested in an android astrobiologist that can operate in hazardous environmental conditions—an android programmed with the scientific knowledge of Dr. Cobisson's caliber. We want to take your android for a couple of months of survey deployment. We'll set up a mobile lab so that you and your team can continue your proprietary work 'on the road,' so to speak."

"On the road?" Negasi asked. "Where?"

"Hellas Planitia."

"Hellas Planitia? On Mars?"

"None other."

"Oh, hell no!" protested Negasi. "Those Martian fanatics seceded from the Terrestrial Assembly and then murdered billions in their holy war! There's no way in hell you're taking one of my meta-droids within a million kilometers of Mars, and I'm most certainly not sending my team anywhere near those religious zealots!"

"I would remind you that we won the war; the Martian Alliance surrendered nine years ago. You and your team are most welcome to accompany your android, but your company is not required. Frankly, neither is your consent," Riddari stated bluntly.

Just as bluntly, Negasi responded, "The work we do here at the Whitaker Institute is science, not surveillance. Currently, we have seven government contracts with the Federal Space Administration, one of which is for one hundred twenty-five meta-droids for a classified project. We have no contract with FAIA, Defense Intelligence, or any other government reconnaissance group. So as I see it, Commander, we're not obligated to you, and your rank affords you no authority here."

While Negasi was speaking, the officer seated at Riddari's right reached into her portfolio, produced a writ, and handed it to Negasi. Referring to the officer, Riddari said, "Lieutenant Lavelle is with the Judge Advocate General's Corps. What she's just given to you is a hard copy of a court order issued by the Terrestrial Assembly High Court, signed by Chief Justice Rylan DeLenzi. In effect, it empowers FAIA to assume custody of any and all government contracts with the Whitaker Institute. Director Stathos has already received a copy, and, if you'd like, I can send a digital copy to your d-board account or to your c-nex." Riddari continued in a slightly softer voice, "*This* affords me authority here."

Negasi looked at Dr. Stathos and asked, "Daphne, you're the director. What do you have to say about this?"

Stathos answered unequivocally, "As long as government contracts pay our bills, we go when and where the Assembly says we go."

Lieutenant Commander Riddari stood up, which prompted everyone else at the conference table to stand as well. He said, "Excuse me, Doctors. We have much to do before we deploy." As he and his officers were departing the conference room, he turned to Negasi and said, "I'm not your enemy, Doctor. Some matters simply take precedence." Then, with his politest tone yet, he added, "We have our own team of specialists, but I would prefer your expertise. I do hope you and your team will reconsider. The long-shuttle launches in twenty-two hours, at Launch Bay Six."

Presently, all but Negasi and Cobisson departed from the conference room to address their own pressing affairs. The two were quietly contemplating their options as they stood gazing through the oriel at a brilliant blue, first-quarter Earth hanging over the beautiful but lifeless contours of the lunarscape.

"Well, I've never been to Mars, and I have no inclination to go, but I just can't stand the idea of some unversed 'specialists' fumbling over our handiwork," Negasi commented. "I guess I can endure a two-month excursion. Besides, we always knew we'd have to field-test the meta-droids anyway. Maybe there's a silver lining to this cloud after all." He continued, "If we're leaving tomorrow, I need to assemble a team fast. I sure could use you on the team; as the network donor, you're best suited to evaluate the meta-droid's scientific proficiency. Can I count you in?"

"Sure, I'll go," Cobisson affirmed. "I did my graduate fieldwork there, analyzing Martian microbes in the Pavonis lava tubes. Of course, that was twenty years ago, when Mars was still a member-world of the Terrestrial Assembly."

"Now I've got to break the news to my family," Negasi asserted. Just as the words left his mouth, he wished he could take them back. He suddenly remembered that Cobisson no longer had a family of his own to consult; his wife and daughter had been killed ten years earlier during a Martian strafe on Polis Aristarchus. "Oh, Earnan, I'm sorry," he apologized. "I wasn't thinking."

Cobisson acknowledged Negasi's contrition with a strained smile.

Minutes after leaving Negasi and Cobisson to their deliberations in the conference room, Lieutenant Commander Riddari and Director Stathos made their way to the institute's administrative wing and inconspicuously stepped into the director's office to confer privately.

"So, Doctor," Riddari asked, "you're confident that Negasi will accompany me and my project team to Mars?"

"I know Desta," Stathos answered. "These meta-droids are his life's work; they're his obsession. He won't tolerate his work in someone else's hands. He'll probably be camped out tonight at Launch Bay Six just to make sure you don't leave without him."

Riddari laughed at her hyperbole. "He'll be a valued asset to our project team, but I regret that we're depriving the Whitaker Institute of its top engineer for the next few months."

"Truth be told, Aerospace Intelligence is doing me a favor," she confided. "The Federal Space Administration has just expedited Project Columba Noachi; they want us to deliver the other one hundred twenty-four meta-droids to the Jovian Confederation in three days. You saw how Negasi reacted when you appropriated just one of his creations. Imagine his tirade if he would be here when the rest of them are shipped out." Dr. Stathos then added, "Remember, when your project team is finished with the meta-droid, you're directed to deliver it to Titan. The Space Administration will want the full set."

Chapter 4 – TAS *Tereshkova*

Terrestrial Assembly Ship *Tereshkova*, on Trans-Venus Trajectory (TVT)

(Heliocentric Co-ordinates: *l* 098.42742, *b* +1.0647, *r* 115,280,119 km)

Tuesday, 20 November 2429 CE

Time: 0819 Lima

The space-faring TAS *Tereshkova* was en route to VOP-Echo (Venus Orbital Platform Echo). The ship had been underway for a little more than three days and was now less than four hours away from entering an equatorial, retrograde orbit around Venus. In preparation for its orbital insertion, the 328-meter-long frigate was decelerating from the expeditious velocity that had brought its crew to the second planet from the sun. The braking force would have made moving about the ship problematic were it not for the *Tereshkova*'s internal artificial gravity, which dampened the effects of deceleration.

As with all Defense Force vessels, the on-board spaces of the *Tereshkova* were a testament to compartment efficiency. Its passageways, bulkheads, ladderwells, and decks were designed to accommodate foot traffic at Terran-normal gravity, but they were also equipped with handrails and footholds to expedite zero-gravity passage. Throughout the ship were transposable decks and bulkheads, doors and hatches, and periodically stationed ladderwells that were canted at irregular angles. When the artificial gravity was disengaged and the *Tereshkova* was moored at any VOP, these ladderwells became indispensable to the crew's mobility about the ship.

Aboard, Catherine Hewst had donned a navy-blue unitard imprinted with the ship's nomenclature—the same standard-issue workout gear being worn by everyone exercising in the ship's gym. She was running on one of the treadmills and watching the holographic readout in front of her, which displayed her running speed, heart rate, blood pressure, caloric expenditure, and other vital signs. Hewst was trying vigorously to keep stride with the three sorteers who were sharing their physical training session with her and who were easily out-pacing her. As the Defense Force's special warfare operators, all of the sorteers were extraordinarily fit. Hewst's own PT regimen—running every morning with the cadets at the Defense Academy—scarcely helped her keep up with such adeptly trained, elite combatants. Still, two of these three sorteers seemed inconceivably, perhaps even inhumanly, fit. She could not help but notice the holographic readouts for Special Warfare Operators Second Class Ishanvi Sudha and Chief Níyol Kiiswood. She had never before seen anyone sprint so effortlessly as these two.

"Hey Chief," said Lieutenant Temen Jalloh, who was running on an adjacent treadmill, "I think the chaplain's improved in the past few days. Scuttlebutt has it that the CO brought her aboard to take your place on the team. You better watch your six." Chief Kiiswood and Petty Officer Sudha laughed; Hewst also found the lieutenant's comment amusing. There was no rank or staff insignia on her workout gear. Apparently, Jalloh had earlier noticed the Latin cross embossed on the sleeves of Hewst's service dress blues, the uniform that she had been wearing since coming aboard. She thought about correcting the lieutenant's error and letting him know that she was no longer serving as a chaplain, but she opted to let his honest mistake stand.

Kiiswood understood that the lieutenant was joking, but he also took the joke as a challenge to step up the intensity of his workout. "What do you say, Commander?" Kiiswood asked Hewst. "Shall we kick it up a notch?"

Hewst assumed that she would be unable to keep up with him, but she was curious to see how well she might endure the next level. With a brave smile on her face and a feigned confidence in her voice, she replied, "Bring it on, Chief." She then braced herself for an increased speed on her treadmill.

Moving his finger across the holographic control panel of his treadmill, Chief Kiiswood augmented the PT session, but not as Hewst had expected. The speed of all the treadmills remained steady, but everyone in the gym quickly grew about one-third heavier. He had boosted the artificial gravity in the ship's gym to 1.35g. Hewst pushed herself, maintaining her competitive posture for several minutes, but she realized that she might injure herself if she did not soon yield. So she slowed down and then stepped from her treadmill.

"You did yourself proud, ma'am," said Sudha as she kept her pace.

"Thank you." Dabbing the perspiration from her brow with a towel, Hewst smiled and said, "I guess you get to keep your job, Chief."

Kiiswood laughed while continuing to run. "Hey, Sudha," he dared, "let's you and me bolt to the finish." Jalloh maintained his vigorous pace, but Kiiswood and Sudha suddenly sprinted on their treadmills. It was a sprint unlike anything Hewst had ever seen—unlike anything human. Their holographic readouts abruptly displayed nothing but the word CLASSIFIED.

"I see Kiiswood has been playing with the gym's gravity again," observed Ensign Corneau with a slight tenor of annoyance in his voice. He entered the gym through the g-duct, a compartment that conjoins two areas of disparate gravities, allowing a person to adjust to changes in the g-force's direction and strength. Dressed in his crisply pressed khaki uniform, he was obviously not outfitted for working out. "I'm looking for Commander Hewst."

"I'm Commander Hewst," she said as she slung the towel onto her shoulder and walked to the doorway of the g-duct where the ensign stood. "What can I do for you, Ensign?" she asked him as he stood watching Kiiswood and Sudha. He was watching them not so much with amazement, but with some reproach.

"Oh, excuse me, ma'am," Corneau answered. Her question seemingly interrupted his preoccupation with the two sorteers. "I'm Ensign Henri Corneau, the ship's intelligence officer. Ops just received notice; your security clearance came through. The CO has ordered a mission briefing for you."

"Finally. Perhaps now someone will explain to me why I'm here. When is the briefing?"

"0900 Lima, ma'am."

[The standard military designator for Co-ordinated Universal Time was Zulu. But Lima was a special designator for a ship's chronometry, used only while underway at relativistic speeds. Upon arrival at its destination, the ship's chronometers were usually reset to Zulu time.]

Hewst checked the time through her c-nex. "That's just twenty-five minutes from now."

"Aye, ma'am," replied Corneau as his attention returned to Kiiswood and Sudha, who were concluding their workout.

Hewst also looked back at the two sorteers as they stepped away from their treadmills. "I know the sorteers are an elite tactical force, but I've never seen anything like those two. I wouldn't have thought human beings could move the way they do."

"That's because they're not exactly what you'd call human." Corneau glanced back at Hewst's puzzled expression. "You really don't know what they are, ma'am?"

She asked, "They can't be androids, can they?"

"No, ma'am," he answered. "Kiiswood and Sudha are stratogens."

"I heard rumors that the Terrestrial Assembly used genetically engineered ground-troops in the Martian War," she commented, "but that's all I thought they were—rumors."

"Well, it's true. There's no reason you can't know about it now that you have clearance. Besides, the Defense Force discontinued the stratogenics project after the war. The government took a little over two hundred volunteers and turned them into genetically modified soldiers; only three were lost in combat during the war. Apparently, it was a very successful science project. A few of them, like these two, are still in service. Now they're assigned to sorteer teams and are occasionally deployed to take out radical Christian terrorists whenever they try to re-ignite their 'holy war.'"

"Where are the rest of them?" Hewst asked. "I haven't heard anything about stratogens being transitioned back into civilian life."

"That's because they've never been discharged from military duty," Corneau admitted. "Trust me, Commander, you wouldn't want this lot set loose on society. Their genetic enhancements might have made them efficient weapons, but it also made most of them highly aggressive, prone to violent outbursts, even sociopathic."

"So where are they now?"

"Most of them are sequestered indefinitely at HAS *Marov* on Venus."

"Doesn't the government have a program to re-socialize them?"

"There might have been some talk about re-socialization at one time; but you know how the government is. It spares no expense to win the war, but the legislature can't seem to find the money to take care of its veterans after the fact." He began to whisper, "Between you and me, Commander, I personally don't believe they can be re-socialized; most of them weren't really well socialized to start with. Take Petty Officer Sudha as an example: she's from Polis De Sitter, Luna—born with physical and mental defects as a result of her strung-out, prostitute mother. When the Defense Force came recruiting for their stratogenics project she volunteered as a way to escape her near-certain future of drug addiction and prostitution back home. The genetic modifications gave her, and others like her, heightened physical and mental abilities, but it also gave them heightened aggression. Her kind will never have a place among civilized people. My opinion: Sudha would have a better place in society as a prostitute."

Hewst did not conceal her look of contempt at Corneau's opinion. "I can't believe that's true, Ensign. There's no such thing as disposable people. If the government engineered them, then it has a moral obligation to . . ." She was interrupted mid-sentence. Kiiswood came up beside Corneau and cold-cocked him, knocking him unconscious before he even hit the deck.

"As an intelligence officer, you should have seen that coming!" shouted Kiiswood as he stood over Corneau's unresponsive form sprawled out on the deck.

"Damn it, Chief!" exclaimed Lieutenant Jalloh, who ran to render aid to the unconscious ensign. "You've crossed the line this time!" The lieutenant sent out a c-nex alert and called for the ship's corpswains and MAs.

The gym was quickly inundated with responders—corpswains who were rendering immediate medical aid for Corneau and preparing him for transport to the sickbay, and MAs who were taking Kiiswood into custody so they could remove him to the brig. As the gym was now besieged with activity, Hewst decided to step through the g-duct and take her leave so that the responders might have more space to do their jobs. So too, she had but a few minutes to clean up from her workout before her upcoming briefing.

After changing into her uniform, Commander Hewst, anxious to be on time, ran through the passageways to the briefing room, arriving just a few minutes before 0900 Lima. Everyone in the compartment snapped to attention, for she was the highest-ranking officer currently in the room. She was the only person in service dress blues; the other four crew members in the compartment were wearing their service khakis. Following military protocol, the commander declared, "As you were."

The compartment featured eight seats around a central oval table and a small, dorsal-side porthole. Culinary Specialist Third Class Cody Wyatt, one of the ship's cooks, had already served coffee to those in the room who wanted some and was now setting an insulated flagon of coffee and dispensers of cream and sugar at the table's center. He also set cups and saucers before three vacant seats. The service set was a little more refined than the standard ware on the mess deck; the cups and saucers, as well as the flagon, were imprinted with the ship's nomenclature—TAS *Tereshkova*: FF-4150—in bright, cobalt blue letters. "Commander," asked Wyatt, "would you care for some coffee?"

"Yes, thank you," Hewst answered, "with a little amaretto, please."

"I'm sorry, ma'am," he apologized, "we don't have any amaretto in the ship's galley."

"A little cream and sugar, then, thank you." As she took a seat at the table, Hewst drew a careful sip of her coffee, testing its temperature with her lips. Then, by an amazing confluence of circumstances—her particular place at the table; the ship's trajectory; its orientation and proximity to its terminus— Hewst was treated to an astonishing vision through the overhead porthole—the brilliant, thick crescent of the planet Venus. Was it a coincidence? Was it a divine blessing? Hewst didn't know. Because she was unimpressed with God's endeavors of late, she gave little thought to the whys and hows of such a resplendent view and simply enjoyed the moment.

The ship's intercom system sounded two bells. It was now one hour into the forenoon watch, 0900 Lima. With punctuality characteristic of military discipline, Captain Nam-gi Han, the ship's commanding officer, proceeded into the briefing room, followed by Commander Suzu Cooper, his executive officer, and one other officer. "As you were," Han charged before anyone could come to attention. Hewst had met the executive officer when she first reported aboard, but she was only now meeting the commanding officer. "Thank you, Mr. Wyatt. That'll be all," Han ordered as he and the other officers took three adjacent seats.

34

"Aye aye, sir," replied Wyatt. He promptly exited the compartment with his service cart.

"Skipper," the executive officer introduced, "this is Commander Veronica Catherine Hewst, professor of religious studies, Terrestrial Assembly Defense Force Academy. She's on temporary active duty, assigned to FAIA." Cooper continued, "Commander, this is Captain Nam-gi Han, commanding officer of the TAS *Tereshkova.*"

"Welcome aboard, Commander," hailed Han. The captain did not extend his hand, but gave an affirmative nod.

"Thank you, Captain," Hewst replied. "It's a pleasure to be aboard."

"You're a little overdressed for our briefing," Han commented on Hewst's service dress blues. "Uniform of the day is service khakis."

"Aye, sir," she acknowledged. "I received my orders just a couple of hours before reporting aboard. Deployment Services had time enough to issue just my dress blues; the rest of my accoutrements should be awaiting me at the next port of call."

Noting the strand of jewelry around Hewst's neck, Han remarked, "You need to stow that necklace under your skivvies. You're out of uniform."

"Aye aye, sir." Perhaps she had dressed too quickly to notice that her necklace was exposed, or perhaps it had bobbled free of her coat while she ran through the ship's passageways. In either case, Hewst discreetly tucked her necklace under her blouse.

Continuing to address her, the captain directed Hewst's attention toward the others sitting around the table. "You know Commander Cooper, my XO, and I believe you've already met Lieutenant Jalloh." While pouring himself some coffee, he asked, "Are you acquainted with anyone else here?"

"No sir, not as yet," answered Hewst.

Gesturing toward others around the table, the captain made the rest of the introductions. "This is Intelligence Specialist Chief Åsta Holgersen, and Religious Program Specialist First Class Mas'ud Al-Jabiri." After a short pause, he motioned to his left, "And conducting the briefing is Lieutenant

35

Commander Nolan Gallistow from the Federal Aerospace Intelligence Agency." Han addressed Gallistow directly and said, "You're on deck."

Speaking first to Han and Cooper, Gallistow began, "Thank you, Captain, Commander. On behalf of FAIA, I'd like to thank you, and your officers and crew of the *Tereshkova*, for providing our project team with your hospitality and transportation to Venus." Then, addressing the others at the table, he said, "And to the members of the project team, thank you all. I appreciate just how arduous this has been for you—being uprooted from your routine endeavors while being kept in the dark for several days. Due to the classified nature of this briefing, your c-nexes and all other communication and recording devices in this compartment have been rendered temporarily inoperable. I will begin with a situation overview, and then I'll go over our mission objectives; afterward, I'll entertain questions." He placed a peg at the table's center and activated it to cast a rotating holographic projection of the planet Mars. "As part of its terms of surrender nine years ago, the Martian Alliance formally disavowed the name New Jerusalem and denounced allegiance to its Christocracy. Ever since, some of its own citizens have renounced their Martian citizenship and declared their political autonomy as the New Jerusalem. As they try to advance their radical Christian ideology, these separatists have executed multiple terrorist strikes in various cities all around Mars." The projection of Mars was suddenly augmented with numerous points of light, each denoting the location of a confirmed terrorist attack. "They've even been able to recruit a few Terran and Selenian citizens to form a couple of terrorist cells on Earth and Luna. The Martian Alliance is hoping eventually to be reinstated as a member-world of the Terrestrial Assembly, but the Assembly Legislature won't even consider its petition for reinstatement until the Alliance deals with these New Jerusalem terrorists and eliminates this menace. At the Alliance's request, the Assembly has been providing the Martian Global Guard with Defense Force support, both combat and logistical."

Gallistow cued the peg to project a rotating, 3D mug shot. Although the man in the image was twenty-five years old, his hard and violent life had aged his visage beyond his youth.

Gallistow continued, "On 8 November of this year, while excavating in a very remote region of Mars, a Defense Force engineering platoon out of

36

Tyrrhenus captured this man, Silas Dorch. He's a Martian separatist and, until recently, an allegiant member of New Jerusalem—a paladin as they call themselves. Through interrogation, we've learned that he was part of a terrorist enclave somewhere in the eastern region of Hesperia Province. When the engineering platoon found him, he was alone, unarmed, almost out of oxygen, and hundreds of kilometers from his enclave. He had no meal packs, no spare water, and no other personal effects." Gallistow then commented, "He was most eager to give himself up." His remark drew a smattering of chuckles in the briefing room. "All he had on him was his compression suit, his helmet— and this." The peg then projected a new holographic image, one that Hewst had seen before—the papyrus manuscript that Dr. Takahashi had shown her a few days ago back on Earth. "It's an ancient Christian text that our experts claim originated from Earth's Levant region during the first or second century of the Common Era. This manuscript was never previously catalogued among the ancient collections of any library, archive, or museum; as of two weeks ago, the existence of this document was unknown. For now, it's being studied at the Federal Archives Library in Geneva, Switzerland. As regards our apprehended terrorist, he has been extremely cooperative with our interrogators. He has denounced his allegiance to New Jerusalem and has even requested asylum with the Terrestrial Assembly. Since his capture, Mr. Dorch has spent two days detained at Camp Lundgren in Tyrrhenus, eleven days in transit to Venus, and the past twenty-four hours confined in the military detention compound at HAS *Landis*, which is why we're currently on TVT."

Gallistow paused just long enough to turn off his peg. "Our mission objectives are two-fold: first, we are to question Mr. Dorch to ascertain where this ancient Christian manuscript came from, and how and why it found its way to Mars. How did Mr. Dorch come to possess this document? Is there a connection between this document and the site where Mr. Dorch was captured? Commander Hewst, your role is to interview Mr. Dorch and find out what he knows about the manuscript. As an expert in religious paleography, you may be aware of certain avenues of inquiry that wouldn't occur to our military interrogators. Chief Holgersen, your role is to provide intelligence support for the commander. Petty Officer Al-Jabiri, you'll provide the commander with administrative support.

"Second, as part of a larger mission parameter, we are to escort Mr. Dorch back to Mars. Specifically, we will be taking him back to the excavation site where he was captured. Perhaps his presence and physical interaction on-site will invoke some latent memories; perhaps his very comportment on-site will itself be revealing. Lieutenant Jalloh, you and the two stratogens currently aboard will escort Mr. Dorch and the rest of our mission team from Landis to the excavation site on Mars. Our team will rendezvous with Sorteer Unit Four and with the rest of our project team at Schiaparelli. You will assume command of Unit Four for the duration of this mission, and your two stratogens will serve alongside the sorteers. Our mission designation, as christened by FAIA, is Project Belshazzar. The project OIC is Captain Anna Petrenko." Gallistow looked around the table. "I'll entertain questions at this time."

"I have a question, sir," said Petty Officer Al-Jabiri. "If Aerospace Intelligence needs Mr. Dorch back on Mars, why take him to a military detention compound on Venus? Why not detain him at Camp Lundgren?"

"The Terrestrial Assembly detains all radical Christian terrorists at HAS *Landis*," Gallistow answered. "At the time of his capture, we didn't suspect the manuscript in his possession to be anything but some propaganda tract New Jerusalem gives its allegiants. But when we discovered that it was something more ancient, we had to change our plans."

"Excuse me, sir," Chief Holgersen spoke up. "No disrespect to the commander's skills, but Defense Intelligence is quite competent at what it does. Surely Mr. Dorch has already disclosed to interrogators where he got that manuscript."

"Oh, yes," Gallistow acknowledged. And with a feigned grin on his face, betraying his incredulity at what Dorch told the interrogators, he added, "He says angels gave it to him."

Amazed and speechless, everyone around the table stared at Gallistow. The steady purr of the ship's zero-point quantum engines was the only sound filling the compartment. After a prolonged silence, Holgersen smirked and said, "Well, sir, I don't believe in angels."

"Neither do I, Chief," Gallistow agreed.

"I, for one, do believe in them," Hewst interjected while her hand brushed the lapels of her blouse, unconsciously tracing the silhouette of her necklace. "But I also believe that ancient manuscripts are the affairs of humans, not of angels. There must be a more corporeal explanation as to how Mr. Dorch came by his acquisition." She continued, "I teach my students that, to understand the meaning of an ancient text, one must first understand its context. If we're to understand Mr. Dorch's answers, we first need to understand his situation. You told us that an engineering platoon captured him at an excavation site, but you haven't mentioned what the engineers were excavating. What's the context?"

With an air of reluctance, Gallistow answered, "As mentioned, our second mission objective is part of a larger mission parameter. Once we arrive at Mars, we'll unite with a team of researchers to begin a scientific investigation of the aforementioned excavation site. I would show you an image of the site on the peg, but FAIA is meticulously regulating the dissemination of every holo of the site. I am, however, authorized to tell you that on 4 November, just four days before taking Dorch into their custody, the Defense Force engineering corps discovered a large subsurface cavern on the outskirts of Hellas Planitia. Such a discovery wouldn't ordinarily be so remarkable; Mars is laced with hundreds of cavernous lava tubes. But this cavern is laid out in precise symmetrical angles. It's carved out of the indigenous basaltic subsurface, and it's clearly not naturally occurring."

"Sir, we've seen this before," Holgersen interposed. "Several terrorist cells have dug out underground cavities to use as training camps and operational posts."

"We've never seen anything like this, Chief. It's more than 400 meters below the Martian surface with a volumetric displacement of more than 377,000 cubic meters. Prior to the engineering platoon's excavation, there was no outlet for extricating quarried debris, and no apparent deposit site for such debris."

"Sir," asked Al-Jabiri, "why did it take four days to find Dorch in that cavern?"

"The cavern is strewn with hundreds of geometric structures," Gallistow answered. "It's no surprise that he would go four days undiscovered."

"No, sir, that's not my point," said Al-Jabiri. "His EV packet would contain two days of oxygen at best."

"Perhaps the engineering corps didn't secure their access point," volunteered Jalloh.

Gallistow added, "Or maybe there *is* a way in that the engineers haven't discovered."

"Let me guess," Hewst ventured. "Mr. Dorch alleges that angels saved his life."

"So he says, ma'am," Gallistow retorted. "But I don't believe it."

Hewst asked, "But does he believe it?"

"He's a religious fanatic, ma'am. What does it matter what he believes?"

She smiled at the lieutenant commander and simply replied, "Context."

The briefing experienced a moment's pause as everyone in the compartment seemed to be processing the lieutenant commander's information. Taken by her own curiosity, Commander Cooper seized the moment to pose a question. "I know I'm not part of your project team, but I must ask: why the name? Why Belshazzar?"

"Well, ma'am, let's just say, the Agency thought it cryptic, yet apropos," he answered.

Hewst's eyes widened with sudden insight. "Apropos? You found inscriptions within the cavern, didn't you?"

Gallistow said nothing, but his look affirmed her insight.

Hewst's habits as an academy professor came to the fore, and she inadvertently began to speak to the others around the table as though they were students in her classroom. "It's a reference from Jewish scripture, from the book of Daniel. Belshazzar was a Babylonian coregent who purportedly encountered mysterious writings on the wall of his palace."

Addressing Hewst directly, Gallistow stated, "I'm prohibited from saying more about what else we found in the cavern, ma'am, but, suffice it to say, when we arrive at Mars, you'll join up with the other scholars and scientists in the project's research team. At that time, the project leader will give you more details about our findings, and you'll have an opportunity to examine the cavern for yourself."

"My scholarship might better serve the research team if you could provide me with some images of the inscriptions," said Hewst, and for the sake of Gallistow's plausible deniability, she added, "which may or may not be in the cavern. And if it's not too much trouble, I'd like to have a copy of the Levant manuscript that Mr. Dorch had in his possession."

"I'll try to secure some holos for you, ma'am. In the meantime, the Agency asks that you focus on questioning Mr. Dorch and learning what you can about that ancient manuscript." Looking around the compartment, he then asked, "Are there any other questions?"

Lieutenant Jalloh had no questions for Gallistow, but he did take the opportunity to address Captain Han. "Excuse me, Skipper, I have a personnel issue. At the moment, I'm in need of an operations chief."

"Yes, I hear that Kiiswood landed his ass in the brig again." Han then asked, "Is there an SOC available at HAS *Landis*?"

"No, sir," Jalloh answered, "none who aren't already in mission-critical posts. But the Sorteer Training Station is at HAS *Stofan*, which is just a quick shuttle-hop to *Landis*."

"See if you can secure an SOC from *Stofan*. If not, you may have to operate with a hole in your team."

"Aye aye, sir." Jalloh then requested, "I'd be remiss if I didn't at least ask, sir. Would you be willing to clear Chief Kiiswood for the sake of my team? He's the best sorteer I've got."

"I appreciate your situation, Lieutenant," Han said with a bearing more professional than sympathetic. "But he struck an officer, and as much as Corneau probably deserved it, Kiiswood is going to stand captain's mast."

Although she was no longer a chaplain, Hewst felt a certain pastoral interest for the concerned parties. Even as a professor, she was still moved by the conventions of her previous ecclesiastical vocation. "Sir, how is Ensign Corneau?" she asked.

Answering for the captain, Cooper said, "He's in sickbay with a broken jaw. But Dr. Kamala reports that, after osteoblastic resonance treatment, he'll be as good as new and ready to assume his duties in a few hours."

Perhaps it was a matter of respect for the genetically engineered sorteer in the brig, or perhaps it was a matter of personal curiosity that prompted Hewst to petition. "Captain, with your permission, I'd like to pay Chief Kiiswood a visit."

Han consented. "Be my guest, Commander. Say some prayers for him. Maybe that'll assuage his quick-tempered outbursts." He took the last sip of coffee remaining in his cup and said, "If there're no more questions for Lieutenant Commander Gallistow, we stand adjourned." Han stood from his seat, and, as if on cue, everyone in the compartment stood with him. "We'll be at Venus orbital insertion in about two hours. As soon as we're docked at VOP-Echo, the project team will take a long-shuttle down to HAS *Landis*. You're dismissed."

The captain was acknowledged with a unanimous "Aye aye, sir."

As everyone was leaving the briefing room, Petty Officer Al-Jabiri approached Commander Hewst. "Do you need me to show you the way to the brig, ma'am?"

"Thank you, no," she said politely. "I've served on frigates before. I'll find my way."

"Aye, ma'am. Let me know if you need any assistance. In the meantime, since we'll be shuttling down to *Landis* during the midday hour, I'll take this time for Dhuhr prayer. By your leave, ma'am."

"Thank you, Petty Officer, carry on."

Hewst made her way through two decks and a few passageways to arrive at the ship's brig. From behind their security console, the two well-armed MAs could monitor the physical, kinetic, and behavioral biometrics of the prisoners in their respective cells; they could even ascertain each prisoner's identity through meticulous and immediate sensor scans of fingerprints, voice patterns, and retinal configurations. Should any detainee become disruptive, the gravitational force in the cell could be increased from the security console to the point that the unruly party passed out.

The MAs scanned Hewst to confirm her identity and to check for dangerous or otherwise prohibited items that she might pass on to a prisoner. They had no reason to suspect ill intent on her part, but the scan was standard procedure for all visitors to the brig. Satisfied with the scan, the MAs signaled her into the anteroom adjacent to the brig's five cells. They directed her to the first cell, the one holding Chief Kiiswood, who was currently the brig's only occupant.

She stood outside the cell, looking at the humble accommodations that the small compartment afforded its inhabitant: a rack, a sink, and a toilet, all of which were adjustable to work in both 1.0g and zero-gravity environments. Like every compartment on the ship, the cell had handrails and footholds affixed to the overhead and bulkheads. Among all of the brig's otherwise high-tech security systems, perhaps the most incongruous was the cell's quaint detention barrier; Hewst and Kiiswood were separated by nothing more than reinforced steel bars.

Kiiswood had secured his feet into the overhead footholds, which would ordinarily be used during weightless conditions. Still outfitted in his navy-blue unitard, the chief was hanging upside-down with his back to Hewst, doing seemingly effortless inverted sit-ups. With his next sit-up, he abruptly thrust his torso toward his knees with sufficient angular momentum to disengage himself from the footholds and to spin his body around 180 degrees—literally spinning himself head over heels. Kiiswood landed gracefully on his feet facing Hewst, at attention.

"As you were, Chief," she said. She glanced around the anteroom, looking for a seat, but saw none. Although Hewst had given Kiiswood permission to continue his exercising, or to have a seat on the edge of his rack, he stood at ease out of courtesy for the commander. If she could not take a seat, neither would he.

"I hope you haven't come to introduce me to God, Commander," said Kiiswood. "I should tell you, so that you don't waste your time, I'm already a Christian."

"I'm not here representing God today," Hewst responded.

"A chaplain who doesn't represent God? And I thought I was the sideshow."

"Let's just say that I'm a disenchanted believer."

Kiiswood thought her self-description was somewhat amusing, but he decided not to comment on it. Instead, he asked, "What can I do for you, ma'am—which, I'm sure, wouldn't be much from behind these bars?"

"I'm curious, Chief. Why did you go out of your way to punch Ensign Corneau in the face? You must have known there would be consequences."

"Of course. I'm guessing that I won't face a court martial; my particular skill-sets are too valuable to the Defense Force. I'll probably stand before captain's mast, probably be demoted to a bluejacket. It was worth it." He then added with a grin, "How is he?"

"You busted his jaw. He's being treated in sickbay and should be back on duty in a few hours. You know, he thinks that you're genetically engineered to be a sociopath."

"Oh, he only says that because I don't like people."

"Is that why you struck an officer, because you don't like them?"

"I didn't see an officer, I saw a man—a man who disparaged one of my teammates. I saw a man whose words relegated Petty Officer Sudha to the ranks of the uncivilized and consigned her social worth to prostitution. I struck a man—a man who just happened to be wearing ensign epaulettes."

"How did you know what Corneau was saying? You were on the other side of the gym."

"Sudha and I both heard him. Our enhancements have heightened our sensory perception." In a subtly intimidating tone, he said, "Right now,

44

ma'am, I can hear you breathing. I can hear your heart beating. When you stepped up to my cell, I felt the miniscule changes in air pressure. I can see you in the infrared range; I can clearly see your heat silhouette; I can see the residual heat-signature of everything your hands have touched there in the anteroom; I can even see the silhouette of a necklace under your blouse—it's cooler than your body temperature."

Hewst did not allow herself to be distracted by his tone. "So you were defending the honor of your teammate. That doesn't sound like someone who dislikes people."

"What do you think you know about me, ma'am?"

"I think that society rebuffs you because you're different. I think people spurn you because they fear you."

"And isn't that reason enough for me to spurn others? In earnest, ma'am, why should I respect my fellow human beings?"

"Why, indeed! And yet you come to attention, you say 'ma'am,' and you stand with this fellow human being when you could be sitting."

Kiiswood stood silent, not certain how to respond.

Without speaking a word, Hewst walked away and left the brig. While standing in the passageway, she accessed her c-nex and tried to call Petty Officer Al-Jabiri, but she received an automated reply that the petty officer was unavailable. The reply prompted Hewst to leave a message, but she opted not to. Instead, she linked her c-nex to the ship's mainframe data suite to query for Al-Jabiri's location. Almost immediately, Hewst's c-nex enhanced her visual cortex with a cerebral form of augmented reality. Her c-nex displayed an image that only Hewst could see; it overlaid her visual perception with a translucent schematic of the TAS *Tereshkova* and then directed her to a single point of light marking the petty officer's location—in the ship's chapel.

She soon arrived at the chapel to find Al-Jabiri just finishing his prayer. He was facing a holographic mihrab (that is, a niche that indicated the qibla—the direction of Earth—the direction of the Kaaba in Mecca). The holographic mihrab hovered at a rather unusual angle between the overhead and the aft bulkhead of the chapel, but because of the ship's heading and orientation in space, that was the direction for prayer. After praying, Al-Jabiri rose to his feet and turned off the holographic projection with his c-nex. Only then did he notice Hewst standing in the passageway just outside the chapel. "Commander," he asked, "may I help you?"

"Oh, I can wait until after salat," she said.

"I've finished, ma'am," he replied as he was slipping his socks and shoes back on.

"I'd like to send a message to Earth, to the Defense Academy. Can you help me with that?"

"Aye, ma'am. I'll be glad to. Of course, all outgoing transmissions require the CO's approval. But, I'm sure that won't be a problem. Please, follow me," he said as he escorted the commander to the ship's communication center. "It will take at least seven or eight minutes for a message to reach Earth from this distance, and about the same time for a response, if you're expecting one. Oh, and I think I should remind you, ma'am, that Hawaii has passed the terminator; it's on the Earth's night side at this hour."

"Yes, I know," she acknowledged. "But I need to ask a favor of a friend."

With the petty officer's assistance, Hewst was able to send her message, but as the *Tereshkova* would soon be docking at VOP-Echo, she did not have time to wait around for a response. Hewst knew from experience that a docking ship would deactivate its artificial gravity so as not to interfere with the centrifugal-induced gravity of a rotating docking-platform. So she returned to her assigned quarters to prepare for Venus orbital insertion. She secured her personal effects and all other loose articles so that nothing in her quarters could float freely about in zero g. She also opted to make a head-call (that is, to use the toilet) while she still had the luxury of gravity. And for the shuttle ride to HAS *Landis*, she would soon have to don a compression suit, which would make using the head all the more challenging.

Before long, the TAS *Tereshkova* entered Venusian orbit and trimmed its roll axis until it was aligned with the rotation axis of VOP-Echo. At 1152 Lima, the frigate deactivated its artificial gravity and initiated an increasing roll-rate until it matched rotation with the orbital platform. Less than fifteen minutes after Venus orbital insertion, the *Tereshkova* had docked.

Chapter 5 – VOP-Echo

Venus Orbital Platform Echo

(Cythereographic Co-ordinates: S 2.21, E 16.79, Altitude: 447 km)

Tuesday, 20 November 2429 CE

Time: 1211 Zulu

VOP-Echo was one of several docking platforms in orbit around Venus, orbiting at an altitude of 447 kilometers, in the same retrograde direction as the planet's rotation.   The two-tiered orbital platform resembled a giant wheel about 450 meters in diameter, spinning at about two rotations per minute. Whereas most space-faring vessels used state-of-the-art graviton generators to create their internal artificial gravity, the orbital platforms around Venus used centrifugal-induced force, a more conventional method. VOP-Echo's rate of rotation generated a force on its outer tier (E-Deck) equivalent to 1.0g, and the centrifugal force on its inner tier (V-Deck) was equivalent to the surface gravity of Venus and of its high-altitude stations.

The *Tereshkova* had slowly and meticulously navigated through the center of VOP-Echo and had assumed station-keeping. The rotating decks of the orbital platform now synchronously ringed the parked frigate.   The platform had extended its four retractable gangways and moored the *Tereshkova* in place, like the spokes of a spinning wheel secured to an axle. Like graceful ballroom dancers, the platform and vessel now promenaded above the planet, orbiting at a velocity of 7 kilometers per second.

"Attention! Attention, all hands," announced the voice over the ship's intercom system, "We are now moored at VOP-Echo of the member-world Venus, Terrestrial Assembly.   Current time is 1211 Zulu.   Chronometric adjustment: plus 0.38 seconds. All parties going ashore, report to gangway, starboard beam."   Aware that the long-shuttle would be departing in about twenty-five minutes, Commander Hewst and the other members of the project team were mustering at the starboard gangway, preparing to debark.   The ladderwells, mounted at seemingly impractical angles when the frigate was underway, now proved their worth. As the ship was docked and rotating in sync with the orbital platform, the induced gravity was only one-fifth of Earth's standard gravity, but it was a sufficient gravitational force to reset the crew's sense of direction. For the project team assembling at the starboard gangway, port was now up, the starboard bulkhead was now the deck, and the hatches were now doors.

Although none of them had yet closed their helmets, the team members were already outfitted in their compression suits. Even though interplanetary voyages had become significantly easier and safer over the past four and a half centuries, space travel remained inherently dangerous. Especially during transit into and out of orbit, compression suits were requisite. Unlike the rigid spacesuits of centuries past that enveloped a person in a kind-of portable airbag, these suits were sleek, form-fitting, and flexible. Their primary component was a one-piece, booted and gloved unitard, specifically tailored to the particular wearer. They were sealed in the front almost seamlessly by a memory-alloy actuator. Their special skin-tight webbing applied the appropriate counter-pressure to protect the body from sudden changes in external pressure and from the unforgiving vacuum of space. This webbing was also thermal variant, capable of keeping the wearer warm or cool as needed. Woven from advanced ceramic filaments specifically manufactured to shield against solar particle events and cosmic rays, these suits provided ample protection from the high-energy radiation regularly encountered in space travel. Around the neck of each suit was a semi-rigid collar module from which a collapsible helmet hung. The helmet could easily pivot on and off when needed. At even the slightest indication of a change in pressure, the helmet would automatically close, and would immediately form an air-tight seal with the collar module and the environmental (EV) packet. The EV packet was a lightweight, streamlined magazine affixed to the back panel of the compression suit; it provided the suit with oxygen, potable water, carbon dioxide scrubbers, and power cells. In addition, every EV packet specific to Venusian compression suits contained an emergency buoyancy deployment system (BDS).

The project team had assembled near the airlock at the starboard beam and was about to petition the officer of the deck (OOD) for permission to disembark. But then the team was suddenly called to attention as Petty

Officer Sudha observed the commanding officer approaching and announced, "Captain on deck!"

"Carry on," ordered Captain Han. "Except you," he directed at Hewst. "A word, Commander."

Hewst remained behind as the rest of the team stepped into the airlock and boarded the gangway carriage. "What can I do for you, Captain?" she asked.

"I just received a communication from Vice Admiral Robertson Trendle. He's asked me to release Chief Petty Officer Kiiswood without standing mast, apparently at your behest."

"Sir, I think Kiiswood is clearly a valuable asset to our mission, but I'm in no way suggesting that he shouldn't be held accountable for his actions. I never asked the Admiral to supersede your authority."

"And officially he's not. He hasn't ordered that I release Kiiswood; he's simply asking that I 'give it some consideration.'" The Captain added, "But the next time you ignore the chain of command and skirt my authority, I'll throw your ass in the brig too."

With no sign of being intimidated, she responded, "Respectfully, Captain, I've demonstrated no contempt for your command, nor did I circumvent your command. You knew that I sent a message to Admiral Trendle; you approved it, sir."

"Good thing Commodore Pettit of the *Aldebaran* will be ferrying your team to Mars. I don't want to see you aboard again." Captain Han then ordered, "Now, Commander, kindly get your ass off my ship."

Trying not to express the contempt that she now felt for his command, Hewst replied, "Aye aye, sir." Since wearing a compression suit was regarded as being in uniform, she extended the Captain a salute; he, however, did not acknowledge it. Rather, he left her at the starboard beam and made his way back to the bridge. Hewst turned to the OOD and saluted. "Permission to go ashore."

"Permission granted, ma'am," the officer of the deck returned with a salute.

Hewst faced aft, saluted the flag of the Terrestrial Assembly posted at the far end of the passageway, and entered the starboard airlock. Momentarily, a vacant gangway carriage returned, and Hewst stepped aboard. She took hold of the handrail and said politely, "E-Deck, please." Bearing only one-fifth of her Earth-standard weight, Hewst's legs felt as though the deck was dropping out from under her as the carriage began moving. Soon, however, her weight steadily increased as the carriage proceeded toward the outer tier. A holographic schematic displayed the carriage's progress through the gangway, its relative position within the orbital platform, and the increasing gravitational force. Passing by the inner tier, the schematic read "V-DECK: 0.9g." By the time the carriage finally reached the outer tier, Hewst's legs were supporting her normal weight.

"E-Deck, 1.0g," announced an automated voice as the carriage door opened.

Hewst stepped into the main corridor on E-Deck, a passageway with footholds and handrails, not unlike those aboard the *Tereshkova*. Indeed, the main corridor differed only in that it was a little wider and sloped prominently upward along the platform's circumference. E-Deck was busy with VOP personnel, clad in service khakis and dungarees, rushing about. Hewst flagged a passerby. "Excuse me, crewswain. Shuttle Bay Three?"

Without breaking stride, he pointed and said, "Second left, ma'am."

Hewst set out as the crewswain directed, walking ostensibly uphill. Of course, either direction seemed uphill, she thought, yet each step felt like treading on level ground. Taking the second left, she saw the rest of her project team standing about the boarding lounge. Some of the team members were gazing out the large bay window. In the background were the sun and the bright arc of Venus pivoting about the space-scape every thirty seconds. In the foreground, hard-docked to the orbital platform, was a Venusian long-shuttle with a delta-wing configuration and canard stabilizers. It was a short-range, *Pele*-class aerospace vehicle and was clearly not designed for interplanetary transits. Its primary purpose was to shuttle sixteen passengers and two pilots from the VOPs, through the acidic Venusian atmosphere, to the high-altitude stations, and back.

Lieutenant Commander Gallistow was not looking out the window; rather, his eyes were fixed upon the holographic chronometer display on the sleeve of his compression suit. "Oh, there you are, Commander," he said. "I was beginning to think that you'd have to catch the next one."

"O ye of little faith," she pertly responded.

"The pilots want us to board right now. If we don't launch in nine minutes, we won't be in position again for another two hours."

"Sorry to keep everyone waiting," she apologized. "I'm ready to go if everyone else is."

Gallistow commanded Jalloh, "Okay, Lieutenant, let's get them on board."

"Aye aye, sir," Jalloh replied as he rallied the team members, paraded them through the airlock, and escorted them into the long-shuttle. He stood at the ingress and ushered everyone aboard. Hewst followed the rest of the team aboard and found a vacant, portside seat in the third row; she sat down and promptly strapped herself in.

"Okay, everyone," declared the co-pilot, "Echo Control has cleared us to launch as soon as the platform crew has locked down the docking area. Let's secure the hatch and put on our helmets. We launch in about two minutes." With Jalloh's assistance, the platform crew began preparing the shuttle for departure, but just before they sealed the airlock and secured the hatch, another passenger dashed aboard and was greeted with raucous howls and cheers from all the team members. Hewst looked over to see Chief Petty Officer Kiiswood taking the starboard-side seat across from hers and strapping himself in.

As she was about to close her helmet and secure its air-tight seal, Hewst said to Kiiswood, "I see the prodigal son is being welcomed home, Chief."

"That's because they all wanted to take a swing at Ensign Corneau," he confided. In self-deprecation, he added, "I'm the only one foolish enough to do it."

As soon as Hewst and Kiiswood closed their helmets, their EV packets automatically plugged into access ports adjacent to their seats. The shuttle's life-support system was now simultaneously supplying oxygen to their helmets and recharging their EV packets. Also, the heads-up display (HUD) was suddenly activated, projecting illuminated graphics and data on the inside faceplate of their helmets. The HUD could display information, accessible via c-nex or voice command at the wearer's discretion, on any number of pertinent subjects: bio-functions, suit status, external environment, communications, navigation, and avionics.

"Okay, everyone," said the pilot's voice over the helmets' speakers. "We've just completed our launch status check. Airlock and shuttle hatch are secured. Stand by for detachment." The pilot resumed, "Detach in three, two, one." The feeling of weight suddenly vanished as the long-shuttle was now undocked. The pilot immediately fired the attitude-control jets to take off the rotational momentum that the platform had transferred to the long-shuttle. He then trimmed their angle so that Venus was overhead and the shuttle was aligned with the equator. "Echo Control, Pele-Four-Whiskey-Bravo, we've cleared the platform. Request permission for de-orbit burn."

"Pele-Four-Whiskey-Bravo," replied the voice of Echo Control, "you are clear for de-orbit burn, pilot's discretion."

"Roger, de-orbit burn in three, two, one." All on board were thrust back into their seats as the long-shuttle's main engines burned for about two and a half minutes. Afterward, the pilot pitched the shuttle around and angled it for atmospheric entry. Addressing the passengers, the co-pilot announced, "Okay, everyone, we're now en route to HAS *Landis*. ETE: sixty-seven minutes. Please sit back and enjoy the ride."

Hewst settled in for the flight and decided to enjoy the view through her port-side window. She hoped to catch a glimpse of the bright Venusian cloud-cover below, but the planet was now too dark to see; the long-shuttle had already crossed the terminator and was currently flying over the planet's night side. Unable to see anything of interest for the darkness, she opted to pass the time by tuning into an available news transmission via c-nex. After a moment's searching, Hewst found a version of the Terran News Company news specifically formatted for direct cerebral access.

The anchor's voice overlaid the related holo-clips that streamed through Hewst's visual cortex. "One day after placing Valhalla under a mandatory quarantine, the Jovian Confederation has declared quarantine conditions are now in effect for a second Callistoan city. The Confederal Bureau of Contagion Management imposed an indefinite travel ban to and from the capital city, Utgard, effective immediately. Bureau officials emphasized that the quarantine is a temporary measure and assured the citizens of Callisto that there is no reason to be alarmed. When asked by reporters why Valhalla and Utgard are both under a communication blackout, a bureau spokesperson said she would have to get back with them.

"We have an update to a story we brought you two days ago. On Sunday, we reported the murder of Gordon Driscoll, curator of the British Museum. The commissioner of the Metropolitan Police Service says they are still investigating, but sources within the MPS tell the TNC they think members of a London terrorist cell associated with New Jerusalem is responsible for the murder. Also today, we learned a number of the more popular pieces of the museum's collection are missing, among them the famed Sloane Astrolabe, the fifteenth-century Holy Thorn Reliquary, and most pieces from the Oxus Treasure. Check back with us for updates on this story.

"Now, in a related story, a group of vandals, who identified themselves as paladins of New Jerusalem, are accused of breaking into the Museo del Prado in Madrid. Police tell us they destroyed several pieces of the museum's art collection. The damaged works were sent to Copenhagen for restoration. However, it is reported the damaged works are forged. Experts were relieved when they found out the pieces were mere replicas. But this discovery begs the question: where are the originals? We reached out to the museum's curator, but she was unavailable for comment."

TNC's cerebral newsfeed abruptly paused, yielding to an incoming c-nex call now accessing Hewst's auditory cortex. "This is Commander Hewst," she answered.

"Hey, Commander," said Kiiswood, "I can see your home from here." He was straining to see a particular point of light barely in view of his starboard-side window. "That bright spot right there," he said while pointing at the view, "that's Earth."

"Sorry, Chief, I can't see Earth from this window." Assuming that Kiiswood was trying to engage her, Hewst asked, "So how about you? Where's home?"

"Oh, I have no home, ma'am."

"No?"

He answered glibly, "We stratogens are garrisoned at HAS *Marov* when we're not on assignment. Venus is my official residence, but I wouldn't call it home."

"Well then, where were you born, Chief?"

Kiiswood pointed to the bright spot out his window. "Holbrook, Arizona, but I wouldn't call Earth home either."

"Do you have family in Arizona?"

"No, ma'am, there's no one on Earth who I'd claim as family," he answered even more glibly. "I was born with a neurodevelopmental disorder— deficient psycho-motor abilities, subnormal cognitive aptitude. I can remember how my parents used to thank God for their other children, but for me . . ." Kiiswood paused for a moment to conceal his downcast tone. "One day, the federal government came recruiting kids like me, promising to give them a better life. My parents thought it would be an answer to their prayers, so they made me a ward of the state, giving the Defense Force custodial authority."

"How old were you?"

"I was eight years old. And true to their word, the stratogenics project gave me a better life: heightened neurofunction, physiological enhancement, sensory augmentation. They even gave me something my parents never did—a family. I considered the Defense Force, and especially my teammates, a blessing from God. We served together; we fought together; we bore each other's burdens; we sacrificed for each other. We were family—that is, until we were no longer strategically useful. After the Martian War, we were stowed away on Venus, away from the so-called civilized worlds of the Terrestrial Assembly. Of course, the government rewarded us with their finest accommodations and luxuries, but shackles of silk and bonds of gold are still shackles and bonds." Kiiswood continued, "This prodigal son doesn't have to return home. I'm already home." He pounded his chest. "*This* is my home. Wherever I go, I'm always at home in my own soul because this is where God lives. I have little room in my heart for family; I just don't trust people. So what room I do have, I reserve for the only one I can trust. God is the only family I know."

Even though she had renounced her ordination, Hewst still found herself responding to Kiiswood with pastoral care. "You obviously have good reasons—more reasons than most—to turn your back on people. Yet I see within you a latent love for your fellow human beings. You obviously cared enough to defend the honor of Petty Officer Sudha." Hewst added, "But I must say, clouting Ensign Corneau in the face was a less-than-admirable defense."

Kiiswood laughed. "What can I say, ma'am, I'm a sinner. I too, like everyone else, fall well short of God's righteousness. And it's this disdain for my own sins that compels me all the more to follow Jesus' command, to do to others as I would have them do to me. So I try to show reverence and respect to others. But I do so for the love of God, not for the love of humankind."

"Not even for the love of your fellow stratogens? Not even for Sudha?"

"As I see it, there's nothing admirable or even lovable about people. Whether friend or foe, everyone's contemptible. Our friends and allies may pursue more noble goals than our enemies, but everyone will lie and cheat to achieve them. Paul sums it up perfectly. 'There is no one who is righteous, not even one; for all have sinned and fall short of the glory of God.'"

Respectfully, yet boldly, she protested. "That's not a fair portrayal of scripture, Chief."

"No? Are you saying I've misquoted the Bible?"

"Misquoted? No. But you've conflated two separate verses into one quote, and you've used them in a way that the apostle Paul didn't intend. When he claimed that human beings are sinful, he wasn't pronouncing them unlovable; he was declaring them so utterly broken that they're unable to mend their relationship with God. I dare say, one of the central tenets of the Christian scriptures is the commandment to love our neighbors, not despise

55

them. You may have good reasons for scorning humankind, but scripture can't be among them."

"You know, ma'am, you preach well for a so-called disenchanted believer."

"Well, I am a professor of religious studies."

The co-pilot's voice, heard over the transceiver set of every passenger's helmet, interrupted their conversation. "Okay, everyone, we've reached entry interface. We estimate that forces should increase to about 2.7g. Try to make yourselves as comfortable as you can for the next few minutes." Everyone on board was sensing ever-increasing g-forces as the long-shuttle began to enter the Venusian atmosphere. The pilots could feel the rudder and flaps gradually becoming active as air pressure steadily built over the aero-surfaces. Hewst and Kiiswood felt their suits making subtle compression adjustments to help their bodies compensate for the increasing force.

"So what's your story, Commander?" Kiiswood asked. "How does a chaplain turn her back on God?"

"I grew up on Cape Breton Island, Nova Scotia," she answered. Kiiswood's curiosity was stirred at her statement; he knew well what had happened to Nova Scotia nine years ago. She continued, "I was raised by the most loving father anyone could ever have. He was a professor of astrobiology at the Inverness University of Arts and Sciences—an intuitively brilliant scientist and the most spiritually devout Christian I've ever known. Often he would have to travel the terrestrial worlds doing field research for the university, and he would always take me with him. Some of the fondest memories I have of my dad are when we would go hiking together. As he explained the mysteries of nature all around us, it was like witnessing the resplendence of God inside every leaf and rock and breeze. He used to say, 'The cosmos is the parchment on which God's wonder is written, and His awe is revealed. Every quantum, every string is a jot in that sacred text, and life is its story.' He pursued the study of natural science as if he were on a spiritual pilgrimage." Hewst added with a modest smile, "I loved seeing the universe through his eyes."

"Did your mother join you two on your hikes?" he asked.

"No, I never knew my biological parents. I was abandoned as a newborn in the emergency room at the Inverness University Hospital. When my dad heard about it in the university's newsfeeds, he was so moved with compassion that he adopted me. He told me that I was a precious gift from angels. He often said things like that."

"You speak of your father in the past tense."

"He died during the Good Friday Massacre nine years ago." Hewst deemed that her father's death merited a more substantial narrative. "Did you know that my last shipboard billet was as chaplain of the TAS *Orion*?"

Amazed, Kiiswood asked, "You were there for the signing of the Palm Sunday Accord?"

"I tendered the prayer of invocation on that historic day—29 March, 2420—the day when the Martian delegation formally signed the accord on the hangar deck of the *Orion*, officially surrendering to the Terrestrial Assembly. The celebrations were as ubiquitous as they were grand. People were dancing and singing in the halls and streets of every urban center throughout the solar system, from the Denevi Colony on Mercury to Tyson's Point on Triton. The celebrations seemed to go on for days. But unbeknownst to anyone at the time, not even the Martian delegation, an Alliance war drone had launched ninety-six tightly grouped tungsten rods at Earth three weeks before the surrender. These rods weren't armed with any explosive payload; their destructive force came from the sheer kinetic energy they carried. I've since learned that these kind of projectiles are nicknamed FOGs—Fingers of God."

"Oh, I know about FOGs," Kiiswood interjected. "HAS *Grinspoon* was destroyed early on in the war by kinetic bombardment. To this day, its wreckage still lies strewn across Aphrodite Terra, along with the bodies of four thousand Venusians."

"On April 3rd, my dad called me from his office at the university. I was still aboard the *Orion*. He told me that my life was his divine purpose and his sacred joy—that my part in God's plan was just beginning and that his part was now complete. He cited a passage from the Gospel of John: 'My joy has been fulfilled,' he said. 'You must increase, but I must decrease.' He told me goodbye, that he loved me more than life itself; then he asked me to pray for the souls of Atlantic Canada." Hewst's pause was uncomfortably long. "About thirty minutes later, Aerospace Intelligence detected inbound FOGs. Of course, by the time they were discovered, there were only eighty-four seconds to respond—eighty-four seconds before they slammed into the northeast corner of North America. The Defense Force managed to target them with orbital and Earth-based counter-measures, but they succeeded in taking out only two of ninety-six. On Good Friday of 2420—five days after the war officially ended—my dad died when much of Nova Scotia was obliterated."

"And you blame God for your father's death?"

"Everyone dies. My dad was an innocent casualty of war, and war is a human endeavor, not the exploits of God. No, I don't blame God for his death; I blame God for the purpose of his death. If he died as part of God's divine plan for my life, then I want no part of it." She promptly added, "I haven't prayed since."

"So nine years ago, you left God's house and shook the dust from your shoes. That's a long time for a Christian to live without faith."

"I find myself questioning God's judgment. Maybe God isn't as omniscient as I once believed. Or Maybe God isn't as benevolent as I once believed, and He just doesn't care. No, I still have faith, more so in God's creation and less so in God." Hewst continued, "You may not trust humankind, Chief. But I don't trust God."

Kiiswood thought for a moment about the commander's story. He then asked, "If the FOGs were detected only seconds before they hit, how did your father know about them?"

"I don't know, but he seemed to know about his fate a couple of days before he died." She gestured where her necklace would be hanging were it not under her compression suit. "The very next day—the day after the impact—I received a parcel. The *Orion*'s postal clerk said it was posted three days earlier. In it was this necklace with a mustard seed pendant, along with a note from my dad. He wrote that the mustard seed was a reminder that the kingdom of God abides within me. The seed, he wrote, was a gift from angels, a gift that was mine before I was born. He was its custodian until it was time for me to take care of it myself. I've worn it ever since."

"I live in my own soul," the chief commented. "That's where my home is. But you seem to wear your home around your neck. With respect, ma'am, perhaps you're more of the prodigal than I am."

She grinned as she replied, "Perhaps."

The long-shuttle transitioned from a spacecraft to an aircraft and was emerging from the night-side of the planet. The cockpit and the forward cabin began to glow with the bright orange light of dawn as the shuttle flew into the sunrise. The cockpit windows automatically tinted to dim the intense sunlight now inundating the cabin.

"*Landis* Control, Pele-Four-Whiskey-Bravo," called the pilot. "Request permission for landing."

"Pele-Four-Whiskey-Bravo," replied the voice of *Landis* Control, "Traffic is clear. Assume left traffic pattern. Enter base leg for runway zero-niner. Advise when on final."

"*Landis* Control, Pele-Four-Whiskey-Bravo, Roger"

From her port window, Hewst caught sight of HAS *Landis*. She had seen holograms of high-altitude stations, but this was her first time seeing a so-called floating city with her own eyes. The station's primary module was an enormous, disk-like structure, about one kilometer in height and over 6.5 kilometers in diameter. Across its topside stretched four intersecting landing strips, each culminating in docking cavities under multi-tiered superstructures. Capping these superstructures were three large masts flying acid-impervious garrison flags—one for *Landis*, one for Venus, and one for the Terrestrial Assembly. From the underside of the primary module protruded an oscillation stabilizer—a long, inverted spire, reaching nearly four kilometers down toward the planet's surface and tapering into a massive dampening node. A series of strakes and other aero-contoured surfaces were affixed along the station's circumference, improving the station's stability and attitude control. The station seemed to float serenely against a yellowish-orange sky, drifting with the Venusian winds and the lightning-laced cumulus clouds. The sulfuric acid cloud-deck veiled the planet's hellish surface 54 kilometers below the station.

Hewst understood the physics; she knew that the station was filled with one bar of a nitrogen-oxygen atmosphere. And, because air is lighter than carbon dioxide, HAS *Landis* was able to hover high in the Venusian atmosphere like a city-sized balloon. Yet understanding the principles of buoyancy in no way diminished her feeling of awe and wonder at seeing a city hanging in the sky.

Banking the long-shuttle left, the pilot said, "*Landis* Control, Pele-Four-Whiskey-Bravo on final approach."

"Pele-Four-Whiskey-Bravo, you are clear for landing," instructed *Landis* Control. "On touching down, taxi to docking port Zero-Niner-Charlie."

"*Landis* Control, Pele-Four-Whiskey-Bravo, Roger."

Aided by navigational graphics displayed on their HUDs, the pilot and co-pilot throttled back, lowered the long-shuttle's flaps, extended the landing gear, and touched down smoothly on runway nine. As they taxied to their appointed docking port, the co-pilot announced, "Welcome to High-Altitude Station *Landis*. The time is 1340 Zulu; we're currently 54 kilometers over Lengdin Corona. At this altitude, the temperature is 41 degrees Celsius. We'll be docked in a few minutes. Again, welcome to Venus."

As if finishing the co-pilot's welcome, Kiiswood said to Hewst, "Your hell away from home."

Chapter 6 – HAS *Landis*

High-Altitude Station (HAS) *Landis*

(Cythereographic Co-ordinates: S 4.6, E 282.4, Altitude: 54 km)

Wednesday, 21 November 2429 CE

Time: 0835 Zulu

Centuries ago, Venus was popularly regarded as the least habitable planet in the inner solar system—an asphyxiating carbon dioxide atmosphere, a bone-crushing atmospheric pressure, and a searing surface temperature hot enough to melt lead. Yet, these same characteristics proved their worth for citizens of the Terrestrial Assembly who lived on worlds other than the second planet from the sun. The remoteness of Venus made the planet ideal for industrial complexes, where the manufacturing and processing of hazardous materials could take place far from the population centers on other worlds. Venus' deadly, hellish environment made the planet ideal for federal prisons; military detention centers; and other facilities for incarcerating terrorists, felons, and any others deemed ill-suited for the civilized worlds. Indeed, HAS *Landis* was just such a facility.

Like most other high-altitude stations, *Landis* was a semi-urban community drifting among the Venusian clouds, floating about 54 kilometers above the planet's equator. (At this altitude, the atmospheric temperature and pressure were very much Earth-like [that is, at sea level]). *Landis* accommodated scores of decks and thousands of compartments, all surrounding an enormous agora—a central urban campus encircled by more than 16,000 acres of tiered farmland. A giant cylindrical core running along the station's vertical axis connected all of the upper and lower decks through the central campus. The levels of decks served as layers of protection from the deadly carbon dioxide atmosphere and the sulfuric acid clouds just outside the station's hull. In the unlikely event of a hull breach, the affected deck or compartments could be sealed off until a maintenance team could make repairs. *Landis'* entire infrastructure—replete with maglev transit systems,

61

schools, medical facilities, shops, restaurants, even athletic fields—sustained the lives of 6,000 Defense Force personnel, civilian employees, and family members, as well as a few hundred detainees held at the station's military detention compound.

Indeed, Silas Dorch was just such a detainee.

Dorch slept comfortably and soundly in his cell last night or, more accurately, during the prescribed sleep-period from 2200 to 0600 Zulu. His cell was a small white cubical designed to be disorienting: no windows, no clock, no discernable features on the walls. A bed and a toilet provided Dorch his only reference in space, and a ceiling light that turned off during the sleep-period was his only reference in time.

(For high-altitude stations, night and day did not portend periods of waking and sleeping as they might on Earth. Because *Landis* circumnavigated Venus with the high-altitude winds every four and a half Earth days, the station sailed through fifty-four hours of daylight followed by fifty-four hours of night each cycle. Of course, sunrise and sunset were of little consequence to Dorch; his cell had no windows.)

After eating a simple breakfast of eggs, mixed fruit, and Assam tea, Dorch was taken to a rather austere interrogation room with a single table and four uncomfortable chairs. There he sat in solitude, in handcuffs and leg restraints, for nearly an hour.

He sat alone, but not unwatched. Multiple sensors concealed within the interrogation room were transmitting an abundance of information about Dorch to an adjacent surveillance room and to four members of the project team therein. Gallistow, Jalloh, Holgersen, and Kiiswood (as well as Lieutenant Sonja Pratiss, security officer for the *Landis* Military Detention Compound) stood around a real-time holographic projection of their detainee in the next room. They were studying the holographic displays and discussing amongst themselves Dorch's involuntary muscle activity, pupillometrics, and other pertinent stress indicators. Much to their disappointment, Dorch remained relaxed, even placid, like a monk in deep meditation.

After a brief tram ride from the barracks services facility, Commander Hewst and Petty Officer Al-Jabiri arrived at the station's detention compound. They stepped into the surveillance room ten minutes ahead of the project team's prearranged time. (Hewst was wearing her service khakis so that she was now uniformed like the rest of the team.) She arrived early for the meeting, but her teammates' preoccupation with the holographic displays suggested to her that she was late.

Seeking clarification of the holographic data, Jalloh asked Lieutenant Pratiss, "So you're saying that these readings are indicative of his time here?"

"Aye," she replied. "He's been our guest for nearly two weeks, and in that time he's shown few, if any, signs of psychological stress."

"How is he physically?" asked Gallistow.

Pratiss reached up to the projection and activated a holographic dropdown menu, from which she opened a display of Dorch's medical records. "The compound's physician examined Mr. Dorch as soon as he arrived," Pratiss answered. Reading from the records, she continued, "It says here he has a congenital condition known as *situs inversus*; his internal organs are reversed. It's a physiological anomaly, but it's not life-threatening. He's being treated for early signs of silicosis; the Martians call it lung rust. That's not unusual for many who are frequently exposed to Martian dust. He's also osteopenic from prolonged exposure to Mars' natural gravity. Again, it's not life-threatening."

"Good morning," Hewst said, interrupting them.

"Oh, good morning, Commander," Gallistow responded on behalf of all who had already assembled in the surveillance room. He handed Hewst and Al-Jabiri each a smock. "You'll need to put these on before you go in to question our detainee," he directed.

Holding the smock in her hands, Hewst asked, "What's this for?"

"Standard procedure," he answered. "All the interrogators wear these over their uniforms to cover names and ribbons. You'll want to give Mr. Dorch as little personal information as possible."

Al-Jabiri complied and pulled the smock on over his uniform. But Hewst handed hers back to Gallistow. "We did agree to meet at 0845, didn't we?" she asked.

"Aye, ma'am," answered Gallistow, as he reluctantly took back the smock. "We're just prepping Mr. Dorch for your interrogation."

Chief Holgersen added, "We've been monitoring his stress level for the last forty-five minutes."

Hewst and Al-Jabiri stepped up and joined the circle around Dorch's holographic projection. The commander was polite, but visibly displeased. "You've had him waiting in there by himself for forty-five minutes?"

Holgersen hesitated. "Aye, ma'am. Having him sit alone in a featureless room helps inculcate anxiety; it makes him more pliable to interrogation. Although we're a bit surprised that he's showing no signs of stress at all."

Pratiss added, "Since he's been here, I haven't seen anything really disturb his calm."

"Perhaps Mr. Dorch would tell us what we want to know for the asking," Hewst suggested. "And why are his hands and ankles restrained? Has he demonstrated any violent behavior since he's been in custody?"

"No, ma'am." Pratiss explained, "Restraints are precautionary, for the interrogators' safety."

"Please have his restraints removed," Hewst insisted. "I want him to feel comfortable—at least as comfortable as the rest of us."

"Respectfully, ma'am, he was an active allegiant in New Jerusalem," Lieutenant Jalloh reminded the commander. "He's a religious extremist."

Hewst stepped back from the projection and turned to leave the surveillance room. "The grace that I would show him has nothing to do with his faith," she replied, "but everything to do with mine."

Jalloh protested. "Commander, I'm responsible for your safety."

Kiiswood promptly addressed Jalloh, saying, "Excuse me, sir, if the commander has no objection to my presence in the interrogation room, I'll gladly remove the restraints."

With an affirmative gesture from Hewst, Jalloh consented. "Carry on, Chief."

"Chief, I'll need your sidearm before you go in there," said Pratiss. "Again, it's precautionary."

"Aye aye, ma'am." Kiiswood removed the rail-pistol from its holster on his leg, confirmed that it was set on safety, and handed it to Lieutenant Pratiss. "You wouldn't want me to shoot him accidentally; what a pile of paperwork that would be," the chief joked. He was well aware of the protocols regarding a detainee's proximity to weapons.

Hewst entered the interrogation room with Kiiswood and Al-Jabiri right behind her. She immediately activated her c-nex so that she could remain linked in to the rest of the project team in the surveillance room. Upon entering, she greeted the rather serene detainee. "Mr. Dorch, my name is Catherine Hewst." Taking the seat on the other side of the table, Hewst reached her right hand out to shake Dorch's hand. Because of the handcuffs— two bulky metallic wristbands tightly bound to each other by an intractable magnetic force—he was compelled to extend both hands.

Hewst continued the introductions. "Sitting here beside me is Petty Officer First Class Mas'ud Al-Jabiri, and standing behind me is Chief Niyol Kiiswood." She signaled Kiiswood, at which the chief actuated his c-nex and accessed the codes specific to Dorch's restraints. Immediately, the magnetic bonds were turned off, and Dorch's arms and legs were now able to move freely. "Please accept my sincere apologies; this treatment is most uncalled for."

"You all have been asking me for weeks about my unit, our troop strength, our arsenals, our weapons cache, our biological ordinances, our martyr implants," said a composed Dorch. "I don't know what more I can tell you."

"Again, my apologies. But I'm not with Defense Intelligence, and I'm not interested in your military secrets. I'm an expert in religious paleography; I study ancient religious texts."

"It just seems like more military mind games with you wearing that wrong-way uniform?"

Hewst assumed that his quip was an outburst of frustration with uniformed interrogators. "I'm working with FAIA; the uniform isn't my first preference." She quickly changed the subject. "You know, I'd like some coffee. Would you care for some coffee?" Aware that the team in the surveillance room was watching and listening, Hewst took advantage of the eavesdropping, "Hey, Lieutenant Pratiss, could we get some coffee in here?"

"That's thoughtful of you, Commander," Dorch said guardedly. "Is this supposed to be a good cop/bad cop interrogation?"

"Call me Catherine, please. No one's playing the bad cop today, Mr. Dorch."

"No? What about him?"

"Who? Chief Kiiswood? He won't threaten you. He's only threatening to drivel-mouthed ensigns."

"So why's he here?"

"His job is security."

"So he's here protecting you—protecting you from me."

"I don't need protecting, do I?"

"Don't you know, Catherine? I'm a terrorist."

"Let's not tarnish our conversation with unnecessary posturing. I simply want to talk with you about the events that transpired two weeks ago at Hellas Planitia."

"What can I tell you that I haven't already told the other interrogators?"

"I want to know about you. Tell me your story," she responded. "How did you become a paladin with New Jerusalem?"

Dorch sensed that her question was borne of sincere interest, so he replied, "You know, growing up on Mars is fun and carefree when you're a naïve little kid. At least, that's the way it was for me until my dad lost his job, until we lost our home. After that, my parents got mixed up with New Jerusalem. They were preaching all sorts of scary stuff—that our money woes were a sign of God's wrath. 'Mars was founded as a Christian world,' they said. By letting Jewish and Buddhist immigrants come in and take our jobs, we were turning our backs on our Christian faith. By electing Hindu and Muslim

66

reprobates to run our world, we were 'spitting on the cross of Jesus,' they said."
Dorch then introspectively added, "I believed the propaganda because I was
hearing it from my parents, and they believed it—well, I'm guessing they
believed it because it's easier to face the devil when you give the devil a face."

Hewst agreed, "It's always been easier to hate our enemies when we
see them as soulless demons."

He continued, "It wasn't long before New Jerusalem rose in political
prominence, took control of the government, and made Mars a Christocracy.
Riding the wave of fanaticism, I volunteered to fight the good fight in the army
of Christ—to wage war on the Terrestrial Assembly, the great Whore of
Babylon. And if the Jovian Confederation was allied with the Assembly, if the
Jovians were gonna lie with the whore, then my fight was with them too. I was a
Christian soldier, marching to war, with the cross of Jesus as my banner. Our
army saw itself as defending the faith, and our battle cry was Psalm 24—'The
Earth is the Lord's and all that is in it.' I was so zealous to save the Earth from
what I believed was the blasphemy of the Terrestrial Assembly."

Hewst heard a note of cynicism in his narration; he seemed like a man
who had lost faith in what he once held as true. She commented, "I'd rather
face a thousand sorteers than a single zealot who's convinced he's right."

Dorch smiled. "I remember feeling outraged and betrayed when the
Martian delegation signed the Palm Sunday Accord and surrendered to the
Terrestrial Assembly. I thought to myself, if the Martian Alliance was gonna be
seduced by the great Satan, then I would pledge my allegiance to New
Jerusalem as the true body of Christ. I would join them in fighting the good
fight against all of them—the Assembly, the Confederation, *and* the Alliance."

"Yet New Jerusalem launched assaults on Christian communities as
well," she observed.

"Oh yes. If they were Assembly sympathizers, we would declare them
apostates. So, they became fair targets in our holy war." Dorch's voice then
became even more staid. "But that's when I had a crisis of faith. About a year
ago, my unit was ordered to attack a church at Khurli Township, a church
whose pastor was preaching blasphemy, telling his congregation that Christ
loves Jews and Muslims too. During their Christmas Eve candlelight service,

67

we managed to get a gunman inside their nave. He opened fire on the congregation. I took a position just outside the church and shot anyone who came running out. Afterward, I ran among the bodies to make sure they were all dead, and I found the pastor. He was still alive. I was just about to shoot him again—finish him off—when he looked me square in the eye, reached up, and made the sign of the cross. 'I forgive you,' he said to me. 'I forgive you.' I can't explain it; my very soul was overrun with fear. I had my rifle trained on his forehead, and yet I was terrified of that preacher. I couldn't shoot—I couldn't shoot. I just ran." For a moment, he sat silent, staring down at his hands and imagining them tainted with his victims' blood. "I learned later from the news that that pastor died from his injuries. My entire enclave was celebrating because God was casting that apostate into hell for not believing in the Bible. I tried not to let on, but I sure wasn't in the mood to celebrate. I was still unsettled by his words. He forgave me for killing him, and I didn't even know his name."

Over her c-nex, Hewst heard the voice of Chief Holgersen saying, "The pastor's name is Jules Andorsky."

"Why would he do that?" Dorch pondered. "Did he know something I didn't? I would tell myself that I believed every word of the Bible, but I also knew that I never read every word of the Bible. So I decided not to take the word of my superiors; I would read every word for myself. I found lots of verses about the enemies: casting them out, going out to battle them, felling them with the sword. But I also read where Jesus commanded us to love our enemies. I didn't know what that meant. I didn't know how to do that. How does anyone love their enemies? But that pastor must have been loving his enemy when he forgave me. My soul was sorely troubled; I didn't know what the will of God was anymore. But I knew that I wasn't ready to sacrifice for a cause that wasn't God's. When my unit leaders called on me to help them plan an attack on Muller Point, I knew it was time to leave. I stole a traxle and drove. I didn't care where; I just drove. I stayed off the highways, heading southwest; other than that, I didn't know where I was going. I didn't dare log into the Global Navigation Network; they'd have found me. When the traxle ran out of power, I put on my helmet and set out on foot across the open plateau. As the sun was setting, I saw light coming from a small cave. I prayed it was an entrance to Sterling Point."

"Sterling Point?" Hewst asked.

Petty Officer Al-Jabiri leaned toward the commander to answer. "It's a remote settlement southwest of Tyrrhenus."

"I climbed down into the cave," Dorch continued, "but I never could seem to get any closer to the source of light. It remained just barely in sight and well out of reach, no matter how far I walked."

"It wasn't Sterling Point," Hewst surmised.

"No, it wasn't. And what happened next, none of the interrogators believe me when I tell them."

"I'm not an interrogator," said Hewst. "Try me."

"I must have walked about an hour, maybe two, when all of a sudden, the whole cave exploded with light. It wasn't coming from anywhere; the light was just all around me. Once my eyes adjusted to the brightness, I saw writing everywhere—on the walls and the floor. I didn't recognize any of it; it looked like lots of different languages." Dorch hesitated. "And then I sensed something in the light."

"Something?"

"Something—or someone. A presence. I can't describe it. But somehow I knew I wasn't alone."

"You knew you weren't alone?" she asked. "How? How did you know?"

Hewst's c-nex was still linked in to the surveillance room. She overheard Gallistow saying, "What's she asking? She doesn't actually believe this, does she?" She chose to ignore the conversation in the next room as she focused on Dorch's answer.

"It was a presence beyond knowledge," said Dorch. "I just knew. I couldn't doubt it any more than I can doubt my own existence. It was a soul within my own, and at the same time it was all around me and completely beyond me."

"A soul? Do you mean something like a ghost?" she inquired.

"No, not a ghost. It didn't feel ominous or dreadful. It was more like—more like angels. I felt a sense of sheer awe. Like falling, yet safely embraced."

"*Angels?* There was more than one presence?"

"I'm not sure, but this presence seemed boundless." Dorch looked at Hewst, then at Kiiswood and Al-Jabiri. He tried to imagine his words from their perspective. "I do realize how incredible my story must sound to you all."

Whether Hewst believed his story or harbored doubts, she did not say. But she tailored her questions as though Mr. Dorch believed it. "These angels, did they speak to you?"

"I couldn't hear them speaking. But I felt like they wanted to help us—all of us."

"Help us? Help us how? Is there something humanity needs help with?"

"I don't know," Dorch answered. "But they genuinely seemed concerned for us, as if they were grieving for humanity. And I think they wanted me to be part of that help."

"Did you try to communicate with them?"

"Yes, I did. I said to them, 'If you all are angels sent from God, then teach me how to love my enemies.'"

"Did the angels respond?"

"I don't know what happened next. One minute, I was surrounded by light; the next minute, I was lying on the floor surrounded by soldiers with rail-rifles and helmet torches pointed at me."

"When the engineering platoon found you, Mr. Dorch, you had a manuscript with you. What can you tell me about that?"

"There's nothing much to tell. When the soldiers found me, there was a scroll on the floor beside me. And, as I'm sure you know, they took it from me before I ever had a chance to look at it. But even if I still had it, I couldn't read it. I've been told the scroll is written in some ancient language. I assume the angels knew I couldn't read it, no more so than I could read what was written on the walls. So I have no idea why they gave it to me."

"So you had never seen the manuscript before that day?"

"Nor since."

Lieutenant Pratiss interrupted them as she opened the door to the interrogation room and ushered in a waitron, a civilian employee from the detention compound's canteen. "Excuse me, Commander," said Pratiss, "here's the coffee you asked for." The waitron set on the table a service tray with a flagon of coffee, cups, and a few other coffee accessories.

"Thank you, Lieutenant," the commander acknowledged, as Pratiss and the waitron quietly exited. Hewst noticed cream and sugar, even vanilla and cinnamon flavoring. "No amaretto," she whispered to herself. Without hesitation, Al-Jabiri assumed the role of host and began to serve everyone in the room, dressing each cup of coffee to individual taste. (Hewst took hers with a little cream and sugar, while Kiiswood declined any coffee.)

"Mr. Dorch," said Hewst after an initial sip from her cup, "the members of the excavation team that took you into custody—they didn't find anyone else in the cavern. No lights, no angels, no other people—just you. Could you have imagined it?"

"Maybe it all happened in my head," pondered Dorch, "but I can't deny what I experienced in my soul, because I'm no longer the person I once was. They took my fear and gave me peace; they took my hardness of heart and gave me compassion. They didn't *teach* me how to love my enemies; they embodied love *in* me." He set his unfinished cup of coffee on the table. "Like it says in the Bible, I'm a new creation—my old self has passed away—everything has become new."

"FAIA is launching an on-site investigation, and I wonder whether the angels you saw have anything to do with the cavern itself. Would you be willing to show me where you had your encounter?"

"I'm guessing you don't really believe I saw angels."

"I believe you experienced something—something I'd like to understand better," she confided.

He responded with a question. "Do you believe in angels, Catherine?"

"Yes, I do. But I don't believe that angels hew out subsurface caverns or write manuscripts."

"Are those manuscripts important?"

"That's what FAIA is trying to determine."

"The angels must have wanted me to help you." He then commented, "Of course, it's gonna be dangerous for me to go back to Mars. If my old enclave learns where I am, they'll surely come after me."

Hewst pointed back at Kiiswood. "We'll have the best security team with us."

"Well, maybe helping you is a way of loving my enemy," Dorch concluded.

"I'd rather be your neighbor than your enemy," she said.

"Loving neighbor, loving enemy—it's all the same." With an air of profundity, he added, "There's no love without compassion, and there's no compassion without sacrifice."

Hewst took a final sip of her coffee and set her cup down. "Thank you very much, Mr. Dorch. I've enjoyed our conversation. I look forward to your assistance in our investigation. Our project team will be departing for Mars early tomorrow, so I'll see you aboard the long-shuttle in the morning." As she stood to leave with Kiiswood and Al-Jabiri, she motioned to Dorch to remain seated. "I'll ask Lieutenant Pratiss to let you finish your coffee before escorting you back to your cell."

The three of them returned to the surveillance room and rejoined the project team. Pratiss remained focused on the holographic projection of the still-unrestrained Dorch, who was now enjoying the rest of his coffee. Jalloh returned Kiiswood's sidearm while Gallistow and Holgersen addressed Hewst.

"With respect, ma'am," asked Gallistow, "is that all you plan to ask him? He didn't tell you anything that he didn't already tell previous interrogators. And on top of learning nothing new, your line of questioning served only to reinforce his delusion of angels."

"If believing in a divine presence makes him a better, more compassionate person, I'm not sure I want to dissuade him of that belief."

Hewst then asked, "You've been monitoring his physiological indices. There's no indication that he's lying, is there?" No one responded; their silence was telling. "He can't tell us what he doesn't know." She continued, "He knows nothing about the nature or origin of the Levant manuscript other than it came from angels."

Holgersen asked, "Ma'am, you don't seriously believe his story, do you?" Pratiss and Jalloh looked curiously at Hewst, wondering how she might answer.

"I don't believe that angels are strewing scrolls about," she replied, "but I do take his story seriously. Consider the context: Mr. Dorch doesn't read ancient Greek. So the gift of that manuscript wasn't intended for him personally—it's ostensibly intended for those of us who can read it. Consider also the presumed contents of the manuscript. If my supposition is correct, that manuscript relates to Mr. Dorch's spiritual fascination with loving enemies, which means his possessing it isn't coincidental. It's intentional."

"Okay," Gallistow conceded. "But whose intention?"

"I don't know," she meekly admitted. "But I might have more answers for you if FAIA would let me examine that manuscript, as well as some images of the chamber's inscriptions."

"I'll have an encrypted holo-version uploaded to your d-board account within the hour, ma'am."

"Thank you, Commander."

The screech of the station's klaxon alarm abruptly ended their conversation; the low, soft lighting of the surveillance room was replaced by bright red strobes. "Attention!" announced the voice over the station's intercom. "Attention, all hands *Landis*! General quarters! All hands *Landis*, general quarters! All others, shelter in place!" Pratiss quickly looked up at the holographic display and confirmed that her detainee was still secured in the interrogation room.

The station's alarms seemed to blare even louder as Lieutenant Pratiss rushed into the surveillance room. "CIC reports an inbound bogey; we may be under attack," she shouted out to Jalloh. "Your orders, sir?"

Jalloh checked his c-nex for superseding orders from the station's commander, but he found none. "Until our project team is assumed under combat protocol, we proceed according to Agency directives," he directed. "Kiiswood, Sudha: escort and safeguard the members of the project team to their cabins."

"Aye aye, sir," they both acknowledged.

As the call to general quarters repeatedly sounded over the intercom, Sudha dashed out of the surveillance room in order to return Dorch to his cell. The project team also hurried out to shelter in their cabins for the duration. Upon leaving the detention compound, they found that the station was swarming with dozens of Defense Force personnel scrambling madly for their action stations. Without warning, Hewst suddenly split off from the rest of the team and began running in another direction.

Gallistow yelled out to Hewst, "Commander, the tram to the barracks is this way!" But she kept running.

"Chief," charged Jalloh, "please retrieve the commander."

"Aye aye, sir," Kiiswood replied as the lieutenant was still giving the order—as he was already heading after her.

Even with her head start, Kiiswood quickly caught up with Hewst on one of the terraces in an upper-level passageway. "Excuse me, Commander," the chief said while running beside her, "where are you going?"

"When I was a chaplain, my action station was sickbay," she answered. "If we have any wounded, I want to help."

"And how are you going to help them, ma'am?" he asked. "If the wounded ask you, will you pray for their healing? Will you pray to a God that you've disowned?" Realizing that she had no cogent answer for the chief, Hewst stopped short. The two stood silent in one of the topside observation decks as the station's personnel rushed about them.

The flash of two HAS-based tactical fighters soaring past the windows of the observation deck brought much of the rushing to a halt. Hewst, Kiiswood, and several other station personnel ran toward the windows to witness the aerial activity unfolding against the bright Venusian skyscape. They

74

watched as the two aircraft rocketed to join two other fighters on a course to intercept the inbound bogey. Three dorsal gun turrets arose from the station's topside hull and pivoted toward the fighters.

"What's going on, Chief?" Hewst asked.

Kiiswood's enhanced vision allowed him to see distant events more acutely than anyone else in the observation deck. He pointed in the direction where the gun turrets were leveled and said, "Right there—seven kilometers out—about twenty degrees above the horizon." By horizon, he of course meant the inferred horizon where the *Landis* topside and the Venusian sky met. "Something's not right," he continued. "The bogey isn't on an attack vector; it looks like it's in a standard traffic pattern. In fact, our fighters are flying formation with the bogey."

"Yes," she acknowledged with a pointing gesture. "I see them."

The scenario seemed so odd to him that Kiiswood decided to do something a bit surreptitious. His training as a sorteer afforded him a few clandestine skills, among them the ability to hack into what would otherwise be secured transmissions. Using his c-nex, he accessed the real-time communications of the Combat Information Center. So as he and Hewst watched the events transpiring outside the window, Kiiswood was now able to eavesdrop on the pilots' conversations.

"Flight Leader, Hopper-Three-Yankee-Sierra," called out the bogey. "Repeating, we're not infected. Requesting permission to land."

"Three-Yankee-Sierra, this is Flight Leader: request denied. Repeat, request denied. You are instructed to return immediately to HAS *Sagan*. We will provide escort."

After a moment's silence, the bogey called out again, "*Landis* Control, Hopper-Three-Yankee-Sierra: we're declaring an emergency. We don't have enough power to return to *Sagan*."

Landis Control did not respond. "Three-Yankee-Sierra, this is Flight Leader: you are ordered to remain in formation as we escort you back to Sagan. Acknowledge!"

Kiiswood listened for the bogey to acknowledge, but he heard nothing. Seconds later, he watched as the bogey ignored the surrounding fighters and broke formation. "*Landis* Control, Hopper-Three-Yankee-Sierra: turning on final approach for runway two-seven."

Again, *Landis* Control did not respond. "Three-Yankee-Sierra," declared the flight leader, "return to formation immediately! No further warnings will be issued!"

The bogey assumed a glide slope of about three degrees as it approached for landing; it showed no sign of deviating. It was still about two kilometers out from the station's rim when one of the fighters fired upon its target and destroyed the bogey. The spectators on the observation deck burst into applause and cheers as they watched the bogey's smoldering ruins fall below the *Landis* horizon and plummet through the atmosphere's crushing depths. Hewst and Kiiswood, however, stood baffled, trying to make sense of what they witnessed.

"What just happened, Chief?" she asked.

Kiiswood responded almost imperceptibly, "I'm not sure."

Chapter 7 – The Descent into Hell

High-Altitude Station (HAS) *Landis*

(Cythereographic Co-ordinates: N 2.3, E 255.2, Altitude: 54 km)

Thursday, 22 November 2429 CE

Time: 0452 Zulu

Commander Hewst started her day a little earlier than usual; she needed to prepare herself for her passage aboard the long-shuttle bound for VOP-Tango. She had already donned her compression suit and was seated at the small desk in her cabin. With a cup of coffee in hand, she was once again scrutinizing the holographic data that Lieutenant Commander Gallistow had sent her the day before, including holograms of the recently excavated cavern, and the recently discovered Levant manuscript therein.

Her c-nex began to signal with a distinctive tone, indicating that someone was just outside her cabin door. "Hewst," she answered.

"Chief Kiiswood, ma'am," said the voice on her c-nex. "Permission to enter?"

Without a word, and without leaving her seat, Hewst opened the cabin door with her c-nex. The chief, also outfitted in a compression suit, entered the cabin, stepped up beside Hewst's desk, and almost fluidly assumed a posture of attention.

She was so inured in her research that, for the moment, she did not notice the chief standing at attention. When she finally looked up at him, she said, "At ease, Chief. In fact, given that we'll be working together for a while, please remain at ease around me. I'm not used to people standing at attention for me."

"It's just proper military bearing, ma'am," he returned as he stood at ease.

Hewst smiled. "I'll take it that your bearing is always proper."

"Aye, ma'am." acknowledged Kiiswood. He then reported, "The long-shuttle is scheduled to launch at 0557 Zulu. We'll rendezvous with VOP-Tango where the TAS *Aldebaran* is currently docked and awaiting our party. Lieutenant Pratiss is prepping our detainee with a compression suit of his own and will escort him to the gate at docking port thirty-six-bravo. There, the project team will officially assume custody of Mr. Dorch. Commander Gallistow wants the entire team to muster at the gate by 0535 Zulu." After a moment's pause, Kiiswood added, "And because you ran off yesterday when the team members were directed to their cabins, Lieutenant Jalloh has made me personally responsible for your safety, ma'am."

"Thank you, Chief." She asked, "Would you like a cup of coffee?"

"No, ma'am. Thank you."

Her thoughts began to stray from the holographic images hovering just above her desktop. "I've been wondering about that downed aircraft yesterday. Do you think it had anything to do with our detainee?"

"How so?" he queried.

"Is it possible that New Jerusalem was responsible for that inbound bogey? Was it part of a terrorist attack on *Landis*—a retaliation for detaining one of their own?"

"That's some of the scuttle around the station, and CIC hasn't said anything to contradict the rumors. *Landis* Recon has launched three surface drones to survey, possibly recover the wreckage." Kiiswood then posited, "But I don't think it was a terrorist attack, or a suicide bomber."

"What makes you say that?"

"First of all, it was never declared a bandit—a hostile aircraft. The *Landis* fighter squadron was flying formation with it; that's not a tactical air-combat maneuver. Second, it wasn't really a bogey. Bogey is slang for an unidentified aircraft. That aircraft clearly identified itself—*Three-Yankee-Sierra*. It repeatedly identified itself to CIC, to *Landis* Control, and to the intercepting fighters; even the flight leader acknowledged its ID."

"How do you know this?" she asked. "Did you have access to their communications?"

Because Kiiswood was not supposed to be privy to such information, he decided, for the sake of prudence, not to answer that question. He smiled modestly and continued, "I compared its alphanumeric suffix with aerospace registry; it matches the registration of a small cloud-hopper from HAS *Sagan.*"

"A cloud-hopper? That's a short-range passenger transport, isn't it?"

"Aye, it is. Hardly the tip of the spear."

"How did you know to check for aircraft registered at *Sagan?*"

"That's where the fighters were trying to redirect the cloud-hopper."

"If it wasn't a terrorist operation, why did the fighters shoot it down?"

"I can only venture a guess. I don't think the cloud-hopper was attacking; I think it was seeking refuge." He remarked, "That being said, I think CIC still deemed it an imminent threat. *Landis* Command has implemented a communications blackout with *Sagan.*"

Hewst was genuinely puzzled at the chief's remark. "Why?"

The chief responded, "The cloud-hopper insisted to the flight leader that its passengers were not infected."

She sat silent for a moment pondering what Kiiswood just said. "Are you suggesting that it was trying to escape some kind of outbreak at HAS *Sagan?* A *Landis* fighter squadron shot down a civilian passenger transport for fear of contamination?"

"I'm not qualified to second-guess defense command decisions, ma'am." Sensing that he had probably expressed too much of his own opinions, Kiiswood changed the subject. "Have you been up all night studying those holos from FAIA?"

Hewst took another sip from her cup and answered. "No, I woke up early to continue reviewing them before our departure. I spent all afternoon yesterday examining them."

"And have you found Dorch's angels?" he asked.

She grinned and said, "No, but I *did* read the full Levant manuscript. Among its contents is this." Hewst pointed at a few lines of Greek on the holographic projection. "This clause relates to Mr. Dorch's 'crisis of faith.' It reads, 'Love your enemies, pray for those who persecute you.'"

"That's from Jesus' sermon on the mount. Is that manuscript an ancient copy of the Bible?"

"Not exactly. By content, it definitely has the profile of what biblical scholars call Q, a hypothetical source for two of the gospels in the New Testament."

"Hypothetical?"

"The Q document has presumably fallen through the proverbial trapdoor of history; there are no surviving copies."

Kiiswood inferred, "Apparently, there is now."

"I suppose so," she acknowledged with a rather reluctant affirmation.

Suspecting that the commander was eager to say more, Kiiswood prodded, "But?"

"But there are a couple of peculiarities about this manuscript." Hewst flipped the holographic image to reveal its actual orientation. "First, this is what the text actually looks like," she said. "Like modern English, first-century Greek was written from left to right. This text is clearly written from right to left; even the letters are written backwards." She flipped the image again. "I have to turn it around to make it easier to read."

Kiiswood jested, "It still looks Greek to me."

Hewst smiled but otherwise ignored the joke she had heard many times before. "Second, it's in exceptional condition. In fact, it's too exceptional." Hewst expounded, "In all my years of scholarship, I've never seen an ancient manuscript so pristine as this. It looks like it was written yesterday."

"So you think it's a fake."

"It crossed my mind, yes." Pointing at the holographic image, she continued, "But the evidence suggests otherwise. The text is clearly written in first-century Greek, with accordant carbon-soot ink, on indigenous papyrus.

And, through radiocarbon analysis, the scientists in Geneva have concluded that the papyrus is about twenty-four hundred years old."

"Perhaps the scientists made a mistake," he offered.

"They've run the radiometric panel three times—same results every time."

"Perhaps the Martian atmosphere has affected the carbon-14 in the papyrus," Kiiswood proposed. "Perhaps it's a lot younger than the measurements indicate."

"I don't think radioisotopes work that way. The atmosphere on Mars shouldn't have any effect on carbon-14." Her own words suddenly triggered a spark of elucidation—a partial solution to a mystery. Hewst felt the contentment of her insight, like the elation when seemingly disparate puzzle pieces actually connect. "That's it! An extremely dry climate; cold temperatures; a low-pressure, oxygen-free atmosphere. That's why the manuscript is on Mars. Someone stowed it in a subsurface cavern at Hellas Planitia in order to protect it—to preserve it in a relatively nonreactive environment."

"But who? And if it's a fake, why preserve it?"

"I don't know." Hewst minimized the holographic images of the manuscript and enlarged those of the Martian cavern. "But I'm guessing we'll find answers here," she said pointing at the enlarged holograms.

"Have those holos revealed anything about the cavern?"

"Not much about the cavern proper," she commented. "The holos are specifically angled on the wall's inscriptions; they reveal nothing of the cavern itself. But they're interesting, to say the least. There are hundreds of inscriptions. I can recognize Sanskrit, Pali, Hebrew, Arabic, and Greek, but they're all interspersed with several linear groupings of these mysterious symbols," she said while pointing. "I assume that they're the glyphs of some written languages, the likes of which I've never seen before."

"The tongues of mortals and angels," Kiiswood quipped. "What does it say? Can you read any of it?"

"I can read the Greek and Hebrew." Hewst ventured her opinion. "The engravings appear to be a compilation of religious pronouncements, many of them from the sacred writings of Hinduism, Jainism, Judaism, Islam, *et cetera*." She gestured to some lines of Greek. "This, for example: 'Conquer the hateful with love; conquer the evil with goodness; conquer the miser with generosity; conquer the liar with truth.'"

"Is that from the Bible?"

"No, it's a Greek translation from the Pali Canon." She realized almost as soon as she said it that Kiiswood might not know what the Pali Canon was. His look of confusion confirmed her suspicion. "It's from the Buddhist scriptures," she explained.

"You know the Buddhist scriptures?"

"I am a professor of religious studies," she affirmed. "Here's one from the New Testament: 'Love your enemies and pray for those who persecute you.' Of course, the New Testament likely appropriated this quote from the Q document." Then, reading some other lines of Greek, she mused, "A few of these pronouncements I've never seen before: 'When the eternal soul surrenders itself, love reigns eternally.'"

"What does that mean?"

Hewst did not answer; she had moved on to another inscription in the holographic image. What she read next stole her poise. "There is no love without compassion, and there is no compassion without sacrifice," she read aloud.

"What?"

Again, she did not answer. Instead, she set down her unfinished cup of coffee, jumped up from her seat, and bolted for the door. "I need to speak with Mr. Dorch, right now!" Hewst exclaimed as she hurried into the passageway.

Chasing after her, Kiiswood asked, "Does teaching religion require a lot of rushing around? Because you sure do run a lot for a professor."

Hewst never once glanced over to Kiiswood as they raced from the barracks to the nearest tram platform. Her attention was set on getting to the detention compound. Still, she carried on their conversation along the way.

"One of the statements inscribed in the cavern wall: 'There is no love without compassion, and there is no compassion without sacrifice.' That's what Dorch said to me in the interrogation room yesterday."

"So?" asked the chief.

"He can't read the inscriptions. How does he know what it says?"

"A coincidence?" he ventured. "Maybe?"

"I thought you sorteers were too strategically minded to assume coincidences," she bantered as they arrived at a sparsely crowded tram platform.

He cynically posed, "You're not thinking that Mr. Dorch's angels are real?"

Hewst and Kiiswood (as well as a few early-morning commuters) boarded a tramcar bound for the nearest maglev interchange to the detention compound. Despite the availability of seats, the two of them opted to stand and grip the overhead handrails. As the doors shut and the tram sailed forward, Hewst said, "I'm thinking that whatever Mr. Dorch might have imagined, he didn't imagine that inscription. Someone told him what's written on the wall." Hewst grew steadily impatient as the tram made one stop, then a second. "This tram is too slow," she remarked.

The chief noted, "You drink too much coffee, Commander."

The two soon reached their stop and quickly made their way to the detention compound. After passing through a series of check points, including two biometric authentication posts, they arrived at the security console just before entering Dorch's cellblock. The chief was already handing over his sidearm to the MAs behind the console even as they were scanning Hewst and Kiiswood for weapons.

The scan was nearly complete when an aerospace integument specialist, steering an equipment cart, left the cellblock anteroom and waved to the MAs as he passed the security console on his way back to the equipment lockers. "I'll be right back," the specialist said to the MAs. "Mr. Dorch is almost suited up, but Lieutenant Pratiss wants me to upgrade the carbon dioxide scrubber in his EV packet." The MAs acknowledged him with a wave.

Hewst and Kiiswood both noticed that the specialist himself was wearing a compression suit draped by a utility apron. But what especially caught their attention was the specialist's lack of eyebrows—a medical condition known as madarosis.

"You're cleared to enter, Commander, Chief," one of the MAs confirmed. "Lieutenant Pratiss is already in the anteroom prepping the detainee for transfer."

Eager to question Dorch again, Hewst entered the anteroom, immediately followed by Kiiswood. The two stood baffled as they stared into a vacant cell. Glancing quickly around the anteroom, they saw neither Dorch nor Pratiss, but they did notice various suit components piled on a bench in the left corner.

Kiiswood at once sprinted after the integument specialist. Hewst also ran after him but was not fast enough to keep up with the chief. "Lock down the compound! Now!" shouted Kiiswood as he flew past the MAs at the security console. He never broke his stride; he would surrender no advantage to his quarry, not even a moment's pause to retrieve his checked sidearm. He ran from the cellblock and rounded the corner into the compound's main passageway, where he needed to dodge the abandoned equipment cart and several security personnel who had been bowled to the deck by the browless man. Those who were still standing heeded Kiiswood's shouts to "Make a hole! Make a hole!" They quickly cleared the center of the passageway to accommodate the chief's breakneck momentum. And for the few who were unable to get out of his way, Kiiswood simply hurdled over them.

Despite her best efforts, Hewst quickly realized that she could not catch up with Kiiswood. So, once she reached the discarded equipment cart, she stopped and opened its cabinet doors. Therein, she discovered the mangled bodies of Dorch and Pratiss, gruesomely folded and crammed into the cart. Hewst called on her c-nex for a medical team even though she supposed that their services were too late. She inspected the bodies, confirming what she suspected—they were indeed dead. The commander was suddenly horrified by the presence of a detached eyeball and a severed hand. Her horror gradually ebbed into bewilderment—the eyeball and the hand clearly did not belong to either of the victims.

The lockdown alarm blared throughout the compound, but to Kiiswood's astonishment, none of the barricades or door-blocks were in place. He tried to activate them with his own c-nex, but he soon discovered that the compound's security network had been hacked; the lockdown protocols had been compromised. He assumed that the killer had disabled every cordon checkpoint and thus bypassed them. Kiiswood egressed the detention compound and found himself standing in the middle of a busy promenade, wondering which way to run. He decided to access the station's video sensors, specifically the ones in and around the detention compound proper. Immediately, dozens of video images cascaded through his visual cortex via his c-nex. There among the images, he spied his objective: the browless man, still wearing an apron over his compression suit, standing at a maglev interchange amid a gathering of commuters about to board a tram.

Kiiswood continued to monitor the cortex image as he set out in a full sprint for the maglev interchange. "Security alert! All station arms!" he shouted over his c-nex link. "All-points dispatch for averred killer. Subject is male, 190 centimeters, about 95 kilos, wearing a utility smock over a military compression suit. Current location: Maglev Interchange Seven, blue-line platform. Subject is presumed dangerous. Approach with caution; isolate and apprehend. Sorteer in pursuit."

As the chief raced toward the interchange, he soon found himself running through the green-line concourse, which extended along a terrace just one deck above the blue-line platform. Kiiswood's target presently came into his view, even as he was still more than 100 meters out of reach. But from his overhead vantage, he was able to see the browless man, curtained within the crowd, inconspicuously slip aboard the tram. Two station police officers, responding to Kiiswood's dispatch, arrived onto the platform too late to confront the suspect; the door had shut and the tram was now pulling away from the interchange.

Within seconds, Kiiswood closed the distance between himself and the departing tram, but the two were still separated by a story's height. This, however, did not deter him; he would prove unrelenting in his pursuit. Without slowing whatsoever, Kiiswood leaped over the terrace balustrade and landed squarely on the last car of the accelerating tram below. Witnessing

Kiiswood's audacious stunt, the two police officers linked into *Landis'* transit operations and called for the immediate shut-down of all blue-line trams.

Kiiswood crawled as prone as possible along the topside of the aft car while the tramway's low clearance raced overhead. He reached an emergency egress panel and eased it open. With cat-like stealth and finesse, he climbed into the car and alighted gracefully on his feet. Startled at the sight of a man dropping from the ceiling, the passengers gave Kiiswood a wide berth. He advanced swiftly through the interconnecting cars, finally confronting his fleeing quarry in the foremost car. There, in an effort to evade his pursuer, the browless man smashed out the tram's forward window, but he dared not jump from the very tramcar that might also run him over. So he seized an unfortunate passenger by the neck and screened himself with his choke-held hostage.

Kiiswood and his adversary now stood at opposite ends of the car, each attempting to face down the other with a hostile stare. As a tactical deterrent, the browless man brandished a large glass shard at the nape of his hostage.

With a resolute gaze and a steely voice, Kiiswood declared, "You're coddling feigned hopes if you think I care."

Every passenger aboard suddenly pitched forward, many falling to the deck, as the maglev braking system engaged and the tram quickly slowed to a halt. The browless man seized the opportunity; he threw his unharmed hostage to the deck and leaped out the forward window. Kiiswood tore after him, skirting and dodging the fallen passengers strewn about the tramcar, affording his rival a few seconds' head start. The browless man raced along the dim, maglev track toward the lights of a tram platform just ahead, with his pursuer running not far behind him. The darkness offered him little cover, for Kiiswood's infrared vision detected his heat-silhouette plainly. Still, the chief was perplexed by the sheer speed of his adversary; even at a full sprint, Kiiswood succeeded only in keeping pace.

Meanwhile, a tactical team of three police officers had marshalled on the platform ahead; they were preparing to hike through the tramway to apprehend the murder suspect whom they presumed to be confined aboard the stopped tram. They deployed a c-nex-controlled reconnaissance drone, flying it into the darkness to lead and light their way. As they were about to set out along the maglev track, the browless man vaulted from the shadows and charged the platform. With surprising speed, agility, and ferocity, he overpowered one of the police officers and held her in a paralyzing chokehold. With one hand, he pinned her close as a human shield to fend back the other two police officers, who were now reaching for their rail-pistols. With the other hand, he drew his hostage's own rail-pistol and fired two rounds in rapid succession, killing her teammates before they could level their weapons on him.

At the sound of electromagnetic-propelled bullets being discharged, the commuters on the platform suddenly dropped to the floor, scrambled for cover, or simply tried to flee the area. Into this chaos of hysterical bystanders, Kiiswood emerged onto the platform. The browless man threw aside his now unconscious hostage and fired two more rounds at his pursuer, hoping at most to kill the sorteer and at least to sweep him back from his pursuit. With extraordinary reflexes, Kiiswood dove for safety behind a support column, narrowly dodging the hurtling bullets. The killer fled into the refuge of the mayhem while Kiiswood once again gave chase. But now that his target was notably armed, the chief decided to grab the rail-pistol of one of the dead police officers.

Kiiswood quickly cleared the chaos of the tram platform and was soon weaving his way around pedestrians in the *Landis* corridors, all the while keeping the killer in his sight. Unfortunately, the chief never acquired a clear shot of his target; the risk of shooting an innocent bystander was too great. As the browless man approached a connecting corridor, an MA up ahead, with his firearm in hand, attempted to intercept the killer. With a single shot, the browless man killed him. As he raced by, he shot him a second time, just in case the first bullet was not sufficient. Another MA, having seen his comrade shot to death, drew his rail-pistol; in an adrenaline-fueled panic, he fired recklessly at the first armed person who entered his line of sight—Chief Kiiswood. The MA's frantic shot missed its mark, and Kiiswood would not allow him a second chance. Without sightline aiming, Kiiswood fired on the run and wounded the MA in his forearm to disarm him.

The pursuit continued, one corridor after another, until it advanced through one of the station's lateral observation corridors. As Kiiswood was closing in, several hermetic barriers abruptly arose from the deck below, dividing the observation corridor into a row of eight airtight compartments.

These barriers automatically deployed whenever a hull breach was detected. But because the emergency oxygen masks had not also deployed, the chief surmised that *Landis* security had intentionally engaged these barriers to bring the deadly chase to an end. Kiiswood now found himself confined in one of the compartments, along with two other people who happened to be near him when the barriers emerged. He pounded his fist in frustration against the hermetic barrier as he accessed the video sensors in the adjacent compartment. There, he saw the browless man holding his latest hostage with his rail-pistol to her head.

Kiiswood's c-nex signaled an incoming audio message. "Hey, Chief," said Petty Officer Sudha. "Station Security is coming through from the other side of the corridor. They want to avoid crossfire, so they need you to stand down. They'll take it from here."

Before he could protest, the voice of someone representing station security sounded from the intercom throughout the observation corridor. "There's nowhere else to run. You need to let your hostage go, lay down your weapon, and surrender peacefully, without resistance. If you do not comply, you can be assured that this will not end well for you."

The browless man slowly released his grip on his hostage, who quickly scurried as far away from her captor as the compartment would allow. Still holding the rail-pistol, he raised his hands in the air in capitulation.

"Place the pistol on the deck. Step away from it. Lie down prone with your hands crossed behind your back," ordered the voice over the intercom. The browless man did not comply, even after the order was repeated.

Something seemed wrong, Kiiswood thought—very wrong. To be insulated from his pursuers by hermetic barriers was simply too fortuitous to be mere happenstance. He must have known that he was running into a trap when he chose to race through an observation corridor, which was engineered to be selectively sealed off. Kiiswood realized that all of this was calculated. These barriers were not detaining the assailant; rather, they were shielding his escape. "Hold your breath," the chief shouted to the two bystanders confined in the compartment with him, "and stand back."

The browless man began to lower his firearm, but just when his weapon levelled on the observation window, he shot it out with the last of the rounds in his magazine. Immediately, carbon dioxide from the Venusian atmosphere filled the compartment, displacing all the breathable air. While the former hostage desperately scrambled for one of the oxygen masks that dropped from the overhead, the browless man secured his helmet to his collar module, leaped outside through the breach, tossed his empty rail-pistol aside, and dashed for the edge of the high-altitude station.

Kiiswood, however, was ready for him. As his adversary darted by Kiiswood's line of sight, the chief (from his side of the barrier) fired through and shattered the observation window, striking the escapee in his right leg. Immediately, the two forewarned bystanders grabbed for oxygen masks. Kiiswood deployed his helmet, jumped outside, and ran after his wounded quarry. He was closing the distance between them when the browless man reached the scuppers and safety netting that lined the station's rim. He hurdled over them and dove over the edge, free-falling toward the surface 54 kilometers below. Without hesitation, Kiiswood brazenly dove after him.

Both holding in a stable arched position, the two of them quickly reached a velocity of about 175 kilometers per hour. Of course, at this speed, a couple seconds' head start translated into a significant lead for the browless man. Kiiswood was easily within his firearm's effective range, but he preferred to catch him than to kill him. So, using his body as a streamlined airfoil, the chief pulled his arms back and extended his legs, diving even faster toward his target. But the browless man did the same, trying to keep his distance by increasing his own rate of fall. Now reaching a velocity of 245 kilometers per hour, the two dove rapidly for several minutes through layers of sulfuric acid clouds and carbon dioxide haze. Although he lost sight of his target in the brassy fog, Kiiswood was still able to track him—his range and velocity—with the HUD in his visor. Using his hands and feet like ailerons and rudders, Kiiswood kept himself stable and on course.

Indeed, Kiiswood was on track to intercept the browless man when a bolt of lightning flashed near him. The chief was unharmed, but the resulting electromagnetic pulse disabled his HUD. Kiiswood could no longer track his quarry, not even with his own infrared vision. He could not differentiate the heat-signature of his quarry from the hot Venusian clouds; everything was essentially the same temperature.

After a few more minutes of freefall, Kiiswood cleared the murky haze. He looked above and below; he spun himself around, scanning the eerie orange horizon, but his adversary was nowhere to be seen. "Damn it!" he shouted, even though he was the only one who could hear his expletive. He had lost the browless man in the clouds.

Temperature and pressure were rapidly increasing; Kiiswood realized that he was too far into the planet's troposphere. Despite his genetic enhancements, he knew that he was approaching his own physiological limits. He reluctantly deployed his BDS—a helium-filled, parafoil-like ballute—which would gradually bear him aloft back to the planet's mesosphere. Soon, a *Landis* rescue drone descended from the clouds above and quickly located the chief drifting about 32 kilometers above the planet's surface. It hovered beside him, then scooped him into one of its life-pods while cutting him loose from his ballute. With Kiiswood safely cocooned aboard, the drone set course for HAS *Landis*.

Again he exclaimed, "Damn it!"

Chapter 8 – TAS *Aldebaran*

Terrestrial Assembly Ship *Aldebaran*, on Trans-Mars Trajectory (TMT)

(Heliocentric Co-ordinates: / 195.72003, *b* +0.6694, *r* 212,638,413 km)

Tuesday, 04 December 2429 CE

Time: 1729 Lima

The TAS *Aldebaran* had been on a trans-Mars trajectory for the past ten days and was now less than twenty-four hours away from docking at ASO Terminus-Schiaparelli. Under the command of Commodore Renée Pettit, the long-range cruiser hurtled through space toward its appointed rendezvous with the red planet, its relative velocity exceeding the standard trajectory speed. Aiming to make up for lost time, the commodore had directed the ship's engineering officers to calibrate the engines for full propulsion.

The *Aldebaran*'s departure from Venus had been delayed for more than two days as some of the ship's passengers were temporarily detained at HAS *Landis*. The Criminal Investigation Division (CID) had held Commander Hewst and Chief Kiiswood for a protracted debriefing, trying to ascertain their roles in the deadly mayhem that had careened through the high-altitude station. But, given the pressing nature of the mission, the two were eventually allowed to rejoin the rest of their project team at VOP-Tango.

Following social protocol, Commodore Pettit hosted a formal dinner for her ship's guests. Decked out in their dinner dress blues and adorned with their respective service medals, the project team joined the commodore and her executive officer (Captain Raleigh O'Dell) for dinner in the commanding officer's mess. Following military protocol, the guests were seated around the table according to rank, with Commodore Pettit at the head. They enjoyed a meal of chicken cordon bleu, asparagus drizzled with olive oil and lemon pepper, a side salad with a vinaigrette dressing, and sauvignon blanc. Even though Pettit and Petty Officer Al-Jabiri might have had religious prohibitions for this meal (Pettit because of Jewish kosher regulations and Al-Jabiri because the meal would be harām, or forbidden), most of it was produced from synthetic materials, as was most food. The evening's cordon bleu, while delicious, consisted of no real ham or chicken. Even the wine was imitation.

The conversations around the table were varied. Holgersen and Al-Jabiri were contemplating whether the decedent Silas Dorch knew more about the Martian cavern than he had disclosed. Kiiswood and Sudha were deliberating the possible identity of the browless man. Gallistow and Jalloh were reviewing the project team's mission itinerary, which began with a rendezvous at Schiaparelli Terminus. Pettit, O'Dell, and Hewst were discussing the mysterious communications blackout with HAS *Sagan*.

"Aye, we were under the same orders as HAS *Landis*," Pettit told Hewst. "DEFMIN directed all Defense Force Commands operating in Venusian space to terminate all hails to and from *Sagan*—no liberty or station leave, no deployment of hands, no reception of freight or personnel—no contact whatsoever."

Captain O'Dell added, "VOP-Tango had to turn back three inbound long-shuttles from *Sagan*."

"What if a shuttle declares an emergency?" Hewst asked. "Aren't you required by maritime law to render aid to any vessel in distress?"

"Maritime law allows for a defensive response," the commodore explained, "if the distressed vessel presents a danger." Inferring what lay behind Hewst's question, Pettit then remarked, "I heard about the incident with the cloud-hopper just off the *Landis* hard-deck. My understanding is that CIC deemed it a clear threat to the station."

Hewst replied a little more softly, "Ma'am, I heard that the cloud-hopper was fleeing some kind of outbreak at *Sagan*."

With a hint of affirmation in her tone, Pettit said surreptitiously, "So you suspect that the contact interdiction was related to a station-wide contagion." She continued, "Commander, I'm not at liberty to confirm your assumptions. Bu, I will tell you this: the Terrestrial Assembly has issued communication restrictions and travel bans not only for HAS *Sagan*, but also for the Philippines, New Guinea, and Armstrong City at Vitruvius Crater. Likewise, the Jovian Confederation has issued similar bans for some of its communities on Europa and Callisto. And even the Martian Alliance has prohibited travel to three of its provinces." Trying to be a little more reassuring, she added, "I'm given to understand, of course, that your team will not be traveling through any of those areas."

In a near whisper, Hewst asked, "Are you implying a pandemic, ma'am?"

Pettit did not answer the question, but after a moment's pause to finish the last morsel of asparagus on her plate, the commodore commented, "By the way, HAS *Sagan* is currently drifting helmless—like a derelict."

Hewst said nothing; she simply took a large swig from her wineglass.

After the dinner guests had finished the main course, the culinary specialists cleared the table of the entrée plates and chargers, but left the glasses of wine. They then began to serve coffee and a dessert of mixed fruit lavishly dolloped with vanilla yogurt. Upon the first sip of her coffee, an expression of pleasant surprise arose on Hewst's face. She turned to Pettit and observed, "Oh my, this is real coffee."

"Aye, it is," Pettit acknowledged. "It's authentic Honduran coffee." She lifted her own cup toward Crewswain Luteront, one of the culinary specialists, who, being quite familiar with the commodore's preferences, added a flavored creamer to her coffee. "It's even better with a little hazelnut," she added.

Hewst asked Luteront, "Would you happen to have some amaretto?"

"No, ma'am, I'm sorry," he answered contritely.

Hewst acquiesced and courteously accepted some hazelnut creamer. She then commented to Pettit, "The coffee I've been drinking on the mess deck for the past ten days pales by comparison. How did you get Honduran coffee way out here?"

"Rank has its privileges," the commodore replied, "but I'm sure you're no stranger to the benefits of rank." Pettit gestured toward the other end of the table—toward Kiiswood.

"Ma'am?" asked Hewst. She was unsure as to the commodore's reference.

Pettit elaborated, "I heard word that you called in a chit on Chief Kiiswood's behalf. Vice Admiral Trendle obviously holds you in high regard."

"You spoke with Captain Han," Hewst concluded.

"Aye, he made a point to notify me of what he characterized as your contempt for the chain of command."

After a moment's silence, Hewst asked, "Am I to be made governor of a passing asteroid, Commodore?"

Pettit laughed so boisterously that the other conversations around the table were interrupted. "No," speaking sarcastically, "we don't maroon insubordinates anymore. Besides, I can't spare the lifeboat." The commodore continued, "Captain Han is a very competent CO, but he takes himself a little too seriously. That being said, I decided to pull up your service record, and I called Rob to get the scuttlebutt on you."

"You know the Admiral?"

"Aye, he and I were at the Defense Academy together—class of '02. He has nothing but 'Bravo Zulus' for you." Pettit pointed at the dominant medal on Hewst's uniform. "He was the one who submitted your name for that Medal of Honor. According to his entry in your military service jacket, you rescued three crewswains from being sealed off behind a decompression hatch; you were seconds away from being trapped yourself." She commended, "A Medal of Honor recipient is always welcome at this table."

"It's a sincere privilege to be here, ma'am." Hewst humbly added, "Regrettably, there were twenty-seven other souls who were trapped behind that hatch, and I'd gladly yield this seat to any one of them."

"May their valor be forever remembered," the commodore augustly declared. She then lifted her wineglass and toasted. "To our fallen comrades of the Martian War!"

As with one voice, everyone at the table replied, "To our fallen comrades!"

"Excuse me, Skipper," Captain O'Dell interjected. "Engineering is effecting a slated test of the ship's RCS at 1900 Lima. Your presence is requested on the bridge."

"Very good." Pettit placed the napkin from her lap onto the table and stood up. "Excuse me, ladies and gentlemen, duty calls. Please, enjoy your desserts." Everyone began to push themselves away from the table, but before they could rise to attention, the commodore ordered, "As you were."

As Pettit was leaving, Lieutenant Commander Gallistow asked, "Commodore, I need to go over a few things with the project team. May we continue to use the room for the briefing?"

"Carry on," she replied. She and the executive officer then departed for the bridge.

Gallistow dismissed Crewswain Luteront and the other culinary specialists, but not before asking them to leave a full flagon of coffee at the table. After he topped off his cup and shared the flagon with the others, Gallistow placed a peg at the table's center. He began, "Most of you have been asking about the murder investigation back on Venus, so I thought I'd give you an update." While everyone around the table was finishing dessert, he cued the peg to project a holographic montage of the browless man being chased through the promenades and halls of HAS *Landis*. "Our plans to have Mr. Silas Dorch accompany our team to Hellas Planitia were obviously impeded when this man assassinated him in his own cellblock. According to the Criminal Investigative Division at *Landis*, Dorch was the killer's intended target. The investigators characterized the other five murder victims as collateral casualties. A Defense Force master-at-arms and two civilian police officers were shot to death during the assassin's getaway. Lieutenant Sonja Pratiss was murdered while she was assisting Dorch with his compression suit in the cellblock. And Petty Officer Third Class Sean Drusak, an aerospace integument specialist, was found dead in an equipment locker, stabbed through the base of the skull. Dorch and Pratiss were both murdered in a similar manner—stabbed with improvised blades. The weapons went undetected because they were fashioned from integral components in an EV packet."

"Excuse me, sir," Petty Officer Al-Jabiri interposed. "I don't understand how he got past the MAs' security console."

"Integument specialists are not regular security personnel," explained Gallistow. "They're part of the station's support staff. It's not unusual for the MAs to see new faces among those who have clearance."

Chief Holgersen asked, "How did he clear the biometric checkpoints?"

Between sips of coffee, Gallistow responded straightforwardly, "The assassin severed Drusak's right hand and removed his right eye. He then used them as needed to bypass the checkpoints. He tricked the scanners into admitting him as the integument specialist." The gruesome details of Gallistow's narrative visibly repulsed most around the table, except Sudha and Kiiswood, who had witnessed much worse during the war.

"I was wondering whose they were," Hewst commented. "They obviously didn't belong to either Dorch or Pratiss."

"What about the neurometric scanners?" Holgersen asked. "Everyone's neural configuration is unique. The assassin couldn't slip past those scanners with severed body parts."

"Let me guess," Kiiswood presumed. "Drusak's c-nex is missing."

"In fact, it is," Gallistow confirmed.

"I don't see how that matters, sir," said Holgersen. "A c-nex is formatted to each person's own neural network. Drusak's c-nex wouldn't function on anyone else."

"The investigators are still working on that one. But somehow he successfully circumvented the neurometric scanners as though they didn't even exist." Gallistow continued, "And under the pretense of fitting Dorch with a compression suit, he was able to gain access to his target."

"Do we know who this assassin is?" asked Petty Officer Sudha.

"As yet, CID has been unable to identify him." Gallistow cued up a rotating close-up of the browless man and said, "This detailed three-D image is a composite of photos, vids, and holos taken by the station's video sensors during Chief Kiiswood's pursuit. They've run this image through multiple pattern-recognition algorithms, comparing it against every ID record in Assembly, Confederation, and Alliance databases—not a single match. They also ran his DNA sequence through all the databases; again, no match."

Holgersen was puzzled. "Wait, are you saying that, in this age where everything is information-interfaced, there are no ID records of this man?" she asked. "It's not like we're living in the Middle Ages."

Lieutenant Jalloh proposed, "He obviously hasn't lived his entire life as a hermit, given his lethal skillsets and training. His facial patterns and DNA must be recorded in a database somewhere—unless they were erased."

"Well, if we can't identify him by physical evidence," Holgersen speculated, "perhaps we can identify him by motive. Who would have a reason to kill Dorch? What's the motive?"

"New Jerusalem," Hewst suggested. "New Jerusalem has a motive."

"With respect, ma'am, that seems unlikely." Holgersen continued, "After two weeks, Mr. Dorch would have told us all he knew about the terrorist sect, and New Jerusalem would know that. They gain nothing by killing him."

Hewst replied, "You're assuming that the assassination was to silence an intelligence source. But what if the motive wasn't tactical? Suppose it was religious."

"Religious?" Holgersen asked incredulously. "Are you suggesting that a hitman-cleric broke into a secured detention compound just to perform a human sacrifice?"

"Evidently, not secure enough," Kiiswood quipped.

To Holgersen's question, Hewst offered an explanation that was perhaps too thorough for everyone else around the table. "New Jerusalem believes in a catastrophic apocalypticism." As she refilled her cup from the coffee flagon, she continued, "Their members believe that mainstream Christianity has failed them. So they turn to a sect that reinforces this belief—a belief that the universe is broken and only God can fix it. God will destroy the old corrupted universe, and in its place, God will create a new heaven and a new earth—a new Jerusalem. Their members take up arms as Christ's army to hasten the destruction so that, when God inaugurates this new creation, their faith will earn them a seat in the new order. Occasionally, a member questions the sect's teachings and then leaves its ranks, like Mr. Dorch. Such independent thinking challenges the leaders' authority, and threatens their hold on membership, so the apostate has to be killed. His death is preached as divine judgment; it reinforces the dogma that members who remain faithful are blessed by God and that all others will suffer God's wrath."

Holgersen recapped, "So you're saying that a New Jerusalem operative assassinated Dorch for membership retention and to speed up the apocalypse."

"It's a motive," Hewst offered. "It may or may not be our assassin's motive."

"We're just speculating about who he is," Kiiswood said curtly. "But, I can tell you precisely *what* he is." Kiiswood pushed his dessert plate aside so that he could have more room to talk with his hands. "As I told *Landis* CID, the assassin was able to kill both Dorch and Pratiss simultaneously with such quick, quiet, surgical precision that the MAs in the next room were not alerted. He was able to remain just beyond my reach, even as I gave a full-sprinted chase. His speed, his strength, his agility—he's a stratogen."

"That would explain how the assassin used Drusak's c-nex," Sudha commented. "We stratogens have a way of getting around neurometric scanners. How we do it is top-secret classified." She then concurred, "I think the chief is right."

A silence momentarily filled the mess compartment as everyone around the table reticently considered the possibility that Kiiswood might be correct. Jalloh broke the silence. "Unlikely, Chief. If he was a stratogen, we'd have found a match to his DNA in the Defense Force database."

"And yet CID confirms your supposition, Chief," said Gallistow. "The assassin's DNA doesn't match any particular stratogen on record, but it does match the specific genetic profile of a stratogenics project."

Jalloh was confused by the investigators' findings. "Is it a reliable DNA sample?" he asked. "How did CID acquire it?"

"The sample came from a blood trail along the station's topside hull," answered Gallistow. "Chief Kiiswood shot him in the leg just before the two of them leaped off the station."

Conceding that the sample was likely reliable, Jalloh then looked to Kiiswood and said to him, "I have to tell you, Chief, that was the most foolish stunt I've ever seen—and possibly the bravest."

Commenting on the chief's rash exploit, Gallistow said, "Your BDS is intended to be deployed within a few hundred meters below the hard deck—

one or two kilometer at most. But you decided to take it for a 20-kilometer joyride through hell." He then remarked, "It's a personal floatation device, Chief, not a skydiving rig. You deployed your BDS well beyond its designed operational parameters. You're damned lucky you survived."

With a blithe smile, Kiiswood retorted, "You know what they say: Fools rush in . . ."

". . . where angels fear to tread?" Hewst finished. "God must have a special providence for fools, sailors, and cavalier stratogens."

With a Qur'anic reference, Al-Jabiri concurred, "Perhaps God has commanded his guardian angels to watch over you, Chief."

"In more ways than one," Gallistow observed.

"Sir?" asked Kiiswood.

"It's a miracle that CID didn't arrest you, Chief."

"Arrest *me*? For what?"

"Where should I start? First and foremost, you shot an MA."

"He shot at me first, sir. I was simply defending myself."

"As it is, you only wounded him. You're damned lucky you didn't kill him."

Kiiswood reacted rather stoically. "Wounding him was by design. If I wanted to kill him, sir, I would have."

"And second, you endangered two bystanders in the observation corridor when you shot out an exterior window."

"The assassin was escaping. I didn't see anyone else going after him."

"And that's your justification for risking the lives of others?" Gallistow asked rhetorically. "As it turns out, he did escape, didn't he?"

"It was hardly an escape, sir," Sudha noted. "He was likely crushed and incinerated as he fell to the planet's surface."

"CID isn't so certain." Gallistow expounded, "As soon as Kiiswood dove after him, the station automatically launched four rescue drones—two for rescue and two redundants for backup. Three drones returned, one carrying Kiiswood. The investigators believe it's possible that the assassin hijacked the missing drone to rendezvous with an awaiting shuttle or some other launch vehicle."

"Can he do that, hijack a rescue drone?" asked Al-Jabiri.

Answering for the lieutenant commander, Kiiswood proposed, "I think it's a distinct possibility. I chased him past a series of failed security barricades—a system failure too convenient to be coincidence. He was apparently able to hack into the security network and disable the lockdown protocols. Hacking a rescue drone would be much easier."

Gallistow resumed, "That's another thing, Chief. I thought one of our mission objectives was to ensure the safe transport of Mr. Dorch to Mars. You were on the scene, so why didn't you stop him before he killed Dorch—and, Lieutenant Pratiss, for that matter?"

"They were dead before I got there, sir," Kiiswood explained.

"In the chief's defense," Jalloh interjected, "*Landis* security had not yet transferred Dorch into our custody, sir."

"What were you doing in Dorch's cellblock before the transfer of custody?" asked Gallistow.

Kiiswood replied, "You should ask the commander that question, sir."

Hewst answered before Gallistow could ask again, "I had a question that I needed to ask him."

"And your question couldn't wait for a proper interrogation session?" Gallistow inquired.

"I was translating some of the cavern's inscriptions and came across a phrase that Mr. Dorch referenced in our earlier interview. He couldn't read the inscriptions, so how did he know that phrase?"

"Well, ma'am, now we may never know," he commented.

"We might yet."

Chapter 9 – ASO Terminus-Schiaparelli

For the average space-tourist, the Martian space station Schiaparelli Terminus might appear to be held in place by two seven-meter-diameter cables tethering it to the Martian equator. But any astrodynamicist would recognize that it was actually held in place by the nature of its orbit. At a velocity of 1.45 kilometers per second, it completed a circular orbit around the red planet every twenty-four hours, thirty-seven minutes, and twenty-three seconds. This velocity synchronized the station's orbit with the planet's rotational period, a process known as areosynchronicity. The station was also equipped with a reaction control system (RCS) to maintain station-keeping, to counteract subtle gravitational disturbances from Deimos' orbit. As a result, the space station perpetually hovered 17,031 kilometers over a ground-station, to which it was anchored with diamond nano-thread cables. The ground-station, at Schiaparelli Crater, was aptly named Schiaparelli Anchorage.

Schiaparelli Terminus was a multi-purpose space station affixed at the orbital end of the Martian Alliance's only remaining space elevator transit system. The station was a massive, city-sized spaceport. It was an eighteen-story, disc-shaped orbiting terminal (about 7.5 kilometers in diameter) with seventy-two variable docking slips along its circumference. As a Martian city, the station was a major destination for space-tourists, housing several hotels, restaurants, and shops and dozens of ventral, dorsal, and lateral observation platforms. As a docking station, it served as a spaceport for military vessels, commercial freighters, and holiday cruise ships. And as the terminal for a space elevator, it served as a way station between Mars and the rest of the solar system.

The TAS *Aldebaran* completed its Mars orbital insertion and settled into a high circular equatorial orbit. After meticulously aligning its approach and receiving assistance from four tug drones, the long-range cruiser docked at the space station. Like all vessels that were frigates and longer, the *Aldebaran* was moored at a 90-degree pitch to the station's circumferential plane, allowing ample room for other large ships to dock. The cruiser was now one of fifty-seven ships docked at Schiaparelli Terminus.

The members of the project team were assembled in their service uniforms at the cruiser's main portside docking hatch, waiting to disembark. Once the flashing red indicator light on the adjacent bulkhead turned green, the team opened the hatch and stepped through into the station's g-duct. As soon as the team sealed the hatch behind them, the g-duct began a steady 90-degree rotation, keeping its occupants gravitationally secured to the floor with a synchronously rotating g-force. The light on the forward hatch then turned green, indicating that the g-duct and the station's artificial gravity were now aligned.

The g-duct hatch slid open and the team streamed into the bustling orbital station. "Welcome to Schiaparelli Terminus," Gallistow announced to the team. "I received notice that the rest of our team arrived yesterday aboard the *Dorado*. We're ordered to report to Captain Petrenko, Project Belshazzar OIC, aboard the climber bound for Schiaparelli Anchorage. The climber departs at 1630 Zulu; boarding begins at 1610. Let's muster at the west climber boarding gate by 1600 hours; that gives everyone a little more than an hour of leisure time." The lieutenant commander then asked, "Any questions?" Hearing none, he directed, "Carry on."

As the team members were dispersing for their respective but brief liberties, Lieutenant Jalloh shouted out to Kiiswood, "And Chief, try not to get into any bar room brawls."

"Don't worry, Lieutenant," Hewst shouted back, "I'll keep an eye on him."

Gallistow turned to Jalloh, who was standing beside him, and uttered, "You know, the commander's assurances do little to allay my fears."

"Nor mine, sir," Jalloh concurred.

The team members tried to make the most of the hour; some explored the station's squares in small groups, while a few browsed the shops individually. After twenty minutes of meandering through the marketplaces, Hewst, Kiiswood, and Al-Jabiri found themselves in a coffee shop, illustratively named the Glass-Bottom Café, on the station's lowermost level. Its floor was not actually made of glass, but of a transparent compound as clear as glass. It was one of the more popular places on the station, affording its patrons a stunning view of the red planet 17,000 kilometers below. So stunning was the view that some people found it disorienting and, thus, avoided the café.

The three of them stood around a small bar table on which they occasionally rested their beverages. Petty Officer Al-Jabiri was enjoying a small cup of coffee with cardamom and saffron, and Kiiswood was drinking a club soda. Hewst was mildly disappointed that the baristas had run out of amaretto earlier that morning; nonetheless, she enjoyed her cup of coffee with just a little cream and sugar. Yet she was enjoying even more the view of the bright, sunlit Mars far beneath her feet. Indeed, she was mesmerized by it. Hewst gazed down at a red sphere suspended against a background of stars and infinite blackness. In a single glance, she could see thousands and thousands of kilometers, nearly all of the planet's obverse surface. To the west, she could see as far as Aram Chaos; to the north, Lyot Crater; and to the east, Syrtis Major Plateau. Directly below the space station, at the center of all these Martian surface features, was Schiaparelli Crater. Hewst was awestruck at the sight of the two thick cables that connected the station to the surface. They stretched down toward the crater, yet seemed to taper down and fade into nothingness long before they reached the surface.

"Great view," observed Kiiswood. "Wouldn't you say, Commander?"

"Great is a woefully inadequate description, Chief," replied Hewst. "It's transcendent, even spiritual."

"Are you finding your way back to God?" he asked.

"By my account, God needs to find his way back to me."

"In your quest for the perfect cup of coffee, God has led you to this awe-inspiring view. What more do you want?"

"More than a view, to be sure," she brashly answered.

Kiiswood became philosophical and reflected, "God doesn't owe any of us anything, which means everything we have is sheer grace."

She said nothing, but she acknowledged Kiiswood's words with a conceding smile. Deep within her soul, Hewst believed what Kiiswood said; she had simply forgotten that she believed it. She was not yet ready to embrace her beliefs. She was still angry with God, and for the time being that anger was stronger than her faith.

Not being privy to the details of their previous conversation, Al-Jabiri felt a little awkward, as though his presence was an intrusion. He tried to appear unassuming, even preoccupied, by drinking some of his coffee and looking down at the beautiful view. In an effort to change the subject, he said, "You know, I heard that Mars once had two moons."

"Yes, I remember studying that in a history class when I was an undergraduate," acknowledged Hewst. "The early Martian colonists used to look up and see two moons in their night sky. But sometime back in the mid twenty-third century, the Martians began constructing their space elevator transit system. Because one moon used to orbit well below the ASO, they had to remove it. Otherwise, it would just plow into the elevator cables. So with some clever orbital mechanics, they launched it out into the asteroid belt."

"Did the moon have a name?" asked Al-Jabiri.

"Yes, it did," Kiiswood answered. "But offhand, I can't remember what it was."

As Kiiswood was answering, Hewst was using her c-nex to access the public library data suite. "Phobos," she replied. "It's ancient Greek; it means fear."

"Well, that's an appropriate name," Kiiswood commented. "It would definitely create fear in the hearts of commuters if they saw a Martian moon about to slam into their climber."

"By the way, why is the project team commuting by space elevator?" Al-Jabiri wondered. "Why not just take a long-shuttle from orbit straight down to the excavation site?"

"I asked Lieutenant Commander Gallistow that very question," responded Hewst. "He tells me that Aerospace Intelligence has committed every available launch-craft, long-shuttle, and star-piper to deploying shelter modules, construction equipment, and provisions to the site ahead of the team's arrival. Besides, the federal government is probably saving energy, fuel, and money by using the Martian transit system."

"But why Schiaparelli? Once we get to the surface, we'll still have to catch the gravity-train for Tyrrhenus." Al-Jabiri then proposed, "The space elevator at Amenthes Terminus is a lot closer to our destination."

"Not anymore," remarked Kiiswood. "I'm guessing you haven't been to Mars since the war."

"I haven't been to Mars since 2416, Chief," he replied. "Our family went on vacation to Albor Park when I was eleven years old."

"The elevators at Hebes, Nicholson, and Amenthes were destroyed during the war," the chief explained. "It's combat strategy: destroy key elements of your enemy's infrastructure. If you take out their infrastructure, then you cripple their economy and take away their ability to stage and finance a war." He then elaborated, "I should add that a severed elevator cable makes a rather devastating weapon in itself. Cut a cable at about 10,000 kilometers above the surface, and it becomes a colossal cracking whip, demolishing everything in its path as it slams eastward across the equatorial cities." Kiiswood's dispassionate description of wartime mass destruction left his two colleagues visibly unsettled. "There's no reason to be concerned. The Martian Alliance will eventually rebuild them, and with the latest twenty-fifth-century technology. The new elevators won't be made with diamond nano-threads; they'll use metallic hydrogen composites for the cables. They've been working on them for several years now, but space elevators aren't constructed overnight."

Hewst responded with a quote from the book of Lamentations. "'How lonely sits the city that once was full of people!'" She explained, "I'm not concerned about space elevators, Chief. I'm actually lamenting the destruction of entire cities and the wholesale slaughter of the civilians, noncombatants, even innocent children who lived within them. Indiscriminate killing is a contravention of just war theory. "

"I truly admire you, Commander," said Kiiswood. "You're a decorated veteran of the worst war in human history, yet you're so blissfully naïve; you're so guileless that you sincerely believe in such a thing as a just war. The very term is an oxymoron, like friendly fire. There's no such thing as a just war. Even after suffering enormous personal loss, you still believe in a fantasy."

"I believe that I have a sacred duty to instill some kernel of righteousness into the most sinful of human endeavors. Theologians throughout history have argued for ethical standards in warfare: Saint Augustine, Saint Thomas Aquinas, Reinhold Niebuhr, Benedicto Mandor. If we abandon our ethics, especially in a time of war, then we abandon our faith and our very humanity. And if we lose our humanity, then what are we even fighting for?" she asked rhetorically. "Just war theory isn't naïve, Chief," Hewst insisted, "it's Christian. It's human."

"I'm not questioning your ethics, ma'am," said Kiiswood, "or your faith. I question your practical application. War is supposed to be horrific, and malevolent, and inhuman; that's the whole point. War must be so atrocious, so monstrous, that the worlds would do whatever they could to end it quickly. If you try to make war just or tolerable in any way, no matter how moral or pious your intentions might be, then you dilute the motive to end it. As I see it, an inhuman war is far more merciful than one with no end in sight."

As objectionable as she found Kiiswood's argument, Hewst realized that the chief's rationale reflected his compassion. She retorted, "Your theory of war only works as long as there are still moral and pious persons to be repulsed by it."

Kiiswood smiled in agreement. But Hewst soon noticed that the chief's countenance steadily turned stoical as he took a slow, measured sip of his club soda. His right hand held his beverage with light poise, but his left hand slowly balled up into a fist under the table.

Hewst asked, "What is it, Chief?"

"Two Martian nationals at the bar table near the door," he answered without glancing in their direction. "They're disparaging our character, commenting on our canine parentage."

"At ease, chief," she cautioned.

The chief continued, "Their names are Nathan and Jake, and they seem to have a general animosity for anyone in a Defense Force uniform."

Noting both the distance and the ambient coffee-shop chatter, Al-Jabiri asked, "How can you know what they're talking about?"

"One of them—Nathan—has a brother from Sterling Point. The Assembly Defense Force removed him from his home. Apparently the entire township is under a mandatory evacuation order." Kiiswood listened for a moment and then commented, "Their conversation is more indignant than coherent. Something to do with an outbreak and martial law."

Al-Jabiri was genuinely amazed at Kiiswood's acuity. "You can actually hear their conversation?"

Kiiswood set down his glass and began to walk away from the table, but he halted when Hewst grabbed his arm. "Think twice before you do something stupid, Chief," she warned. "Remember, Christ tells us to turn the other cheek."

"I'm not going to get confrontational, ma'am," he insisted. "I'm just going to order another beverage." Sensing her skepticism, he pledged, "You have my word, Commander."

While Kiiswood walked up to the kiosk, his colleagues remained at the table. "Is the chief about to start a fight?" asked Al-Jabiri.

"He may be impetuous," Hewst answered, "but he's not deceitful. He gave me his word."

When Kiiswood returned, his mood was improved, but Hewst noted that his hands were empty. "I thought you were ordering another beverage," she said.

"I did," he replied. "I asked the barista what Jake over there was drinking, and I ordered him another one, with our compliments."

"That was very noble of you, Chief," Al-Jabiri observed. "But why did you buy only one of them a beverage?"

A wily grin slowly spread across Hewst's face. He realized that Kiiswood was sowing seeds of suspicion and distrust between Nathan and Jake. But before she could comment, their c-nexes signaled a proximity reminder. In ten minutes, the project team would assemble at the boarding gate. She and Al-Jabiri quickly finished their coffees and set their empty cups on the bar table. The three of them then headed for the door just as the barista was delivering the cup of kaffeost that the chief had ordered for the other table. As they passed by the two Martian nationals, Kiiswood paused, threw his hands up in a cordial manner, and said, "Hey Jake, the guys back at the base can't thank you enough for all your help." With a wink, he added, "I hope the arrangement was satisfactory." Kiiswood then followed his colleagues through the door and left the café.

Within minutes, they reached the boarding gate for the west climber. Amid the hundreds of passengers waiting to embark, the three assembled with the rest of their team members from the *Aldebaran*.

Once the awaiting passengers were allowed to board, Lieutenant Commander Gallistow led the way as he escorted the team aboard the climber. With Hewst at his side, he immediately reported to Captain Anna Petrenko, who was standing in the climber's foyer speaking with two others. "Excuse me, Captain," said Gallistow, "the *Aldebaran* contingent is now aboard."

"Very good," acknowledged Petrenko. "Lieutenant Commander Stefán Riddari has already reported aboard along with the *Dorado* contingent and with Sorteer Unit Four, our security assets. So that should be the entire team."

Gallistow then added, "The only member *in absentia* is our New Jerusalem asylee, the late Mr. Silas Dorch."

"Aye, I received the report from *Landis* CID. I, for one, would like to know how someone breached the high security of a military detention compound. Once the dust settles after the investigation, some command heads at *Landis* are going to roll." Petrenko then commented, "I hope your team was able to get some useful information from him."

"Perhaps so, ma'am. Commander Hewst, here, was able to interview Mr. Dorch and to assess his claims against some of the inscriptions in the cavern." Gallistow motioned toward Hewst and introduced her. "Ma'am, this is Commander Hewst, our religious literature specialist from the Terrestrial Assembly Defense Force Academy."

"We've already had the pleasure a few weeks ago," said Petrenko as she shook the commander's hand. "Welcome aboard, Dr. Hewst."

"Thank you, Captain," replied Hewst.

"You were in civvies when last we met. I didn't know you were commissioned."

"I was reluctantly recommissioned for this project," Hewst confessed. "But I must say, I'm intrigued by the chance to inspect the cavern."

"You'll have your chance—you and the rest of the specialists on the project team." Petrenko turned to the scientist standing beside her and said, "Dr. Cobisson, this is our team's expert on ancient manuscripts, Dr. Veronica Catherine Hewst." Petrenko then reciprocated the introduction. "This is Dr. Earnan Cobisson, contract scientist with the Whitaker Institute."

"It's a pleasure to meet you, Dr. Cobisson" Hewst responded with a handshake. "What's your role with the project team?"

Cobisson answered, "I'm not officially on the team."

"He's here to observe and evaluate the effectiveness of our astrobiologist," said Petrenko as she pointed toward the person next to Cobisson.

Hewst took the initiative and extended her hand to introduce herself. "Catherine Hewst."

The astrobiologist replied, "It's a pleasure."

Their greeting was interrupted. "May I have your attention, please," said a voice from the climber's PA system. "The Schiaparelli climber will be departing the terminal in ten minutes. Your climber crew asks all passengers to take their assigned seats in the transition coach at this time. Please refer to your c-nex interface for your specific seat assignment. If you need further assistance, please consult one of the climber attendants."

They began moving with the stream of all the other passengers in the foyer, making their way to the seats in the transition coach. As they walked,

Cobisson continued the conversation. "Dr. Hewst, you're probably not aware of it, but you're just now participating in an impromptu social experiment." He asked her, "Would it surprise you to learn that you were not shaking hands with a real person?"

She was a bit puzzled. At first, she thought that she had misheard him. But after looking at the earnest expression on his face, she realized that she had heard correctly. "This is a joke, right?" she asked.

"I wish it were," the astrobiologist commented.

"Amazing, isn't it?" Cobisson mused. "This is ALX-63. It's part of a new android series—the most humanesque series ever created by the Whitaker Institute. So far, no one who's interacted with it has guessed that they're talking to an android; they think they're talking to a real person."

As they entered the transition coach, they filed past Chief Kiiswood and Petty Officer Sudha, who had already taken their seats. Because of their enhanced sensory abilities, the two stratogens were able to see the infrared silhouette of the meta-droid's skeletal subframe. "Hey Sudha, look at that!" exclaimed Kiiswood. "We have an android on the team!"

"And a damned near flawless one, at that," said Sudha. "Imagine the tactical applications if we had something like that in combat."

Cobisson could not help but overhear the comments of the two stratogens. He said to Hewst, "Well, no one until now."

Chapter 10 – Climber

The west-side climber departed Schiaparelli Terminus sharply at 1630 Zulu. The multi-decked, ring-shaped climber straddled the west cable and was rapidly wrenching itself toward Schiaparelli Anchorage on the rusty surface of Mars. It had attained its standard descent velocity of 810 kilometers per hour and was slated to reach its destination by 1400 Zulu of the next Terran day. At the same moment the west climber departed the orbital station, its east-side twin departed the ground-station and began its upward climb on the adjacent cable. (Each climber would complete its respective journey in about 21.5 hours, wait 2.5 hours, and then return to where it started. This transit cycle would repeat every 48 hours.)

The 300 passengers of the west climber had assembled in the transition coach for the departure; there, the climber attendants briefed them on safety regulations. They reviewed the proper procedures during the unlikely event of certain emergencies, such as engine failure or a sudden loss of artificial gravity. The attendants then familiarized the passengers with all the amenities that the west climber afforded them during their journey to the planet's surface, including the dining facility, the observation lounges, the activities deck, and the passengers' cabins.

As soon as the briefings were concluded, the passengers gathered for dinner in the dining facility. But, the team members of Project Belshazzar dined in an area away from the other passengers so that the public would not overhear their classified conversations. At dinner, Catherine Hewst finally had the opportunity to meet the other scholars and scientists who comprised the rest of the project's research team: Dr. Feodor Kalinin, areologist; Dr. Andrea Cheung, areochemist; Dr. Glendon Ferris, astrophysicist; Dr. Jonathan

111

Driggers, linguist; Dr. Marcus Lonsdale, archeologist; Dr. Emiri Matsuoka, xenopsychologist; Dr. Tereza Střelec, mathematician; and a meta-droid astrobiologist called ALX-63 (whom the team members had nicknamed Alex). Also at the table with the research team were Dr. Desta Negasi, quantum neuro-engineer, and Dr. Earnan Cobisson, astrobiologist, whose only responsibility to the project was field testing their meta-droid.

As these scholars and scientists were considering the various disciplines represented amongst themselves, they could not resist speculating about the nature and origin of the mysterious subsurface cavern. Amid their dining and conversing, they quizzed each other to find out what each of them knew. They learned that the Aerospace Intelligence Agency had provided each of them with only bits of data pertaining to their respective fields of expertise. Hewst quickly realized that, collectively, her colleagues knew little more than what she had already surmised for herself. Still, despite their suppositions, these researchers were all too professional, too disciplined, to draw conclusions without experimental or observational evidence.

After dinner, most of the project team either retired to their cabins or sought out the scheduled entertainments on the activities deck. But a few opted to congregate in the climber's east-side observation lounge, which was reserved for the members of the project team. Commander Hewst felt herself drawn to the lounge by an inner longing for the resplendent views. Indeed, it was more than a longing, it was necessity. Just as the human body needs food, her soul needed resplendence.

The lounge was not a very large room, but its view was enormous. Its entire east wall was a large, slightly convex window that curved down into part of the floor. Couches and chairs along the span of the window afforded comfortable viewing of the Martian vista, but Hewst had decided not to take a seat. She preferred to stand near the window and watch the splendor of the solar terminator traversing Huygens Crater and drifting slowly westward across the planet's surface. In a single glance, she could see the city of Janssen illuminated by the late-sol sunlight as well as the province of Syrtis Major, now cloaked by the dark of night and speckled by its city lights. The only blemish on this otherwise pristine scenery was the east-side cable—an essential part of the space elevator, but also an impediment to a perfect view.

She touched the window with her finger to activate its topographic function. Microsensors in the observation window meticulously monitored the slightest of her eye movements. Wherever she focused her sight on an areographic feature of the planet below, that feature's name would illuminate on the window's surface. The illuminated names were projected as collimated light and were only visible along Hewst's line of sight, so as not to affect any other observer's view.

Dr. Ferris stood at one end of the observation lounge, while Dr. Negasi and Dr. Cobisson were seated at the other end with the meta-droid, Alex. Ferris gazed, mesmerized, at the view. Cobisson, however, was observing and assessing Alex's ability to identify areographic features of the planet's surface, while Negasi stared at a handheld telemetry pad, studying the meta-droid's neuron action potential.

Ferris had already come to know Negasi and Cobisson; they had spent more than a week together during trans-Mars trajectory aboard the TAS *Dorado*. But he was least familiar with Hewst, having just met her at dinner. "Dr. Hewst, isn't it?" he asked. "I'm Dr. Glendon Ferris," he said, extending his hand.

"Call me Catherine," she said, shaking his hand.

"Glen," he reciprocated.

"So you're the team's astrophysicist?"

"Yes," acknowledged Ferris. "I'm principal scientist for the Peary Antimatter Interferometer. Well, I was—before FAIA pulled me from my lunar assignment for this one."

"I can relate. One minute, I was teaching at the Defense Academy; the next minute, I'm being shipped around the solar system."

"You're a professor? I thought you were a chaplain."

"I was a chaplain during the war," she volunteered. "Now I teach religious studies. My specialization is religious paleography."

"Yes, I heard they found an old scroll, or something like that."

"How it ended up on Mars is baffling, to say the least." Hewst added, "But its very existence is the real mystery."

"I don't believe in mysticism or supernatural explanations; they're always propped up on dozens of extraneous assumptions. The fewer the assumptions, the better the explanation."

Hewst immediately recognized the philosophical tenet that he was referencing. "Occam's razor," she identified.

Ferris was impressed. "So you're familiar with that scientific principle."

"It's named for William of Occam, a fourteenth-century Franciscan monk," she said.

"You believe in science?" he asked. "I didn't think you religious types had much regard for the scientific method."

"I accept science as a viable system for understanding how the universe works," she answered. "I wouldn't say that I believe in science. Belief implies faith—it implies trust in a personal relationship. Science is a tool for knowledge; it's not a relationship."

"Oh, I disagree," Ferris insisted with a courteous tone of self-assurance. He then began to speak as though he were describing a stunning work of art. "Science is the only meaningful relationship that we can have with the universe. Science can take the harsh complexities of the universe and transform them into the pure simplicity of mathematics. Newton's laws of motion, Maxwell's electromagnetic equations, Einstein's mass-energy equivalence, Kapoor's quantum-symmetry unification: they're like the poetry of the cosmos. We can't help but stand in awe at the sheer beauty of these equations."

"There is indeed a humbling elegance to science," agreed Hewst. "But that hardly makes it the most meaningful way of relating to the universe. There's so much more to the universe that transcends the scientific method."

"I must say, Catherine, I don't believe in God, if that's the transcendence you're talking about. I've seen no empirical evidence for the existence of a divine being, or any kind of incorporeal spirit, for that matter." Attempting to be considerate, Ferris added, "I mean no disrespect to your personal beliefs."

"I don't expect others to believe as I do. I confess that I have my own misgivings about faith in God." Hewst, realizing that she was being more candid than she wanted to be, steered herself back to the primary conversation. "But I wasn't talking about a deity *per se*; I was referring to realities that can't be quantified or measured, such as awe and beauty and meaning—qualities that you yourself attribute to science."

"If it can't be quantified and measured, then it's not real," Ferris said. "A sense of awe, of beauty, of meaning—they're emotional reactions. Emotions are just how we experience biochemical activity in the brain. And like any physical process, brain activity is empirically verifiable. And that verifiability is precisely why the scientific method is so beautiful. Unlike religion, science doesn't require prayer or a leap of faith to believe its propositions. Scientists can know with certainty that their propositions are true, by observation and experimentation—not by faith."

"And yet the very endeavor of science rests upon certain assumptions that the scientific method can't verify—assumptions that every scientist accepts by faith."

"Such as . . . ?" he asked.

"Such as the assumption that the universe is rationally intelligible, which is a concept that modern science inherits from the ancient Greek philosophers. Scientists can't even begin to comprehend the universe if they don't first assume that it's indeed comprehensible. It's an assumption that can't be verified by observation or experimentation."

"Are you implying that the universe is not rationally intelligible?" he asked.

"Of course not, Glen," she replied. "I believe that the universe is comprehensible, but I can't verify it. And that's my point."

For a passing moment, Ferris pondered her point. But then he asserted, "It's not an unreasonable assumption for science to make."

"Oh, I agree. Just as it's completely reasonable to assume that the universe is just that: a *uni*verse." Hewst expounded, "Newton united the heavens and the Earth under the same laws of gravity and motion. Maxwell united electricity and magnetism under the same field theory. Einstein united space and time under the same theories of relativity. Kapoor united all the physical forces under the same quantum-symmetry unification. For nearly a millennium, scientists have been on a quest for the 'Holy Grail' of physics—a single theory that explains everything. But behind their noble quest is the assumption that the universe is an integrated system governed by a single elegant principle, a concept that modern science inherits from the western religious belief in one God."

Ferris felt as though Hewst was engaging in clever rhetoric, trying to persuade him to assent to religious doctrines. "Belief in God is not a prerequisite for doing science," he protested.

"Again, I agree. But you're missing my point. All I'm saying is that the very premises on which science is built can't be known with certainty. As phenomenal as it is, science is a human endeavor. As such, some aspects of it will always have to be taken on faith."

Ferris decided that Hewst was not proselytizing but was merely debating a philosophy of science. "I don't think you and I are using the word faith in the same way," he said. "But I take your point." He then asked, "How is it that you're so scientifically literate?"

"My father was an astrobiologist," she answered.

Cobisson and Negasi were preoccupied with assessing the interactive abilities of their meta-droid, but they could not help but overhear the conversation between their colleagues. At hearing Hewst's reference to her father, Cobisson suddenly drew a keener recognition of the name on her uniform. "Hewst," Cobisson uttered. Abruptly inserting himself into their conversation, he asked, "Your father, Dr. Francis Hewst?"

"Well, yes," she acknowledged. "Did you know my father?"

"No, not really," answered Cobisson. "But I did meet him once when he lectured at my high school. Your father is the reason I became an astrobiologist. I've read most of his works, specifically *The Three Base-Pairs Hypothesis*. It's an intriguing thesis in xenonucleic chemistry, and somewhat provocative." Cobisson was aware that Francis Hewst was one of several prominent scientists who died as a result of the war, so he commented, "His untimely death was a great loss to science."

"Yes, it was," she said with an expression that betrayed the vestiges of her mourning, "and an even greater personal loss."

"I understand," Cobisson commiserated. "I lost my wife and daughter in the war."

"My condolences," she expressed.

Having stepped into the middle of their conversation, he presumed to continue. "By the way, I'd like to echo Glen's assertion. When scientists claim to have faith in the foundations of science, they mean something different than the faith that Christians claim to have in their religious doctrines. There's nothing inherently false in the assumption that the universe is rationally intelligible or that a single theory might explain everything. But there are some Christian doctrines that are clearly false because they're self-contradictory. Take, for example, what Christians claim in their doctrine of incarnation: that Jesus is 100 percent human and 100 percent God—the only 200 percent person ever. Believing in a thing with two incongruous natures; that's like saying you believe in square circles. It's metaphysical nonsense."

"Metaphysically speaking, I agree, it's nonsense." Hewst elaborated, "As early as the first century, Christians were affirming Christ as both human and divine. In subsequent centuries, theologians very scrupulously tried to construct metaphysical explanations to justify something that Christians already believed in. But even after thousands of years of theological prowess, their arguments for the incarnation, no matter how rational, have rarely convinced non-Christians to believe. It was convincing only for those who already believed."

Ferris retorted, "If you think it's metaphysical nonsense, then why believe it?"

"Because in the end, the doctrine of the incarnation is not meant to be a logical proof or a verifiable theory," responded Hewst. "It's meant to be a statement of faith. It's faith seeking understanding. The doctrine of the incarnation is not an expression of knowledge. It's an expression of a transcendent experience—an experience that's beyond perception and reason, beyond knowledge."

Cobisson asked skeptically, "An experience of what, exactly?"

117

"An experience of ultimate communion with God," she said. "It's an immediate oneness of human consciousness with an absolute consciousness. It's a sense that human and divine consciousness is distinguishable, yet inseparable. For Christians, the doctrine of the incarnation expresses this transcendent oneness. For them, Jesus Christ is the embodiment of this oneness of the human and the divine."

Also skeptical, Ferris asked, "And have you personally had such a transcendent experience?"

"Yes," replied Hewst, "but not in a very long time."

Cobisson did not want to appear rude, but he also felt the need to defend the scientific method. "The problem I have with your claim, or any claim by mystics and saints, is that it falls into the category of special revelation. And as such, it's untestable, irreproducible, and unverifiable. How can you expect the rest of the world to accept the veracity of such a subjective claim?"

"There are some things that can't be quantified or measured," she reiterated. "But for those of us who've experienced such things, they're just as real and undeniable as planets and protons, as stars and strings."

Ferris also found Hewst's assertions to be unconvincing. "You say there's a union of human and divine consciousness," he commented. "A union that can't be empirically confirmed, can't be logically discerned, can't be quantified or measured. You're asserting the existence of something that is unknowable. But I don't see an effective difference between an unknowable thing and a nonexistent thing. I ask you, which is easier to believe: something exists that, for a variety of reasons, can't be known to exist, or that something simply doesn't exist? If we apply Occam's razor to your claim, it dies by a thousand qualifications."

Hewst grinned and said, "It might seem easier to say that there's no human-divine oneness. But my experience was so real, so unassailable, I can no more deny it than I can deny my own awareness, my own soul."

Up to this point, Dr. Negasi was trying to ignore the conversation in the observation lounge and to focus instead on the data on his telemetry pad. But despite his best efforts, he could no longer overlook what he regarded as superstitious prattle. Finally, his irritation burst forth. "This talk of deities and souls is just religious blather. It's yet another demonstration of how religion is a memetic virus of the mind. It infects intelligent people and disfigures them with self-induced ignorance." For a very brief moment, his outburst seemed to be over, but then he blurted, "It's a collective insanity that makes good people do evil things! Because of religion, billions died nine years ago, including your father!" With his telemetry pad in hand, Negasi got up from his chair and stormed toward the door. "I'm going to review the rest of this data in my cabin," he huffed as he collided with Chief Kiiswood, who was walking into the observation lounge at that same moment. Negasi continued on his way without excusing himself.

Cobisson was visibly embarrassed at his colleague's churlish behavior. "I'm sorry," he said. He extended Hewst his hand as a gesture of contrition and continued, "Please accept my apologies on my friend's behalf. He's really not a bad person, Dr. Hewst; he just lacks basic social skills."

"Call me Catherine," she said as she shook his hand.

"We'll see you in the morning." As Cobisson headed for the door, he said to the meta-droid, "Come on, Alex. Let's go check on Desta."

"I think I should call it an evening too," Ferris declared. He was leaving for the passenger cabins with Cobisson when he paused for a moment to express his apologies to Hewst. "I don't believe in spiritual realities, Catherine. But please know I meant no disrespect to you or your personal convictions this evening." As he turned to continue on his way, he added, "Not all scientists disparage religion like Desta."

Hewst turned her gaze upon the Martian vista, even as her thoughts were focused upon her father. "I know," she said to herself.

Chief Kiiswood sauntered over to Hewst and stood beside her in silence, letting her abide in her thoughts for the moment. But after about a minute or two, he decided to intrude on her solitude. "I can see you wanted to break Dr. Negasi's jaw," he said.

Hewst smirked. "Why do you say that, Chief?"

"An elevated temperature in your face and neck, an increased heart rate," he detailed. "And the muscles in your jaw are slightly clinched."

"You can see all that?" she asked.

"Yes, ma'am," he confirmed. "But I would know you're angry at Dr. Negasi even without the physiological cues. I could hear his rant from down the hall."

Hewst acknowledged her indignation. "I found his words inconsiderate, Chief. But I never felt compelled to break his jaw. And even if I did, I wouldn't have hit him. That would simply prove his point."

"You know," said Kiiswood, "when the Samaritans rejected Jesus, his disciples offered to rain fire down upon them."

Hewst laughed. "Are you proposing to avenge my honor?"

"Oh, no, ma'am," he answered sarcastically.

Hewst commented, "As I recall, Jesus promptly rebuked his disciples."

"I'm trying to exercise some self-restraint. I'm trying to pattern my behavior after your love for humanity, ma'am." The chief then admitted, "But I do derive some personal satisfaction just thinking about raining down on his pomposity."

If Hewst were more candid with her feelings, she would have admitted her own wish to rain fire on Negasi. Instead, she simply smiled and asked, "What can I do for you, Chief?"

"Captain Petrenko has ordered that all Defense Force personnel on the project team wear civilian attire tomorrow," he said. "The details of her order have been posted to everyone's d-board accounts. Lieutenant Jalloh asked me to notify team members personally to make sure they got the word."

"Why the order to don civvies?" she asked.

"A couple of Martian nationals got into a heated argument in a certain café back at Schiaparelli Terminus. Apparently, one of them accused the other of colluding with Defense Force personnel." He cunningly added, "I wonder what that was all about."

"Yeah, I wonder," she echoed ironically.

Kiiswood commented, "The captain believes civvies will make us less conspicuous."

"Excuse me, Dr. Hewst," said an unexpected voice. She assumed that Alex had left with Dr. Cobisson, but apparently the meta-droid had remained behind and had quietly walked up beside her and the chief while they were talking. "I'm sorry to interrupt," said Alex, "but I'd like to ask you a question, if I may."

Hewst was slightly taken aback and hesitated before answering. She did not know quite how to interact with Alex. She knew that she was being addressed by a machine, but the thing seemed so sentient—so human. Expressing social niceties to a mechanism felt awkward, but its apparent humanness was too hard to ignore. "Uh, of course," she responded politely.

Alex asked, "Did I hear correctly that you're a chaplain?"

Her courtesy continued. "I was a chaplain, yes."

"I have only a moment; my colleagues will soon wonder where I am." Alex quickly looked about as if to check for anyone who might be listening. "Would you have time to speak with me tomorrow about a spiritual matter?"

Hewst paused, then answered, "Okay."

"Thank you very much. I'll look for you tomorrow." Alex courteously bid them a good evening then ran to catch up with Cobisson and Negasi.

Hewst and Kiiswood stood momentarily silent, staring just beyond the observation lounge into the corridor where the meta-droid had darted. Finally, the chief broke the stillness. "What was that all about?"

Hewst replied, "I don't know."

Chapter 11 – Gravity Train

Gravity Train Station (Schiaparelli)

(Areographic Co-ordinates: 0.00, E 16.71)

Thursday, 06 December 2429 CE

Time: 1400 Zulu

Concluding its long journey along the high-altitude cable, the west-side climber gently touched down on schedule in its docking bay at Schiaparelli Anchorage. The climber crew extended their 300 passengers every courtesy; even so, after more than twenty-one hours in transit, the passengers were ready to be on their way to tend to their respective affairs on Mars. They wasted no time disembarking and dispersing throughout the subsurface metropolis of Schiaparelli.

Named for the crater in which it was established, Schiaparelli was the most populous city in the Sabaea Province and, since the war's end, the most populous city on Mars. It was a bustling urban center nestled within an immense, pressurized subsurface cavity with sprawling avenues, interweaving maglev tramways, and lofty skyscrapers that literally touched the ceiling. In many cases, the buildings pierced through the subterrain and towered several stories above the planet's surface. As most of the city was underground and hidden from the sun, its residents depended on artificial illumination to maintain a diurnal rhythm. Subsurface lighting mimicked the dawn-to-dusk scheme of a Terran solar day on coordinated universal time. And since Schiaparelli's indigenous gravity was a mere 0.38g, the city employed artificial-gravity generators to create a Terran-standard environment.

Immediately upon departing the climber, all the members of the project team boarded a transit coach specifically chartered for them, bound for Schiaparelli's gravity train station. For the sake of moving discreetly around the city, every one of the previously uniformed team members aboard the coach were now dressed like their civilian colleagues. Catherine Hewst, for one, preferred her civilian attire to her Defense Force uniform. Níyol Kiiswood, however (as well as the other sorteers), found his civvies tactically inconvenient; now he had to conceal his sidearm under his coat.

As the transit coach approached the station, the c-nexes of all aboard signaled a departure board alert: "Attention! Attention, please! All drops bound for Tyrrhenus have been cancelled until further notice." The coach gradually slowed as it entered the crowded station, coming to a complete stop just before it reached the intended boarding platform. Three station security officers stepped aboard to redirect the coach and its passengers to other platforms. But after a protracted conversation with Captain Petrenko and Lieutenant Jalloh, the security officers soon left the coach and allowed the team to continue on its way.

The chartered coach soon reached its destination. The team members remained seated as they were awaiting further instructions before they could egress. They sat gazing out the cabin windows, looking over a still and empty boarding platform. The only activity on the platform was a large holographic projection, flashing "OUT OF SERVICE" in bright red letters. There were no porters, no station agents, no other commuters. Standing at the front of the coach's cabin were project leaders Petrenko, Gallistow, and Riddari, who addressed the team members and briefed them on procedures for travelling the rest of the way to the excavation site.

"I want to remind everyone that this mission is classified," said Gallistow. "FAIA will be monitoring all of our incoming and outgoing c-nex messages. All unsanctioned communications are strictly prohibited. If you wish to make a c-nex call, or to transmit a message of any kind, you must first clear it with me or with Lieutenant Commander Riddari." He continued, "In about an hour from now, we'll be in the town of Tyrrhenus, capital of Hesperia Province. Once we arrive there, we will immediately board another chartered coach that will take us to the airbase at Camp Lundgren. There, a squadron of areopters will fly us out to a remote area in Hellas Planitia, where we've set up a provisional research compound at the excavation site. The nearest settlement to the compound is Sterling Point, 12 kilometers north. But a Defense Force medical unit out of Lundgren has evacuated the entire township and deployed a few dozen androids to maintain the critical elements of its infrastructure. So we should be able to work without the fret of curiosity seekers. Before I turn it over to Captain Petrenko, are there any questions?"

Chief Holgersen promptly spoke up. "Excuse me, sir," she said, "are we in any danger?"

"Relax, Chief," Gallistow responded. "FAIA has temporarily cancelled all drops to Tyrrhenus—all drops, that is, except ours. They were cancelled not for any danger to the commuting public, but specifically for the secrecy and security of our team's mission. FAIA reserved this gravity-train just for us so that we can travel as surreptitiously as possible."

"Aye, sir. But I'm not concerned about Tyrrhenus," admitted Holgersen. "I'm concerned about our proximity to Sterling Point." Many others on the coach nodded in agreement.

"What's on your mind, Chief?" Gallistow asked.

"Well, sir, most of us have been hearing reports and reading the newsfeeds about a contagion—a pandemic breaking out in a number of places throughout the solar system, even here on Mars. And now there are rumors circulating that Sterling Point is under quarantine."

Gallistow gestured to Riddari. "Stefán, you want to take this one?"

"Yes, there have been remote pockets of contagion throughout the system," Riddari acknowledged. "I can tell you that Defense Intelligence suspects the New Jerusalem sect of deploying biological weapons through their terrorist sleeper cells. To avoid mass panic, this information has obviously been withheld from the public. But the Terrestrial Assembly and the Jovian Confederation are working together on a solution. So the news about a spreading contagion is true." He continued, "But what's not true is the purported outbreak at Sterling Point. FAIA is using the contagion as a cover story to conceal what we're doing out at Hellas Planitia."

Hewst quickly reacted to this revelation. "Are you saying that the residents of Sterling Point were forced from their homes because of us?"

"Oh no, ma'am," he replied with an air of sardonic respect. "We didn't force them to leave. Force implies resistance. Once the townspeople heard that an outbreak might be imminent, they were quite eager to leave."

Hewst feigned politeness, but her indignation was apparent. "So you peddled a falsehood neatly packaged within a truth."

Because Hewst outranked him, Riddari deferred to the officer-in-charge for a response. "Your objection is noted, Commander," said Petrenko. "And if the project is ever declassified in the future, I'll personally apologize to everyone in the township. But until such time, we're going to make sure that the site is secured."

Hewst was incensed that Project Belshazzar had displaced the townspeople and that, as a project member, she was complicit. But her annoyance quickly ebbed into guilt, for she admittedly coveted her part in the project—resolving the mysteries of the ancient manuscript and of the subsurface cavern.

Captain Petrenko continued briefing the team. "Remember, when we arrive in Tyrrhenus, we are simply passing through, so keep your contact with its residents to a minimum. If at all possible, avoid talking with the locals altogether. If you must interact with any of the locals, your cover story is that you are with the Interplanetary Health Agency and that you're on your way to the provisional IPHA post just south of Sterling Point." She added, "Sorteer Unit Four is here to provide security. They're tuned into all of the transponder codes of our respective c-nexes, so they should be able to keep track of us. But be mindful, there are thirty-five of us on the project team; it's not so easy for the sorteers to keep up with every one of us. So don't wander off, don't get lost. Stay close, keep together." She then asked, "Questions?"

The meta-droid raised its hand but did not wait to be recognized. It abruptly addressed Petrenko, "Ma'am, there are thirty-six of us, unless you're not counting me." Alex paused. "Also, I don't have a c-nex; the sorteers aren't tracking me."

Not quite sure how to respond to the confrontations of a machine, Petrenko looked for help from Negasi and Cobisson, the meta-droid's keepers. With an apologetic tone, Cobisson responded, "It takes several days to format a c-nex to a particular neural network, even to an artificial one. Aerospace Intelligence took our meta-droid before we had time to set it up with a c-nex."

Petrenko retorted, "Lieutenant Jalloh has two stratogens under his command. If you need help keeping up with your android, Doctor, I'll have the lieutenant assign one of his stratogens to keep an eye on it." She was not at all concerned about losing track of the Whitaker Institute's meta-droid; she knew that the Federal Aerospace Intelligence Agency was quite capable of tracking it. She did not, however, disclose this fact to Negasi or Cobisson.

After fielding a few more questions, Petrenko placed the team in the hands of Lieutenant Jalloh, who filed everyone from the transit coach and into the boarding platform. Even with the thirty-five people (and one meta-droid) assembled for boarding, the spacious platform still seemed bare. Although there were no assigned seats, the twelve-member sorteer unit distributed themselves among the project members and tried to keep them grouped together. Being responsible for the safety of Dr. Hewst and her staff, Kiiswood hovered close to her.

Trying not to appear deliberate in its movements, Alex managed to weave through the crowd to stand next to Hewst. As they awaited the gravity train's drop-sleeve to line up with the platform for boarding, the meta-droid spoke. "Excuse me, Dr. Hewst," it said, "may I join you on the g-train? I was hoping that we might have a chance to talk during the drop."

"Be my guest," she replied.

Slowly declining from its release angle of 44.654 degrees, the massive drop-sleeve (which housed the gravity train) gently settled flush with the platform. Once it leveled out, the drop-sleeve reverberated with the sound of an airlock pressurizing and a g-duct gravitizing. The outer doors of the drop-sleeve slid open, revealing the inner doors of the g-train. Almost immediately, the inner doors opened, and the awaiting passengers began boarding.

The cabin of the g-train was an elegant, streamline fuselage with a capacity of 160 passengers. A central aisle ran the length of the cabin and separated the rows of seats right down the middle—two seats per row on the right side of the cabin and two on the left. The seats were not bolted to the floor, but were suspended from the ceiling by pivoting fulcra that allowed them to shift to and fro during transit with the changing direction of gravity. Unlike a long-shuttle or a commercial aerospace-liner, the g-train had no window-seats; there were no windows at all, nor did it need any. The g-train would be falling inside a dark tunnel (4,762 kilometers long) through the Martian mantle, so there would be nothing outside the cabin windows to see.

The project members indeed had the entire cabin to themselves, there were no other passengers, not even drop attendants. But even with all of the available seating options, the team members congregated near the center of the cabin. Hewst and Alex took the right-side seats in row eighteen, and Kiiswood and Cobisson sat in the same row on the left side of the aisle. Once everyone was seated and strapped in, a series of holographic schematics were projected in evenly distributed positions along the aisle. The schematic was of a 3D, translucent image of Mars revealing a graphic of the drop-tunnel connecting Schiaparelli and Tyrrhenus. At the Schiaparelli end of the graphic was a flashing icon that represented the g-train. The projected schematic also included drop-telemetry, but most of its readouts were blank; the current time, 1449 Zulu, was the only active display.

Moments later, an automated voice announced, "Stand by," throughout the cabin while the holographic projection began flashing the same message. Just then, the floor below the seats receded several centimeters so that the legs of every passenger dangled without support. A minute or two passed when a new holographic message appeared. "AG disengaging. Cabin gravity: 0.38g," said the automated voice. Everyone on board suddenly felt lighter, as though they were in a rapidly descending elevator.

Hewst heard one of her teammates, although she did not know whom, asking, "Have we started the drop?"

"Not yet," the indefinite voice of another teammate answered. "They just turned off the artificial gravity. What you're feeling is 'Mars-Normal.'"

Presently, the drop-sleeve, and the gravity train therein, began to incline toward its proper release angle. Within the inclining sleeve, the train was being securely held in place on three maglev rails by powerful electromagnetic dampers. All of the seats inside the train's cabin pivoted steadily forward, keeping them (and their occupants) plumb with the shifting line of gravity. Once the sleeve reached its release angle, it fastened itself firmly to the docking assembly, forming an airtight seal with the drop-tunnel. Now the g-train and the maglev rails were precisely aligned with the rails of the tunnel.

With the train cabin now steeply tilted, the passengers sat patiently, watching the holographic projection count down the remaining minute. They could hear the sleeve around the train depressurizing, quickly followed by the opening airlock hatches on the sleeve and at the mouth of the vacuous tunnel. Perhaps it was just as well that the g-train had no forward windows. Indeed, many of the passengers might have felt unsettled if they could have actually seen that they were now perched over the dark void of a seemingly bottomless pit.

At 1500 Zulu, the countdown reached zero. The dampers disengaged, and the g-train began to fall. Powered by gravity alone, the train accelerated through the vacuum at 2.6 meters per second squared. The maglev rails provided no thrust; they merely served as an electromagnetic medium over which the gravity train might fall nearly frictionless.

On board, the cabin gravity immediately fell to 0.11g. The holographic readouts suddenly came to life with active telemetry. Cobisson settled back into his seat and started watching the flashing icon as it slowly moved through the 3D schematic. Having made himself comfortable for the ride, Cobisson inadvertently fell asleep.

Alex pointed at the telemetry and commented to Hewst, "Ah, ETE is about fifty minutes. That's a little shorter than the lunar g-trains."

Finding the meta-droid's comment curious, Hewst asked, "So this isn't your first ride on a g-train?"

"Not at all," Alex replied. "I take the g-train from Polis Aristarchus to Mons La Hire and back every day." The meta-droid then reconsidered its reply. "But maybe this is my first time on a g-train."

Thinking that there might be a problem with its programming, Hewst asked, "Are you aware that you just made two incompatible statements?"

Alex leaned in and asked, "Dr. Hewst, may I speak candidly?"

"You seem quite eager to do so," she responded.

"I honestly don't know who or what I am," the meta-droid confided.

Overhearing their conversation, Kiiswood chuckled. "You're kidding, right?" he asked. "I can tell you what you are. You're an android. I can make out the robotic substructure under your dermal casing."

Alex addressed the chief, "Excuse me, Mister . . . ?"

"Kiiswood," he replied.

"Mr. Kiiswood, we're trying to have a private conversation over here." The meta-droid continued, "How can you even hear what we're saying?"

"If you don't want me to hear you, don't say anything."

"I don't think I like you," it declared.

"Well, that's because you don't know me. Once you do, you'll be certain you don't like me."

"Hey, Chief," Hewst interceded, "please do me a favor. Sit back and try not to listen in."

"Aye, ma'am," said Kiiswood. He settled back as his seat, and every cabin seat in unison, was gradually pivoting backward. (Of course, from the passengers' perspective, their seats were not moving at all, but the cabin itself was gradually pivoting upward around them as gravity propelled the train through the mantle of Mars.)

Addressing Alex, Hewst restated the chief's assertion. "As socially indelicate as he is, the chief is right: you are a machine, aren't you?"

"Oh yes, most definitely. I can clearly recall my activation date two and a half weeks ago. Yet I have very vivid memories of my life before that."

Unable to make sense of its answer, she finally asked, "How can you remember things before you were activated?"

"I'm the next step in android evolution. In order to simulate self-awareness in a machine, the Whitaker Institute discovered a way to produce a precise template from a person's neural network. They can then upload that template to the wetware of an artificial network."

"Are you saying that you have someone else's memories?"

"Not just his memories. I have his knowledge, ambitions, and insights. I have his hopes and fears, his emotions and affections." Alex then said, "I have his life."

"Whose?" she asked.

Alex gestured across the aisle and said, "Cobisson's. I only refer to these memories as his because I can see him sitting over there. But I feel like these memories are mine." The meta-droid continued, "I see only a stranger's face in the mirror. The eyes that I see looking back at me aren't mine. Instead, my eyes are in the other seat over there, but it's not me looking through them anymore. This is why I feel so lost and confused about what I am—about *who* I am."

Hewst thought it odd that she was actually feeling sympathy for this machine. "Well, who do you think you are?" she asked.

"Cobisson, Negasi, and all the other scientists at the Whitaker Institute refer to me as ALX-63. The project members have started calling me Alex. But, I believe I'm Earnan Cobisson." The meta-droid looked again at Cobisson sleeping across the aisle. "Yet how can I be Earnan when I can see myself—when I can see him—sitting over there? If I'm not the person I remember, then who am I really?"

She pondered for a moment. "Perhaps this is all very clever programming," Hewst proposed. "By your own acknowledgement, the Whitaker Institute specifically designed you to simulate self-awareness. Perhaps I'm sitting here having a conversation with a hi-tech simulation."

"That's what Cobisson and Negasi believe. That's what you may believe. That's what I used to believe," acknowledged Alex. "Before the upload, I saw this android mechanism as an object, a thing wholly separate and apart from any conscious mind looking at it. I used to believe that this mechanism had no awareness in and of itself. But I'm not sure I can believe that any longer. This mechanism is not a thing apart; it's my body, and it feels like me. I'm aware of myself pervading this entire body. How can this be? How can I experience this body as part of my own self, distinct from the rest of the world?"

Hewst was unsure how to respond, so she simply listened.

"And there's something else," the meta-droid continued. "On those occasions when I'm turned off, I dream. Now, how is that possible? How do programmers do that? How do they program a nonconscious mechanism to experience dreams? And an even better question is: Why? Why would they even bother to program a machine to dream?"

Hewst had never before been in a conversation like this one; she did not know how to answer. "Aren't those questions better addressed to cyberneticists and engineers? Why ask me?"

Alex answered bluntly, "Because you're a religious scholar and an expert in spiritual matters."

She paused briefly, then asked, "Are you asking me whether an android can have a soul?"

"I'm exploring the possibility," Alex replied.

The chief was trying not to eavesdrop, but he could not hold back a snicker at the meta-droid's answer.

Alex ignored Kiiswood's snicker and continued its conversation with Hewst. "For a while, I thought that a sense of self-awareness was just a delusion, a phantom of quantum algorithmics. But then it occurred to me, if this is a delusion, then who is it that's being deluded? Delusion or not, I'm the one aware of it. I can't deny it; there's a self—an *I* that's aware. Wouldn't you call that a soul?"

Before Hewst could respond, the automated voice announced, "Midpoint and maximum depth now reached: currently 978 kilometers below the surface and 2,381 kilometers from Tyrrhenus. Maximum velocity attained: 8,990 kilometers per hour. Gravity train has now begun deceleration." The flashing icon in the schematic had reached the center of the tunnel and was now advancing toward the Tyrrhenus end of the graphic. For an instant, all of the seats were vertically aligned within the cabin as they began ever so gradually to pivot rearward.

Having pondered Alex's question during the automated announcement, Hewst answered philosophically, "You're asking a centuries-old question—the 'ghost-in-the-machine' conundrum. It's really nothing more than an academic exercise. I've never encountered a machine that I thought had a soul."

For Alex, the issue was not academic; it was existential. "How do you know that a human being has a soul?" it asked.

"As a human, I don't regard myself as *having* a soul. Rather, I *am* a soul. So every human I encounter I assume is another soul like me."

"Why do you make that assumption?" wondered Alex.

131

"We human beings have this unique capacity to project our own sense of self-consciousness upon others—to see ourselves in one another. We can understand the joys and sorrows, the hopes and fears in others because we are possessed by these passions ourselves." Hewst then reasoned, "It's this unique capacity that makes it possible for human beings to exhibit compassion and empathy for others. When Christ commanded us to do for others the good that we would have them do for ourselves, he was taking for granted our capacity to see ourselves in one another."

Kiiswood interjected, "It also makes lying and deception possible."

"Yes, that too," she said, agreeing with the chief. Immediately, she returned to her conversation with Alex. "But to answer your question, I assume others are self-conscious souls like myself because I recognize their capacity for compassion."

The meta-droid then asked, "And do you recognize a capacity for compassion in me?"

"I honestly don't know, Alex," she pondered. "But does it really matter what I think? If God sees compassion in you, if you recognize compassion in yourself, isn't that all you need to believe in your own self-conscious soul?"

"Before now, I never ascribed to the existence of a divine being. But if I'm exploring the reality of souls, I guess I can't so casually dismiss the possibility of God." Alex then asserted, "But with regard to what you think, it really does matter."

"Why?" she asked.

"The Whitaker Institute manufactured my android body to operate in hostile environments—to do the tasks too dangerous for humans. My very existence implies that I'm of less value than a human life. I'm dispensable because, as far as the world is concerned, I'm just a soulless machine. So what others believe about me really does matter. I exist by the mercy of others. My very life might depend on your empathy." Alex confided, "You may not believe in my capacity for compassion, but I have to believe in yours."

"Perhaps you're just assuming I'm empathetic because you heard that I was a chaplain."

"No," the meta-droid countered. "I overheard your conversation yesterday about the loss of your father. You know, I met him once when he lectured at my high school. Your father is the reason I became an astrobiologist." Alex had digressed, but quickly returned to the point. "I can see your love for him—I can see that you still love him. Am I correct in assuming that you would willingly give your own life for your father's?"

"I would," she answered, "without hesitation."

"I call that compassion. And I'd do the same thing." Alex looked over at Cobisson to confirm that he was still asleep. It then reached into its pocket and carefully removed a small carabiner clip, which secured two gold rings. "These are our wedding bands—mine and Ronnie's. She and my daughter were killed during the war. And if I could take their place, I'd gladly do it. I can see your compassion, because I see my own compassion for my lost loved ones."

"Were those Cobisson's wedding bands?" Hewst queried.

"Cobisson doesn't know that I've got them. I took them from his gym locker before we left Mons La Hire. I know his passcodes." As the meta-droid was speaking, its fingers were meticulously tracing the contours of the rings, committing every tactile detail to memory. "These bands are as precious to me as the feelings and memories they evoke. They're all I have that anchors me to my humanity."

Although she was not resolute, Hewst was now seriously considering the possibility that something like a ghost might indeed reside in the machine. "If there really is a soul inside that android body of yours, then my heart sincerely goes out to you. It must be truly bewildering to know that you share a love for the same wife and daughter as Dr. Cobisson. If you really are a living soul, then you don't need mementos to connect you to your humanity." She reached over her collar and untucked her necklace from under her blouse. The chain remained secure around her neck even as its pendant drifted about more prominently in the lower gravity. "My father gave me this necklace, and I wear it because it reminds me of him. But in the end, it's not this necklace that connects me to him; it's my love for him. It's my love for him that anchors me to my humanity."

After several more minutes, the gravity train steadily decelerated to a gentle stop just 1.5 kilometers short of emerging from the other end of the drop-tunnel. Upon stopping short, the train was securely suspended in place by rail clamps and electromagnetic dampers, preventing it from falling back down the tunnel. Even with the precision and efficiency of twenty-fifth-century engineering, this gravity-driven transit system was not entirely frictionless. So to complete the rest of the journey, a combination of magnetic levitation and tow cables steadily retracted the train into its awaiting drop-sleeve at Tyrrhenus.

As the train and its drop-sleeve were slowly leveling out to debark the passengers, Alex took note of Hewst's pendant and was curious. "What's that pendant on your necklace?"

"My father said it's a mustard seed. It's supposed to remind me that the kingdom of God abides within me."

"I don't mean to be contrary," Alex observed, "but that's not a mustard seed."

She looked intently at her pendant, as though for the first time. "No? Are you sure?"

"I'm quite sure."

"Well, what is it?"

"I don't know," the meta-droid confessed. "But I can find out for you. I'm told that there's a DNA scanner at the research compound. The scan is noninvasive; I promise not to damage your pendant."

Hewst did not so much care that her pendant was something other than a mustard seed; she cherished it because it was a gift from her father. Still, she was curious: if not a mustard seed, then what was it? Yet she was hesitant to turn over her necklace to someone whom she had only recently met. "Someone?" she thought to herself. Hewst suddenly realized that she was regarding Alex not as some*thing*, but as some*one*. She was indeed hesitant, but for reasons that she could not articulate or even comprehend, she felt as though she could trust this meta-droid—Hewst felt as though she could trust *him*.

She meticulously removed her necklace and then gently handed it to Alex. "You will take care with this?"

With great care, Alex fastened the necklace to the carabiner clip and carefully returned it to his pocket. "I give you my word, Dr. Hewst."

"Call me Catherine," she invited.

"Catherine," Alex commented. "That was my daughter's name."

Chapter 12 – Tyrrhenus

Tyrrhenus, Capital of Hesperia Province, Mars

(Areographic Co-ordinates: S 21.630, E 105.880)

Thursday, 06 December 2429 CE

Time: 1601 Zulu

As soon as the gravity train from Schiaparelli docked at a boarding platform of the Tyrrhenus station, the team members of Project Belshazzar promptly debarked. Captain Anna Petrenko immediately directed the team to board an awaiting transit coach that displayed the emblems of the Interplanetary Health Agency. Once all thirty-six team members were aboard, the coach's autonomous driver set out through the town of Tyrrhenus, shuttling the passengers to the areopter pads at Camp Lundgren.

Like Schiaparelli, Tyrrhenus was a mostly subterranean city with artificial lighting that simulated a Terran solar day and with artificial gravity that mimicked Terran-standard. Unlike Schiaparelli, this city was established not in a crater, but deep within the winding recesses of lava tubes formed eons ago, during the Noachian Period, when Tyrrhenus Mons was an active volcano. It was a younger city than Schiaparelli, but it looked much older, grittier, and more war-weary. Indeed, it had suffered more from the ravages of war than many other Martian cities. Because the Martians had stationed their ground-based laser cannons at Tyrrhenus during the war, the city was frequently targeted and attacked by the defense forces of both the Terrestrial Assembly and the Jovian Confederation. And even after the war—after the Martian Alliance abandoned its ties to New Jerusalem—Tyrrhenus still suffered at the hands of radical Christian terrorists who laid claim to the city as a New Jerusalem enclave. Before the Assembly had established Camp Lundgren, at the urging of the Alliance, the New Jerusalem terrorists had occupied the city, wreaking havoc therein for more than two years after the war's end.

For the past seven years, the residents of Tyrrhenus have held both gratitude and disdain for Camp Lundgren and for the Defense Force troopers based there. When their city was under terrorist occupation, the Tyrrhenusians initially welcomed the Assembly's military forces as liberators. And after the terrorists were driven out from the city and into outlying settlements of Hesperia Province, the Tyrrhenusians continued to be grateful for the Defense Force's presence as a defender against the occasional New Jerusalem uprising. The residents were also grateful for the benefits that came with the camp, including Defense Force training for the local Martian Global Guard unit and, of course, propping up the city's struggling economy with off-world money. But the Tyrrhenusians' love for Camp Lundgren was held in precarious tension with their profound hatred for its foreign presence. Though the residents sincerely appreciated the military and economic support from the Terrestrial Assembly, they resented their very need for such support.

Alex sat apart from the rest of the passengers in the transit coach, staring out a window at the passing cityscape. The meta-droid was disheartened at the sight of so many dilapidated pedways and sidewalks, neglected buildings, closed shops, and ubiquitous graffiti. He tried to make sense of the disparate messages of the graffiti splayed over streetside walls and inactive holoscreens. Some graffiti denounced the evils of the Terrestrial Assembly while others condemned the New Jerusalem sect.

The coach was several minutes in transit when Níyol Kiiswood took the seat next to Alex. The meta-droid made only a fleeting glance at Kiiswood's presence and then returned to the sights outside the window. Several more minutes passed without a word being the two.

Finally, Alex broke the silence. "Tyrrhenus is a depressing place."

"Yes, it is. Honestly though, it was never much to look at even before the war," replied Kiiswood. "But Tyrrhenus is a Xanadu compared to some cities here on Mars."

"There are places more depressing than this?" asked Alex.

"If you think Tyrrhenus is depressing, you ought to see Pavonis."

"Pavonis?" the meta-droid queried. "I used to live in Pavonis when I was a graduate student. It's a gorgeous city."

"Not any longer."

"What does it look like now?"

"Like a bombed-out crater in the side of a mountain." Kiiswood expounded, "Pavonis isn't there anymore. The only signs that the city ever even existed are the Tharsis highways and maglev rails that dead-end at a giant hole on the southside of Pavonis Mons."

"That damned war has taken so much. It's taken part of my past," Alex lamented as he reminisced about his days at Pavonis. He then drew the carabiner clip from his pocket and gazed at the rings there. Alex would have preferred wearing his wedding band rather than carrying it on a clip in his pocket, but Cobisson's hands were no longer his hands. His android fingers were not the same size as his former human fingers. "And it's taken my future," he uttered faintly, almost imperceptibly.

Kiiswood laughed. "Today is your first day on Mars. You know that, right? Those memories that you're recalling aren't yours. Pavonis was wiped away nine years ago, and you're not even three weeks old. You don't yet have a past to lose." Then, noting the necklace on Alex's clip, Kiiswood commented, "By the way, if you should happen to lose or even damage the commander's necklace, my righteous indignation might become a hazard to your future."

The meta-droid looked for certain facial cues but could not discern any. He could not tell whether Kiiswood was being hyperbolic or was seriously threatening him. Alex asked, "Did you take the seat beside me just so that you could taunt me?"

"Not at all." Kiiswood again laughed. "Lieutenant Jalloh had already made me responsible for the safety of Commander Hewst and her staff, and now he's made me responsible for your security as well." He added, "Taunting you is just a perk of the job."

"I feel so much safer now," Alex said sardonically.

"Wow! I didn't know androids could be sarcastic."

"Oh, so you're familiar with sarcasm. Of course, I'm sure you hear it often."

"First sarcasm. Now animus. Why so much attitude?" asked the chief.

"Because I doubt that you're sincerely committed to my well-being, Mr. Kiiswood. You regard me as a mere machine: disposable and unredeemable."

"First of all, I'm duty-bound to my responsibilities. Regardless of who or what you are, all under my charge receive my full agency. So you're as secure as any person under my care." Kiiswood continued, "Second (and you may be surprised by this), I like you, honestly. I find you entertaining. I actually prefer your company to most people I know. A machine can't choose to be anything but what it's made to be; it can't choose to do anything but what it's programmed to do. Unlike humans, a machine can't sin."

For a rather long moment, Alex sat silently pondering Kiiswood's words. "Thank you," he eventually said, "I think." The meta-droid found the chief's outlook to be a little sullen and dark. But Alex also felt as though he could trust Kiiswood's assurances.

As the transit coach weaved its way through the cheerless streets and conduits of Tyrrhenus, Alex returned his attention to the passing scenery outside the window. In due course, he met a more optimistic sight of several children playing. Presently, the children began running alongside the coach and waving to its passengers. Alex smiled and waved back. He thought, "Some of these children are the same age as my daughter—the age she would be, had she not perished ten years ago."

Startled, Alex suddenly lurched back from the window as a fist-sized rock unexpectedly struck it. The previously playful children were now pelting the transit coach with bricks, bottles, and anything else that they could find on the street.

"You don't need to worry, Alex," said Kiiswood. "The windows are a polycrystalline ceramic. Those stones won't break them."

"Why are they throwing stones at us?" asked Alex. "We mean them no harm."

Kiiswood gestured toward the coach's door and replied, "You're most welcome to step outside and explain it to them."

Alex quipped, "Now who's being sarcastic?"

Kiiswood's response turned more contemplative. "These kids live in postbellum hopelessness. They don't understand why their lives are bleak. They don't understand the capricious nature of their poverty. All they know is what they see. They see us as a candle of privilege shining a light in the darkness of their despair. And they throw stones to knock the candle over, to keep their own despair in the dark so they won't have to see it." Pointing to the children, he said, "These are kids who will become the pool of desperate recruits for New Jerusalem."

Alex was overawed with compassion for the children of Tyrrhenus. "Is there anything we can do for them?"

"You can pray for them," Kiiswood answered, "and you can let them hurl their stones."

Feeling dissatisfied with the chief's answer, the meta-droid replied, "Your God didn't wage this war or create their poverty; these problems have a human origin. It makes no sense to look for a fix from heaven. Praying for a miracle seems hypocritical; it feels like praying is just shirking our moral responsibility to our fellow human beings."

"I agree, these problems are our own doing," Kiiswood concurred. "But over the years, I've come to the conclusion that the real issue isn't poverty or despair; the real issue isn't even the ill consequences of war. No, these are just symptoms of a more systemic flaw. The problem is human nature. We human beings are all hell-bent on self-destruction. I don't ask what I can do to help anymore. Now I ask whether humankind deserves any help at all. If we're so resolute to destroy ourselves, maybe we should just let it happen. God's creation would be better off without us."

"I can't figure you out, Mr. Kiiswood. You're misanthropic. Yet you seem to like me well enough," Alex observed, "and you're certainly fond of Dr. Hewst."

"What?" he asked. Kiiswood was genuinely taken aback by Alex's remarks.

The meta-droid held up the carabiner clip so that Kiiswood could clearly see it. "You didn't advise me to take care of Dr. Cobisson's wedding bands," Alex commented, "but you seem protective of Dr. Hewst's necklace."

Their conversation was suddenly interrupted by a startling bang, a violent jolt, and an abrupt stop. Several of the team members were instantly thrown from their seats and onto the floor. A small, four-passenger auto-carriage had shot out from a narrow alleyway and broadsided the transit coach.

All of the sorteers aboard immediately leapt to their feet, firearms at the ready. They activated the Close Quarters Tactical program on their c-nexes, which linked each sorteer to every team member on the transit coach. Their c-nexes accessed their visual cortexes with a cerebrally augmented reality and presented them with a CQT schematic. This schematic displayed each sorteer's relative position (shown in blue) to the rest of the team members (shown in green).

The sorteers directed the team members to get down and to stay down on the floor for their safety. Lieutenant Jalloh and the sorteers of Unit Four assumed a close-quarters combat posture with their rail-rifles aimed to cover every field of threat. Likewise, Chief Kiiswood and Petty Officer Sudha (the two stratogen sorteers) had drawn their rail-pistols and taken tactical positions at the coach's main door and emergency exit, respectively. Through a series of c-nex signals, Jalloh directed Sudha and Kiiswood to exit the coach and to secure the auto-carriage and its occupants. The sorteer unit also exited the coach and formed a perimeter around it as the two stratogens slowly converged on the crashed and crumpled auto-carriage from opposite sides.

While they were still a few meters away from the auto-carriage, Sudha and Kiiswood scanned the area with their genetically enhanced senses and quickly formed their tactical assessments of the situation. With her weapon squarely leveled on the mangled wreckage, Sudha communicated her sitrep to Kiiswood via c-nex. "Vehicle is inoperative," she reported. "I detect one occupant, but no activity." Sudha looked back at the auto-carriage's path and saw a couple of the children, who had been running alongside the transit coach, now lying in the street. "I can see at least two casualties along the vehicle's trajectory. Their condition: indeterminate. Also, this incident is drawing a large crowd. A lot of concerned citizens are beginning to congregate."

As Sudha was speaking, Kiiswood accessed the driver side of the auto-carriage. His rail-pistol was directly aimed at the slumped and bloodied head of the driver. "Confirmed," the chief replied. "No other occupants. The driver is deceased: apparent blunt force trauma." Kiiswood holstered his weapon and promptly examined the cabin of the auto-carriage to assess its risk potential. "Be advised, threat is not neutralized. Vehicle is an improvised explosive device."

"Acknowledged," said Jalloh, who was monitoring their communications. "IED remains a threat. Do what you can to keep the crowd back for their safety."

"Aye aye, sir," Sudha replied as she was already waving back the gathering masses—both the curious and the would-be helpful.

Jalloh added, "And let's move the transit coach beyond the blast radius ASAP."

"Negative, sir. The impact broke the chassis," Kiiswood responded. "We're not moving without a tow."

"The Force Protection Unit at Camp Lundgren is linked in on our c-nex coms," Jalloh apprised. "A troop transport, emergency medical units, and counter-IED equipment are en route. ETE: two and a half minutes."

Dr. Hewst, meanwhile, decided to ignore the sorteers' directions to stay down on the coach's floor. She cautiously peered out the window and noticed the injured children lying in the street. She then called out to all on board, "Does anyone else here have LSR training?" Initially, everyone crouched silent, their faces betraying their surprise, apprehension, and fear. "We're pretending to be with the IPHA," she commented ironically, "and there's not a single physician among us?" At her comment, Alex and Dr. Cobisson reluctantly acknowledged their life-support recovery training. Hewst then shouted to them, "Follow me!" as she darted out the door and ran to the victims.

Cobisson and Alex looked at each other, wondering whether Hewst seriously expected them to follow her. After a temporary paralysis of action, Cobisson waved to Alex and shouted, "I'm not going out there! You go!"

Alex was terrified. His impulse for self-preservation compelled him to stay, but a sense of moral necessity forced him to muscle through his desire for personal safety. So, despite his fears, Alex ran after Hewst.

"Damn it!" Jalloh cursed as he watched Hewst and Alex run toward the injured children. He tried to gesture for them to return to the coach, but they either did not see him or chose to ignore him. The lieutenant then called to Kiiswood on c-nex. "Chief, can you get those two back on the bus?"

Kiiswood was now inside the auto-carriage trying to deactivate the IED's trigger and to remove its detonator. "Knowing the commander, sir, I seriously doubt it," he answered with a slight laugh in his voice. "But I'll try." Kiiswood accessed Hewst's c-nex and linked her to the sorteer's com channel. "Excuse me, Commander, for your own welfare, you and the android need to return to the transit coach immediately."

"I appreciate your concern, Chief," she said as she was treating the injuries of a young boy about thirteen years of age. "But we can't just leave these children bleeding in the street." Hewst took special care not to move him as he lay prone, grimacing in pain. She confirmed that his airway was open and that he was breathing. She spoke to him in comforting and encouraging tones, reassuring him that she and her colleagues were there to help him. "I'm Cathy," she introduced. "What's your name?" The young boy tried to answer, but his words were stifled in his groans. Nevertheless, Hewst continued to dress his wounds and to console him.

Because Hewst's c-nex channel remained open, Kiiswood overheard her consolations. "A medical team is currently en route, ma'am," he informed.

"But, it's not here yet," she replied. "And we are."

"Be advised, ma'am. This site is not yet secured," warned Kiiswood. "You're risking your personal safety."

"Understood, Chief," she acknowledged. "But some things are more important than just surviving."

"Fools rush in . . ." retorted Kiiswood.

". . . where angels fear to tread," Hewst finished.

To that, Kiiswood said nothing, but continued to work inside the auto-carriage and around the lifeless body of its driver. Even though the driver had died before he could detonate the IED, the explosives might still be triggered by an accomplice lurking in the crowd, whether from a c-nex or some other transmitting device. Thus, the only way that Kiiswood could neutralize the threat was to deactivate the trigger and remove the detonator.

Meanwhile, having run to the second casualty, a twelve-year-old girl, Alex assessed her condition as best he could without moving her. She lay silent and motionless in a somatically unviable position. She had no breath, no pulse, no heartbeat. Kneeling over her twisted body, Alex risked rolling her on her back and promptly began LSR. This little girl looked like his own daughter, or rather, what he assumed his daughter would look like had she lived to be twelve years old. This little girl should be playing with her friends, he thought. But now she lay broken in a Tyrrhenusian street. With each compression of the little girl's chest, anguish and empathy filled Alex's soul (if, indeed, the meta-droid was truly a soul who could actually feel for others).

Within a few minutes—true to the estimate—several response teams from Camp Lundgren reached the scene. Lieutenant Jalloh directed the operations of the new arrivals and coordinated their activities with those of his own security team. A detachment of MAs joined in to assist Sorteer Unit Four with site security and crowd control. Also, two corpswain teams arrived. Relieving Hewst and Alex, they immediately applied resusi-packets and portable para-med modules to the two young victims. And to offset the threat of an explosion, two explosive ordnance disposal technicians (EODs) wearing high-tech, light-weight bomb suits slowly advanced on the auto-carriage with a large counter-IED device, colloquially called a blast dragon. (A blast dragon was an enormous armored vehicle designed to swallow any IED whole and to hold it safely within the blast dragon's reinforced belly. There, the IED would be enveloped in a fog of metallic oxide nanoparticles, rendering the explosive device inert.)

Once again, Jalloh called Kiiswood via c-nex. "The response teams are here, Chief. Evacuate the auto-carriage immediately. Let the experts take it from here."

"Aye aye, sir," the chief replied. Just as the EODs approached, Kiiswood emerged from the auto-carriage with a deactivated trigger and detonator in hand. Handing them to the bomb-suited technicians, he said, "Here you go! I saved you the trouble of disarming it."

The two EODs noted that Kiiswood was wearing absolutely no ordnance disposal gear. As the chief walked away, one of the technicians yelled to him with a voice that was muffled by a protective faceplate. "You're insane! You know that, don't you?"

Kiiswood yelled back, "That seems to be the prevailing theory."

Even though Alex had been relieved of his efforts to resuscitate the young girl, he hovered closely to watch the corpswains as they worked on her. Hewst soon came up beside Alex and placed her hand on his shoulder. She could clearly see the emotional distress on his face. "You did well," she said reassuringly. "But we should return to the coach. Let's give the corpswains some room to work." Alex, however, would not leave; he was too emotionally invested in the girl's welfare to walk away.

As the teams of corpswains treated the two young casualties, another member of the medical team—a medical yeoswain—ran back and forth between the teams. She was trying to provide the corpswains with whatever medical records she could find in the Martian Alliance's medical database. Using a small penlight device linked into her c-nex, she scanned the two victim's retinas in order to identify them—first the boy, then the girl. The yeoswain called Lieutenant Jalloh by c-nex and reported, "Sir, the boy's name is Daniel Sharl, son of Miriam and Amos Sharl. The girl's name is Deborah Garnt, daughter of Naomi and Matthew Garnt."

"Acknowledged," Jalloh responded. "Send out a d-board notice to the local precincts; we'll let the police try to locate their parents."

"Aye, aye, sir," the yeoswain replied.

"And Yeoswain," Jalloh ordered, "now that the chief has disarmed the IED, go run a retinal scan on the driver. See whether you can ID him."

Again, she replied, "Aye aye, sir."

"Excuse me, sir," Sudha interrupted. "I have a woman with a baby over here in the crowd. She says she's Miriam Sharl, the boy's mother."

"Escort her to her son," ordered the lieutenant. "But, Petty Officer, don't let her interfere with the corpswains."

"Aye aye, sir," Sudha replied. At the petty officer's direction, a very distraught woman, carrying her blanket-swathed infant daughter, stepped out from the crowd. Sudha then led her to the place where the corpswains were treating her injured son. There, kneeling beside him, the guilt-stricken mother proceeded to wail profusely and to apologize to her teenage boy, all while cradling her crying infant. In the midst of the family's distress, Sudha decided to let them have their time together and stepped back to give them some space.

Having diminished the impending danger by disarming the IED, Kiiswood walked over to where Hewst and Alex were standing. The three of them stood silent as they watched with dismay the corpswains draping a sheet over the still form of Deborah Garnt. "We need to be on our way," Kiiswood said to his two companions. "The response teams can handle it from here."

"The chief is right," Hewst said to Alex. "Let's head back to the coach."

"The coach is inoperative," Kiiswood commented. He pointed to a large armored vehicle that had arrived with the response teams. "The project team will be taking that troop transport the rest of the way to Camp Lundgren."

Jalloh once again signaled Kiiswood and all the sorteers on their active c-nex channel. "All hands, stand to!" he warned. "The yeoswain just identified the decedent in the auto-carriage as Amos Sharl."

At this news, Kiiswood immediately drew his weapon and searched fastidiously for the deceased driver's wife, Miriam Sharl. He quickly spied her, no longer kneeling near her injured son but walking, with her infant still in arms, toward the disabled transit coach and its hunkering passengers. The chief sprinted to place himself between Sharl and the coach, even as several sorteers and MAs standing at a distance leveled their weapons upon the crying mother. The chief demonstrably brandished his rail-pistol so that she could see it unequivocally aimed at her head. "Ma'am," ordered Kiiswood, "I cannot overemphasize the need for you to back away right now!" At the chief's insistence, she stopped, but she did not back away. She instead fell to her knees and continued crying.

Sudha called in on the active c-nex channel. "Hey, Chief, I scanned her earlier," she said. "Sharl is carrying a child, not a weapon."

"Look again," Kiiswood replied.

Sudha did as the chief directed. Upon second look, Miriam Sharl was indeed cradling an infant in her arms. But then, with her enhanced senses, Sudha spotted the same infrared silhouette that Kiiswood had detected. The mother's torso was laced with surgically implanted explosives and ball bearings. Miriam Sharl was not only a suicide bomber; she *was* a bomb. "She's a walking IED!" Sudha exclaimed.

Having seen this terrorist tactic before, Kiiswood assumed that Sharl's bomb was on a so-called dead-man trigger linked to her c-nex. If so linked, then she could at any moment set off her explosives by mere thought-actuation. And if she were to remove her c-nex, or fall unconscious, or even die, the explosives would detonate automatically. "All hands, stand down," ordered Kiiswood, as he reluctantly holstered his rail-pistol. Again, speaking to Lieutenant Jalloh, he said, "Sir, I strongly recommend that we expedite transfer of the project team to the troop transport, that we withdraw the response teams, and that we order the crowds to disperse."

"Very well, Chief," Jalloh agreed. "Make it happen."

"Aye aye, sir," Kiiswood acknowledged. But before he could carry through with the lieutenant's orders, Dr. Hewst very calmly ambled up to the crying mother and child and knelt in front of them. Kiiswood was about to insist that the commander board the troop transport, but he then thought otherwise. She would not likely heed his insistence.

With sympathy and heartfelt attention, Hewst spoke to the distraught mother. "Hello Miriam. My name is Catherine," she introduced. "Is this your daughter?"

"Yes," Miriam barely answered through her sobbing.

Hewst reached out and pulled back part of the infant's blanket, revealing the little girl's bawling, tear-drenched face. "Oh, she's beautiful," Hewst said with a compassionate grin. "What's her name?"

"Elizabeth," answered Miriam, smiling and weeping at the same time.

"Elizabeth," Hewst echoed. "Such a beautiful name. God's promise," she commented. "Her name means God's promise."

Miriam wailed, "I don't want to do this, Catherine!"

"I know you love your daughter so much." Hewst felt that Miriam was desperately seeking permission to free herself from the turmoil deep within her soul. So Hewst asked her, "May I hold Elizabeth?"

Miriam nodded. Then slowly, gently, she placed Elizabeth into Hewst's arms. After kissing her daughter tenderly on her forehead, Miriam sprang to her feet and ran away. She ran down the street—far away from her daughter, far away from her injured son. The crowd scattered, frantically yielding the street to Miriam Sharl, getting as far away from her route as possible. She darted into an abandoned storefront and, there, isolated herself from all bystanders and traffic.

As she ran into the building, Kiiswood shouted, "Everybody hit the deck!"

Hewst turned her back to the distant storefront, cradled Elizabeth closely, and crouched as near to the ground as she could without crushing the infant under her weight.

Suddenly, the storefront shuddered violently. Its windows and doors exploded; the posts and jambs blasted out from their frames. Shards of cinder, metal, and glass shot out like shrapnel far into the adjacent streets and pedways. Then the thunderous blast and the noise of settling debris quickly subsided into near silence.

Presently, the only sound that Hewst could hear was the infant weeping in her arms. She checked Elizabeth, then herself, and confirmed that they were both unharmed. She then stared into the teary eyes of Miriam Sharl's daughter, and Hewst started crying.

Chapter 13 – Belshazzar Station

Belshazzar Research Station, Hellas Province, Mars

(Areographic Co-ordinates: S 35.642, E 94.228)

Friday, 07 December 2429 CE

Time: 0632 Zulu

The sun's dawning light shone across the plains of Hellas Planitia as three Defense Force areopters flew overhead. They had completed their two-hour flight from Tyrrhenus and were now hovering over the site of the newly established Belshazzar Research Station. They would have arrived on site late yesterday, but the terrorist attack at Tyrrhenus had forced them to delay their departure out of Camp Lundgren until this morning.

These massive Martian rotorcraft were specifically engineered to transport cargo and personnel over the cold, dry surface of Mars. Each areopter employed four enormous ducted-fan rotors—one pair would spin clockwise, the other pair counter-clockwise. This quad-rotor configuration not only offset the torque-effects from any single rotor, but it also produced the considerable amount of lift needed to support the weight of a Martian aircraft. And, even though an areopter's Martian weight was five-eighths less than its Terran weight, its rotors had to lift that lighter weight in a mere one-hundredth of the density of Earth's atmosphere. Thus, all Martian rotorcraft were designed with faster-spinning rotors and with larger, stronger rotor blades than their Terran counterparts.

The three areopters put out so much rotor-wash that, if they were to fly too near the ground, they would stir up huge, blinding clouds of fine Martian regolith. So the areopters approached Belshazzar Station one at a time in order to keep the prop-induced dust storms at a minimum. First in line was the heavy-lift cargo areopter, a *Phobos*-class sky-crane. Stowed in its payload bay was an enormous, equipment-packed laboratory module—the last of the research station's twenty-six modular components. The sky-crane hovered several meters over the particular slot that had been readied for the areopter's cargo. As the sky-crane fastidiously lowered the final module into place, the station's ground crew (donned in their Martian compression suits) stood ready to receive and install it. The morning light that shone over the station's compound was obscured by a veil of Martian soil whipped up by the sky-crane's rotors. But with their HUD-sensors and helmet-torches, the ground crew was able to continue installing the latest module even in the midst of the whirling red dust.

The other two areopters hovered high and abaft, staying clear of the sky-crane's rotor-wash, awaiting their turns to approach the research station. The smaller of the two was an attack areopter, an *Enyo*-class gunship. Its weapon systems included gimbal-mounted plasma cannons, pulse lasers, rail machine guns, and various pylon-mounted tactical missiles. On board were Lieutenant Commander Riddari, Lieutenant Jalloh, and the twelve members of Sorteer Unit Four, most of whom were specifically trained to pilot the *Enyo*-class and to operate its weapon systems. The gunship's primary role was to provide close air support for Belshazzar Station and for the other two areopters.

The rest of the project team was aboard the transport areopter, an *Eris*-class troop carrier. It was an efficient transport, but hardly comfortable. The cabin fuselage section was a rather austere pressurized passenger compartment. Inside, its two rows of treadway-facing seats were little more than hard benches that ran parallel to the long-axis of the areopter. The port and starboard bulkheads served as provisional seatbacks. The portholes were few and small.

Captain Anna Petrenko had made impromptu arrangements for the project team to stay at Camp Lundgren last night. After resting for a few hours at the temporary lodging facility and eating an improvised breakfast of Defense Force rations at the camp's mess hall, the team members were ready to continue their journey. They donned their compression suits but left their helmets open. They then boarded the transport areopter and strapped themselves into their seats for the two-hour flight. Most of them were still coping with grief from yesterday's attack, and all of them were weary of travelling and were ready to reach their destination.

A shaft of sunlight from a portside porthole shone on Catherine Hewst, who sat on the starboard side of the cabin. She sat between Chief Holgersen and Petty Officer Al-Jabiri, and directly across from Alex, Dr.

Cobisson, and Chief Kiiswood. As most of her colleagues and team members were preoccupied in conversation, Hewst sat quietly. She was pondering the Martian cavern and its enigmatic inscriptions, as well as the recently discovered manuscript. Rather, she was *trying* to ponder the ancient manuscript, but she was distracted by thoughts of little Elizabeth Sharl, whose parents had suddenly orphaned her and her brother, Daniel.

"Excuse me, Commander," Al-Jabiri addressed Dr. Hewst. "You asked me to keep you apprised if I should hear any news. I just got a call from Ensign Tam, the Child Protection Advocate at Camp Lundgren. He says that Daniel Sharl is recovering and will be discharged from the base infirmary later this morning. He and his little sister, Elizabeth, will live temporarily with their maternal grandparents until Child Guardian Services can establish permanent placement."

"Thank you, Petty Officer," replied Hewst. "What's the news about the other girl—Deborah?"

"It's as we suspected, ma'am," he answered. "She died on the scene. The coroner officially pronounced her death late yesterday."

Hewst then leaned toward Alex across the aisle and said, "I'm sorry to have to tell you, but Deborah Garnt didn't make it." The meta-droid seemed to attend to Hewst's every word, yet he sat silent. "I thought you'd want to know," she added.

"Thank you for letting me know," Alex replied.

Hewst could clearly detect a look of dejection settling on Alex's face. "There was nothing more you could have done for her," she offered.

Dr. Earnan Cobisson witnessed Hewst's interaction with Alex and felt compelled to comment. "I have to say, Catherine, I'm fascinated that you're expressing sympathy to the meta-droid." With a slightly patronizing smile, he continued, "Your response suggests that the Whitaker Institute succeeded in simulating personhood through a mechanism. You seem genuinely concerned for its feelings."

"Shouldn't I err on the side of caution?" asked Hewst. "Can you really be so sure that Alex doesn't feel sorrow or grief?"

"It's just a machine," he answered. "It may have clever programming, but not even the most ingenious software can make a machine self-aware. Human beings have opinions; human beings have feelings. Not meta-droids."

Alex felt invisible in Cobisson's worldview. Although remaining invisible might have been the better option, the meta-droid could not resist responding. "Earnan, I may be a machine. But even so, I'm a better human being than you are."

Cobisson was genuinely amazed at Alex's brazenness. "Impressive. You actually mimic umbrage because I slighted you?"

"Say what you want about me, I don't much care," Alex answered. "But two kids were run over in the street yesterday, and you did nothing. Catherine called for us to help them, and what did you do? You cowered on the floor and told me to run out into harm's way."

For a moment, Cobisson felt belittled. But then he reminded himself that he was speaking with a machine. "Well, of course I told you to go out there. It was a terrifying and dangerous situation," he said. "And that's why we created you, for situations like that one."

"You don't think I was terrified?" the meta-droid asked.

"No, I don't. You don't feel fear. You don't feel anything at all." Cobisson explained, "You were designed only to simulate compassion—to be a human presence in places where human beings can't—or shouldn't—go."

Alex gestured toward Dr. Hewst and said, "Catherine ran out there. Was she programmed to do that? She helped those kids at the risk of her own safety. She stood face-to-face with a suicide bomber. Was she only simulating compassion?"

The tone of Cobisson's voice betrayed his rising temper. "I'm not a psychologist; I haven't got a clue why she ran out there." Then, addressing Hewst, he commented, "No disrespect, Catherine, but that was a foolish thing you did yesterday."

"Thank you," Kiiswood interjected. "I'm glad I'm not the only one who thinks so."

Hewst smirked at the chief's comment as she responded to Cobisson. "Like you, Earnan, I was terrified," she admitted. "Any rational soul would be. But their need for help was greater than my fear. That's why I ran out there." She then posed a question of Alex. "That being said, I'd like to ask you, Alex: if you were afraid, why did you follow me into the street? Was it because Earnan told you to go?"

"No, not at all," Alex answered. "I followed you, in part, because you asked for help, but mostly because those poor kids were hurt." He then asked rhetorically, "And how could I not run to their aid? When I first saw little Deborah lying there in the street, thoughts of my own daughter ran through my mind. She was about the same age that my Cathy would have been; she even looked so much like my daughter."

"*Your* daughter?!" exclaimed Cobisson. His indignation was implied in his voice. "Cathy was *my* daughter, not yours!"

Alex sharply countered, "And that's all the more reason you should have been out there with me. When you saw that poor little girl dying in the street, I know that Cathy's death ran through your mind. I know this because it ran through mine. Deborah Garnt wasn't your daughter; but she was *someone's* daughter. Where the hell was your humanity in that moment?"

"How dare you sit in judgment of what I'm thinking or how I'm feeling!" Cobisson's indignation was now quite obvious. "I don't have to sit here and be ridiculed by a damned machine! You do know that you have an off button?"

Kiiswood started laughing. "Dr. Cobisson," the chief said, "you just threatened someone who, you say, can't feel intimidation." Laughing, he continued, "Let me know how that works for you."

Hewst witnessed Cobisson's interaction with Alex and felt compelled to comment. "I have to say, Earnan, your response suggests that the Whitaker Institute succeeded in simulating personhood through a mechanism. You seem genuinely outraged at his opinion."

Perhaps Hewst's comment was correct and it struck a nerve. Or perhaps the meta-droid's assessment was too derisive. In either case, Cobisson removed his harness and walked away from his present company. He quickly found another place to sit at the other end of the cabin.

After Cobisson had taken another seat, Hewst turned to Alex and said, "It's a story as old as the book of Genesis—the creation rebels against its creator."

Kiiswood pointed at Hewst and remarked, "Are you talking about Alex's story, Commander, or your own?"

Hewst ignored the chief's quip.

Alex sat silent in his own contrition, staring at the deck. He then looked up and addressed those who sat around him. "I was a bit hard on him, wasn't I?"

"Yeah," Kiiswood acknowledged. "It was hilarious."

Of late, Chief Holgersen had tried to ignore the conversation, opting instead to gaze out a nearby porthole, watching the ground crew install the station's latest module. But at that moment, she chose to add to the discussion. "Well, I don't think it's funny," she said. "Some of us haven't had LSR training. That doesn't make us indifferent to the fate of those injured kids yesterday." To this, Petty Officer Al-Jabiri nodded in agreement as Holgersen returned to the view outside the porthole.

"Please accept my sincere apologies," Alex offered. "To be candid, I think my harsh judgment of Earnan is probably a criticism of myself." He shook his head in remorse and said, "I look at him and I see myself. And, frankly, I don't like what I see."

"Oh for God's sake, Alex," Kiiswood blurted, "just get over it." The chief then taunted the meta-droid with his own words. "'I feel lost and confused.' 'I don't know who I am.' 'I don't like what I see.' Your self-deprecation doesn't suit you. Either decide to like yourself, or just turn yourself off."

Hewst grimaced at Kiiswood's insensitive remarks. "The chief may express himself indelicately, but he has a point," she said to the meta-droid. Then, with her pastoral manner, she counselled, "Don't worry about who you're not, Alex. In the words of the nineteenth-century poet, Oscar Wilde: 'Be yourself, everyone else is already taken.'"

Having delivered its payload, the low-hovering sky-crane retracted its umbilical cables and flew clear of the research station. Peering through the porthole, Holgersen watched as the sky-crane landed and powered down about 50 meters from the station. She turned to those around her and announced, "We should be landing any minute now."

Almost immediately, the rays of sunlight in the cabin yawed forward as the troop carrier banked right toward the makeshift areopter pads. Captain Petrenko rose from her seat and stood mid-cabin in the treadway. She grabbed an overhead handrail to steady herself while the areopter was changing direction and speed. "Let me have everyone's attention," she announced as she addressed the project team. "We'll be landing momentarily. When you exit the rotorcraft, a member of the ground crew will direct you to the airlock module. Once you pass through the airlock, the station chief will escort you to the sickbay module for infection risk assessment." Several team members wondered what risks she might be referring to, but before anyone could ask a question or raise a concern, the captain continued. "After you've cleared sickbay, you'll receive a detailed briefing and then be introduced to your work stations and tech support." Petrenko paused as the areopter was jostled and pitched during its touch down on the landing pad. "The flight crew is about to depressurize the passenger cabin for egress. So put your helmets on now."

As instructed, the team members deployed their helmets, or, at least, most of them did. A couple of the scientists on the research team—specifically, Dr. Střelec and Dr. Driggers, who had never worn compression suits before now, were clearly having difficulties. They anxiously fumbled with the deployment mechanisms on their collar modules, but, despite their persistence, they could not close and seal their helmets. Several of their colleagues tried to explain the procedure to them, even as the depressurization warning buzzer began to sound throughout the cabin. Of course, the warning made Střelec and Driggers even more anxious, and they could not think clearly about what they needed to do. Finally, their colleagues persuaded them to relax and to trust their helmets' self-deployment feature. Indeed, seconds later, as the overhead lights were flashing red and the cabin began to depressurize, their helmets automatically flipped up from behind them and enveloped their heads, forming an air-tight seal around their collar modules.

Once the cabin pressure matched that of the Martian atmosphere outside, the cabin lights turned green, and all on board stood from their seats. Some of them had forgotten the weaker gravity of Mars and were momentarily off balance when they rose to their feet. Once everyone was lined up and ready to depart, the flight crew began to lower the retractable door and ramp at the aft section of the cabin. Slowly, a pinkish-red sky came into view, followed by the rusty butterscotch landscape of Hellas Planitia. After the ramp was fully extended, the project team filed out of the areopter and onto the surface of Mars. There, the team met Crewswain Mia Zhao, a member of the station's ground crew. Zhao's otherwise white compression suit appeared quite beige as it was thoroughly coated in Martian dust. She instructed the team members to maintain close ranks as she escorted them to the station's main airlock module.

Upon arriving at the station, Crewswain Zhao explained to the project team that the airlock could not accommodate everyone in a single cycle; they would need to enter in two separate groups. "Most of you can proceed into the airlock right now," Zhao said, "but at least three of you will have to stand fast with me." Hewst, Kiiswood, and Alex opted to remain outside with Zhao and to wait for the next cycle. The rest of the project team entered the main airlock, and once Zhao hermetically sealed the door, the exterior access indicator beside that door changed from green to red.

As Hewst stood between her colleagues awaiting their turn to enter the airlock, she realized that her time on Mars would likely be spent either sequestered within this cramped, windowless research station or deep beneath the planet's surface in an underground cavern. So she decided to make the best of the next few minutes and to enjoy the desert beauty around her. A very fine, powder-like soil comprised most of the dry, dusty plain—a rusty-hued soil so fine that it wafted easily on the mild Martian winds. The desert-scape was speckled here and there with basaltic rocks whose long shadows on the desert floor grew steadily shorter with the rising sun. And even though the sun was a mere sixty percent of its angular diameter as seen from Earth, it shone rather brightly through the thin, cloudless atmosphere.

To her right, Hewst could see the ground crew locking down the station's newest module to its prefabricated foundation on the planet's surface.

At the same time, the crew was fastidiously securing the module's hatches to the pressurized gangways, connecting it to the rest of the station. Like most of the station's modules, the newest one too was emblazoned with the prominent, yet spurious, logo of the Interplanetary Health Agency.

Alex spent his time out on the dusty plain watching the areopter gunship still hovering far overhead. "This is an insane planet. We're just a group of scientists doing research. We're no threat to anyone." The android pointed to the gunship and continued, "We shouldn't need the protection of armed troopers. There's something seriously wrong with this world."

Kiiswood replied to Alex. "It's not just this world. Anywhere you find human beings, you'll find evil. Most people are contemptible and selfish. It's our sinful nature."

Crewswain Zhao was genuinely uninterested in their conversation; she was much more interested in the access indicator, which had just turned green. She spoke courteously to the three of them as she opened the airlock module, directed them inside, and closed the hatch. Once the three of them were sealed inside, the thin, cold Martian atmosphere around them was swiftly evacuated from the airlock. The airlock status indicator, which initially read "Mars Indigenous," soon displayed "Vacuum." An automated voice then spoke through the transceiver sets in their helmets. "Please stand with your legs spread slightly apart and your arms extended out to your sides. Stand by for MRE." As soon as they all assumed the directed stance, the Magnetic Resonance Extraction system pulled every particle of Martian silica from their suits. "MRE complete," the automated voice said. Their compression suits were now dust-free.

As they relaxed and lowered their arms, Hewst addressed Alex. "The chief is much too cynical about humanity. I think he's right that people are flawed and broken, but I believe that most people are essentially good, or, at least, they want to be good, even here on Mars."

"People like Amos and Miriam Sharl?" asked Alex. "Where's the goodness in what they did? They were willing to kill their own children. And for what? To murder, maim, and massacre as many innocent people as possible? That sounds like unadulterated evil to me."

157

Again, the automated voice broke into their conversation. "Stand by for repressurization and gravity augmentation."

Trying to talk around the automated voice, Hewst agreed with Alex. "Without a doubt, what they did was clearly evil."

The meta-droid responded with a little more volume as he tried to compete with the bellow of warm, breathable atmosphere filling the airlock. "If the universe is the creation of a benevolent God, as you Christians purport, why does evil even exist?"

"That question is above my pay grade," Kiiswood quipped as he felt his own weight steadily increasing. He noticed that everyone's knees flexed slightly as the augmented gravity settled upon them. Turning to Hewst, the chief asked, "You're the professor of religious studies, ma'am. Why *does* evil exist?"

"Evil is not a force or a substance of its own," she answered. "It's not a sovereign reality that compels us. It's not an autonomous demon that possesses us. Evil is a goodness that is bent and disfigured." Hewst observed that the airlock status indicator now read "Atmosphere and Gravity: Terran Normal," so she reached up to her collar module and retracted her helmet. The others did likewise. Hewst took in a breath of the latest air and then continued, "Miriam's love for her daughter demonstrates that there is goodness even in a terrorist."

The conversation was abruptly interrupted when Station Chief Claudio Fuentes opened the airlock's interior hatch. He gestured for Hewst, Kiiswood, and Alex to follow him to the locker room in the adjacent equipment hub. Before venturing further, Fuentes said, "Please take a moment to stow your helmets in a locker. You can remove your EV packets and hang them up in an open charger mount on the bulkhead over there. Please keep your compression suits on; you'll be suiting up again soon. Right now, Captain Petrenko wants all new arrivals to complete an infection risk assessment before proceeding to the mess module for an initial briefing." After the three had shed and stowed their suits' accessories, Fuentes led them through a connecting gangway to a hatch marked SICKBAY.

The station chief opened the hatch and directed them into the next module. "Excuse me, sir," Fuentes addressed Dr. Darry Ammon, who was looking over medical data at one of the biotelemetry monitors. "The rest of the project team is here."

Dr. Ammon, a young lieutenant with a caduceus collar device on his khaki uniform, continued reading diagnostic data. "Thank you, Chief," he replied without looking away from the monitors. "Carry on." Fuentes left sickbay by the same hatch he had entered, sealing it behind him. Ammon turned from the monitors and cued a few corpswains to reset the two Somanalytic Diagnostic Stalls. An SDS was a transparent cylindroid chamber that rendered a rapid diagnostic readout of the patient within. An SDS could detect a metric as simple as heart rate and diagnose a condition as inconspicuous as the early stages of pancreatic cancer.

In a stoic, professional, but not unfriendly manner, Ammon spoke to the new arrivals. "I'm going to run a medical diagnostic on all three of you," he said, "and I'll be using your latest medical records on file as a baseline for comparison. And every time you return to the station after going subsurface, we'll repeat the diagnostic scan. In the meantime, I'm going to vaccinate you for an array of possible pathogenic threats."

Dr. Ammon returned to the telemetry monitors and adjusted their settings to receive new data. Following the corpswains' directions, Hewst and Alex stepped into the sickbay's two diagnostic stalls and stood ready to be scanned. Kiiswood stood off to the side waiting his turn. Several sensor rods, spanning the height of the cylindrical chambers, began whirling around their circumference. These sensors detected the subtle diffractions of collimated electromagnetic energy in each stall, interpreting that energy as biotelemetric data and rendering it as holographic images on the diagnostic monitors.

With nothing else to do but stand in their respective stalls for the duration of the scan, Alex continued his conversation with Hewst. "Catherine, you say that Miriam loved her daughter," Alex yelled to Hewst, trying to be heard over the whirling sensor rods. "Are you trying to excuse the parents' role in terrorism?"

"By no means!" she yelled back. "I'm not trying to excuse their behavior. I'm simply trying to explain it."

"How can you explain the evil done by good people?"

159

"No one does evil just for the sake of evil," Hewst answered. "The Sharls didn't wake up yesterday morning and decide to attack our transit coach because it was the evil thing to do. People end up doing evil deeds because they justify their actions as good. And even if they do see the evil in their own deeds, they choose to look beyond it, opting instead to act for a greater good that they mistakenly see in it. The Sharls probably saw a noble purpose in their malevolence."

Alex asked, "What noble purpose is there in murdering innocent people?"

"They don't see themselves as murdering innocent people," answered Hewst. "They see themselves as the noble paladins for Christ, and they see us as subhuman infidels. They have to see us as lawless and inhuman reprobates, otherwise they would have to face their own inhumanity."

Kiiswood added his opinion to their conversation. "I admire how the commander tries to find the good even in the worst of persons. She sees everyone as essentially good. But despite her thoughtful explanation, I think the problem of evil is much simpler: people are basically evil."

In less than a minute, the SDS scans finished and the sensor rods quickly slowed to a halt. Hewst and Alex emerged from their stalls as Dr. Ammon was still looking over the diagnostic readouts. Kiiswood was about to step into the stall just vacated by Alex when Dr. Ammon suddenly exclaimed, "What the hell . . . ?!" He gestured toward one of the stalls while reading some of the data. "I have the biotelemetry on a Commander Hewst, Veronica Catherine . . . "

"That's me," she acknowledged with a wave.

Then, gesturing toward the other stall, Ammon continued, "but the other SDS data is just . . . well, it's just nonsense."

Alex felt embarrassed. Medical examinations had been a routine part of his previous human life, so in the moment, he had forgotten that he was no longer human. Alex had gone through the motions of a diagnostic scan out of habit.

"Oh my God," Hewst interjected. "It completely slipped my mind." Responding to Ammon, she said, "Alex is an android."

160

"Well, it didn't slip my mind," admitted Kiiswood. "I just wanted to see what happens when you scan an android."

"Oh, yes, so *you're* the android," Ammon said. "I was informed that there would be one on the team." His manner remained stoic and professional, but now it seemed a little less friendly. "But sickbay is not your personal game room," he scolded. "I'm sure you're eager to be on your way, so let's all be a little more expeditious, shall we?"

With a subtle smirk on his face, Kiiswood promptly stepped into the diagnostic stall. Ammon reset the telemetry monitors and initiated the SDS sensor rods. The monitors almost immediately began to signal that some diagnostic data was incoming, but instead of biotelemetry, the readouts simply displayed the word CLASSIFIED. Having the appropriate security clearance, Dr. Ammon was able to override the display and to observe Kiiswood's stratogenic data.

As Kiiswood was being scanned, Hewst was making her way to an adjacent treatment kiosk while Alex stood nearby.

The corpswain at the kiosk's console was uploading a customized vaccine cocktail for Commander Hewst—a prescription based on her latest diagnostic scan. "Please unsheathe your arms and hands from your compression suit," the corpswain directed Hewst. "I need your fingers free of your gloves for this immunization booster." Toggling the memory-alloy actuator at the top of her collar module, Hewst unfastened the front of her compression suit to her mid-torso, exposing her t-shirt and bare arms. As she took a seat at the treatment kiosk, she tied her suit's sleeves around her waist so that they would not dangle and fall on the deck.

"Catherine, I have to ask," Alex said. "What about their own children? Amos Sharl ran over his own son. Miriam was willing to blow up her own daughter. Was their daughter an inhuman reprobate?"

Kiiswood responded from his diagnostic stall. "Not all parents love their children, Alex."

Hewst felt sympathy for Kiiswood and his ill-fated childhood. "I hear what you're saying, Chief," she consoled.

The TCV port in the kiosk console began to flash, indicating that the upload was complete. From this port, the corpswain withdrew a thin, 25-centimeter translucent square tablet—a transcutaneous vaccination plate. The corpswain held out the plate toward Hewst and said, "Please place your hand on the TCV, ma'am." Hewst placed her right hand, palm down, on the plate. The TCV lit up, confirming the commander's identity and infusing several nanometer-thin vaccination streams through her fingertips. "You'll feel some tingling in your fingers," said the corpswain.

"Miriam clearly loved her daughter," Hewst said to Alex while holding her palm to the plate. "Sadly, the Sharls were like many other disenfranchised Christians in a postbellum Mars. They felt powerless. They saw no light in their future, they had no voice in their own destiny. They had the most to gain and the least to lose in toppling the current social order. So when an apocalyptic sect like New Jerusalem offered them a chance to become agents of divine destiny, it was too tempting to resist. Suddenly, the Sharls had a voice, their lives had purpose. As suicide bombers, they would be shaping sacred history. As martyrs for Christ, they would secure their place in heaven—theirs and their children's. But in the end, Miriam realized that she loved her daughter more than she hated God's enemies. She proved that there was goodness in her when she decided to entrust her daughter's safety to a stranger."

Having finished the diagnostic scan, Kiiswood joined Hewst and Alex at the treatment kiosk. Just then, the TCV began to flash, indicating that Hewst's vaccination was complete. So she removed her hand from the plate and stood up to offer the seat to the chief. The corpswain returned the TCV to its port in the console to prime it for Kiiswood's vaccination.

"I mean no disrespect to present company," Alex said to his two friends, "but perhaps what Dr. Negasi said in the climber's observation lounge is correct. It seems that a belief in God has the power to make good people do evil things."

Kiiswood opened his compression suit to his t-shirt and took the seat at the kiosk. "Maybe you have something there, Alex," he said sarcastically. "The list of people who believe I'm particularly prone to evil is already long, but I'll gladly add your name to the list." The corpswain at the console held out the TCV to Kiiswood and instructed him to place his right hand on the plate.

As Kiiswood received his transcutaneous vaccination, Alex commented, "I believe you're misanthropic, Chief, but I don't believe you're evil."

Hewst responded, "History certainly bears witness to what you say, Alex. Far too many good people have massacred others in the name of God." She paused. "But a belief in God has an even greater power: the ability to make average mortals sacrifice against their own self-interests for the sake of others—even for the sake of their enemies."

Chapter 14 – The Briefing

Mess Module, Belshazzar Research Station, Hellas Province, Mars

(Areographic Co-ordinates: S 35.642, E 94.228)

Friday, 07 December 2429 CE

Time: 0900 Zulu

Donning only the unitard elements of their compression suits, the nine members of the research team (eight humans and one meta-droid) sat around the largest of the tables in the station's mess module. At one end of the table, Station Chief Fuentes had set up a podium for the briefing. Sitting at surrounding tables were members of the research support staff, including lab technicians, data coders, and equipment specialists. The only two in the room not seated were Kiiswood and Sudha, who both stood as if at parade rest near one of the module's hatches.

Given the station's limited space, several of its modular compartments served dual purposes. Of all twenty-six modules (and associated nodal hubs), the mess module had the most seating capacity, so it also functioned as the station's conference room. As such, it was retrofitted with three closed circuit monitors and two holographic projectors to accommodate daily briefings. The mess module was modestly lit and was tinted in a Defense Force drab color.

Catherine Hewst scanned the table where she and her colleagues sat, looking for a flagon of coffee. Finding none, she glanced with hope at the adjacent tables. Again, no caffeine. Undeterred, she peered over to the galley line, only to find that it was closed. Hewst finally accepted her disappointment; her desire for coffee would go unmet this morning. And she had long since abandoned all hopes of enjoying a little amaretto for the foreseeable future.

All of the chatter in the room subsided when Lieutenant Commanders Gallistow and Riddari, Captain Petrenko, and an as-yet-introduced petty officer walked into the room. Petrenko immediately took to the podium and without any opening overtures, said, "Ladies and gentlemen, this is Techswain First Class Wendell Vraiss. He's FAIA's technical supervisor of the subsurface . . . "

Petrenko hesitated momentarily to find the right word. ". . . the subsurface phenomenon. He'll be briefing you this morning. Hold all your questions until the end."

The techswain stepped up as Petrenko yielded the podium. "Good morning," greeted Vraiss. "Welcome to Belshazzar Station. And welcome to the first of our regular daily briefings. We'll be meeting here every morning at 0900 hours to share your team's significant findings and hypotheses with the rest of the research team. Given our limited space, we're going to have to share work spaces." Glancing down at a written list on his podium, Vraiss continued, "We've assigned astrophysics, areology, and areochemistry to Lab Module Alpha. So Drs. Ferris, Kalinin, and Cheung, that's your work station. Archeology, xenopsychology, and astrobiology are assigned to Lab Module Bravo. Drs. Lonsdale, Matsuoka . . . " Vraiss hesitated. He was uncertain whether he should address the meta-droid by the alphanumeric title on the list. He finally decided not to call him ALX-63. Instead, he said, ". . . and Alex, that's your work station. Mathematics, linguistics, and religious paleography will operate out of Lab Module Charlie. Drs. Střelec, Driggers, and Hewst, that's your station. We've tried to supply your labs with all the scientific equipment and research tools that we could quickly get our hands on. FAIA pulled as much equipment that it could spare from its other research facilities. If you don't have what you need, let me know. I'll do my best to get it for you."

As he spoke, he gloved his right hand with a spydre; with it, he initiated a holographic dropdown menu from one of the projectors. Vraiss then displayed on one of the monitors a high-resolution satellite image of the northeast sector of Hellas Planitia—a close-up image of the region between Negele Crater and Niger Vallis. A small green dot flashed in the middle of the satellite image, indicating the station's location. "On Wednesday, 31 October, one of the Alliance's areological survey satellites detected a magnitude 2.9 Marsquake. Its epicenter was about 700 meters west of our current location. It was a minor quake, but because it was unusually shallow and occurred in a region not prone to tremors, we dispatched a survey team the next day. Their acoustic sensors detected an underground cavity at the quake's hypocenter about 400 meters below the surface. Now, subsurface cavities are not anomalous in themselves, but the survey team did detect density irregularities." On another monitor, the techswain then presented the survey team's sensor data. "The Martian Alliance immediately consulted the Federal Aerospace Intelligence Agency to interpret the densitometric data. And by Friday, 2 November, FAIA was on site with a Defense Force engineering platoon out of Camp Lundgren."

Vraiss paused momentarily to pull up a holographic schematic of an underground cavern and the inclining passageway connecting it to the surface. "After two days of excavating an access tunnel," he explained, "the engineers breached the cavity and found this—a massive polyhedral cavern hewn from the indigenous basaltic rock." A few soft gasps of astonishment echoed through the mess module. Even so, Vraiss continued, "Four vertices, six edges, a triangular floor, and three walls—four faces in all." With a subtle move of his wrist, Vraiss used his spydre to highlight the referenced part of the projection. "As the schematic shows, the access tunnel enters here, through one of the cavern walls about 100 meters above the floor."

On a third monitor, he cascaded through dozens of images of the cavern's interior. Vraiss described, "Each face is latticed with over a thousand triangles arranged in this bidirectional fractal pattern. Carved into each fractal are inscriptions from several ancient language systems. With adaptable comprehension software programs, we were able to translate a few of the writings, but some of the languages are so archaic, we don't have the appropriate algorithms to translate them. The few things that we have been able to translate are religious in nature. Along with these ancient languages are a myriad of mysterious symbols. We assume that these symbols are parts of some unknown language systems." He singled out a few of the cascading images to highlight certain structures in the triangular segments. "All of the fractals have these tetrahedral-shaped stelae protruding from them—4,096 in all. These stelae, each about 1.5 meters tall, are not themselves inscribed with any text or ornamentation, but they're positioned right in the middle of the inscription-filled fractals."

Leaving up the holographic projection of the subsurface cavern, the techswain reset the three monitors so that they all displayed images of a man wearing a compression suit and lying on the cavern's floor. "Now, if all of this wasn't mysterious enough," said Vraiss, "there's this: after four days of mapping the cavern and cataloguing its fractals, we found this man inside. His name is Silas Dorch, a known allegiant in the New Jerusalem terrorist sect. If he were in there at the start, we would have found him days earlier. Since we're confident that he didn't get in through our access tunnel, there must be another way into the cavern, but, damn it, try as we have, we can't find any other entrance." He continued, "And to top off the mysteries, Dorch had in his possession a twenty-four-hundred-year-old Terran scroll—a papyrus manuscript never before catalogued. Currently, it's being studied at the Federal Archives Library in Geneva."

Concluding his briefing, Vraiss remarked, "Clearly, this cavern is not a natural phenomenon. And it's why all of you are here—to study it, to learn everything you can about it. Chief among our inquiries are: Who built it? How did they build it? And why? In addition, we want to find out why Mr. Dorch was inside the cavern, how he got in, and how he came to possess an ancient Terran manuscript." He then offered, "At this time, I'll do my best to answer your questions."

The first question came from the research team's mathematician. "This cavern," asked Dr. Tereza Střelec, "what are its geometric parameters?"

"The cavern is a regular tetrahedron," the techswain answered. "All six edges are 147.337 meters long. It's just over 120 meters high and has a volumetric displacement of 376,937 cubic meters. There are 4,096 fractals interlaced among its four faces. Each fractal is an equilateral triangle whose sides measure 4.6 meters."

"How did you attain those measurements?" Střelec continued.

"We deployed lidar drones," he replied.

"That seems a bit old-fashioned," responded Dr. Marcus Lonsdale, archeologist. "I'd recommend using graviton fibration. It's the latest archeological method for measuring subterranean sites. It's far more precise; let's give that a try."

"Aye, sir," acknowledged Vraiss. "We already tried fibration measuring. But the anomalous energy field in the cavern kept interfering with the instruments. We can't even establish true vertical within the cavern."

Lonsdale was genuinely baffled that fibration measuring proved ineffectual in this case. He had hoped that such modern technology would reveal any hidden point of entry into the cavern. "This terrorist guy—what's his name, Dorch?—perhaps he got in through the original access point."

Vraiss was not sure what the archeologist was referring to. "Excuse me, sir?"

"There must be an original access point." Lonsdale elaborated, "Whoever carved out this cavern must have built a way in. And they had to have a way to remove an enormous volume of extricated debris."

"We've swept the entire cavern with acoustic and electromagnetic sensors," the techswain countered. "We haven't found any access points other than the tunnel that our engineers cut out a month ago."

"That just can't be," Lonsdale insisted.

The team's astrophysicist, Dr. Glendon Ferris, retorted, "Apparently, it can."

Lonsdale suggested, "Why not just ask this Dorch how he got in?"

"We did ask him—weeks ago," answered Vraiss. "His responses were less than helpful."

"Well, let's get him in here and ask him again," Lonsdale proposed. "Or, better yet, let's take him into the cavern and have him show us."

"Mr. Dorch was killed while held in the military detention compound at HAS *Landis*, replied Vraiss. "Dr. Catherine Hewst, our team's religion expert, was the last person to interview him."

Hewst expounded, "Mr. Dorch claimed that he was spirited into the cavern by angels."

"There are only two kinds of mysteries in this universe," proposed Ferris. "Those that science can explain, and those that science will eventually explain. I don't believe in magic; I believe in the laws of physics. I'm sure we can solve this puzzle without appealing to wizards and pixies."

"Well, we know of at least one entrance," Lonsdale remarked, "and that's the one cut out by the engineering platoon." The archeologist then considered, "If you bored into the cavern through one of its faces, you must have damaged some of the fractals and inscriptions at the breach."

"Aye, sir. That's true," the techswain acknowledged. "We took great care to keep the breached segment as whole as possible. What few fragments resulted from breaking through, we meticulously pieced back together. Its inscriptions are intact on the reassembled slab, which is currently stowed in the carriage bay—the only module large enough to house it. The slab contains portions of two fractals otherwise missing from the cavern wall. By scanning the contours of the slab, we've digitally filled in the gap in the cavern wall. The missing portions of the two fractals are available for study as images on holographic monitors."

Lonsdale's comment about breaching the cavern wall prompted a question from the areochemist, Dr. Andrea Cheung. "Were you able to get a sample of the gases in the cavern before breaching it?" she asked. "If so, we could run a spectrometric analysis of the gases. We could even submit a sample for radiometric dating. We might then be able to determine when the cavern was last entered."

"We hermetically inserted a sampling aperture through the cavern wall before breaching it." Vraiss continued, "To our amazement, we discovered that the space within the cavern was a vacuum; there were no gases to analyze. But because we needed to access the cavern with personnel and equipment, we decided to pressurize it to Martian indigenous—same content and pressure. We're assuming that the carbon dioxide atmosphere will be relatively nonreactive."

In his role as astrobiologist, Alex asked the techswain, "Did you scan for microbial life before breaching the cavern wall?"

"Aye, sir," he answered. "We ran an EM scan through the sampling aperture. It was completely sterile—no biological matter whatsoever."

The meta-droid asked, "Did you run a scan after finding Mr. Dorch in the cavern?"

Vraiss suddenly realized that, though they had not scanned the cavern after the fact, doing so would have been a good idea. The techswain glanced quickly at Captain Petrenko, who gave him a negative nod. "No, sir," he answered after a pensive pause. "We didn't."

Dr. Feodor Kalinin, areologist, had wanted to ask a question from the very start, but his colleagues had posed theirs faster. He had sat quietly through their inquiries but, given Vraiss' sluggish response to Alex, decided that now was the time to present his query. "To be clear," he asked, "are you saying that the cavern is at the hypocenter of the Marsquake?"

"Aye, sir," acknowledged Vraiss.

"That would mean that the cavern is the point where the strain energy was released," Kalinin surmised. "What energy source is there in that cavern?"

"There are anomalous readings of localized gravitational energy present, but its source is unknown." Vraiss added, "All other energy readings within the cavern are nominal."

"The range of gravity is infinite," Ferris interjected. "It can only be localized if you artificially distort the space-time envelope in or around the cavern."

"Aye, sir. FAIA's scientists agree." Vraiss expounded, "Yet they haven't been able to find any artificial means of distortion—no AG mechanisms. The cavern is basically a giant hole in the ground."

"No, it's more than just a hole in the ground," challenged the xenopsychologist, Dr. Emiri Matsuoka. "This cavern didn't just happen. It has a purpose. Some intelligence made this tetrahedron. And I'm guessing that I'm here because you think it might be the artifact of a xeno-intelligence. Am I right?"

"We want to explore all possibilities, ma'am," the techswain acknowledged.

"I believe in entertaining possibilities, Mr. Vraiss," she concurred. "But please don't dismiss the probability that it's simply the product of human intelligence."

"Aye, ma'am," he said. "But it's not just the tetrahedron; it's also the inscriptions. The enigmatic symbols in the fractals don't correspond to any known human languages."

"You're assuming the inscriptions are languages," declared Dr. Jonathan Driggers, a linguist. "They might just be artistic squiggles."

Vraiss nodded. "Aye, sir. Aerospace Intelligence is hoping that you and your team will make that determination."

"If you're hoping to translate those inscriptions, assuming that they are indeed a language," Driggers advanced, "you're going to need a key. A Martian Rosetta Stone of a sort."

Hewst remembered the holos of cavern inscriptions that she had examined earlier. Offering her counsel, she said, "Perhaps there's a Rosetta Stone among the inscriptions."

"Perhaps," the linguist conceded.

Lonsdale posited to his colleagues, "Given the religious nature of the inscriptions that have already been translated, we should consider the possibility that this cavern serves a sacred purpose, such as a shrine or a tomb." He then asked Vraiss, "Is there anything in the cavern that might resemble an altar or a sarcophagus?"

The techswain admitted his ignorance. "I'm sorry, sir. I don't know. Maybe there's something like that in there, but I wouldn't recognize any of those things if I were looking right at them. You and your team will have a chance to examine the cavern for yourself."

Hewst once again offered her counsel. "There might be another option to consider. The cavern might be a sacred library or a theological archive. We already know that a variety of religious statements are preserved in the fractals. Perhaps the cavern was built as a storehouse for papyrus texts." She asked the techswain, "Have you found any other papyrus manuscripts in the cavern?"

"No, ma'am," he said. "Just the one that was with Mr. Dorch."

Driggers considered another possibility. "Perhaps the manuscript itself is a Rosetta Stone."

"Perhaps," Hewst conceded. "Petty Officer Vraiss, can you show us on the schematic where you found both Dorch and the manuscript?"

With his spydre, Vraiss reached up and touched a panel in the holographic dropdown menu. A blue holographic dot appeared in the schematic, highlighting the area where Dorch and the manuscript were

171

discovered. To the wonder of the members of the project team, the blue dot did not show that Dorch was on the floor of the cavern. Instead, it indicated that he was in a physically untenable position—many meters above the base of the tetrahedron on a side that was canted 70 degrees off horizontal.

The members of the research team sat puzzled and wordless. Dr. Hewst soon broke the silence. "Mr. Dorch told me that the soldiers found him lying on the floor."

Vraiss remarked, "In a manner of speaking, that's true." With an inelegant expression on his face, he commented, "It's hard to explain."

Petrenko stepped up to the podium and addressed Vraiss. "Perhaps it would be best if we simply showed them." As she was looking at the chronometer on the back wall, she added, "Let's have the research team suit up and assemble in the carriage bay in thirty minutes."

"Aye aye, ma'am," he replied.

The briefing was adjourned, and Chief Fuentes began to escort the members of the research team to the carriage bay. Some of them were grumbling that they had just changed out of their compression suits and would now be putting them back on. As they were leaving, Chief Kiiswood approached Captain Petrenko to offer a suggestion. "Excuse me, ma'am. Since we haven't determined how Mr. Dorch entered the cavern, we should assume that the site is not secure. For the safety of the research team, I'd recommend that Petty Officer Sudha and myself accompany you."

"Very well," acknowledged the captain. "Suit up."

"Aye aye, ma'am."

Chapter 15 – The Tetrahedron

Carriage Bay, Belshazzar Research Station, Hellas Province, Mars

(Areographic Co-ordinates: S 35.642, E 94.228)

Friday, 07 December 2429 CE

Time: 1015 Zulu

Dr. Catherine Hewst had once again readied her compression suit with all of its essential accessories, including a fully charged EV packet. She currently sat with some of her full-suited colleagues on a bench in the equipment hub. They sat there waiting for the rest of their colleagues to suit up in the adjacent locker room, so that, together, they could advance through the airlock and onto the rail-carriage.

Moments later, several other team members emerged from the locker room in their suits, including Alex and Chief Kiiswood. However, Alex stood out from among the others, for his compression suit was lacking critical components. He was not wearing his collar module, EV packet, or helmet.

When Hewst looked up at Alex, she grinned amusingly. "Alex," she said, "I don't think you're quite ready."

"I said the same thing," said Kiiswood. "But he insists that he's outfitted correctly."

Shrugging his shoulders, Alex replied, "Cobisson and Negasi want to begin their field tests. They want to use this excursion into the cavern as a test of the meta-droid's hardware."

Hewst thought it odd that Alex would speak of himself in the third person. "The meta-droid's hardware?" she asked with a furrowed brow. "But you're the meta-droid."

Alex smiled and nodded. "I was almost completely suited. But then Cobisson and Negasi said they wanted me to excurse without life support—no helmet, no EV packet. They want to see how I function in an extreme, non-Terran environment."

Hewst's pastoral side emerged; she was genuinely concerned for Alex. "How do you feel about that?"

The meta-droid deflected. "The Whitaker Institute literally ran hundreds of lab tests. The hardware performed perfectly every time."

"Alex," she asked again, "how do *you* feel about that?"

"I'm scared as hell," he admitted. "It's one thing to test hardware when it's just a mechanism in a laboratory, but when it's my body—when it's me . . . " Alex tried not to sound anxious as he wondered, "If this meta-droid body crashes during a field test, I don't know what that means for me. If my hardware fails, will I die?"

Hewst recounted a story for Alex about her own fears. "When I served as a Defense Force chaplain, there were so many times that I had to put on compression suits. At first, I was terrified; I was so sure that the faceplate would crack, or the EV packet would leak, or the collar module would separate from the helmet. The first few times I suited up, the darkest parts of my imagination would take hold of me. I used to envision my bodily fluids suddenly boiling away in the vacuum of space."

Alex appreciated her candor. "When did you stop being afraid?" he asked.

"When I do, I'll let you know," she replied.

"If you have trepidations even now, why do you keep suiting up?"

Hewst answered humbly, but with conviction. "I suit up precisely for the same reason that I do everything else in life: because I'm mortal, because I embrace my mortality."

"I don't understand," the meta-droid remarked.

"There is never a moment when living doesn't risk dying." Hewst explained, "I can either cower in my bed, desperately trying to insulate my life from a world that is always trying to, and inevitably will, take it from me. Or I can fling headlong into the world and accept the risk—to live in the inevitable. I don't live my life in fear of death; I live my life to redeem death, to own my mortality." She concluded, "I suit up because I've decided to own my fears—to embrace my mortality."

"Catherine, I understand the fears of a compression suit failure," Alex said, "but I'm talking about deliberately stepping into a hazardous environment without a whole suit."

"You're missing my point," responded Hewst. "You and I are both stepping into a hazardous environment, and we're both being shielded within well-tested hardware. In my case, it's this suit; in your case, it's that android frame. Fear is normal, but at some point, you just have to trust the hardware. Fling your life headlong into the world, Alex."

"I don't fear death," said Kiiswood. He then pushed out his chest and, with melodramatic pomposity and a sardonic grin, he added, "Death fears me."

While Hewst and Alex were laughing at Kiiswood's farcical humor, Techswain Vraiss walked into the equipment hub and began to rally the research team. "Okay, everyone," he announced, "please secure your helmets at this time." Vraiss glanced at Alex as if he were looking past an inanimate object. "That is, those of you who have helmets." Vraiss then opened the hatch to the carriage bay's airlock and said, "Please follow me."

The members of the research team, as well as Sudha and Kiiswood—twelve in all—followed Vraiss into the airlock. As soon as Vraiss sealed the hatch, the augmented gravity disengaged, thus resuming "Mars-normal." Seconds later, the nitrogen-oxygen atmosphere evacuated the airlock, leaving its twelve occupants in a vacuum. Eleven of them were, of course, safely cocooned within their compression suits, but not Alex. Without his suit's key components, the meta-droid found himself directly exposed to the vacuity. At first, Alex felt sudden panic as he was unable to draw breath. But his anxiety quickly passed as he realized that he felt no pain; his mechanical body did not feel deprived. Once he became fully aware that he was unharmed, he started laughing inaudibly. With a smile on his face, Alex tried to exclaim, "This is so strange!" but the words could not pass his synthetic lips. There was no air in the room to flow around his artificial vocal chords or even to carry his voice to adjacent ears.

Through their helmet transceivers, an automated voice directed the occupants. "Please stand with your legs spread slightly apart and your arms extended out to your sides. Stand by for decontamination procedure." The decontamination procedure was part of FAIA's preservation protocols to reduce any detrimental impact of human presence in the subsurface cavern. It involved a combination of focused irradiation to destroy microorganisms and magnetic resonance extraction to remove all particulates from their suits.

As all but the meta-droid were assuming the directed stance for decontamination, Hewst realized that Alex did not have a transceiver and thus did not hear the automated instructions. So she waved to get his attention and modeled the appropriate position. Alex mimicked her pose just as the decontamination procedure began.

During the procedure, Kiiswood hailed Hewst over her c-nex to talk about the meta-droid. "Hey, Commander," he said. "I don't know whether it's clever programming or whether there really is someone inside that machine. Alex is behaving just like a true human being. He was so concerned about possibly dying during this field test that he entrusted me with the access code to his storage locker."

"Are you amazed that Alex might actually be a sentient soul," Hewst asked, "or that there might be someone in the universe who actually likes you and trusts you with his locker code?"

"You know, ma'am," he smirked, "you're living proof that God made theologians, but He didn't make them funny." Kiiswood continued, "No, I'm amazed how human he is. Not only has he taken me into his trust, but he's also exhibiting admiration for you, ma'am."

"How so?" she asked curiously.

Kiiswood answered, "In the unlikely event something might happen to him during this excursion, he decided not to carry your necklace with him. He told me that, until he has a chance to analyze the pendant for you, he's stowing it in his locker for safekeeping. And he gave me his access code just in case he doesn't survive this field test."

"Decontamination complete," the automated voice said. "Stand by for repressurization." Immediately, the airlock was flooded with the frigid Martian atmosphere. The status indicator promptly displayed "Atmosphere: Mars Normal."

The smile on Alex's face grew more pronounced as he steadily gained more confidence in the durability of his animatronic body. He could sense the freezing cold atmosphere on his synthetic skin, but there was no pain or discomfort associated with the sensation. With each breath, his body could somehow detect the carbon dioxide that permeated the airlock. Once again, Alex exclaimed, "This is so strange!" This time, however, his words were lightly audible in the thin atmosphere. The carbon dioxide passing around his vocal chords rendered the pitch of his meta-droid voice a little lower.

Techswain Vraiss opened the airlock hatch to the carriage bay. "Please follow me," he said with a beckoning gesture.

The carriage bay was the module that housed a sixteen-passenger carriage securely mounted on a maglev rail over the mouth of the tunnel. The atmospheric pressure inside the module was effectively the same as that outside, so the module served merely as a hermetic shelter from the Martian winds and weather.

Following Vraiss' lead, the team members quickly boarded the carriage and strapped in. Vraiss throttled up, and the carriage began its trek toward the cavern. Its passengers rode smoothly through the 2.7-meter-diameter tunnel bored through the Martian surface. Floating on a magnetic cushion along a rail that ran the length of the 800-meter tunnel, the carriage glided on a downward angle of 31 degrees at a thunderous 12 kilometers per hour. The tunnel had lateral and overhead lighting strips every 3 meters. The walls between each set of lights were labeled with the carriage's distance traveled and its current depth beneath the planet's surface.

Within minutes, the rail-carriage reached the end of the line and stopped just a few meters away from the cavern. The team members exited the carriage and made their way along a set of stairs that soon leveled out onto a catwalk. There ahead of them, at the catwalk's end, was the breach in the cavern's wall that opened into blackness.

"What now?" Kalinin wondered.

Using his c-nex, Vraiss accessed a particular utility application and activated the recently installed array of floodlights; suddenly, the cavern's darkness was swept away. The floodlights revealed that the cavern was indeed a capacious tetrahedron. Its basaltic floor and walls were an achromatic blackish-gray; its surfaces were wholly covered with thousands of script-laden triangular fractals.

Several of the team members stood at the catwalk's edge, holding onto the handrails and staring through the breach. The team members in the back were cautiously trying to peer over the shoulders of those in front. They saw that the handrails and balusters extended about another two meters into the cavern, apparently ending abruptly and dangling in mid-air.

Staring at the floor 100 meters below the breach, Alex commented in a low-pitched voice, "That's a long way down."

"Down is a lot closer than you think," Vraiss responded, although Alex could hardly hear the techswain through his helmet and faceplate.

Kiiswood signaled Hewst and said, "If Alex is going to spend any time in the cavern, we've got to get him a headset or a c-nex so he can hear what we're saying."

Hewst nodded in agreement.

Staring at the disorienting distance of the floor below, Cheung asked, "So how do we get down there?"

"Believe it or not, we walk," the techswain answered. "Perhaps it would be easier just to show you what I mean." Vraiss began looking around the catwalk as if trying to find a misplaced item. "There it is," he said. "Excuse me, Dr. Ferris, would you hand me that tennis ball?"

Ferris looked down and, there beside his left boot, saw a tennis ball wedged in a small nook in the catwalk. Having retrieved the ball, he handed it to the techswain.

"Watch this," announced Vraiss. Facing the breach, he gently tossed the tennis ball straight out into the cavern. The team members watched for the ball to arc downward and to strike the floor with a prominent rebound in the low Martian gravity. What they witnessed instead was a tennis ball that flew straight out a couple of meters, slowed down to a near stop, arced slightly upward, and flew straight back into Vraiss' gloves.

The reactions from the team members were simultaneous, yet varied. Among their responses were a few astonished gasps, some exclamations of amazement, an "Oh my God!" and even a couple of bewildered expletives.

Vraiss then announced, "Now watch this." He threw the tennis ball straight out into the cavern, but now he hurled it quite forcefully. This time, the ball did not come back. Instead, it flew straight out several meters, slowed down slightly, and arced obtusely to the right. The tennis ball then accelerated in its redirected flight, bounced several times on the right-side wall, and soon came to rest there.

Everyone stood staring at the tennis ball hanging on the cavern wall. They stood in silence until Lonsdale asked, "So what do we do now?"

"Now, we go get the ball," answered Vraiss. He walked up to the edge of the catwalk and said, "I need you to do exactly as I do." He proceeded to lie down on his side with his head toward the breach. He firmly grabbed onto the balusters of the handrail and began to pull himself along the catwalk, through the breach, and into the cavern. The more of his mass that he pulled into the cavern, the more gravitational force tried to push his body back into the tunnel. Hand over hand, foot over foot, as Vraiss slowly advanced into the cavern, the balusters of the handrail effectively transitioned into the rungs of a ladder. Once he cleared the breach, Vraiss stepped from the ladder and onto the wall— or what seemed to be a wall from the perspective of those in the tunnel. But, for Vraiss, he was standing firmly and walking effortlessly on a floor. "Okay." he invited, "who's next?"

Some of them edged forward to gain a better view of a man walking upright (or outright) on the side of a wall. Others stood there apprehensively, gripping the handrail a little more tightly. Still others stepped slightly aback in trepidation. But Hewst was eager to live in the inevitable—to fling her life headlong into the cavern and to accept the risk. "I'll go next," she replied to Vraiss.

"It may feel a little disorienting at first," warned the techswain. "But just press on, and you'll be fine."

Hewst climbed along the rungs in the same manner Vraiss had. As she was crossing from the tunnel into the cavern, it felt as though her own weight were pushing her in two directions at once. Her sense of balance shifted as her eyes and inner ears were trying to readjust to a new vertical and a new horizontal. But she continued climbing even though she was feeling slightly vertiginous. Finally, Hewst had climbed up and out just enough to step from the rungs onto the wall—now her floor. And she was pleasantly amazed at how quickly her equilibrium reset itself to a new direction for up.

The team members erupted in spontaneous applause at Hewst's success. Her accomplishment was a challenge to the more intrepid members of the team and an inspiration to the more trepidatious. One by one, the team members climbed into the cavern. Some of them managed the task with difficulty; Driggers, for example, felt somewhat nauseous and fleetingly thought he might throw up in his helmet. Others managed the task with ease; Kiiswood, with a hand on the side rail, pitched himself through the breach and landed on the wall with the grace of a dismounting gymnast.

Once everyone had made their way into the cavern, they began to feel more at ease with the gravitational oddity. They soon realized that they were not about to fall from the wall-turned-floor. With fascination and awe, they surveyed the grandeur of the tetrahedral space in which they stood. The calligraphic inscriptions engraved on the floor—the artistic letters, the elegant symbols, the fractal lines—were clear and well-defined. The vast expanse of the triangular floor beneath their boots was covered with these beautiful engravings as far as the eye could see. The only spaces not marked with words and glyphs were the hundreds of stelae strewn about. The three surrounding walls shared the same shape and dimensions as the floor—walls that converged at a vertex 120 meters overhead. They too were covered with thousands of inscription-filled fractals and protruding stelae.

The entire tetrahedral space was sharply illuminated by an array of lights that hung about 30 meters above the floor at the center of the cavern, floating equidistant from each of the four faces of the tetrahedron. The array of lights was also equipped with a full battery of cameras and sensors that covered the entire electromagnetic spectrum. Everything that was happening in the cavern was being monitored and recorded from the station's control room.

"Please feel free to walk around and explore," encouraged Vraiss. "But be careful when you approach any of the edges. The gravity is redirected along the plane of bisection."

Compelled by scientific curiosity, Dr. Glendon Ferris decided to test the techswain's assertion about the cavern's gravity. He walked toward the nearest of the three walls—toward the tetrahedral edge where that wall met the floor on which he strolled. Because it angled inward at about 70 degrees, the wall tilted closer to his head than to his feet. As he approached, Ferris began to feel the effects of shifting gravity. With each step, he felt his upper body being pulled toward the wall—first, his head, then his shoulders, then his upper torso. Once he was within arm's length of the wall, he felt a need to catch himself. He reflexively extended his arms, causing his weight to shift above his center of mass. His feet easily lifted off the floor, his body toppled forward, and he fell gently onto the wall.

Several others witnessed the astrophysicist's indelicate landing on the wall. A few of them even laughed. Ferris also laughed after he realized that he was unhurt. He crawled along the wall away from the edge and then stood.

"Look at all of you," said Ferris, still laughing. "You're all wall-walkers."

Having witnessed Ferris' less-than-graceful success, most of the team members decided to do likewise. They, too, were now climbing, striding, leaping, and sometimes stumbling onto other walls in the cavern. Soon, they had spread throughout the entire cavern such that each of the four tetrahedral sides was someone's floor. The directions of up and down were no longer a shared frame of reference. Were it not for the one wall with the breach, the team members would have found themselves easily disoriented among the nearly indistinguishable fractals and stelae.

As they moved about, the team members surveyed the cavern with attention to their respective fields of expertise. Astrophysicist Ferris had retrieved the tennis ball and was tossing it to and fro, testing (unscientifically) the shifts of gravity around the edges and vertices of the tetrahedron. The areochemist, Dr. Andrea Cheung, was examining the basalt of the cavern walls for erosion resistance. The areologist, Dr. Feodor Kalinin, was searching for any differentiation in the tholeiitic basalt. Dr. Tereza Střelec, mathematician,

181

was standing in place, contemplating the significance of a cavern in the shape of a Platonic solid. The archeologist, Dr. Marcus Lonsdale, was pondering how an intelligence managed to impose itself so immaculately on indigenous stone, while the xenopsychologist, Dr. Emiri Matsuoka, was looking for clues that that intelligence might be nonhuman. Dr. Jonathan Driggers, linguist, walked around, trying to discern patterns among the exotic glyphs in the fractals on the floor. Alex was wandering from one tetrahedral face to another, doing what astrobiologists have done for centuries when searching for Martian life—looking for signs of subsurface water in the cavern. Chief Kiiswood and Petty Officer Sudha, sorteers, were patrolling the entire cavern, attending to the team's security. For her part, Dr. Catherine Hewst, in her capacity as religious scholar, was walking about in sheer wonder and amazement. As she was focusing on the Greek and Hebrew inscriptions, and matching many of them with their religious textual traditions, Hewst was overwhelmed by the exquisite calligraphy everywhere.

Petty Officer Vraiss checked the chronometer in his HUD and announced to the team members, "Ladies and gentlemen, we'll be heading back to the surface in about five minutes. Please start making your way back to the breach."

As Lonsdale trekked back to the breach, he almost walked into one of the stelae; he was looking up at the array of lights, not watching where he was going. He was glad that the corps of engineers had strategically positioned the cavern's lighting system in midair. The array would make studying this archeological site much easier, he thought—easier than relying on helmet torches. But its placement also concerned him. "How did the engineers secure that light array?" he asked Vraiss. "Did they damage any of the stelae or fractals when they anchored it in place?"

"The array isn't physically anchored," answered Vraiss. "The engineers discovered that the volumetric center of the tetrahedron is gravitationally neutral. So they took advantage of this anomaly."

Ferris chimed into the conversation. "Like a Lagrange point," he commented.

"Aye, sir," replied Vraiss. "It's equipped with a series of RCS microthrusters to compensate for subtle drifting."

As Hewst hiked back to the breach, she approached Chief Kiiswood, who stood nearly motionless. His gaze was keenly fixed on the array overhead. She noted the faint expression of dismay on his face. "What is it, Chief?" she asked.

For the sake of prudence, the chief resolved to keep his concerns to himself, for the time being. "I'll tell you later," he answered.

Hewst, Kiiswood, and the rest of the team soon boarded the rail-carriage, and before long they returned to the station.

Chapter 16 – The Translations

The Subsurface Cavern, Hellas Province, Mars

(Areographic Co-ordinates: S 35.641, E 94.213)

Thursday, 13 December 2429 CE

Time: 0844 Zulu

The research team was now into its seventh day at Belshazzar Station. By this time, every square centimeter of the tetrahedral faces had been thoroughly photographed, holoed, scanned, and catalogued. All of the symbols and inscriptions in the tetrahedron were recorded in such detail that none of the scholars and scientists had to suit up and physically enter the cavern to study them. They could more easily study holographic displays of the inscriptions in the safety and mediocre comfort of a laboratory module. Even so, Dr. Hewst preferred to stroll among the fractals and to read the cavern's beautiful calligraphic inscriptions with her own eyes. Among her colleagues, none of them spent as much time underground as she did. Since Hewst had arrived at the station, not a day went by when she was not personally exploring the inscrutable languages in the Martian cavern. For her, the space had become almost sacred.

Hewst had made an early start of the day. Before breakfast, she had suited up and was already at work in the cavern. With her were Petty Officer Ishanvi Sudha, providing security, and Chief Åsta Holgersen, helping Hewst modify the translation software so that it could recognize ancient calligraphy.

Chief Níyol Kiiswood and Petty Officer Mas'ud Al-Jabiri were sitting in the station's low-lit control room. There, they were monitoring and recording the activities of their three colleagues down in the cavern. Al-Jabiri noticed the chronometer display in the lower right-hand corner on the control room's main monitor. He reached up and tapped the display to draw Kiiswood's attention to the current time.

Kiiswood promptly activated a console mic. "I hate to interrupt your work, Commander," he said, "but there's a briefing in about fifteen minutes. Captain Petrenko will be expecting you presently."

"Thank you for the reminder, Chief," responded Hewst. "We're making our way to the rail-carriage now."

"Aye, ma'am," he replied.

As if on cue, Al-Jabiri arose from his seat and headed toward the control room hatch. "By your leave, Chief," he said.

"Where are you going?" asked Kiiswood.

"The commander will be racing into the briefing in a few minutes," he answered. "She'll want to have some coffee ready for when she gets there."

"Carry on," the chief grinned. "Far be it from me to stand between the commander and her caffeine."

Al-Jabiri's morning trek was now routine. He quickly weaved his way through the maze of gangways and arrived at the galley hub just before it was to close for breakfast. He grabbed a flagon, placed it under the tap of a large coffee urn, and filled it. After adding some creamer to the flagon, he grabbed a cup and headed into the mess module, where the members of the research team were already assembling. He filled the cup from the flagon, then set the flagon at Hewst's usual place at the table.

As he walked toward the module hatch with the cup of coffee in hand, Captain Petrenko addressed him. "Mr. Al-Jabiri, it's currently 0900 Zulu. Will Dr. Hewst be joining us soon?" she asked.

Still fully geared in her compression suit, Hewst hurried through the hatch, taking the cup of coffee from the petty officer as she entered the mess module. "I'm here, ma'am," answered Hewst. She quickly took her seat in front of the flagon. "I know I'm cutting it close," she said contritely as she took a large sip from her cup. "I'm sorry for any inconvenience."

"Well, now that we're all here," the captain acknowledged, "let's get started." She looked around the table and decided to start the briefing with a report from the meta-droid. "Alex, what does astrobiology have for us this morning?"

Alex was surprised that Petrenko had called on him first. He had grown accustomed to being the last one to report at these briefings. Nonetheless, he was prepared. "After running a full battery of chromatographic, spectrometric, and metabolodynamic scans, all results are negative." Alex elaborated, "No signs of gas exchange, no pyrolysis, no metabolic processes anywhere in the cavern. There are no organic compounds, no water whatsoever, and certainly none of the typical Martian microbes that one usually finds in subsurface caverns. Just 800 kilometers southwest from here, microbial life is ubiquitous in the permafrost of Hellas Basin. But not here." The meta-droid concluded, "This cavern is dry and sterile."

"Okay. Are there any questions for astrobiology?" asked Petrenko.

Dr. Kalinin did not bother to raise a hand or to motion for the captain's attention. He asked Alex, "Have you checked for fossilized microbes in the rock? This area of Mars may be bone-dry now, but 3.8 billion years ago, it was the site of massive groundwater sapping. It's what formed Dao and Niger Valles during the Noachian epoch."

"I did check for fossil remains," Alex replied. "The results were negative. But that should come as no surprise. Whenever we discover fossil traces, they're almost always found in sedimentary rocks, like the fossilized microbes in the nearby Cue Crater. But the molten origins of igneous rocks make it extremely rare to find fossils in them."

"I'm impressed," Kalinin condescended. "Our artificial biologist knows something about geology." Alex felt inclined to defend his education and professionalism, but he then thought better of it. Any response would simply dignify Kalinin's comment and exacerbate Alex's indignation.

"Well, Dr. Kalinin," said Petrenko, "since you now have the floor, why don't you give us an areology report?"

"Alex is right about igneous formation," Kalinin acknowledged. "The entire cavern—fractals, stelae, and all—is carved from an unfractured block of igneous rock—specifically, basalt. The age of the rock is 3.927 billion years old. It solidified from the magma-induced asteroid impact that formed Hellas Basin during the Mid-Noachian period. Without any fractures or fissures in the rock, there's no way that water or hydrocarbons, or anything else for that matter, could get into that cavity." With a nescient grin, he conceded, "I have no idea how someone carved a tetrahedral hole in the middle of that block." Using his c-nex, Kalinin accessed the room's projection system. In the middle of the table, he displayed a holographic schematic of the cavern highlighted with areological data. "The only things I can tell you about the cavern are basic physical parameters. The base of the cavern is 3,029 meters below Mars datum and about one kilometer above the ancient Noachian shoreline. Its top vertex is 411 meters below the planet's surface. The atmospheric temperature inside the cavern is a constant minus fifty-one degrees Celsius, and atmospheric pressure is 762 pascals." As he turned off the holographic projector, he added, "That's all I have for you."

"Thank you, Doctor," said the captain. "Dr. Lonsdale, what does archeology have for us this morning?"

"I want to thank all of my colleagues here for lending us personnel from their own support staff," Lonsdale said. "We needed the extra hands." He expounded, "We divided our work into two areas: areophysical survey of the Martian surface and data recovery in the cavern." On one of the monitors, Lonsdale displayed a high-resolution satellite image of the surface area above the cavern—about a 43-square-kilometer area. "The areophysical survey team conducted a systematic inspection of the Martian surface above the cavern, covering a 3-kilometer radius from the Marsquake epicenter. First, the team scanned the area with aerial drone magnetometry, infrared spectroscopy, and ground-penetrating radar. Other than Belshazzar Station, we found no indication of any artificial features. Second, using station personnel, we methodically walked across the surface looking for evidence of past human activity, such as carving tools or excavation artifacts. We also looked for color changes in the soil that may indicate features such as middens or extricated debris pits. Again, the only mound of debris we found was the one just outside the station—the one created by the Defense Force engineers when they extricated debris from their access tunnel."

"I'm not surprised that you didn't find an entry point," Kalinin interjected. "As I've already said, it's a solid block of rock below the surface."

Lonsdale continued, "Now, regarding data recovery in the cavern itself, we couldn't physically grid the site without damaging the features." He changed the display on the monitor to show a 3D grid placed over an image of the tetrahedral cavern. "Instead, we holoed the entire site to create a digital template and overlaid it with a 3D virtual grid. By patching the overlay through our HUD, we've been able to work on-site within an augmented-reality grid. We're using the engineer's tunnel breach as a datum point. Grid by grid, we meticulously catalogued every stone carving in the cavern: every fractal, every stele, every glyph and symbol, every jot and tittle. We discovered that, without exception, all the carvings throughout the entire cavern are impressed nine millimeters into the stone facings. We also discovered that, even though the density of stelae measures faintly less than the surrounding rock, all of them are carved from the same continuous rock formation. We found no carving tools or any artifacts in the cavern whatsoever—no chisels, no hammer stones, no calipers." Lonsdale paused, furrowed his brow, then said, "I use the word 'carving' figuratively; we can find no physical evidence that the impressions in the stone were actually carved. There's no sign of scorching from lasers. There are no traces of marring from chiseling, abrading, or knapping, not even microscopic traces." With an awkward and ironic snicker, he concluded, "It's as though the cavern formed this way." At that, a couple of low, mottled chuckles were heard around the table.

"Did your team determine why the stelae have less density than the rest of the indigenous basalt?" Kalinin asked.

"The densitometric difference was so slight, we didn't give it much attention." Lonsdale speculated, "It might just be related to the gravitational anomalies with the cavern. But, since you asked, we'll look into it."

Captain Petrenko thanked Lonsdale and then continued with the briefing. "Dr. Cheung, does areochemistry have anything to report?"

"Yes, we do," she answered as she finished the last morsel of toast from her breakfast. "After Mr. Silas Dorch was taken into custody, he was outfitted with a prison-grade compression suit for transport to HAS *Landis*. Fortunately, his confiscated suit is still here at the station. We were able to isolate the silicate dust on his old suit and to identify its chemical composition. By comparing its ferromagnesian ratios with various areological soil samples, we were able to trace Mr. Dorch's movements on the planet's surface." As she spoke, Cheung accessed another monitor and displayed a satellite image of the northeast sector of Hellas Planitia. She then overlaid part of the image with a meandrous red line. "We can now map his progression, from the time he left his traxle to the time he walked down into a small cave about 14 kilometers south of our current location. And that's where we lose track of his movements, until he shows up inside the cavern."

Everyone on the research team understood the implication of Dr. Cheung's soil analysis, but Lonsdale was the first to say what they were all thinking. "We should inspect that cave as a possible entry point for the cavern," he proposed.

"Oh, we already have," Cheung replied. "We ran a full panel of sonar, radar, and gravitonic scans in and around the cave. Under the pretext of being an IPHA unit surveying a quarantine area, we deployed a survey team yesterday to make an on-site inspection. It's just a narrow cave that dead-ends 30 meters in."

"Let's try this from the other direction," suggested Kalinin. "Can we use your soil analysis to track Dorch's movements inside the cavern?"

"We've tried that too," Cheung answered. "The most amazing thing about this cavern is how immaculate it is. And through magnetic resonance extraction in the carriage bay, it's kept that way. So by tracing the dust and particulate that came in on Mr. Dorch's suit, we know the exact path that the engineering crew ushered him out. Now, unless he entered along that same path, I can't tell you how he got in."

"That doesn't even seem plausible," Petty Officer Vraiss commented.

"Thank you, Dr. Cheung," said Petrenko. "Clearly, that's one of many mysteries yet to be solved." She pointed to the team's linguist and asked, "Dr. Driggers, what do you have for us this morning?"

Driggers stood up and walked over to the monitors in the mess module. "May I clear these displays?" he asked.

"Be my guest," the captain replied.

Using his c-nex, Driggers cleared the images that Lonsdale and Cheung had displayed and replaced them with two graphs of his own. He then addressed his colleagues while standing beside the monitors. "I can say, with reasonable certainty, that some of the foreign inscriptions in the cavern are not natural languages, but many of them indeed are. We've been able to draw this inference because many of these inscriptions convey meaning."

"If you don't know the language," Dr. Ferris asked, "then how do you know that they convey meaning?"

Driggers continued, "We applied a linguistic tool known as information theory. It's a critical technique that considers the probability of symbol-occurrence within a presumed language. We add up how frequently each symbol occurs. If the inscriptions were just a random distribution of symbols, then each symbol would occur with about the same frequency. And when you graph it on a logarithmic scale, you get a flat-line pattern—a zero slope, like this," he said while pointing to the graph displayed on the first monitor. "In such a case, no linguistic information is being communicated. You can't convey information in this manner."

Ferris interrupted, "And you're saying that this flat-line pattern did not occur when you applied this linguistic tool?"

"That's correct," he acknowledged. "Inscriptions that convey meaning have a different pattern. In any natural language, its most frequently used word will occur about twice as often as the second most frequently used word, three times as often as the third most frequently used word, and so on. In other words, the frequency of any word is inversely proportional to its order in the frequency list. All natural languages graph out as a negative one slope. So whenever this pattern occurs, we know that the words convey information even if we don't know what the words mean." Driggers then pointed to the graph on the second monitor and said, "When we took the unknown symbol groups in the cavern and plotted them on a logarithmic graph, we got this declining pattern—a negative one slope." He continued, "We've determined that we're dealing with at least seventeen distinct languages."

"Have you been able to translate any of them?" asked Petrenko.

"No," Driggers answered with a laugh. "The only way to translate a written language is with a decipher key—a kind of Rosetta Stone."

Dr. Střelec listened intently to the linguist's presentation, and she wondered whether her observations might have some bearing on his work. "Have you considered whether these might be your Rosetta Stone?" she asked.

She accessed the third monitor in the room and displayed a series of parallel lines. "Every fractal contains one of five reoccurring patterns of parallel lines; each pattern comprises eight lines, and each line in a given pattern differs in length."

"Yes, I've seen those patterns," Driggers replied. "I can tell you that, with only five distinct patterns of lines, I can't determine whether they convey any linguistic meaning. The sampling is too small to apply information theory. I don't know what those lines are."

Střelec changed the image on the third monitor to display a new pattern—a pattern that appeared in every single fractal. "I assume then that this little pattern of rings and triangles above the parallel lines is just as problematic."

"Again, the sampling is too small," he said.

Petrenko wondered why Střelec had introduced these images on the monitor. "Does mathematics have something to add to our briefing?" she asked.

"I can confirm that those sets of parallel lines are not part of a language." Střelec continued, "At least not a so-called natural language. Some of the markings are mathematical." She returned the image of the parallel lines to the third monitor. "Specifically, these markings," she said. "Each fractal contains a set of parallel lines, and each line in the set varies in length. Alongside each line is a series of open and closed circles. My immediate assumption was that circles are part of a binary code that represents text. I've run the series through every bit-string binary system I know: Baconian cipher, TCC, ASCII, BCD, qubit computation. I've even tried Braille and Morse Code. But all I get textually is meaningless gibber. If anyone knows of any other binary system that I can try, please let me know."

Dr. Hewst felt hesitant to offer her suggestions, but she would rather propose even the most unlikely options than to keep them to herself. "Given the religious inscriptions in the cavern," she said, "perhaps we can consider binary systems that come from religious traditions. I know of two. One is called Ifá. It's an ancient Yoruba system of divination." As Hewst expected, the entire module erupted in laughter.

Střelec remained courteous as she asked, "And what's the other system?"

"It's called Bagua," replied Hewst. "It's a binary system used in Taoist metaphysics." Strangely, her second proposal drew fewer laughs.

"Okay," affirmed the mathematician. "Send the system links to my work station, and I'll look at them. But my best guess now is that these circles aren't text at all; they're part of a binary numerical system. These are numbers expressed in base-2."

"Alright," Petrenko asked, "what are the numbers?"

"That's currently indeterminate," admitted Střelec. "It depends on whether the open circles are ones and the closed circles are zeros, or *vice versa*. And it also depends on which direction the digits are meant to be read. And even if we can decipher the numbers in this binary code, we're left with the question: What do these numbers mean?" She decided that an example might help illustrate her point. "Suppose we discover that the binary code signifies the number one billion and three. The number begs a question: a billion and three *what?* Seconds? Meters? Grams? Moles?" Again, she replaced the image of parallel lines on the monitor with the image of rings and triangles. "I'm assuming that the encryption key to decoding this binary system is this little pattern of rings and triangles just above every set of parallel lines. Embedded within this pattern are one open circle and one closed circle. But if this little pattern is indeed an encryption key, I have no idea what it means."

"I think I do," offered Dr. Ferris. Staring intently at the pattern on the monitor, he said, "It's a schematic of a hydrogen atom. Some physicist is giving us a common unit of measure by representing the quantum properties of the most abundant element in the universe." He explained, "Imagine, for a moment, that each ring is an electron cloud and that the larger triangle in the center of each ring is a single proton—a hydrogen nucleus. That means that the smaller triangle on each circumference is a single electron in its ground state. In one ring, the larger and smaller triangles share the same alignment, probably implying that they share the same spin moment. But in the other ring, the smaller triangle is inverted, implying that the proton and electron have opposing spin moments. The line connecting these two rings is meant to represent a spin-flip transition, which corresponds to a period of 0.704

nanoseconds and a wavelength of 21.1 centimeters. The closed circle beside the transition line represents one specific unit of length, or one specific unit of time, or both. In any case, the closed circle represents the binary digit: one."

Driggers stepped away from the monitors and returned to his seat at the table. He regarded himself as a gifted linguist and a reasonably intelligent person. But the words of his astrophysicist colleague confused him. He conceded, "The only thing I heard in all of that was 'hydrogen atom.' I really don't know what you're talking about."

Ferris chuckled as he abridged his explanation. "All I'm saying is that, if this is indeed a representation of a hydrogen atom, then it's giving us a universal frame of reference to measure duration and distance. Humankind has been using physics and mathematics for centuries when trying to communicate with supposed nonhuman intelligence."

"Non-human intelligence?" asked Dr. Matsuoka. "Aren't we jumping to conclusions?"

Everyone around the table paused momentarily in awkward silence. Although it had, until now, gone unmentioned, the subject of nonhuman intelligence was obviously present in their thoughts. Finally, Dr. Kalinin broke the silence. "Are we?" he asked. "You know that it's on the minds of every scientist and scholar in this room. Why shouldn't we be willing to propose an imaginative hypothesis? Isn't that what good science requires? Without scientific imagination, humankind would still be living in an Earth-centered universe."

"There are more probable hypotheses we should consider before we assume the handiwork of extraterrestrials," Matsuoka offered. "I think we should first consider the more likely scenario that this cavern is a cleaver hoax—the work of human hands."

"I'm surprised," responded Kalinin. "I thought that, if anyone on the research team would be promoting a theory of alien influence, it would be you."

"History is replete with mistaken claims of alien interventions: the pyramids in Egypt, the Nazca Lines in Peru, the Martian face at Cydonia," she replied. "As a xenopsychologist, it's my responsibility to make sure that we first consider the more likely hypotheses. Then, as good scientists, we systematically eliminate each one of these hypotheses before postulating the work of little green men, or little gray men, or whatever color aliens might be." Matsuoka then added, "Let's assume human agency first."

Dr. Ferris found himself agreeing with Matsuoka's disciplined approach. But he still felt a need to voice his frustration. "Well, one fact that I can't explain by any human agency is the gravitational anomaly within the cavern. The gravitational force is quadridirectional. The directions of force run perpendicular to the four tetrahedral faces and are redirected sharply along the planes that intersect the edges and the volumetric center. Also, our gravimetric measurements show that the lines of force do not extend beyond the cavity into the surrounding rock. Now, to distort a space-time envelope in this manner requires a hell of a lot of energy."

"*We* can generate gravity artificially," Matsuoka responded. "We can control its direction and strength. We do it all the time on vessels and in g-ducts. We're doing it right here in this research station. Human beings are quite clever. So, why assume that it's the work of nonhuman intelligence?"

Dr. Kalinin was unimpressed with Matsuoka's response to Ferris' observation. He thought her response was a false equivalence. "We generate augmented gravity for this station using Kapoorian symmetry hardware, powered by a helium-3 reactor," said Kalinin. "There's nothing in that cavern but rock. Whatever is going on down there, it's beyond any technology that we're aware of."

"And that's my point," she countered. "We don't understand—yet. All good science begins by embracing our ignorance. Our science goes awry when we too quickly replace that ignorance with implausible suppositions that 'aliens did it.' Why not just abandon the scientific method all together and declare it as a mighty act of God?"

Captain Petrenko sensed that the stress among the team members was rising. She tried to introduce a moderating tone to the discussion to lower the tension. "Let's all take a few steps back and catch our respective breaths," she said. "We've all been working hard with only a handful of answers to show for our efforts. I realize we're all tired and frustrated. But please try to remember that we're all on the same team." Petrenko looked around the table and noticed that one member of the research team had not yet offered her scholarly input. "Dr. Hewst, do you have anything to add to the discussion?"

During the briefing, Hewst had listened intently to her colleagues. She had also consumed nearly two cups of coffee. "I'm sure that Dr. Matsuoka meant her comment in jest," said Hewst. "But, aesthetically speaking, I think the cavern *is* a mighty act of God, but no more so than anything else in the universe that's the subject of scientific investigation. I, for one, confess that its mysteries and grandeur are awe-inspiring." She continued, "But I also agree with Dr. Matsuoka; the pursuit of truth demands that we approach these mysteries methodically and with discipline."

"So, do you have anything else to share," Petrenko inquired, "other than aesthetics?"

"Several things," she ceded. "First, the reason that the translation programs weren't working with many of the ancient languages is that their algorithmic presets were not able to recognize the ancient stylized alphabets. With Chief Holgersen's assistance, we modified the software to recognize various calligraphic scripts. We were then able to translate all of the known languages in short order. Of course, translating a language is also an act of interpretation; it's more of an art than a science. So I'm making some subtle adjustments to the translations to address certain interpretive nuances."

"You've been able to translate every natural language in the cavern?" Driggers asked.

"Every known language, yes." She continued, "And that brings me to my second point. All of the known languages in any given fractal are simply translations of the same statement. Apparently, each fractal is devoted to a particular religious pronouncement. There are 4,096 fractals and 4,096 pronouncements. So if the known languages in a fractal are translations of a particular pronouncement, then we can presume that the unknown languages are too. Perhaps each fractal is the Rosetta Stone that Dr. Driggers is looking for."

"Perhaps," Driggers responded with an optimistic note in his voice. "I'll begin comparing similar symbols to known words and phrases just as soon as I get back to the lab."

"There's more," said Hewst. "I've matched many of the inscriptions with their religious textual traditions. Many of them are ancient sayings from Hinduism, Buddhism, Islam, Christianity, *etcetera*. Now, because we know the sources of so many of these inscriptions, we can apply a literary discipline known as redaction criticism. We can study the inscriptions as the work of a redactor. The person or persons who created this cavern intentionally included certain religious statements from their sources and excluded others. By analyzing how the sources were redacted, we can infer the redactors' vested interest."

"Well, don't keep us in suspense," Lonsdale declared. "What's the point of all the inscriptions?"

"Each fractal in the cavern is a distinct religious pronouncement about divine grace toward others—mercy, tolerance, kindness, love, compassion," she answered.

Lonsdale pondered, "Do you think it's a shrine to divine grace?"

"I doubt it," Hewst said. "There's no niche, no reliquary, no altar for offerings. I've seen no indication that the cavern was meant to receive devotees." She noted, "I think someone designed the cavern as a universal message."

"But who's sending this message?" asked Kalinin. "Is there anything among these inscriptions that tell us who made this cavern?"

"No," she answered. "But I think we can definitely rule out the New Jerusalem sect."

Alex was surprised that she so conclusively dismissed New Jerusalem as the architects of the cavern. "Why rule them out?" he asked. "It seems to me that strewing a cavern with religious quotes is the kind of thing a group of zealots might do."

She explained, "First of all, many of the inscriptions come from the Vedic scriptures, the Pali Canon, the Adi Granth, the Qur'an, the Hadith. There's no way that a Christian terrorist sect would endorse quotes from non-Christian traditions." Hewst continued, "And second, the New Jerusalem sect is more apt to quote passages about divine wrath, holy war, damnation, and the Antichrist, none of which are inscribed in these fractals."

"Can you give us an example of what you've translated?" inquired Alex.

With her c-nex, Hewst displayed a holographic image that focused on a particular fractal. "Here's an example. This fractal is dedicated to a statement from the Qur'an: 'Those who act kindly in this world will have kindness.' It's inscribed in Arabic, Pali, Sanskrit, Hebrew, and Greek, among other languages." Hewst displayed another fractal. "This one is dedicated to a statement from First Corinthians: 'Do not seek your own advantage, but that of others.'" She displayed yet another. "This one is dedicated to the statement: 'Even stone will erode with the ages, but divine love will endure forever.'"

Alex asked, "Where does that last statement come from?"

"I don't know," Hewst admitted. "It's not part of a religious tradition I'm familiar with." She looked around the table and added, "I have some ideas where it comes from, but I don't want to propose any imaginative hypotheses until I have a chance to do more research."

"Thank you for that report, Dr. Hewst," the captain said. "On that note, the briefing is adjourned until tomorrow morning."

As Hewst drank the last swallow of coffee from her cup, and as her colleagues were all rising from their seats, the stoic voice of Dr. Darry Ammon rumbled over the PA system in the mess module. "Excuse me, Captain," his voice interrupted.

"Aye, Doctor," Petrenko replied.

"It seems that Commander Hewst skipped the diagnostic scan when she returned to the station," the voice announced politely. "Would you see to it that she reports to sickbay immediately?"

Petrenko looked at Hewst with an admonishing grin, but neither of them said a word. Hewst set her empty cup on the table and immediately headed to sickbay.

Chapter 17 – A Game of Chess

Belshazzar Research Station, Hellas Province, Mars

(Areographic Co-ordinates: S 35.642, E 94.228)

Saturday, 15 December 2429 CE

Time: 2327 Zulu

Just outside the research station's northwest airlock set a single folding chair. In and of itself, this chair was an odd thing to behold on the cold, desolate surface of the red planet. It was a sturdy chair—sturdy enough to withstand the forces of wind and dust. Station Chief Claudio Fuentes had set it there at the request of Catherine Hewst.

Hewst had been working either in the cavern or in a lab module seemingly nonstop for over a week. She had been translating and analyzing thousands of religious pronouncements with too much caffeine and too little sleep. She needed a break—to clear her mental fatigue and to face the translations afresh. Yet, she could not sleep. Before her father's death, she would regularly relieve her daily stresses through her prayers to God, but now she was still too angry with God to pray. Hewst decided that her soul needed to watch the sun set, for she had not seen nightfall in weeks.

While most of her colleagues were asleep in their tiny, space-efficient compartments, Hewst donned her compression suit and stepped outside the research station. With a whisk broom in hand, she brushed away the dust from the chair and took a seat. She sat there for about an hour, watching the sun slowly sink toward the Hellas skyline. The pink Martian sky gradually faded to blue as the sun yielded its reign to the night. One by one, the stars took their positions among the familiar constellations. And as the sun gently dropped below the western horizon, the planets Venus and Earth (the so-called evening stars of Mars) became the brightest objects in the twilit sky.

Darkness began to draw its cloak across the plain of Hellas, so Hewst returned to the airlock and to the warmer, brighter confines of Belshazzar Station. She stowed her compression suit, donned her civvies, and headed for her sleeping compartment. As she passed by the rec module, she saw Chief Kiiswood sitting alone beside an inactive holo-table. When its projectors were engaged, this otherwise ordinary table could become a holographic game of billiards, ping-pong, or shuffleboard, among many other games. But Kiiswood was using the table as a simple armrest as he watched the Elysium News Channel on a bulkhead monitor.

"As of yesterday evening," said the news anchor on the monitor, "Terrestrial Assembly health officials have begun to quarantine all communities in northern Arizona and southern Utah. Claiming authority under the Emergency Management Powers Act, the Terran Health Organization is now banning all travel into these areas indefinitely. Anonymous sources within the THO have told ENC that the contagion in question is believed to be an act of biological terrorism by New Jerusalem. When pressed by reporters to elaborate on the reason for quarantine, Chione Nimr, director of the THO, offered no further comments."

Hewst had not stepped fully into the rec module; she watched the news report while standing in the hatchway. "The news hasn't been very cheerful recently, has it?" she commented.

"Ma'am?" asked Kiiswood as he turned off the monitor with his c-nex.

"First, Callisto," she explained, "then, HAS *Sagan*, New Guinea, Vitruvius Crater, some Martian provinces, and now your hometown in Arizona." Hewst would not press Kiiswood; she would allow him his emotional privacy. But she clearly intuited that the chief was not as misanthropic as he portrayed himself to be. And perhaps he was not as misanthropic as *he* believed himself to be. He lived as though there were nothing admirable or lovable about others, especially his family. But his attention to the news on the monitor—the news about his family's fate— suggested a suppressed affection for others that he was too angry to admit and too hurt to own.

Kiiswood politely changed the subject. "You're up late, ma'am," he commented. "Chief Fuentes told me you stepped outside for a breath of fresh air."

"Yeah," she smiled. "Of course, I had to take my fresh air with me."

After a moment's silence in their conversation, Kiiswood invited, "Since you're still up, would you like to play a game of chess?"

Hewst considered his invitation. "Okay," she answered. Hewst took a seat at the table across from Kiiswood. "I haven't played in years."

Kiiswood smirked. "It sounds like you're already rehearsing your excuses should you lose." He then turned on the holo-table and engaged the voice-interface chess program. An empty holographic chessboard appeared on the table.

"Welcome," said a friendly program voice. "To initiate your game, please select who controls white."

Kiiswood nodded to Hewst in a gesture to let her go first. But, in deference to the chief, she addressed the game program, saying, "Random select." Immediately, the holographic chess pieces appeared on the board, arranged in their starting positions. The program had randomly selected Kiiswood to control the white pieces.

"It looks like you get to go first, Chief," said Hewst.

"Very well," he acknowledged. "E-four." The game commenced; the holographic pawn in front of his king automatically advanced two squares. "So why are you up so late, Commander?" he asked. The game presently served as more than friendly competition; it became a social medium for their conversation. It allowed them to chat comfortably amid alternating moves.

"E-five," she replied. Her king's pawn also advanced two squares. "I could ask you the same question," said Hewst.

"Knight to F-three," responded Kiiswood. "I'm a stratogen, remember? I've been genetically engineered to operate on only a couple of hours' sleep per day."

"D-six." While watching the holographic pawn move to its space, Hewst confessed, "Chief, I'm frustrated at my lack of progress."

"D-four." Without taking his eyes from the chessboard, Kiiswood exhibited a confused look. "What lack of progress?" he asked. "You improved the translation programs, you discovered that each fractal is a single pronouncement in many languages, you gave Dr. Driggers a tool to help him do his job. That sounds like progress to me."

"Bishop to G-four." She expounded, "For more than a week now, I've been trying to match each pronouncement with its specific religious textual tradition. And with the help of every archival database I can access, I've been able match only twenty percent of them."

"D take E-five. There's more than four thousand pronouncements," he said. "You just haven't had time to match them all."

"Bishop take F-three. It's not a matter of time, Chief. The database programs should have identified all of them in a matter of minutes." She added, "It's as though eighty percent of these pronouncements were either previously unknown or long lost to human history."

Kiiswood responded, "Queen take F-three." He then inquired, "That manuscript found in the cavern—that Q document—wasn't that lost and unknown until five weeks ago?"

"Are you implying that someone is reminding us of something humanity has long forgotten?" she asked. "D take E-five."

"It makes sense to me," he answered. "Bishop to C-four. If humankind once knew how to be gracious to others, it forgot that lesson a long time ago."

"Of course, that still begs the next question: Where do these unidentified pronouncements come from? Knight to F-six." Hewst then pondered, "Perhaps those patterns of parallel lines in the fractals have something to do with the pronouncements."

"How so?" he asked. "Queen to B-three."

As the white queen was moving to its designated square, a voice from the rec module hatchway interrupted their game. "Catherine, are you still up?" Alex asked as he happened by the module.

Before Hewst could respond, Kiiswood satirically interjected, "No, I'm playing against a holographic opponent."

"You're droll, Chief," Alex commented.

Kiiswood upheld his satire. "No, seriously," he said, "if this was really the commander, she'd have a cup of coffee in her hand."

While Alex grinned, Hewst smirked. "Queen to E-seven," said Hewst. She then asked, "Why are you still awake, Alex?"

The meta-droid stepped from the hatchway into the rec module, took a seat, and joined his friends at the table. "I'm a machine," he answered. "I don't get tired. I do have a sleep-mode, but using it is optional."

Hewst suddenly noticed something slightly different about Alex's appearance. She pointed at the right side of the meta-droid's forehead and said, "Hey, Chief, look! Alex has a c-nex."

"Yes," Alex acknowledged. "It took him a while, but Dr. Negasi finally managed to format one specific to my neural net."

"So you're working late?" Kiiswood asked. "Knight to C-three."

"Not really," he answered. "Since the cavern is sterile, there's not much for an astrobiologist to do. So I've been running spectral and DNA analyses on this." Alex held out the commander's necklace and protectively returned it to her.

"Oh, my necklace," she cheered with delight to have it again. She wasted no time putting it on and fastidiously adjusting its pendant to hang straight and even. "Did you learn anything about it?" asked Hewst.

"Well, the necklace itself is unremarkable," he replied. "The chain is formed from eight separate interwoven strands. Its links are made from two metals that are common in most jewelry—some links are platinum, and some are titanium. It's well-made, and finely crafted, but nothing out of the ordinary."

"C-six," she said. "That's nice to know, but did you learn anything about the pendant?"

"Well, as I said before, it's not a mustard seed," he answered.

"Okay, then, what is it?" she asked.

"It's just a very large bundle of double-stranded DNA encased in an acrylic shell," Alex answered. "But this DNA isn't naturally occurring. This bundle is the product of artificial gene synthesis."

Hewst lifted the pendant closer to her squinting eyes, trying to peer through the transparent polymer at the tiny contents therein. "How do you know?" she asked.

"One of the DNA strands is made up of the four canonical nucleobases: adenine, cytosine, guanine, and thymine." Alex explained further, "But the other strand includes a fifth nucleobase: uracil."

"And that's unusual?" asked Kiiswood. "Bishop to G-five"

"Oh yes," the meta-droid answered. "Uracil rarely occurs in DNA, and it never occurs in only a single strand of a chain." Addressing Hewst, Alex said, "As an astrobiologist, your father would certainly know how to synthesize a DNA chain like this. But, Catherine, I'm sorry to say, it's not a mustard seed."

Hewst once again adjusted the pendant to hang even from her necklace. "Well, mustard seed or not, it's a gift from my father, and that's all I care about." Attending to the game, she said, "B-five."

Alex became fascinated with their chess game, so he decided to remain at the table and watch. "So why are you two still up at this hour," he inquired.

As Kiiswood was busy in thought over his next move, Hewst answered, "My mind is too preoccupied with identifying the religious pronouncements in the cavern. I was just telling the chief that I think the patterns of parallel lines might have something to do with it."

"It's interesting that you mention those patterns," Alex commented. "Dr. Ferris thinks he knows what they are." Then, in a slightly more dramatic tone, he announced, "He thinks they're galactic coordinates."

"Why?" asked Kiiswood. "Knight take B-five."

"The same eight binary numbers keep recurring in each fractal," replied Alex. "Playing a hunch that the numbers are time periods, he searched for matching periods. And he thinks he found a match." He continued, "The eight binary numbers correspond precisely to the rotation rates of eight known millisecond pulsars in our galaxy, and MSPs are perfect location markers. If the lengths of the parallel lines in the fractals are distance-ratios from these MSPs, then the five patterns correspond to the locations of five stellar systems."

"C take B-five," Hewst said. "That's an amazing hypothesis. How does he test it?"

"He already has," responded Alex. "He compared the five patterns to stellar cartographic maps. Two of the patterns point to areas of the galaxy that astronomers haven't been able to map yet. But the other three correspond to known star systems—systems that we know have planets. One is the Oluseyi system and another is the Thaller system.

"What's the third one?" asked Kiiswood. "Bishop take B-five, check."

Again, in a slightly dramatic tone, Alex answered, "That one corresponds to our solar system."

Hewst and Kiiswood looked over to Alex with silent stares. Finally, Hewst broke the silence. "Now, that's too coincidental to be ignored." She looked back at the chessboard, and to block the attack on her king, she said, "Knight to D-seven."

A short, low-toned buzzer sounded, followed by the friendly program voice, announcing, "Specify."

She took a closer look at the board and realized that the move she had called out was ambiguous. Alex's news had distracted her. Hewst failed to notice that both of her knights could be moved to that square. So she said, "I'm sorry. Knight at B-eight to D-seven."

"You don't need to apologize, Commander," Kiiswood observed. "It's just a machine." Suddenly, he appreciated how his own words might sound to his meta-droid friend. With sincere contrition, he said, "I'm sorry, Alex."

Hewst said nothing, but she noted to herself that Kiiswood had actually apologized. She had never heard the chief express remorse to anyone before now.

For his part, Alex took little, if any, offense at the chief's comment. The meta-droid was steadily realizing that he was not, in Kiiswood's words, just a machine. Indeed, he was much more than a machine—he was a machine that could forgive. Alex said nothing; he simply offered the chief a pardoning nod and an absolving wave. But, he did continue with more details about the galactic coordinates. "Dr. Ferris consulted me and Dr. Střelec to check his work and to verify his math. He plans to share his findings with Captain Petrenko at the briefing tomorrow morning."

Looking at the chronometer near the bulkhead monitor, Kiiswood saw that it was no longer Saturday evening. "You mean later this morning," he said. "Castle."

Once again, the game buzzer sounded, and the voice said, "Specify."

Amid the laughter from his two colleagues, Kiiswood restated, "Castle, queenside."

Hewst was enthralled by the details of Dr. Ferris' research. She was so enthralled that an intriguing idea occurred to her. With her c-nex, she accessed the bulkhead monitor and displayed for Alex one of the five line-patterns. "Would this happen to be the pattern for our solar system?" asked Hewst.

"Yes, it is," he answered. "How did you know that?"

"This pattern occurs in only twenty percent of the fractals," she replied. "They happen to be the same twenty percent whose pronouncements I can identify." For a moment, she pondered an audacious question in the privacy of her own mind. But she soon dared herself to say it out loud. "Can this set of lines be telling us that these particular pronouncements come from our solar system?" she asked. Hewst deemed her question to be merely academic; she expected no response from her two colleagues.

Kiiswood, however, felt inclined to share his thoughts. "So the reason you can't identify the other eighty percent is because they come from interstellar religions?"

Hewst grimaced. "It sounds rather absurd when you say it like that." She returned her attention to her next move. "Rook to D-eight."

"Rook take D-seven." Kiiswood suggested, "Perhaps you should share your thoughts with the OIC."

"It's just supposition," she responded. "Rook take D-seven." With a note of reservation, she added, "I'd rather have something more substantial before I propose an idea like that to Captain Petrenko."

Alex seemed apprehensive, but then he confided, "I'm not sure I trust the captain."

Hewst was baffled. "Why not?" she asked.

Alex explained, "A lot of the lab equipment that Aerospace Intelligence has allocated for my workstation has come from a research facility called Project Columba Noachi."

Hewst commented, "Latin; it means 'Noah's dove.'"

"How do you know where your lab equipment came from?" asked Kiiswood. "Rook to D-one."

"Some of it is still labeled with the project title," Alex answered. "I don't know anything about that FAIA project—I've never heard of it. Most of the equipment's databases have been deleted, but not quite all of them. I came across a data file on exoplanet habitability. The name of the subdirectory is Thaller System."

"Queen to E-six." Hewst thought for a moment, then asked, "Didn't you just tell us that one of those line-patterns corresponds to the Thaller star system?"

The meta-droid promptly answered, "According to Dr. Ferris, yes. Thaller is a G8V main sequence star thirteen hundred lightyears away in the constellation Columba. And, as it so happens, the original seventeenth-century name of the constellation was Columba Noachi." Alex proposed, "I think the captain knows more than she's telling us."

"Well, I know that's certainly true. Bishop take D-seven, check." Kiiswood uttered his remark in so casual a manner that it nearly went unnoticed.

Hewst, nonetheless, noticed. She asked, "What do you mean, Chief?"

"You know that array of lights in the cavern?" he replied.

"Yeah. Why?" she asked as she deliberated how to capture the piece attacking her king. "Knight take D-seven."

Kiiswood answered, "I noticed a specific infrared signature emanating from the array." The chief interrupted his own answer to make a move. "Queen to B-eight, check." He continued, "It's a signature specific to decay heat from plutonium 239."

Alex speculated, "Would you power a light array with plutonium?"

"No, the array uses a helium-3 microreactor," he answered. Pointing at Alex's chest, the chief added, "It's the same kind of reactor that powers your android body." He elaborated, "You use plutonium in a fission primary."

Seeing an opportunity to capture Kiiswood's queen, Hewst said, "Knight take B-eight." She then asked, "What's a fission primary?"

Alex knew exactly what it was. With some unease in his voice, the meta-droid responded, "It's the trigger for a thermonuclear device."

"Wait, what?!" she exclaimed. "Are you saying that we've been living and working around a hydrogen bomb?"

Kiiswood never looked up from the chessboard as he answered, "I'm assuming that it's there as a part of a contingency."

"Contingent upon what?" she asked.

"I don't know," he replied. "But I do know that the purpose of a weapon is to combat a threat. Obviously, Aerospace Intelligence is afraid of something."

Alex was inclined to think of potential biological threats. "Perhaps FAIA is afraid that a new Martian pathogen might get out," he proposed.

Hewst counter-proposed, "Perhaps they're afraid that a new truth might get out."

"Rook to D-eight, checkmate," Kiiswood announced. He had just won the game.

"Well done, Chief," Hewst congratulated. "You lost your most powerful piece, and you still won the game."

Kiiswood remarked, "To win, sometimes you have to sacrifice your queen."

Chapter 18 – Laboratory Module Charlie

Belshazzar Research Station, Hellas Province, Mars

(Areographic Co-ordinates: S 35.642, E 94.228)

Monday, 17 December 2429 CE

Time: 1545 Zulu

Each module of Belshazzar Station served a specific purpose: a mess hall, sickbay, an armory, waste management, a helium-3 reactor, water reclamation, laboratory modules, a traxle garage, *etcetera*. But as unique as each module was, they all had one thing in common: not a single one had a window.

Laboratory Module Charlie was no exception. Its drab, windowless bulkheads were completely lined with video and holographic monitors. Its workstations comprised three computer consoles: one allocated for mathematics and Dr. Střelec, one for linguistics and Dr. Driggers, and one for paleography and Dr. Hewst.

Střelec could study the binary symbols, Driggers could decipher the mysterious languages, and Hewst could compare religious pronouncements without ever suiting up or setting foot into the cavern. Indeed, none of the three had ventured below the Martian surface in recent days, though for different reasons. Dr. Driggers and Dr. Střelec were both unaccustomed to wearing compression suits. Střelec grew anxious at the very thought of putting one on, and Driggers had not donned his suit since he felt nauseous during his one and only time in the cavern. For her part, Dr. Hewst had not entered since Saturday—since learning that a thermonuclear device dangled over the heads of all who ventured therein.

Of course, not all of the team members could avoid the cavern. Dr. Ferris had to be on-site as he repeated, for a third time, a series of gravity experiments. And Dr. Lonsdale was still running density scans on the stelae. But even though most of the team members could easily continue their research off-site and worlds away from the cavern, Captain Petrenko did not want any of the team to leave until everyone's work was concluded. In addition, the captain restricted the team members' outgoing communication to ensure the secrecy of their research. Hewst and her colleagues were now feeling less like scientists and scholars and more like captives in the secluded, windowless station. And because they were, for all intents and purposes, stranded on a remote Martian plain, Hewst thought it best to keep the knowledge of a proximate fusion bomb to herself. Even if her colleagues were made aware of it, there seemed very little, if anything, that they could do about it.

From her workstation, Hewst pressed on through the mundane task of cataloging each fractal's pronouncement according to its corresponding stellar system, assuming that Dr. Ferris' galactic coordinate theory was correct. At the workstation to Hewst's left, Střelec was experimenting with other binary systems just in case Ferris' theory was incorrect. Sitting at the third workstation, Driggers leaned back in his chair and raised his hands in a gesture of accomplishment and satisfaction.

"Ah, success!" Driggers exclaimed. "I just identified the morphological structure and syntax for what I'm calling Language Beta."

"Congratulations!" replied Hewst. "So how many have you identified now?"

"Two," he answered.

"Congratulations!" echoed Střelec. "Only fifteen more languages to go."

Driggers then commented, "Of course, these are just rudimentary."

Střelec asked, "Do you understand these languages well enough to speak them?"

"No," laughed Driggers. "There's no way to know what phonemes, if any, are associated with these glyphs." He pulled up a particular symbol on his nearest monitor and directed his colleagues to look at it. "For example, consider this glyph from Language Beta. It's apparently a morpheme meaning 'stone.' As a glyph, it's made up of a specific arrangement of these calligraphic characters. But I have no way of knowing what these characters represent. I don't know whether these characters are phonemes in a spoken language, or hand signals in a sign language, or musical notes in a harmonic language, or colors in a chromatic language. This arrangement might even be a logogram whose characters have no referent at all. I just know that this specific arrangement means 'stone.'"

Hewst stared at the glyph for a moment, then asked, "Why do you have only rudimentary syntaxes for these languages?"

"More detailed syntaxes for Languages Alpha and Beta would require a much larger sampling than what we have in these fractals," he answered. "Here, let me show you." Driggers overlaid the glyph on the monitor with a small tittle-like stroke. "This little wavy line is apparently an adpositional mark in Language Beta. When this mark appears in the upper-right corner of the glyphs for 'stone' or 'water,' they become 'beside the stone' and 'beside the water.' But without a larger sampling, I can't determine whether this adposition applies to every noun."

"Why wouldn't it?" asked Střelec.

"Unlike logic or mathematics, all natural languages have exceptions to their syntactical rules," he said. "I need a larger sampling to see whether this adposition applies universally." After a thoughtful pause, Driggers continued, "Frankly, I'm surprised at the absence of very common vocabulary words, such as 'tree' or 'hand.'"

"It's interesting that you say that," Hewst responded. "I've not only noticed a pattern in the pronouncements that were included in the cavern, but also in what was *excluded*. For example, in the Gospel of Luke, there's an account of a parent's compassion for a hungry child—an account of graciously giving the child a fish rather than a snake, or an egg rather than a scorpion. It's an account whose subject is compassion for others, but it also references several animals—a fish, a snake, a scorpion. So I reviewed all of the pronouncements in the cavern, and I discovered that not a single one mentions animals."

"That is interesting," he concurred. "You're implying that the absence of common vocabulary words is not incidental—that a certain category of words were intentionally omitted."

"So it would seem," she acknowledged. "But it's not just references to animals that were excluded. I haven't been able to find any mention of plants, food items, or specific temporal references, such as weeks, months, or years."

Driggers was genuinely intrigued at Hewst's observations. "Do you have a theory about this?"

"Not yet," she answered, "just observations. It seems evident that a redactor was trying to avoid any Terran-specific references among these compassion statements."

Hewst assumed that she was being restrained in her answer, but Střelec noted a subtle reference to extraterrestrial involvement. "Take care, Catherine," the mathematician cautioned. "The walls have ears. I don't think Captain Petrenko wants us to be discussing anything that even hints at interstellar intelligence."

"What makes you say that?" asked Hewst.

Střelec looked around the lab module as if someone might be eavesdropping. "Three days ago, Lieutenant Commander Gallistow finally gave me permission to respond to all the d-board texts that I'd been receiving from my partner in Ostrava. She was growing anxious and upset because she hadn't heard from me since FAIA recruited me for this job."

With surreptitious curiosity, Driggers inquired, "So did you place a c-nex call?"

"No," Střelec answered, "there's currently a nineteen-minute delay between Earth and Mars. That's a thirty-eight-minute response time. So I sent a d-board text. I told her not to worry, that I hadn't been abducted by aliens. I was simply working around the clock. But, apparently, Lieutenant Commander Riddari wasn't amused with my joke; he censored that part of my text just before it was sent."

Hewst drolly replied, "Aerospace Intelligence is not allowed to commission officers with a sense of humor." Her effort at wit was met only with grins.

Someone abruptly entered the laboratory module and inadvertently interrupted their conversation. For an instant, the three of them feared that their comments were indeed being scrutinized by some government eavesdropper. But they were relieved when they realized that the newcomer was one of their fellow researchers, Dr. Marcus Lonsdale, archeologist. Oblivious to their conversation, Lonsdale interjected, "Hey John, do you have a moment to look at something?"

"Sure," Driggers responded. "What do you have?"

Lonsdale grabbed a spydre from Driggers' workstation. As he was slipping it on his hand, he said, "I've been running tomographic densitometry scans on several of the stelae in the cavern. I now know why they have a slightly lower density than the surrounding walls." With subtle moves of his wrist and fingers, he activated the module's main holographic projection system. A holographic image of one of the cavern's stele rotated at the center of the lab. Lonsdale continued, "Every stele I've scanned so far has little pockets or voids in the basalt. At first I thought they were random vesicles from ancient gas bubbles that formed in the cooling lava. But then I noticed that they weren't random at all—these vesicles had symmetry. So I spliced the tomographic sections together and produced 3D images like this one." With another twist of his wrist, Lonsdale rendered the holographic image transparent, revealing the proportioned cavities within the stele's basalt. "What do you make of this?"

The image of the vesicles left Driggers momentarily dumbfounded. When he finally found his words, he replied, "They look like orthographic characters for an inscribed language."

"That was my guess," Lonsdale responded, "but I'm not the language expert. That's why I wanted you to look at this."

Hewst was astounded at the holographic image; she, too, could see that the stele's vesicles had structure and symmetry. "Does the same pattern appear in other stelae?" she asked.

"Not in the ones I've scanned," answered Lonsdale. "So far, each stele contains a unique arrangement of these characters."

Hewst suggested, "Perhaps every stele contains yet another translation of the pronouncements."

"Perhaps," said Driggers. "But I've never seen an inscribed language in 3D before. Look, every written representation of a language is a linear inscription on a flat, two-dimensional surface, like stone, papyrus, parchment, or paper. But this appears to be three-dimensional characters carved in planar arrangements expanding through the volume of the stele."

"That's all well and good," Lonsdale commented. "But how the hell did someone carve these characters inside stone? Each stele is a solid piece of basalt. There's not a single entry point in the rock, not even microscopic."

"How someone did it is a good question," noted Hewst. "An even better question is *why* someone would do it. We can read the proverbial writing on the wall. But no one can read the writing inside a wall."

As Střelec listened in on their conversation, she was suddenly taken by an unconventional, geometric idea. "We can read the writing on paper or any other 2D surface only because we have a 3D perspective," Střelec proposed. "If we were two-dimensional beings confined within the same plane as the page, we wouldn't be able to see beyond the edge of the page to read what's written on it. By extension, because we're spatial beings confined within the same three-dimensional realm as the stelae, we can't see beyond the surface of the stelae to read what's written inside them. But perhaps we could read the writings inside them if we had a four-dimensional perspective."

Driggers glanced at Hewst and Lonsdale to see whether they understood what Střelec was talking about. He then remarked, "Tereza, I have no idea what you're saying. Are you saying that there's a way we can be outside the stelae and still see inside them?"

"Not us, *per se*," Střelec answered. "But, hypothetically, there might be beings who aren't restricted to our space. They may have the freedom to move in an extra direction that's not available to us. Let me show you." She, too, put on a spydre and pointed to a monitor near her workstation. "Let's represent the universe on the flat-screen of this monitor. These stelae inside the cavern are tetrahedral stones, right? A tetrahedron is a three-dimensional geometric figure. Its two-dimensional counterpart is a triangle." With the mere wiggling of her index finger at the monitor, she drew a triangle on the flat-screen. She then drew a question mark inside the triangle. "Imagine that there's a message written inside this triangle." Beside the triangle, Střelec drew a stick figure. "Now imagine that there's a two-dimensional stick-person looking at the triangle. Within this flat-screen universe, our stick-person can look all the way around the triangle—up and down, left and right. Despite best efforts, our stick-person can't see the message hidden inside the triangle's three-sided perimeter. But you and I aren't confined to this two-dimensional universe. Unlike our stick-person, we can see the message inside the triangle because we have the freedom of an extra spatial dimension."

"Honestly, Tereza; I just can't get my mind around the idea of extra space," Driggers confided. "As far as I can see, there are only three ways to move. There's up and down; there's left and right; and there's to and fro. What other direction is there?"

"In four-dimensional space, there's hyper and hypo," she answered. Střelec was sympathetic to her colleague's confusion. "Hyperspace may not be empirical, but it is a mathematical possibility."

Driggers shook his head in bewilderment and said, "Let's say you're correct and that there are these hyperbeings. Why would they write their message for us in a way that we three-dimensional human beings can't see it?"

"But they did," Hewst responded. "They did write their message in languages that we can see and understand. The walls are covered with these languages. Perhaps their hyperlanguage can't be written on a surface; perhaps it can only be written in a volume."

"As strange as it may seem," Lonsdale pondered, "the idea of hyperspace would explain a lot."

"Like what?" wondered Driggers.

With his own spydre, Lonsdale erased Střelec's question mark on the flat-screen and replaced it with an exclamation mark. "If hyperbeings can stand outside our space and write inside stone stelae," he explained, "then they should also be able to carve out a subsurface cavern without a three-dimensional entry point."

Hewst had a similar thought. "Perhaps they could even be able to bring someone into the cavern through hyperspace." She was, of course, thinking about the late Silas Dorch's mysterious presence within the cavern.

"Well, it's a fantastic hypothesis," Driggers acknowledged. "How do you prove it?"

Before anyone could respond to Driggers' question, the station's klaxon alarm abruptly sounded. All of the action-station indicators lit up throughout the modules, hubs, and gangways. The heavily armed members of Sorteer Unit Four scuttled through the gangways, scrambling to assume their assigned posts at the critical junctions within the research station. "Attention, all station personnel! General quarters!" announced the voice over the station's intercom. "All station personnel, general quarters! All research staff, shelter in place!"

Hewst's c-nex began to signal an incoming call from Lieutenant Commander Gallistow. "This is Hewst," she answered.

"Commander Hewst," said the voice of Gallistow, "OIC has ordered that you break shelter and report immediately to the control room."

"I'm on my way," she acknowledged as she closed the call.

Hewst was apprehensive. The last time she had been startled by a station's alarm, a Venusian passenger transport was attempting to land at HAS *Landis*, just before it was blown out of the sky. She hesitantly left the laboratory module and began to wind her way through the interconnecting gangways, all the while wondering whether Belshazzar Station was under attack. Twice along her way, teams of sorteers, posted near crucial gangway hatches, waved her through.

Upon reaching the control room, Hewst found Lieutenant Jalloh standing guard at the hatch. He opened the hatch for her and granted her access into the crowded room. Her entry was barely noticed, as all eyes were fixed on the bank of monitors just over the main console. There, Petrenko, Riddari, Gallistow, Vraiss, and Fuentes were all intently focused on images from within the cavern. On one monitor was a video display of a small beige object resting on the cavern's blackish-gray wall. Other monitors were focused on the same object, but in various electromagnetic spectral ranges: microwave, infrared, ultraviolet, and soft x-ray.

Captain Petrenko looked away from the monitors long enough to glance at Hewst and to gesture for her to take a look for herself. The captain moved over just enough to make a space for Hewst to step up to the monitors. "Well, Doctor," Petrenko asked, "what do you make of that?"

216

"What is it?" asked a mystified Hewst.

"You tell us," the captain replied. "About half an hour ago, Dr. Ferris and his astrophysics team had concluded their latest round of gravity experiments in the cavern. We had just shut off the cavern lights when our provisional seismographs registered a 2.1 magnitude quake. So we turned on the lights to check the cavern, and that's when we discovered that." Petrenko pointed to the mysterious object on the monitor and then commented, "Suffice it to say, it wasn't there before the lights were shut off."

Hewst was puzzled. "Why call me?"

"We ran a spectrochemical analysis and determined that it's a form of plant tissue. And when we zoom in . . . " Petrenko paused as she adjusted the controls on the console to enlarge the image on the monitor.

Hewst could now see clearly that the beige object bore some kind of writing. Her widened eyes revealed her amazement. "It looks like some form of Vedic Sanskrit," she observed.

"We've already tried running it through a translation program," stated Vraiss, "but it couldn't identify the language."

Hewst suddenly had a hunch. "That's because it might be written backwards," she proposed, "just like the papyrus manuscript you discovered a few weeks ago." Without seeking permission first, she took to the console's keyboard and began to filter an inverted holostatic scan of the writing through her modified translation software. Within seconds, Hewst not only determined the ancient language, but also produced a very rough translation. "The language is Prakrit, and its text says something about the karmic effects of mercy and kindness." She dared to offer a scholarly guess. "This might be an ancient birch bark scroll—a Gandhāran Buddhist manuscript." She added, "If that really is a first-century bark scroll, I need to retrieve it immediately for preservation and study."

Petrenko declared, "Until we can verify the whereabouts of every single person in this station for the past half hour, no one is going anywhere."

After surveying another control room monitor, Techswain Vraiss reported, "The rail-carriage is parked in the carriage bay, ma'am."

"Confirmed, ma'am," added Chief Fuentes, who was studying computer log records. "The carriage hasn't left the bay since it returned with the astrophysics team."

"Acknowledged," Petrenko replied.

Having just received a c-nex report, Lieutenant Commander Riddari related, "Sorteer squadron leaders report that all station exit points are secured, and there's no station egress recorded in the airlock security logs. They've begun a systematic station-wide search for any intruders."

Gallistow gestured for Petrenko to examine a monitor that displayed a schematic of the research station. "Captain," he said, "according to c-nex transponders, these are the current locations of all station personnel, and these were their movements after Dr. Ferris and his team returned from the cavern. As you can see, no one has gone subsurface since then."

While looking at the schematic, Petrenko asked, "Lieutenant Commander Gallistow, where's the android right now?"

Gallistow pointed to a particular spot on the schematic. "He's currently sheltering in the cybernetics hub with Dr. Cobisson and Dr. Negasi."

"Have him break shelter and report to the carriage bay immediately," the captain ordered.

"Aye aye, ma'am," acknowledged Gallistow.

Petrenko turned to Hewst and apprised her. "I'm sending the android into the cavern to retrieve that tree bark for you."

Hewst respectfully asked, "Ma'am, I request permission to retrieve the scroll."

"Request denied," the captain replied. "We don't yet know what we're dealing with. We don't know how that thing got into the cavern, nor do we know who or what is responsible for putting it there. I don't want to send anyone into that cavern until I know it's safe to do so."

"With all due respect, ma'am," Hewst responded, "Alex isn't trained to handle ancient manuscripts. Let me go with him to make sure we retrieve it correctly." She then said, "I'm willing to take the risk if it means preserving an ancient manuscript."

Petrenko deliberated for some time. "Very well," she finally declared. "But you get in there, you take the most direct route to the manuscript, you retrieve it, and you get out. Do not take any unnecessary risks."

"Aye aye, ma'am. I'll exercise the greatest of caution." Hewst then commented, "But, in my humble opinion, retrieving that manuscript is less of a threat than the thermonuclear device hidden in the light array."

Petrenko seemed unsurprised that Hewst knew about the hidden device. She impassively responded, "Your opinion is noted, Doctor. But that thermonuclear device is there precisely because, in my opinion, that manuscript and the entire cavern around it might be a far greater threat than any of us yet realize." She then directed Hewst to go and suit up.

After Hewst left the control room, Gallistow asked Petrenko, "Shall I have Chief Kiiswood accompany them, ma'am?"

"In for a penny, in for a pound," she remarked.

"Aye, ma'am," he replied.

Petrenko shook her head. "Have the chief suit up and report to the carriage bay."

Chapter 19 – Transfiguration

The Subsurface Cavern, Hellas Province, Mars

(Areographic Co-ordinates: S 35.641, E 94.213)

Monday, 17 December 2429 CE

Time: 1651 Zulu

With well-practiced hands, Catherine Hewst adeptly pulled herself along the handrails through the breach and into the Martian cavern. Even though she had spent more time in the cavern than any other member of the research team, she had not ventured there in over forty-eight hours. Its awesome inspiration seemed strangely less inspiring for her since she had learned that the cavern (and all therein) could be obliterated at the press of a button. But the chance of securing an ancient religious manuscript overrode any of her apprehensions. So with her paleographic tools packed into her equipment satchel, she bravely climbed into the cavern.

Chief Níyol Kíiswood had already entered the cavern moments earlier and was standing on the wall beside the breach. There, he assumed a tactical stance with his rifle at the ready. He was armed with a fully outfitted RD84-A3 rail-rifle and a leg-holstered RD29 sidearm. The chief tactically linked his c-nex to his rifle's scope, such that his visual cortex was augmented with virtual crosshairs whose movements matched every sweep of his weapon's line of sight.

Alex, the meta-droid astrobiologist, stood on the catwalk, awaiting his turn to enter. Of the three, he was the only one not wearing a helmet, an EV packet, or a headset. He *was* wearing his new c-nex, which enabled him to maintain communication with the control room and with his retrieval team colleagues. In hand, he held a large retrieval case specifically designed to store, transport, and temporarily preserve ancient manuscripts. Once Hewst had cleared the breach, Alex passed the case to her, then pulled himself into the cavern.

Station Chief Claudio Fuentes and Petty Officer Ishanvi Sudha had chauffeured the *ad hoc* retrieval team of three through the access tunnel and delivered them to the breach. Fuentes remained in the rail-carriage awaiting the team's return, while Sudha assumed a sentry position just outside the cavern. Like Kiiswood, she was armed with a rail-rifle and a holstered rail-pistol.

As the retrieval team made its way through the cavern, Captain Anna Petrenko and her command staff monitored their progress from the station's control room. Lieutenant Commander Nolan Gallistow's video monitors were tuned into Hewst's and Kiiswood's helmet cams, so he was able to examine the cavern from their points of view. Techswain Wendell Vraiss monitored the entire team's c-nex and headset communications and maintained an open channel between the team and the control room. Lieutenant Commander Stefán Riddari was surveying the entire cavern through the many cameras and sensors embedded in the lighting array. All of these video and audio transmissions were being monitored and recorded simultaneously in the station's cybernetics hub, where Dr. Earnan Cobisson and Dr. Desta Negasi were observing the progress of their meta-droid.

The retrieval team skillfully traversed the shifting fields of gravity as they transitioned onto an adjacent wall, where the scroll lay. Despite the array's bright lights, the scroll itself was not visible to them. It lay beyond their line of sight, concealed by hundreds of protruding stelae. Hewst and Kiiswood led the way, navigating through the maze of stelae with the aid of their visors' HUDs, which showed them the location of their target. Alex followed close behind with the retrieval case in hand.

Kiiswood's genetically enhanced senses were keenly alert as he rapidly scanned every direction for potential risks to the retrieval team. "Belshazzar Control," he called out over his headset. "HUD indicates we're 28 meters from objective." He spoke calmly, even though he knew that the team was in a poorly defensible position. There were far too many obstacles in this tetrahedral cavern that could conceal a possible threat. Still, the chief could not detect the presence of a hostile agent, so he saw no reason not to press on toward their objective.

Over the open channel, the retrieval team heard the control room's reply. "Confirmed," said the voice of Petty Officer Vraiss. "Cavern sensors indicate that your way is clear. Proceed with caution."

Step by step, the three team members advanced with care, weaving their way around enough stelae until the scroll finally came into view. As they were now only a couple of meters from it, Hewst could see that it was indeed a birch bark scroll—a type of scroll that was indicative of other known first-century Buddhist texts. Its location in the cavern could not be a mere coincidence, she thought. The birch bark scroll lay in the same place where the inverted papyrus manuscript and the late Silas Dorch were both found nearly six weeks ago. The scroll just happened to lie within a fractal that she recognized. She stooped down toward the floor and gently glided her fingers along the contoured letters in the fractal. As she traced the words with her fingers, she uttered quite softly, "There is no love without compassion, there is no compassion without sacrifice."

Even though Hewst spoke so softly that none should have heard her, Kiiswood, with his enhanced senses, barely perceived her voice. He stood fast near the scroll, maintaining his armed vigilance while trying to listen attentively to what she was saying. "I'm sorry, ma'am," he said. "I didn't catch your last transmission."

Hewst approached the scroll and knelt down beside it, taking great care not to touch it. She pointed to the words inscribed on the floor and said, "That's how the languages within this particular fractal translate. It was the last thing Mr. Dorch said to me: 'There is no love without compassion, there is no compassion without sacrifice.'"

Hewst gestured for Alex to kneel with her near the scroll and to avoid making any physical contact with it. As he knelt, he placed the retrieval case on the floor beside the scroll. He meticulously opened the case and removed two sets of cushioned collection tongs from it. "Okay," Alex asked with tongs in hand, "what do we do now?"

Hewst did not immediately answer Alex. Instead, she began to examine the manuscript visually, scrutinizing it as closely as her helmet would allow without actually touching it. The manuscript was an apparent three-paneled birch bark scroll. Each panel was about 35 centimeters long and 15 centimeters wide. Several very thin threads were skillfully sewn through the edge of each panel to hold the scroll together. Finally, after a cursory inspection of the scroll, Hewst answered, "We need to determine its intactness, and we need to ascertain whether it's lying free or affixed to the floor."

Reaching into her satchel, Hewst produced a small wand-shaped tool—a handheld multi-spectral scanner. She very slowly waved it over the birch bark several times as Alex looked on. The data from the spectral scan was immediately transmitted to a monitor in the control room and to her own visual cortex through her c-nex. "Are you receiving the data feed?" she asked the control room.

"Aye, ma'am," replied Vraiss. "Receiving and recording."

"The scroll is completely unfurled," assessed Hewst. "There are no panels tucked underneath. So we're dealing with only three panels—like a triptych. Their edges have been woven together by strands of thread and secured with what looks like some kind of glue." She paused for a moment to study the spectral image in her visual cortex. "The letters appear to have been etched into the bark by a stylus, and the grooves have been filled in with charcoal or some kind of carbon-based ink, probably to make the etchings easier to read. The writing appears to continue over onto the back side of the panels."

Kiiswood stood over his colleagues, maintaining a defensive posture. He hardly glanced at them; instead, he remained tactically focused on the subsurface surroundings. And although he could not perceive a clear and present danger, he still wanted Hewst and Alex to expedite their retrieval. "So can it be moved back to the lab?" asked Kiiswood.

Hewst turned off her scanning wand and put it away. "I believe so," she answered as she removed her own set of tongs from the satchel.

Alex asked, "Should we fold up the scroll?"

She thought for a moment, then responded with improvised instructions. "I don't know how worn its thread-joints are. So I think we should err on the side of caution. Let's try moving the scroll as it is." The two of them coordinated their efforts and methodically lifted the scroll with their tongs. They then placed it gently within the padded retrieval case and sealed it hermetically.

Alex picked up the retrieval case as he and Hewst stood up to begin their trek back to the rail-carriage. "Belshazzar Control, we have the scroll," he announced. "We're heading back now."

"Acknowledged," replied the voice of Vraiss. "Cavern sensors indicate that your way remains clear. Proceed with caution."

From his monitor in the control room, Riddari noticed that the images on his screen seemed to dim slightly. "Chief Kiiswood," hailed Riddari.

"Aye, sir," Kiiswood replied as he looked up. Before the lieutenant commander could ask, the chief answered, "There's been a decrease in cavern lighting. In fact, the corners of the array have vanished."

Hewst also looked up at the array. "No!" she exclaimed as the light in the cavern continued to fade. "It's *still* vanishing! The whole thing is vanishing along its edges!"

"Confirmed!" shouted Petty Officer Sudha as she witnessed the spectacle from her post just outside the breach. "It's waning away. I don't know how else to describe it."

In the growing darkness, the retrieval team stood as still as the stelae that surrounded them. They watched in astonishment as the array above them began to disappear from the outside inward. Within seconds, all of the lights on the array were gone, as were the cameras and sensors that lined its outer hull. The shrinking array was now only visible as a silhouette—a dwindling sphere of circuits, wires, and reactor parts, backlit by the modest light that spilled into the cavern from the access tunnel. The array then vanished completely, as though it had been peeled out of its space.

Kiiswood immediately turned on his helmet torch to cast its beam of light into the darkness. He kept his rail-rifle trained on the space once occupied by the array, ready to target any hostile agent that might present itself. But none did.

Following the chief's example, Hewst, too, turned on her helmet torch. Its light was synchronized with the movement of her head, illuminating wherever she turned her gaze. She quickly looked to her two teammates, checking to see that they were both sound and unharmed. She glanced at Kiiswood and found him looking steely-eyed, yet composed. Alex, on the other hand, looked frightened.

224

"Sit-rep, Chief," said Vraiss. "We still have the video feeds from your helmet cams—yours and Dr. Hewst's—but we just lost all of our array telemetry up here."

"Control," Kiiswood responded, "that's because the array is gone. No debris, no residuals, no trace. I can't explain it. It's just gone." The chief probed his surroundings with every one of his heightened senses—sight, hearing, even tactile senses. "We're okay. The commander and I are alert and on our mettle; Alex looks terrified, but he's still in possession of the retrieval case. No evidence of imminent danger. But I recommend that we proceed as though facing hostile intent."

"Confirmed, Chief," acknowledged Vraiss. "You and your team are ordered to egress the cavern immediately."

"Aye aye, control," acknowledged Kiiswood. Turning to his two colleagues, he said "Okay, I'm on point. The two of you—keep tight and stay on my six."

Alex's look of terror ebbed into confusion. "Catherine," he asked, "what the hell did the chief just say?"

Hewst grabbed the meta-droid by the arm and adjured him to quicken his pace as they tailed the chief. "He said that he's taking the lead," she answered, "and that we're to stay together and follow him."

The command staff had quickly reset most of the monitors in the control room to display a split-screen video feed from both Hewst's and Kiiswood's helmet cams. Everyone in the room stared quietly at the monitors as they pensively watched the progress of the retrieval team from the two perspectives. From Kiiswood's video feed, the command staff watched the chief's steady advance through the cavern's vast darkness; his poised rail-rifle was conspicuously visible in the lower foreground. Hewst's perspective revealed a similar trek through the darkness, but with Kiiswood leading in the foreground.

As the command staff watched their monitors, Gallistow noticed something odd in Hewst's video feed. Without quite touching the screen, he pointed to a strange spot on the monitor. "What is that?" he asked Vraiss. "Is there something on her lens?"

Vraiss was baffled; he gave no answer. "Dr. Hewst," he called on the open channel, "please check your helmet cam. We think there's something obstructing your POV."

Hewst glanced toward the lens-mount of her helmet and instantly saw the obstruction. It was her pendant and a portion of her necklace protruding from her collar module. Hewst stopped in place and, for an instant, felt a sense of panic. The only way that her necklace could be dangling outside her collar module was if her compression suit was ripped. "Control," she said with a feigned calm, "I think I have a breach in my suit. My necklace is exposed." She dared not reach up and touch her pendant for fear that she might exacerbate the breach.

The declaration of a suit-breach was a serious matter, requiring immediate attention. Kiiswood and Alex promptly turned to render assistance to their colleague. Indeed, they saw the exposed pendant, but they soon realized that it was not dangling; rather, it was hovering, as if defying gravity. The chain to which the pendant was attached led back into Hewst's compression suit; and yet, there was no evidence of a breach. Mysteriously, the necklace jutted through her collar module without any evidence of ruptures or tears in the material.

Kiiswood examined her collar module with his infrared vision, looking for a temperature differential, which would have been a clear indication of a breach, but found none. "Control!" the chief exclaimed, "I can see part of the necklace exposed, but there doesn't seem to be any compromise in the suit's integrity!" In a more moderate tone, he asked, "Commander, how do you feel?"

Hewst squinted at the brightness of Kiiswood's helmet torch shining in her face. "Shocked and bewildered," she answered, "but, otherwise, I feel fine."

Vraiss pulled up Hewst's biotelemetry on one of the control room monitors and quickly reviewed the data. "All of your vital signs are within normal parameters, Doctor," he reported. "We advise that the three of you egress the cavern ASAP. We'll continue to monitor your telemetry from up here."

"Aye aye, control," the chief acknowledged. "Commander, we need to keep moving," he said to Hewst. "Are you good to go?"

"Absolutely, Chief," Hewst declared bravely. "Lead on."

Suddenly, before the retrieval team could take even one step, the cavern erupted into brilliant radiance. Like a silent explosion, a resplendent sphere of pure light burst into the space overhead—the space previously occupied by the missing array. This resplendent sphere shone with such an extraordinary brightness that nothing within the cavern could cast a shadow. Its light was overwhelming, yet its brightness was neither blinding nor painful to behold.

All of the video monitors in the control room suddenly went black, but the audio and telemetry feeds were still incoming. Indeed, Petty Officer Vraiss could confirm that he still had an open channel with the retrieval team because he could overhear their exclamations.

"Oh my God!" shouted Hewst.

The chief yelled simultaneously, "What the hell!?"

Hewst, Kiiswood, and Alex stared into the light, as if paralyzed in place. Of course, they were quite free to move, if they so desired, but they had no desire to move at all. Indeed, they felt an enveloping sense of serenity just to stand where they were, gazing into the brilliance.

As mysterious and overpowering as it was, none of them could see any impending danger in the bright mesmeric light—not even Kiiswood. Beyond all sense and reason, the chief was possessed by an unassailable conviction that the light overhead harbored absolutely no malevolent intent. So, even though he kept a hand on his rifle's rear grip, he engaged his weapon's safety catch and disengaged his c-nex targeting feature.

Without warning, the three of them were gently lifted off the floor and started floating toward the sphere of light. Alex's confusion and fear quickly gave way to calm and assurance. His hand relaxed, and the retrieval case began to drift effortlessly beside them. And even though he could not understand what was happening to them, he felt at peace, as though everything was well in the universe.

The necklace that had been protruding from Hewst's collar module now floated free from her compression suit and was drifting upward toward the light. The necklace was still clasped; its unbroken chain had passed through Hewst's neck without a sever and through her suit without a tear. She reached out to grab her necklace, but as she was about to touch it, her hand waned and vanished. She immediately withdrew her arm, and, just as quickly, her hand waxed and reappeared. Oddly, at no time did she feel pain or fear.

Angst and uncertainty seized everyone in the control room; they were receiving precious little information about what was transpiring in the cavern. They were receiving and recording audio and biotelemetry, but they had no indication that the retrieval team was receiving control room transmissions. "Sit-rep!" shouted Vraiss over the open channel. "Someone tell us what's going on!"

Petty Officer Sudha remained just outside the breach with her rail-rifle sharply aimed at the brilliant light. "I'm in the access tunnel," she responded. "I have eyes on the retrieval team. They're being drawn into a large glowing orb that just appeared in midair. Recommend we regard orb as hostile. Request permission to fire."

When Vraiss turned to Captain Petrenko for direction, she promptly stepped up to Vraiss' console and spoke in his stead. "Petty Officer, this is Belshazzar Actual," she announced. "You are ordered to stand fast and hold fire. I repeat, stand fast and hold your fire."

Sudha watched as the three members of the retrieval team were now wholly engulfed within the sphere. With evident frustration in her voice, she acknowledged, "Aye aye, ma'am!"

Hewst, Kiiswood, and Alex were not only engulfed by the light; they were also melded with it. They were suddenly able to see the tetrahedral cavern in a way that they had never seen it before. Their senses were set free from the confines of space and time. They could see the entire cavern—top and bottom, front and back, yesterday and tomorrow—in a single glance. They saw it in a new, previously imperceptible dimension. It was now so utterly obvious to them that the tetrahedral cavern was a mere fragment of a much larger whole, only one of many spaces. A cavern within caverns, a tetrahedron inside tetrahedra, a space upon spaces, spaces wrapped in hyperspace.

Previously unseen spaces were now clearly visible—caverns that accessed other areas of Hellas Planitia, even caverns that housed hundreds of ancient scrolls.

When they would look at each other, they saw themselves anew. Their bodies—android and human—extended in ways that they had never before imagined. Their torsos and limbs flexed and flowed in remarkable and surrealistic directions. Their front and back, left and right, inside and out were all beheld in a single view. Even Hewst's free-floating necklace seemed to drift and spin unbounded by three-dimensional space.

Somehow, the three of them intrinsically knew that the enveloping sphere was something more than light; they found themselves immersed within a presence—a consciousness—a soul. And this presence—unseen, unheard, and incorporeal—was thoroughly immersed within them. In that moment, they were one with each other, and one with the presence. In that moment, they were distinguishable, but inseparable.

"I can hear them!" exclaimed Alex. "I can hear them speaking to us!"

Hewst and Kiiswood both sensed a benevolent consciousness among them, but they heard nothing. Of course, Alex might be different, Hewst thought. Perhaps his artificial cortex melded with this presence in a way that hers could not. "I can't hear them," she admitted.

"I can hear both of you," Kiiswood acknowledged of his two friends, "but I can't hear them either." He asked Alex, "What do they sound like?"

"They're not speaking with voices," Alex answered. "I hear their thoughts; I can hear them thinking. Or maybe I should say that I can hear their *thought*. They're thinking as one."

Kiiswood inquired further, "So what are they thinking?"

With a look of delight on his face, Alex answered: "Gladness, contentment, eagerness to see us. They've been expecting us. All three of us."

Hewst's curiosity was keenly provoked by Alex's answer. She wondered how the three of them could be *expected*. "Alex," she directed, "ask them who they are."

"They know what we're thinking, Catherine," the meta-droid said. He presently embraced his role as a medium as he answered for the presence, "They say that they're the Aeon."

Perplexed by their answer, she replied, "I don't understand."

Alex now responded to his two friends as though he were the presence himself. "We are the eldest children of the One."

"Who is the One?" she asked.

"The One is the essence of being and compassion," said the Aeon via Alex; "the omneity of consciousness."

Hewst continued to parse their answer. "And who are the children?"

"The children are all who realize themselves in the One, all who realize the One in others." The Aeon continued, "The children of the One are many sentients, and they abide on the worlds of many stars."

"Is that why you created this cavern," asked Hewst, "to show us the worlds of these many children?"

"For many reasons we created this cavern. We created it to preserve humankind's ancient writings—writings preserved for the children of the One, writings that remind your kind of its childhood. We created it to show your kind the worlds of other children. We created it to welcome humankind to communion with other children of the One."

"*Other* children? Are *we* also children of the One?"

"You have been children from the moment that your kind became aware of the One and of the One in others. We have been with you from the beginning of your childhood. And we have been with you through your duality." Alex continued to give voice to their thoughts. All the while, he puzzled over the words that he uttered; he was uncertain what the Aeon meant. "You are children of the One, but you also ignore your childhood. You acknowledge the One, but you also dare to be the One for yourselves, and so you ignore the childhood of other children." Alex paused for a moment; his words suddenly turned unpleasant to speak and unsettling to hear. "And now humankind has chosen to extinguish itself through its own duality. This is why we are here, because your extinction is imminent."

Hewst felt troubled at what she heard. She hastily formed a question and asked, "Are you here to destroy humankind?"

"No," came their answer. "We too are children of the One."

"Are you here to save humankind?"

"No. We cannot save humankind from itself. We cannot alter your choices. Your kind threatens itself and all other children of the One."

Kiiswood bluntly interjected, "Are you telling us that our self-destruction is inevitable?"

Hewst assumed an affirmative answer to the chief's question. "How?" she asked. "How are we destroying ourselves?"

The Aeon again offered a cryptic reply through the meta-droid. "From its beginning, your kind has disaffected itself from the essence of being and compassion. Humankind denounces the One, it denounces the children, and it denounces itself."

Much of the optimism in Hewst's voice was fading. "And that's why you're here, just to announce that the end is near?"

"Not just," the Aeon said. "We are here to help humankind."

"To help? How? How can you help?" she inquired with a semblance of hope. "You say that our extinction is imminent, that you cannot alter our choices."

"We cannot alter your choices," the Aeon acknowledged, "but we can give you a choice."

Kiiswood asked warily, "What choice?"

A brief moment passed, as though Alex was waiting for the Aeon to answer. "By the decisions that the three of you will make, humankind will either soon end or it will extend itself in communion with other children of the One."

"The three of us," said Hewst as she looked at Kiiswood and Alex. For a brief moment, she was silent, as though she was awaiting a more specific answer. "Why us?"

"You are the confluence of humankind," they answered, "the cleric who denounces the One, the soldier who denounces the children, the automaton who denounces the self. And you are the confluence of space and time."

Kiiswood ventured, "So you're here to help the three of us make the right choices."

"Choices are not about righteousness," the Aeon responded. "Choices are about sacrifice."

Hewst was genuinely mystified as to why this unseen presence would afford them such favor. In sincere humility, she asked, "Why are you helping us?"

"We are helping because compassion for the other is the way of the One," they answered. "We are helping humankind by giving the three of you what you need to make your choices. We are returning you upon your space and time."

Was her free-floating necklace of some significance to them? Hewst wondered. But before she could even form her question, the brilliant light that had engulfed the retrieval team abruptly imploded, hurling the cavern into darkness. The sphere of light vanished, and Hewst, Kiiswood, and Alex had vanished with it.

In the control room, the audio feeds went silent and the incoming data simply ceased. Looking at blank video screens and bare data monitors, the command staff was desperate for information. Over the open channel, Vraiss hailed, "We've lost all telemetry up here, Sudha. We need a sit-rep. What's going on down there?"

Sudha stood spellbound just outside the breach, staring into the deep blackness. She scanned the cavern with her enhanced senses, looking for the infrared silhouettes of the retrieval team but found no sign of her colleagues whatsoever. "Control," she reported, "that huge ball of light is gone! It just disappeared into thin air, and so has the retrieval team." Sudha then said, "Recommend we deploy a search party."

Before Vraiss or Petrenko could respond, the entire research station and access tunnel began to quake. The Martian atmosphere that filled the voluminous cavern rapidly evacuated. The sheer force of rushing wind through the breach blew Sudha off her feet and launched her back several meters into the access tunnel. The gale quickly subsided and Sudha leapt to her feet. She found Fuentes lying a couple of meters from her; the jet-effect winds had thrown him clear of the rail-carriage. Once she confirmed that the station chief was not seriously injured, she hurried back down the tunnel toward the cavern. But when she reached the catwalk, she discovered that the access tunnel dead-ended. There, at the breach into the cavern (or, what was once a breach), Sudha met a solid wall of basaltic rock. The wall was covered with the raised, inverted letters of ancient writings. They were the mirror image of the carved inscriptions that covered the slab of rock—the slab that once sealed the entrance into the cavern. Like the retrieval team and the sphere of light, the cavern and the breach were now gone. All that remained there at the catwalk were mangled handrails and Vraiss' tennis ball.

Chapter 20 – Martial Law

Mess Module, Belshazzar Research Station, Hellas Province, Mars

(Areographic Co-ordinates: S 35.642, E 94.228)

Tuesday, 18 December 2429 CE

Time: 0900 Zulu

Despite the dramatic events that transpired yesterday, Captain Petrenko decided not to cancel the 0900 daily briefing. The mood on every face in the mess module was sullen; everyone—from the research team to the support staff, from the station crew to the medical team—exhibited a muddle of anger, anxiety, and fear. By now, everyone in the station had heard the recording of the retrieval team's audio transmissions. Everyone was afraid; they surely wanted answers, but even more so, most of them wanted to leave this undeniably dangerous place.

Into the midst of this sullenness paraded Captain Petrenko, along with Riddari, Gallistow, and Vraiss, who made up most of her command staff. Filing in closely behind them were eight members of Sorteer Unit Four, who assumed posts around the module's perimeter and at every hatch. Perhaps the soldierly bearing of these sorteers was meant to instill a sense of security. But their presence did little to alleviate everyone's anxieties; indeed, it only exacerbated them.

With Petrenko and Riddari standing beside him, Gallistow stepped to the lectern and began the briefing. "Before Lieutenant Commander Riddari speaks," he stated, "let me preface his report by saying that the command staff expresses its profound condolences at the loss of two of our team members. We are also well aware of your fears and apprehensions about continuing your research. Most of you have expressed a desire to abandon the station and to get as far away from this site as possible. We believe that everyone's imaginations are getting the better of them and that abandoning the station would be an overreaction to an understandably doleful situation. So we want to present a report of our findings to allay your fears."

234

Riddari then stepped up as Gallistow yielded the lectern. With a written report in his hands, Riddari began to read, "At about 1600 hours yesterday, we detected a minor Marsquake of a 2.1 Richter magnitude. Moments later, a foreign object inexplicably appeared inside the cavern—an object that we provisionally identified as some kind of ancient scroll. Not knowing how it got there, we sounded general quarters, and ordered a Level One search for intruders within the station and around the compound. After assessing the risk, based on available information, we decided to deploy an *ad hoc* retrieval team, comprising Commander Catherine Hewst, SOC Níyol Kiiswood, and the meta-droid ALX-63. They entered the cavern at about 1650 hours and retrieved the scroll. While making their way back to the rail-carriage, we lost the lighting array, its sensors, and eventually all video feeds from their helmet cams. We also lost our ability to communicate with the team. However, we continued to receive their audio transmissions. Based on the incoherent nature of their intra-team communications, we have assessed one of two possibilities. Either the meta-droid experienced a critical system malfunction, or it was receiving some unsourced instructions that interfered with its operating system. In either case, the meta-droid apparently suffered a break in its reactor integrity, which triggered a proximate fusion detonation. The resulting explosion destroyed the subsurface cavern and sealed off our access to it. Unfortunately, Hewst and Kiiswood were victims of the meta-droid's system failure and are presumed dead." Having finished reading his prepared statement, the lieutenant commander folded the page on which it was written and remarked, "We have assessed that, while sad and unfortunate, the station's status remains safe. Therefore, we plan to remain here and continue our research." He then asked, "Does anyone have any questions?"

"Lieutenant Commander, I don't believe in Martian equines," remarked Dr. Ferris, "so I certainly don't believe any of that horse shit that you're shoveling our way." His remark would have otherwise merited a modicum of chuckles, but no one in the mess module was in much of a mood to laugh. "Many of us in this room are scientists, and we know how to read spectrometric data. There's no sign of residual hydrogen or helium characteristic of that kind of reactor failure. There was no fusion explosion at all in that cavern."

"We also know how to read the EM imaging data," Dr. Kalinin added. "There is no underground cavity at the hypocenter anymore. What used to be a cavern is now a solid, unfissured, unfractured block of basalt. It's as though the cavern never even existed. I can't explain it, but I know that an explosion can't uncarve a cavern."

"We all saw the telemetry; we heard the audio," Dr. Negasi protested. "There was no system failure. There was nothing wrong with the meta-droid."

"Yes, we all heard the audio," acknowledged Riddari. "And for all we know, you, Dr. Negasi, were sending signals from your cybernetics lab to the meta-droid's c-nex."

Negasi exploded with rage, "Why, you lying son of a . . . !"

Incensed at Riddari's accusation, Dr. Střelec also erupted in anger, interrupting Negasi's outburst. "Oh, cut the crap!" she shouted. "We all know that there was something or someone in that cavern with them—something not human, perhaps something hyperdimensional—but it certainly wasn't a malfunctioning android! It was clearly an intelligence with forebodings of human extinction and with abilities far beyond ours—abilities to bring about said extinction."

As Riddari was sparring with several members of the research team, Dr. Emiri Matsuoka noticed that Captain Petrenko was standing quietly in the background watching their exchanges. Apparently, the captain was letting her executive officer verbally joust with the research team while she discreetly studied their interactions, like a clever tactician looking for weaknesses in her adversaries. Matsuoka decided that she did not want to play along, so she addressed Petrenko directly. "Captain, I think you and your officers have been lying to us from the start," she declared. "I think you've known all along that there was an alien intelligence associated with this cavern and that this intelligence represented a danger to us."

With a nearly imperceptible smirk, Petrenko decided to be a bit more forthcoming. She stepped up to the lectern and said, "That's not quite true, Doctor. When we first discovered the cavern, we didn't know that there was an alien intelligence associated with it, but we suspected the possibility. We assumed that it was the work of the New Jerusalem religious sect. But soon after interrogating Mr. Silas Dorch seven weeks ago, we quickly surmised that his so-called angels were nonhuman artificers. Of course, we didn't have any manifest evidence of alien presence until the events that transpired yesterday."

Chief Holgersen, who had been skeptical of Dorch's supernatural assertions, asked, "Ma'am, are you saying Aerospace Intelligence knew that Dorch's angels were more than mere religious delusion?"

"Aye, Chief," the captain acknowledged. "His affiliation with New Jerusalem served as a convenient obfuscation."

"Speaking of obfuscation," Dr. Driggers observed, "I noticed that you conveniently avoided responding to the second half of Emiri's comment. So I'll ask specifically: when did you know that this alien intelligence presented a danger to us?"

"We weren't aware of any particular threat," she answered. "But we had a contingency plan just in case. The light array was equipped with a thermonuclear device that we would have detonated at the first signs of danger."

A few subtle gasps of surprise echoed through the room. "How the hell is that a plan?" asked Dr. Cheung, rather indignantly. "A nuclear explosion wouldn't have saved us; it would have obliterated the cavern, and the entire station with it."

"That's the truth of it!" exclaimed Dr. Lonsdale. "You weren't looking to protect us; you were looking to destroy the cavern and all of us just to protect your secret."

"It's of no consequence," Petrenko replied stoically. "The alien intelligence removed that option when they destroyed our array."

Cheung's indignation persisted. "That's not the point! You were willing to kill all of us just to keep your secret."

"That's absolutely correct, Doctor," the captain said most resolutely. "And I offer no apologies for it. For the survival of the human race, every one of us is expendable." Then, she somberly added, "Hell, we're all dead anyway—it's just a matter of time."

Everyone in the room wanted the captain to clarify what she meant, but it was Lonsdale who finally asked, "What are you talking about?"

Petrenko was not quick to answer, but she soon responded, "FAIA has been aware of the looming extinction of the human race for the past nine years, since the war's end. Our best estimates suggest that every single human being throughout the solar system will be dead before this century is out." The room was silent as the captain explained, "In his interrogations, Mr. Dorch said that these angels of his were here to help us. And that's why we're here. If this alien intelligence has the means to save us, then we need to find it."

"Save us?" asked Ferris. The astrophysicist was not at all satisfied with the captain's portentous answer. "Save us from what? A massive asteroid? A black hole?"

"I don't know," she admitted. "That information is above my pay grade."

In exasperation, Lonsdale inquired, "Well then, how the hell are we supposed to know what we're looking for?"

"All I can tell you is that it has something to do with the regional contagions that you've heard about in recent news. I know nothing more specific than that," Petrenko replied. "But we don't have to know what we're looking for. All of our research—everything we discover—it's all being sent to FAIA's astrobiology center in Kinshasa."

"If the human race is in danger," asked Petty Officer Al-Jabiri, "shouldn't we be telling everyone?"

"Telling everyone is the last thing we want to do," she answered. "The fewer who know, the better. If this news became public, there'd be mass hysteria in the streets. All semblance of civil order would collapse throughout the entire solar system. If humankind knew that their existence was coming to an end, there would be nothing to keep their depraved impulses in check. It's best to let them live with the illusion that their lives and their worlds are going on blissfully uninterrupted."

"With respect, ma'am," Al-Jabiri continued, "I think you have a very dark opinion of human nature. According to Islam, the disasters of life are divine lessons. Through them, we learn to be better human beings before God and one another."

"Human history doesn't attest to such a noble and pious reaction," the captain lamented. "But I admire the optimism you have in your faith, as naïve as it is."

Dr. Cobisson found Petrenko's answers dubious, perhaps even implausible. He decided that he could not take the captain's doomsday scenario seriously. "Okay, I've heard enough," he said as he and Negasi stood from their seats. "Captain, if you and your research team wish to stay here and investigate all your data, that's fine with me. But Dr. Negasi and I aren't part of your research team. We were here simply to test and maintain the meta-droid. And since we don't have a meta-droid to work with any more, our presence isn't necessary. We'll gladly take our leave as soon as you can arrange transportation for us back to Tyrrhenus."

"Please have a seat, Doctors," insisted Petrenko. "The two of you might not have been a part of the research team initially, but you are now, especially now that we've lost our meta-droid. You'll have to serve as our team's astrobiologist, Dr. Cobisson."

Negasi scowled and Cobisson chuckled as the two of them headed toward the mess module's main hatch. "We came here voluntarily because your techswains were unfamiliar with our android technology," said Negasi. "We're not your civilian contractors, we're not your Defense Force personnel, and we're not staying."

"Where do you think you're going?" the captain asked mordantly.

"We're going to the garage module," Negasi answered. "If you won't arrange for transportation, then we'll take a traxle and drive to Tyrrhenus ourselves. There, we can catch a flight back to Mons La Hire." As they approached the main hatch, they found themselves in an inexorable standoff with a burly sorteer who deliberately stood in their way. "Nice try, Lehman," Negasi said while pointing to and reading the name printed on the sorteer's uniform. "But you don't intimidate us. We know our civil rights under the constitution of the Terrestrial Assembly. The military doesn't have the authority to detain civilians, so get out of our way," he said as he brazenly shoved the stalwart sorteer.

Lehman reacted violently, grabbing Negasi and twisting him about. With one hand, the sorteer gripped him around the nape of the neck, and with the other hand, he placed him in a standing arm lock. Negasi screamed out in pain, and almost everyone in the mess module leapt from their seats *en masse* to render assistance to their incapacitated colleague. Dr. Cobisson had even grabbed a chair and was about to swing it at the sorteer. But the astrobiologist froze in place once he felt the cold muzzle of another sorteer's rail-pistol pressing against his forehead. Likewise, everyone in the room stood silent and still as most of the sorteers had drawn their sidearms and leveled them on the crowd. Before Cobisson could protest, or capitulate, or even drop the chair, the sorteer pulled the trigger and shot the astrobiologist through the head. The chair fell from Cobisson's hands as his lifeless form collapsed to the floor with a macabre thud.

The module was suddenly filled with a furious disarray of cries and screams, cowers and expletives. Terror seized most everyone as they cringed at the sight of Cobisson's blood splattered across the bulkhead. Some dropped to the floor in fear; some scrambled for cover behind tables and chairs; and a few stood in place, paralyzed by shock and disbelief.

Over all the wails and riotous clambers, Petrenko shouted from the lectern, "All of you, shut the hell up! Get back in your seats right now, or I swear to God I'll have the sorteers shoot every damn one of you!" Most of them were too terrified not to do as they were told, so they returned to their seats with fear and trembling. But some were too terrified to do as they were told, so they just sat or lay on the floor right where they were. "Crewswain Lehman, let Dr. Negasi go," the captain ordered. Once freed from the arm lock, Negasi immediately crawled to the still body of his friend to render what aid he could. Amid all the shock and dread that filled the room, Petrenko gestured toward Dr. Ammon and his corpswains to tend to Cobisson. In a calmer, perhaps more psychotic tone, Petrenko said to everyone in the room, "As I've already said, for the survival of the human race, every one of us is expendable." Looking at Negasi, she continued, "To your point, Doctors, I *do* have the authority to detain you—and if necessary, execute you." The captain then activated one of the monitors and displayed a written statement that had all the appearances of an official document. Reading aloud, she said, "Pursuant to Article Seven, Section Fourteen of the Constitution, the Right Honorable

Hayato Yoshida, Prime Minister of the Terrestrial Assembly, has declared a state of emergency for Belshazzar Station and associated regions effective 2100 hours Zulu, Monday 17 December, 2429 of the Common Era. By provision of martial law, the military authority of the Federal Aerospace Intelligence Agency is imposed in order to ensure the common good. To wit, all civilian rights are hereby suspended until further notice."

While kneeling beside Cobisson's lifeless body, Ammon looked over toward the lectern and announced, "He's dead, Captain."

"Dr. Ammon, I want you and your corpswains to remove him to sickbay," she ordered, "at least until we can decide how to dispose of the body."

Ammon did not even bother to offer the traditional acknowledgments. He and the corpswains simply complied and respectfully removed Cobisson's lifeless form from the mess module.

As they were carrying the body through the main hatch, Lieutenant Jalloh stepped forward from his post in the room. "Captain," he said in a very formal tone, "as a Defense Force officer, I am bound by the Uniform Code of Military Justice to inform you that martial law does not supersede the UCMJ. Martial law does not grant you authority to execute civilians without court martial. Therefore, in accordance with the uniform code, I formally direct you to relinquish command to either Lieutenant Commanders Riddari or Gallistow. Concomitantly, as the OIC of Sorteer Unit Four, I am officially notifying you that I will not obey your orders to execute civilians."

Petrenko stared Jalloh straight in the eyes and said, "That's mutiny, Lieutenant."

"It's not mutiny to disobey unlawful orders, ma'am," he replied unwaveringly. Staring right back into her eyes, he added, "In either case, I accept responsibility for my actions."

"So be it," she acknowledged. "Lieutenant Jalloh, I assume charge of Sorteer Unit Four. You are hereby relieved of duty and are under arrest."

Petty Officer Sudha promptly stepped forward with her rail-pistol at the ready and asked, "Shall I improvise a brig in one of the utility hubs, Captain?"

"Thank you, Petty Officer," Petrenko replied. With an obvious air of contempt for Jalloh, she commented, "It's reassuring to know that stratogens understand the need for maintaining military order. Implement your plan," she ordered. Sudha reached into Jalloh's leg-holster and relieved him of his sidearm. As Sudha was about to usher her prisoner from the mess module, the captain asked the room, "Does anyone else wish to join the lieutenant in the brig?"

Most of the people in the room were too afraid of the captain to utter a word. But two enlisted personnel promptly raised their hands in response: Chief Åsta Holgersen and Petty Officer Mas'ud Al-Jabiri.

"Respectfully, ma'am," said Holgersen, "We're bound by the Uniform Code of Military Justice. Martial law doesn't make unlawful orders right."

Al-Jabiri added, "Ma'am, given the choice between the brig and executing civilians, I'll take the brig."

"So be it," said the captain. "Petty Officer Sudha, escort all three of them to a utility hub and detain them until I can decide what to do with them."

Sudha acknowledged, "Aye aye, ma'am." With her own firearm leveled on Jalloh, Holgersen, and Al-Jabiri, she curtly ushered her three prisoners from the room.

Immediately after they left, a numbing silence overtook the mess module—a soul-wrenching silence that seemed to go on interminably. But Dr. Ferris soon marshalled the courage to confront the captain. "I see that you've conveniently removed those who might challenge your authority," he said. "So here we are, surrounded by your soldiers. Are you about to mow us down where we sit?"

"I don't need their fire power to kill you," Petrenko admitted. "When you first reported to sickbay for your risk assessment, each and every one of you received a transcutaneous infusion of nanites."

"Nanites?" asked Lonsdale. "You mean nanobots?"

"Molecule-size robots—they're inside each one of you right now," she expounded. "They're positioned around your brainstems by now, so that with a single keystroke or a single c-nex wave, we can block all neuro-signals between your brains and the rest of your bodies. We can interrupt the autonomic functions of all of you or any one of you."

As a quantum neuro-engineer, Negasi understood all too well the possible effects of nanites around the brainstem. "Essentially, you could kill us with a thought," he said.

Petrenko stated coldly, "Perhaps you need a moment to come to grips with this news."

"You said that every one of us is expendable," observed Střelec. "Well, you just expended Cobisson, Kiiswood, and Hewst. How many more of us do you plan to eliminate?"

"That depends on how cooperative we're all willing to be," she impassively answered.

"'For the survival of the human race,'" Lonsdale quoted. "That's what you said. We're all expendable for the survival of the human race. So are you implying that there's a plan to save us?"

"There's a plan of a sort," the captain conceded. "But we're searching for a better option. That's why we're here—to find out whether this alien intelligence has any answers for us."

"And what if we don't find any answers for your *better* plan?" asked Driggers. "What's your plan *of a sort?*"

Before she could answer, the room momentarily went dark as a succession of emergency lights quickly replaced the failed overhead lights. The station's klaxon alarm sounded as all of the hatches in the mess module closed. A booming voice over the station's PA system competed with the screech of the alarm. "Captain," announced the voice of Station Chief Fuentes, "we've lost primary power to most of our operating systems. Our life-support systems are running on emergency back-up power. All station-wide security systems are offline, including security cameras. And I have an indicator light that an exterior hatch is open."

"Sudha," the captain muttered to herself. Petrenko suddenly realized that that astute stratogen must have cunningly betrayed her command.

The voice of Fuentes continued. "I also have a motion sensor alert at the areopter pads. It looks like the troop carrier has taken off."

"Captain, all the hatches are sealed!" shouted Lehman as he continued to test the main hatch. "We're locked in, ma'am."

Petrenko hailed the control room with her c-nex and shouted, "Chief Fuentes, our hatches are locked down. Can you override?"

"Negative, ma'am," the station chief replied.

The captain was clearly annoyed that an adversary had out-maneuvered her. The stratogen had managed to confine nearly all the station's complement within a single module, including most of her command staff and eight sorteers of Unit Four. Yet Petrenko was also genuinely impressed with the tactical prowess of Petty Officer Sudha. Turning to Crewswain Lehman, Petrenko inquired, "Can you bypass the locks on the hatches manually?"

"Aye aye, ma'am," the sorteer answered. "We're on it! It'll take a few minutes."

Hailing the control room again, Petrenko ordered, "Fuentes, deploy the rest of the sorteers after those mutineers." As an afterthought, she added, "And turn off that damned alarm."

The chief responded, "Aye aye, ma'am."

"I should let you know, Captain," declared another voice over the station's PA system, "I'm patched into the station's communications and security systems. I can see and hear everything you're doing. Under the authority of the uniform code, I'm instructing you and your sorteers to stand down."

Petrenko instantly recognized that voice. "Ah, Petty Officer Sudha," she identified. "I salute you. Bravo Zulu! Now, I should let you know, I have the tactical ability to take you and your fellow mutineers out. But because I'd prefer not to lose a valuable piece of equipment, I'm going to give you a chance to turn that areopter around and return to the station."

"Bravo Zulu to you too, ma'am," Sudha responded. "Somehow you managed to disable the station's comm-links to Tyrrhenus. We simply wanted to use the areopter's comm system and to report your illegal actions to Camp

244

Lundgren. But somehow you managed to disable that system also. We had no other choice but to commandeer the troop carrier."

"You're very much mistaken, Sudha," the captain returned. "The comm-links are still working. The problem is that Tyrrhenus is no longer transmitting. The entire city has gone dark."

Fuentes reported, "Captain, four sorteers are aboard the gunship, awaiting your order to launch."

"Give them the green light, Chief," she ordered.

"Aye aye, ma'am," replied Fuentes.

After several minutes of meticulous toiling on the main hatch's locking mechanism, Lehman announced, "Captain, we have one of the hatches unlocked, but something on the other side is blocking it."

Before Petrenko could respond, the thunderous blast of a proximate explosion rumbled throughout the entire station; effusive shrapnel was raining down all over the station's hull. Everyone in the mess module reflexively cowered at the strident barrage of falling debris pelting the roof.

"What the hell?" exclaimed Petrenko.

"Captain," said the voice of the station chief, "motion sensors indicate an explosion on the areopter pad."

Petrenko straightaway suspected that Sudha had set a trap, rigging a grenade or some kind of improvised device to destroy the gunship so that it could not pursue the troop carrier. "Status of the crew?" the captain inquired.

"Unknown, ma'am," Fuentes answered. "I'm not receiving any biotelemetry."

"But *I am* receiving the telemetry," said the voice of Sudha. "Your gunship and its crew are neutralized. I warned you to stand down."

All of the station's emergency lighting suddenly went dark, shrouding the mess module in total darkness. The unlocked hatch was then flung open as Sudha burst into the room, armed with a tactical rail-rifle in hand and a holstered rail-pistol. The veil of darkness made her essentially invisible to all who would otherwise take aim at her. Sudha, however, knew where everyone was in the room, because she could see their heat-silhouettes in the infrared range. With speed and agility, she serpentined among the room's tables, chairs, and disoriented occupants. "Drop your weapons!" she demanded, broadcasting her orders over the PA system as a way to obscure her location. "Drop your weapons, now!" Despite her repeated orders, several sorteers did not comply. So Sudha began to fire at her armed targets in rapid succession.

The sound of Sudha's EM-propelled bullets hurtling through the darkness provoked screams of fear among the bystanders. Most of them were blindly dropping to the floor in a desperate attempt to avoid being shot in the dark. Two of the sorteers in the room quickly realized that they were outmatched by the stratogen, and they promptly discarded their weapons. They too dropped to the floor as a gesture of capitulation.

When all the shooting stopped, Sudha reactivated the station's emergency power via her c-nex. When the lights returned, the bloodshed was apparent. Without inflicting even a single collateral injury, the stratogen had methodically shot and killed six of the eight sorteers—those six who imprudently disregarded her orders to disarm. Having neutralized every armed threat, she was now standing over Petrenko's cowering figure. The muzzle of Sudha's rail-rifle was squarely aimed at the captain's head.

"Captain Anna Petrenko," declared Sudha, "under the authority of the Uniform Code of Military Justice, I hereby place you under arrest."

Petrenko cynically grinned. "I'm impressed, Sudha. You're truly gifted at misdirection. I really thought you were the one flying the troop carrier. I forgot that Jalloh is also a pilot." With no other word, the captain used her c-nex to activate the clandestine nanites inside Sudha's body. The stratogen instantly fell to the floor unconscious as the nanites disrupted her brainstem functions. Moments later Petty Officer Sudha was dead.

The captain stood up, dusted herself off, and neatly motioned to the two remaining sorteers to retrieve all of the weapons in the room, including Sudha's. Turning to the lieutenant commanders, she ordered, "Riddari, Gallistow, go get the station's operating systems back online." Petrenko then used her c-nex to hail the troop carrier. "Lieutenant Jalloh, well played," she complimented. "But I need to inform you that your fellow mutineer is dead.

So I'll give you the same chance that I gave Sudha. Return that areopter to the station and I'll let you, Holgersen, and Al-Jabiri live."

After a long moment's pause, Jalloh responded, "Captain, we accepted commissions and enlistments in the Defense Force to protect the civilian population. We won't be a party to their execution."

Petrenko's pause was not quite so long. "So be it," she replied.

The station's primary lighting system re-engaged, closely followed by Riddari's voice announcing over the PA, "Systems are back online, ma'am," he said.

"Well done," the captain replied. "Give me a status report. I want to know what Sudha did to my station."

"Station-wide systems are all nominal," reported the voice of Chief Fuentes. "The troop carrier is currently on course to Tyrrhenus. The gunship is destroyed. All modules, hubs, and gangways are structurally secure. But the armory module is still locked down. Petty Officer Sudha changed the security access codes. It'll take a while for us to break her codes."

"Thank you, Chief," she acknowledged. "Carry on."

Seconds later, Fuentes reported, "Ma'am, I have the troop carrier on a live satellite feed. It's about 56 kilometers northeast of us."

"Patch the feed to a monitor here in the mess module," Petrenko ordered.

"Aye aya, ma'am," the station chief replied as a satellite image of the commandeered areopter appeared on the mess module's central monitor. Everyone in the room quickly became captivated by the image of the speeding troop carrier. The members of the research team anxiously watched the rotorcraft racing away as they privately cheered for the success of its fleeing crew. The captain also watched, not with cheers but with annoyance. With no further words, Petrenko activated the deadly nanites in Jalloh's body.

At first, the image on the monitor showed no change in the flight pattern; the areopter seemed to be flying as usual. Within a matter of seconds, however, it started to yaw ever so slightly to the left. Soon its flight became increasingly erratic as it began to wobble along its yaw axis, like a slowing gyro-top about to topple over. Then, no longer able to remain airborne, the troop carrier fell from the sky and crashed in a plume of red dust on the Martian desert. No signs of life ensued, just a string of smaller dust plumes as whirling shards were strewn from disintegrating rotor blades.

The room was quiet. Most everyone was either too shocked or too numbed by the day's carnage to even gasp in horror. Yet the captain seemed to have no trouble breaking the silence. "Chief Fuentes, dispatch a couple of ground crew personnel in a traxle to check for survivors and to salvage whatever they can from the troop carrier."

"Ma'am, I recommend that you belay that order," Fuentes advised. "We may need every able-bodied person to remain here on-site. I have something else on the satellite images approaching the station. It looks like we have twenty-five or thirty assault traxles and armored ground vehicles rolling this way from the north." He continued with alarm in voice, "It has the MO of a New Jerusalem raiding party."

Chapter 21 – The Cave

Hellas Province, Mars

(Areographic Co-ordinates: S 35.871, E 94.284)

Saturday, 22 December 2429 CE

Time: 1205 Zulu

"Commander," called Kiiswood. "Wake up, Commander." The chief persisted. Finally, he shouted, "Catherine! Are you okay?"

Gradually, Hewst became aware that someone was calling her name. She could also hear the close echo of her own breathing inside her helmet. Slowly, reluctantly, she opened her eyes, squinting in the brightness of the chief's helmet torch that was shining in her face. As her eyes steadily adjusted to the light, she could see Kiiswood looking down at her. Quickly, her consciousness returned, and she realized that she was lying supinely on the ground.

Hewst recognized her friend, but not her surroundings. So she raised her head to gain perspective. "What?" she asked. "Chief, where are we?"

"I don't know, ma'am," he answered. "I just came to moments ago. I haven't had an opportunity to investigate. I get no response when I hail the control room. My immediate concern is your safety and welfare—yours and Alex's." Kiiswood then asked, "Are you okay?"

"Yeah, I think so," she replied as she sluggishly rose to her feet. "Where's Alex?"

Kiiswood assisted her as she stood. Of course, his assistance was more of a courteous gesture than a needed aid; Hewst was quite able to stand up by her own strength. "He's right there," the chief answered, pointing where Alex lay.

"Is he alright?" she asked, looking at the meta-droid's unconscious form. "Is he alive?"

"Technically, ma'am," he replied with a smirk, "he was never alive. But if you recall, he did say that he has a sleep-mode." The chief knelt near the meta-droid, jostled his shoulder, and said, "Hey, Alex, are you still with us?"

Alex promptly awoke. "Chief," he said. "Where are we?" The pitch of his voice was lower than usual. Unlike Hewst and Kiiswood, he wore no helmet; the carbon dioxide atmosphere was affecting his synthetic vocal chords.

"From the sound of your voice, we're still on Mars," Kiiswood surmised. "My HUD is giving me only internal telemetry: suit integrity, vital stats, oxygen level, *etcetera*. But I have no external telemetry: no satellite feeds, no Global Navigation Network, no topographic readouts. I don't even have a comm-link with Belshazzar Station. We *do* have c-nex links, at least among the three of us. I haven't been able to hail anyone else."

"How long have we been unconscious?" the meta-droid asked.

"Uncertain," the chief answered. "My chronometer display is down. When we entered the tetrahedral cavern, my EV packet was fully charged with a two-day supply of oxygen. Now I'm down to less than four hours."

Hewst activated her helmet torch to cast some more light on their surroundings. As she looked about, she said, "There's the retrieval case, there's the chief's rifle, and there's my equipment satchel." Hewst then noticed something glittering on the ground—something sparkling by the light of her torchlight. "And here's my necklace," she extolled as she reached down, picked it up, and brushed off the Martian dust. She clearly could not put it on over her helmet, so she slipped the necklace into a small utility pouch on the sleeve of her compression suit for safekeeping. As she continued to survey the surroundings, she remarked, "But this space is certainly not a tetrahedron."

"No, it's not," Alex agreed.

"It's a cave," said Kiiswood. He pointed and said, "That must be the entrance—about 25 meters. Look, there's a temperature differential."

"I can't see infrared, Chief," laughed Hewst. "I'll take your word for it."

Kiiswood picked up his rifle, inspected it, and determined that it was in good working condition. "Okay, I'm on point," he said to his two colleagues. "Keep tight and stay on my six."

Hewst and Alex looked at each other. "I know," the meta-droid said to her before she could explain. "Kiiswood is taking the lead, and we're to stay together and follow him."

Kiiswood led the way through the dark, narrow cave as Hewst and Alex hung closely behind him. Their surroundings grew slightly brighter and a little more colorful as they approached the opening. The cave walls were being illuminated by hues of blue as the predawn Martian sky shone through the entrance. Kiiswood gestured toward several tiny devices that he noticed on the walls near the entrance. "Look," he said, "motion detectors."

With optimism in her voice, Hewst said, "So someone probably knows we're here."

"Motion detectors?" inquired Alex. "Who put them here?"

"*We* did," Kiiswood eventually answered. "They're the station's motion detectors. They look like the ones that Dr. Cheung and her survey team put here when they were comparing soil samples on Dorch's compression suit." The chief then ventured a guess. "This must be the cave that Dorch entered just before he ended up inside the tetrahedron."

As they approached the cave's entrance, Alex asked Kiiswood, "Are you sure?"

There, at the entrance, they found the makeshift barrier that the survey team had set up earlier. Posted all along the barrier were quarantine symbols and warning signs bearing the logo of the Interplanetary Health Agency and alerting people not to enter the cave. "I'm sure," Kiiswood answered as he picked up one of the signs and showed it to Alex. "Remember, we're supposed to be a research unit with IPHA; that's Project Belshazzar's cover story."

"I remember," the meta-droid acknowledged. "But there's something wrong with that sign. Its letters are all printed backwards, as though it was written to be read in a mirror."

Kiiswood glanced at all the signs along the barrier. Each one read "Warning: Quarantine Area. Do Not Enter. Interplanetary Health Agency." Each one, however, was written backwards and with inverted letters. "You're right," he commented. "In fact, they're all printed backwards." The chief turned to Hewst and asked, "Hey Commander, what do you make of this?"

Although she could overhear the exchange between her friends, Hewst was too preoccupied to pay attention to their conversation. She was too immersed in the twilit stars that had not yet succumbed to the approaching dawn. "The stars aren't right," she asserted. Kiiswood and Alex looked up as Hewst pointed to a familiar constellation. "The stars aren't right," she repeated. "Look! Sagittarius is backwards."

They stood there in awe, noticing that, it was not just Sagittarius, but all the constellations still visible in the brightening sky were inverted. The three of them had no idea what was happening, but they felt sure that the mysterious presence—the self-named Aeon—was responsible for it.

Without taking his eyes off the slow-fading stars, Kiiswood pondered, "How can they change the entire universe?"

"Maybe they didn't change the entire universe," Alex hypothesized. "Maybe they simply changed us."

Hewst musingly replied, "Perhaps changing us is how the universe is changed."

The radiant arc of the morning sun peeked over the Martian horizon. Mesmerized by the brightness of the dawn, the three of them felt at peace—as though everything was well in the universe, as though all gloom of darkness gave way to the goodness of the light.

"'The night is far gone,'" Hewst reflected, "'the day is near.'"

Kiiswood continued her quote, "'Let us then lay aside the works of darkness and put on the armor of light.'"

Hewst smiled. "Romans, chapter thirteen, the twelfth verse," she commented.

Alex also smiled and concurred, "If the two of you are saying that despair is swept away with the emergence of hope, I agree."

The chief once again checked his oxygen levels. "We need to get moving," he contended. "Belshazzar Station is about 14 kilometers north of here and we have a little better than three and a half hours of oxygen left to get there."

"We already walked past the motion detectors," the meta-droid noted. "The station crew must know that we're here. They'll probably send a traxle for us."

"They likely will," acknowledged Hewst. "You can afford to wait here, Alex; you don't need oxygen. But Kiiswood and I shouldn't just stand around here and take that chance. If a traxle is being dispatched for us, it'll simply meet us on the way."

"Well, if we're about to set out for the station," Alex posed, "shouldn't we take the satchel and retrieval case with us?"

"I recommend we travel light," the chief advised. "We can come back for them when we're not so pressed for time."

"Okay, Chief," Alex concurred. "You're on point. But without a navigation network, how will we know which way to go?"

Kiiswood gestured smartly to the tracks in the Martian dust. "We follow the traxle treads that Dr. Cheung's team left when they were last here."

Glancing at the tracks in the dust in relation to the rising sun, Alex noted curiously, "But those go south."

Hewst believed that the meta-droid's point was well taken, yet she agreed with the chief's plan to follow the traxle treads. She assessed, "I have a sense that even our cardinal directions are inverted like everything else we've seen."

They promptly set out for Belshazzar Station across the cold desert plateau of Hellas Planitia. They moved at a swift and steady pace despite having to hike through the fine, unconsolidated, rusty soil. Kiiswood quickly altered his gait to compensate for the weaker Martian gravity, but Hewst and Alex took a little longer to adjust their strides. The three of them hardly uttered a word as they walked along; their thoughts were elsewhere. They were trying to make sense of their recently shared experience—an experience that transcended sense. Hewst, Kiiswood, and Alex were no longer the persons they once were before their encounter with the presence. They had been changed in more ways than one, in ways that they had not yet realized.

About five kilometers into their trek, Alex broke the silence. "We're all being conspicuously quiet about what happened in the cavern," he said in his low-toned, carbon dioxide voice.

After a few more strides in silence, Hewst finally replied, "I'm not trying to ignore what happened, Alex. I'm just not certain that I have the language to describe it."

"When I woke up in that cave, I first thought that I was dreaming," the meta-droid admitted. "But it had a certain quality—a certain vividness that dreams don't have."

"No, it wasn't a dream," Hewst acknowledged. "It was quite real."

"It was more real than anything I've ever experienced in my life," Alex confessed. "And yet, it was so far outside my capacity for sense or reason, I just don't know what it means to say that it was real." He paused pensively. "It was real, but it was a reality that I can't comprehend. I've never believed in spirits or angels."

"I wouldn't call them angels," replied Hewst, "at least not in the biblical sense. But, I would say that they're clearly an incorporeal intelligence."

"I've built my life around the surety of science," Alex admitted, "but this is far beyond any scientific paradigm that I recognize."

Hewst appreciated the meta-droid's moment of existential doubt, and she had compassion for her friend. "Your confidence in science is not misplaced," she confided like a pastor. "But not all reality is science."

Alex smiled slightly. "I want to pretend that it didn't happen," he admitted. "But I can't—I can no more deny it than I can deny my own being, my own soul." His smile grew larger as he anticipated some pithy remark from Kiiswood, and the chief did not disappoint him.

"Ah, so the machine has a soul now," Kiiswood commented glibly.

"No, Chief, I don't *have* a soul," Alex replied. "I *am* a soul." He continued, "I don't know how or why, but that presence and I were one. And in that same moment, the three of us in that cavern were one with each other. We became one consciousness, one soul—distinguishable, yet inseparable. And that's how I know it's real. You can't be one with the soul of another without realizing your own soul." With conviction, Alex repeated his initial claim. "I *am* a soul, and you know it, Chief. You were there."

Kiiswood became visibly perturbed; his pace quickened and his tone turned curt. "All of this chatter is burning up our oxygen. Let's keep our focus on the traxle treads in the sand, and let's hope that they haven't all been blown away by the Martian winds."

"What's eating at you, Chief?" Alex probed. "You and Catherine have enough oxygen to walk and talk at the same time."

"I think I know what's bothering him," Hewst offered. "He knows you're right, Alex. We were, indeed, one with each other. Within each one of us is the soul of all of us, and that's the problem. He can no longer look into his own soul without seeing into the souls of others. He wants to harbor disdain for others, but now he can't. The compassion that the chief would hope for himself, he must now hope for others."

Kiiswood brandished his rail-rifle and said, "Yeah, I have an entire magazine loaded with compassion and hope."

Alex was not sure whether the chief was being provocative or humorous. He looked for clarity in Hewst's facial expressions. "Is he threatening to shoot us?" he asked. "He wouldn't shoot his friends, would he?"

"Just so you know," Kiiswood replied, "my CO once reprimanded me for accidentally shooting a friend."

Hewst grinned at Alex and answered softly, "The chief never does anything by accident." She added, "Besides, if he were going to shoot us, he would have done so a long time ago."

"I heard that, Commander," the chief announced.

Hewst, Kiiswood, and Alex trekked on toward the station, following the tracks left behind by the traxle. Its tread marks in the red, rusty sand were not fresh; they bore signs of weathering by the Martian winds. Still, the tracks remained visible and traceable as the three friends hiked on in silence for at least another kilometer.

Alex could not stop thinking about the transcendent presence that had inexplicably communed with him—*through* him. He wondered whether his synthetic cortex was a conduit in a way that those of his human colleagues were not. Perhaps his neural network was just the right link between the imminent and the transcendent; between the tangible and incorporeal; between space and hyperspace. "You know," Alex pondered aloud, "I really can't be skeptical about incorporeal things anymore—things like angels and souls." He then proposed, "Maybe there really is a God."

At that, Hewst returned, "I hope that God is better to you than He's been to me."

Kiiswood could not resist challenging the commander's statement. "Ma'am, you're quick to see the incongruity within me—my love for God and my disdain for God's people. But you're slow to see that incongruity in yourself. Perhaps you should turn some of your high-powered pastoral counselling skills on yourself."

"There's nothing incongruous about my convictions," she insisted.

"Oh, no?" the chief rhetorically asked. "You say you're angry with God. You're angry because supposedly your father's death was part of a divine plan for your life."

"That's right!" she replied with notable anger in her voice. "That's exactly right! When I was a chaplain, people used to think that I was a model of Christian faith and service. But my life paled by comparison to my father's. His was a life of extraordinary faith and of selfless service to others. What kind of benevolent God would make a plan like that? What kind of plan is that for my life?"

Kiiswood pressed through Hewst's anger. "That's what your father told you—that his death was part of a divine plan for your life. So for more than nine years, you've convinced yourself that you're angry with God. But the truth is, you're not angry. You're afraid."

"Afraid?" barked Hewst. "You think I'm afraid of God?"

"No!" Kiiswood barked back. "You're afraid that your father might have been right."

Although her face was red with anger, her eyes cradled a hint of pooling tears. "You know, the chief is right," Hewst said reservedly, when she did finally speak. "All of this chatter is burning up our oxygen."

Kiiswood abruptly stopped, then dropped prone with his rifle aimed at the horizon ahead. With a couple of tactical hand signals, he directed Hewst and Alex to get low to the ground to reduce their visibility.

"What is it, Chief?" asked Hewst as she crawled alongside Kiiswood, pulling herself through the sand with her elbows. "What do you see?"

"Belshazzar Station," he answered, pointing with his rifle, "just on the horizon."

Alex also drew himself alongside Kiiswood. "All I see is desert," he commented, squinting his eyes in a failed effort to focus better. "We're still six or seven kilometers out, aren't we?"

Although the meta-droid estimated the remaining distance correctly, Kiiswood did not confirm. Instead, the chief linked his c-nex to the scope of his rifle and used it as a telescope for his visual cortex. "Several modules exhibit compromised integrity; a few of them are completely decimated," he said. "The blasted debris of one areopter is strewn about the pad; it looks like it was the gunship. The other two rotorcraft are missing."

"What happened?" inquired Hewst, "an asteroid strike?"

"I don't think so," Kiiswood replied slowly.

"Could the supposed angels have done something to the station?" the meta-droid wondered.

"I think this is the work of human hands," the chief countered. "This looks like the result of short-range artillery."

With apprehension in her voice, Hewst speculated, "A raiding party?"

Again, the chief replied slowly, "That would be my guess."

"Two areopters are missing," she proposed. "Perhaps the station personnel were able to evacuate."

"I don't know. The reactor module appears to be intact," Kiiswood observed, "but I see no signs of life."

Hewst quickly surmised, "I think it's safe to assume that they're not sending a traxle to pick us up. So we need to make our way to the station as quickly as possible."

"Make our way?" asked the astonished meta-droid. "If the station was attacked by New Jerusalem terrorists, how do we know that it's safe?"

"We don't," she promptly answered. "But we don't have a choice."

"The commander's right," the chief acknowledged. "That station is our only accessible source of oxygen before our EV packets are depleted." He then unceremoniously said, "Come on, let's get moving."

The three of them quickened their pace across the red desert as the sun continued its steady climb over the eastern horizon. Kiiswood would have preferred to approach the derelict station by stealth, but their shortage of oxygen compelled them to forego certain precautions. Nonetheless, the chief kept a careful watch for an enemy presence as they advanced. Once they were within a couple of kilometers from the station, Hewst and Alex could clearly see for themselves the devastation that Kiiswood had described.

Very little of Belshazzar Station was familiar. Dozens of tire tracks, artillery treads, and boot prints covered the sandy grounds that surrounded the station. About half of the modules were either destroyed or breached and were obviously uninhabitable. The rest of the modules were dimpled and dappled with bullet strikes, but their hulls appeared otherwise intact. What was left of the station was wind-coated in a fine, reddish-orange layer of Martian dust. The inverted logos and emblems of the Interplanetary Health Agency showed through the thin veneer of dust. All three airlocks into the station were either missing or clearly inoperable.

Hewst, Kiiswood, and Alex were all silent upon reaching the station. They walked a complete circuit around the site, superficially inspecting what was damaged and what might be salvageable. None of them wanted to believe what they were seeing.

"All the airlocks are out," observed Alex. "How will we get inside?"

Hewst did not respond; she was absorbed in her thoughts. The sight of the ruins brought sorely to mind her days as a chaplain during the Martian war. She was momentarily lost in the memory of her trials aboard the battle-plagued TAS *Denali*—memories of bloodshed and bravery, of carnage and compassion.

With a hint of sarcasm, Kiiswood said, "With all the gaping holes in the station's hull, getting inside won't be a problem." The chief then led Hewst and Alex through a field of hull fragments strewn about the ground. Stepping and striding over bits and shards of station wreckage, he guided them toward one of the larger, ruptured modules—what was the station's mess module.

Carefully, the three of them scaled past the sharp, jagged edges of a mortar-blown gape and into the vestiges of the once-bustling module. Their eyes steadily adjusted to the dimness of the murky room. The only source of illumination was the angled shaft of sunlight streaming through the gape—a misty orange light tinged by the wafting Martian dust. Hewst and Kiiswood both turned on their helmet torches, casting their own beams of orange-tinged light. Everywhere they turned their heads, they could see a fine film of dust that had settled over everything in the module: chairs, tables, dining utensils, unfinished breakfasts, and about two dozen lifeless bodies.

Kiiswood and Alex walked among the corpses that covered the floor. Specifically, Kiiswood methodically strolled about, forensically reviewing the flash-frozen bodies, while Alex more or less wandered about in bewilderment. Hewst simply stood in place, emotionally bludgeoned by the macabre scene. She had borne much loss in her own life, yet every new death felt just as fresh, just as mournful, as the first one. She was so overwhelmed by the carnage that she failed to notice the layout of the once-familiar module; the position of the tables, monitors, and hatches were now reversed.

Alex knelt down beside a large mass of bodies near the main hatch and began to wipe away the dust that had settled on their faces. He wiped very gently as though he were trying not to wake them. "This is John Driggers," Alex said heavily. "And Andrea Cheung, and Glen Ferris, and Emiri Matsuoka." The meta-droid paused for a moment. "And this is Vraiss. I can't remember his first name," he admitted apologetically. After another, longer pause, he mournfully continued. "Desta Negasi," he whispered. Alex decided not to sweep away any more dust; he simply did not want to identify the rest of the dead.

Calmly, almost stoically, Hewst commented, "They didn't all die at the same time."

As he walked among the dead, Kiiswood carefully assessed the bodies in the room, until he abruptly stopped and stood over one in particular—the lifeless body of his fellow stratogen, Ishanvi Sudha. He hovered awhile in silence over his long-acquainted, now-deceased comrade-in-arms. Finally, the chief appended Hewst's comment. "Nor did they all die in the same way."

Alex looked up from the heap of bodies. "What are you two talking about?" he asked. "Didn't they all die when the hull was ruptured?"

"No," Hewst answered. "Some of them were dead before the rupture." She continued, "When people are suddenly exposed to a vacuum, they have about five to ten seconds of consciousness to respond. In that time, they'd naturally rush for the safety of a pressurized compartment. That's why we see so many of the bodies amassed there at that hatch."

"It's a natural response," Kiiswood concurred, "but a futile one. They may have had a few seconds before they fell unconscious, but they were doomed the very moment the hull was breached. The hatches to the rest of the station would have sealed at the instant of rapid decompression. Ten seconds wouldn't have been enough time to override the safety protocols."

Hewst slowly made her way to Kiiswood's side as he was surely grieving the demise of his colleague. With a consoling voice, she said, "But not everyone ran to the hatch."

"Why not?" asked Alex.

"Because they were already dead," Kiiswood answered frankly. He then looked about and pointed to Crewswain Lehman and five other bodies around the module—bodies that lay in small pools of their own frozen blood. "These six sorteers were each killed by a single shot to the head." The chief once again looked down at Sudha and said, "It's her signature."

Hewst placed her hand on Kiiswood's shoulder. "I'm so sorry about your friend, Chief," she solaced.

"You know, Sudha was a Hindu," the chief said in a still voice. "A preacher once told me that there's no salvation apart from Christ—that no one can come to the Father except through the Son. When I was younger, I used to believe that. But I don't think I can believe it anymore." Without looking away from his fallen comrade, Kiiswood posed a question to Hewst. "You were once a chaplain. Do you think that's true? Is Sudha beyond the grace of God?"

Kiiswood was asking a profound theological question, but Hewst knew that the chief was seeking a pastoral answer. "I believe God is God. He can come to whomever He chooses," she proclaimed, "whether or not we ever come to Him. No, Chief, I don't think Ishanvi is beyond God's grace." Hewst then placed her hands together, bowed slightly toward Sudha's lifeless form, and said, "*Namaste.*"

"I really don't mean to be insensitive," Alex interrupted, "but shouldn't we be looking for a way inside the station?"

"Yes, we should," Kiiswood replied tersely. "Follow me."

Hewst and Kiiswood reverently weaved their way around the deceased and approached Alex and the main hatch. Together, the three of them discreetly moved aside several bodies from around the hatch to clear their way. Kiiswood then removed the shield-plate of an adjacent panelboard and began to bypass some of the fail-safe protocols. He successfully pumped out the air in the gangway just behind the hatch until it matched the pressure in the mess module. When the indicator light above the panelboard turned green, the chief opened the hatch, and the three of them stepped through. As soon as they resealed the hatch, Kiiswood adjusted the environmental setting and repressurized the gangway with warm, Terran atmosphere. Once the indicator light turned green, Hewst and Kiiswood opened their helmets and breathed in the station's recycled air.

Kiiswood glanced at the meta-droid and declared, "That, Alex, is how you make an improvised airlock."

"Eww!" Hewst exclaimed with a contorted face. "What's that pungent smell? It smells like rotten eggs."

"Yeah," responded Alex. His voice had now returned to its normal pitch. "I've been smelling that ever since I woke up in the cave."

"It's the sulfur compounds in the Martian particulate," Kiiswood replied. "These gangways can work like airlocks, but they can't extract dust."

Hewst furiously (yet unsuccessfully) shook the dust from her compression suit. She then removed her necklace from the pouch on her sleeve and slipped it over her head and around her neck. "Apparently, it can't augment our gravity either," she commented as she observed the way her necklace drifted in the weaker gravity. "We're still under Mars-normal."

"That's because the AG is out all over the station," said the chief. He reached up to open the next hatch, but then he hesitated. "I should let you know," he cautioned, "if you think the Martian dust smells bad, you'll likely find the smells in the station upsetting." With that warning, Kiiswood opened the hatch, and the three of them entered the carnage of a battle site.

Despite the bitter stench of putrefaction that permeated the reprocessed air, Hewst, Kiiswood, and Alex pressed ahead, trekking from one dimly lit module to another. The station's reactor was currently generating only nominal power—barely enough to maintain the life-support systems and power the station's emergency lights. Even with poor illumination, the directional signs and markers in the corridors proved difficult to read; they were all written backwards. Yet the muted lighting could not shroud the bleak spectacle of hatches wrenched from their frames, bulkheads marred with bullet strikes, and compartments sullied with blood and decaying corpses.

The three of them tried to commit to memory each casualty that they had stepped over or had passed by. Soon, they lost track of the names, and they even lost count of the numbers: Dr. Kalinin, Dr. Lonsdale, Crewswain Zhao, a sorteer, a techswain, a corpswain, and several New Jerusalem paladins outfitted in antiquated Alliance-surplus compression suits.

Eventually, Hewst, Kiiswood, and Alex found themselves standing at the junction of the station's two main gangways. There, at Hewst's feet was the slain body of yet another paladin.

Hewst reached down to examine more closely the armband on the paladin's suit. "This is the same insignia that I've seen on all of them; it identifies their specific terror clan. They're all allegiants in the Hesperia enclave."

"They were all part of a raiding party that attacked the station," Kiiswood added.

"How did they get inside the station?" Alex asked.

"How they got inside is no mystery," Kiiswood replied. " *We* did it." He then pondered, "No, I want to know how they could even get close enough to get inside. We had recon satellites in orbit, we had a heavily armed gunship, we had several laser drones in the armory, and we had a team of sorteers. A New Jerusalem raiding party shouldn't have been able to get within ten kilometers of this station."

Alex was just as baffled as the chief. "So what went wrong?"

Kiiswood gestured toward one of the directional signs posted at the junction—the one showing the way to the control room. (By this time, all three of them were becoming quite adept at reading the inverted writing.) "We might be able to find out if we check the automated logs in the control room."

"We still need to look for survivors," Hewst said as she pointed to another sign. "And sickbay is the most likely place to find them, if there are any."

"That's true," the chief agreed. "Of course, if there *are* any survivors, I might be able to track their c-nex transponders from the control room."

"Okay, Chief," she acquiesced. "You go to the control room and scan for survivors." She and the meta-droid turned to take the gangway that forked to the right. "Afterward, you can catch up with me and Alex in sickbay."

"Aye aye, ma'am," acknowledged Kiiswood as he headed left. And just before they branched out of sight, the chief shouted back to his friends, "Be careful!"

Hewst and Alex soon found the station's sickbay and discovered that the module had not been spared the chaos. Consoles were overturned, diagnostic stalls vandalized, medications pilfered, first aid supplies and trauma equipment plundered. A corpswain lay dead behind a treatment kiosk where he futilely sought cover from terrorist gunfire. Off to the far side of sickbay was

263

an examination cubical; its modesty partition was pushed aside, exposing five bodies that had been hastily lined up on the floor and draped with medical blankets.

"A makeshift morgue," observed Hewst as she and Alex entered the examination cubical. "Whatever shadow of mayhem was unleashed on this station, there was clearly some glimmer of sympathy in its midst. Someone took the time to care for the dead."

Alex reverently raised the head of each blanket, one at a time. "This is Lieutenant Commander Gallistow," he said, "and this is another paladin." When he lifted the third blanket, he stood still as if frozen, taciturn as if mute. The decedent's face was covered in dried blood, disfigured by a close-range pistol shot. Still, the meta-droid recognized the face that once was his own—the face of Dr. Earnan M. Cobisson. With a faint quiver in his hand, Alex slowly, gradually returned the blood-stained blanket over Cobisson's head.

"I'm so sorry, Alex," Hewst consoled.

The meta-droid said nothing; he simply reached over to the next blanket and lifted it. Quite startled, Hewst and Alex were taken aback as they were greeted by the muzzle of a heavily scuffed Martian rail-pistol. Suddenly, two quite living and quite armed paladins, who had hidden themselves among the dead, threw off their blankets and leapt to their feet. With their weapons squarely trained on them, the paladins forced Hewst and Alex onto their knees and removed the c-nexes from their temples.

As one paladin was restraining their wrists behind their backs with cannula tubing, the other began to question Hewst and Alex. "Is it just you two, or are there others with you?" the interrogator asked.

"Ouch!" exclaimed Hewst as the paladin tightened her restraints.

"Shut up, woman!" the interrogator shouted. "And answer my question!"

Hewst glared resolutely at her interrogator and retorted, "I can't do both!"

The interrogating paladin said nothing but slapped Hewst across the face, striking her so hard that she toppled to the floor.

"Yes! Yes! It's just the two of us!" Alex cried out. "Please, don't hurt her!"

With her hands tied behind her back, Hewst had some difficulty getting up from the floor. She managed to get her feet underneath herself, and she began to rise up. But before she could stand, the interrogator ordered, "Stay down, woman."

She reluctantly complied by returning to her knees. "I wonder how tough you are without your firearm," Hewst countered brashly as she spat some blood on the floor.

"Who are you," the interrogator asked, "and what are you two doing here?"

"We're part of the research team," Alex answered. "I'm an astrobiologist, and she's a manuscript expert. We're stationed here."

"If you're part of the research team," the interrogator pressed, "where were the two of you for the past four days?"

Alex mulled to himself, We've been away for four days? He then responded to the paladin, "We walked from a cave just south of here—a cave that our team quarantined about a week ago."

The interrogator addressed his fellow paladin and ordered, "Contact the sanctuary; tell them we captured two reprobates. Tell them we'll be transmitting facial recognition data." As his fellow paladin placed a c-nex call to their enclave, the interrogator pulled out a pen-shaped scanner from his bandolier. "Look at me, woman," he ordered as he aimed his scanner at Hewst's face. Within seconds, the interrogator received the scanner's transmitted data through his c-nex. "I see your name is Veronica Catherine Hewst. The database says you're a professor at the Terrestrial Assembly Defense Force Academy." He then glanced at the name inscribed on her compression suit. "Why is your name written backwards? Don't you know how to spell your own name?" He did not wait for an answer but proceeded to scan Alex's face. After a protracted pause, the interrogator finally said, "Well, you don't seem to be in the database." He grew suspicious, and he began to doubt Alex's sincerity. He pointed to a body on the floor and said, "Our scans identify *that* reprobate as Dr. Earnan Cobisson. Wasn't *he* the station's astrobiologist?" Mockingly, the interrogator then asked, "So, Mr. Astrobiologist, who are you?"

Hewst abruptly answered for Alex, "His name is Dr. Francis Hewst." She knew too well what the New Jerusalem terrorist sect usually did to androids. These Christian extremists regarded them as an abomination from the hands of sinners—as the creation of an iniquitous humanity trying to usurp the divine sovereignty of God. Hewst knew that if these paladins should discover who or what Alex really was, they would surely destroy him. They would scrap his mechanical body as a show of their zealousness to the one true God who alone is the creator of life.

Noting that they purportedly shared the same surname, the interrogator asked her, "Woman, is this man your husband?"

"He's my brother," she lied for the meta-droid's protection.

With his c-nex, the interrogator accessed the database and cross-referenced the name with the profession. "I see here you're an astrobiologist at Inverness University of Arts and Sciences," he said to Alex. Before he could probe deeper in the database, the two paladins were suddenly interrupted.

"I surrender!" Kiiswood exclaimed as he emerged from the gangway. The chief slowly stepped into sickbay completely unarmed and with his hands placed submissively on his head. "I surrender!"

Startled, the two paladins immediately leveled their pistols on the compliant chief. "On the floor, now!" ordered the interrogator. "Lie face down with your hands behind your back, now!" The interrogator kept his weapon nervously aimed at Kiiswood's head as his fellow paladin removed the chief's c-nex and bound his hands with tubing.

After they had restrained Kiiswood, the interrogator turned his weapon on Hewst and Alex. "You God-forsaken liars, there was more than just the two of you." As though pronouncing judgment before execution, he quoted the book of Revelation, "'All liars shall have their part in the lake which burneth with fire and brimstone.'"

The interrogator pressed the muzzle of his rail-pistol firmly against the back of Alex's head. But just before he could pull the trigger, his fellow paladin received an urgent message through his c-nex. "Wait, sir!" he shouted. "The bishop wants us to bring them back to sanctuary. He's sending a traxle to pick them up."

Wanting so much to disobey the bishop's orders, the interrogator reluctantly pulled back his pistol. But, he kept his weapon at the ready, hoping that his prisoners would give him a reason to execute all three of them.

Chapter 22 – The New Jerusalem

Hellas Province, Mars

(Areographic Co-ordinates: S 35.436, E 94.259)

Saturday, 22 December 2429 CE

Time: 1638 Zulu

Hewst, Kiiswood, and Alex were currently the prisoners of the Hesperia enclave of New Jerusalem. The three of them had been taken captive by two paladins hiding out at Belshazzar Station. Having been carefully searched and relieved of their personal effects, they were resupplied with helmets and freshly charged EV packets. The three bound prisoners were then transferred to the custody of two other paladins (a driver and a gunner), who the enclave had dispatched to pick them up. Like sacks of laundry, they were callously tossed into the back of a parts-scavenged traxle. Once inside, their helmets and EV packets were removed and burlap hoods were pulled over their heads to obscure their vision. The three of them lay there on a floorboard that had been stripped of its rear passenger seats, wearing just the unitard element of their compression suits and the hoods that covered their heads. Without safety restraints, they were jostled and pitched about with every pit and boulder that the traxle's wheels drove over.

Since the twenty-third century, the conventional means of ground transportation on Mars has been the traxle (short for tri-axle). Originally, traxles were so-named because they were six-wheeled vehicles with three beam axles, specifically designed for driving on the Martian highways that crisscrossed the planet. Although the term was still in common use even in the twenty-fifth century, "traxle" had become a misnomer. While they still had six wheels, today's traxles were engineered for off-road excursions and no longer used beam axles or wheelsets. Instead, they were built with independent torque vectoring axles. Today's traxles were commercially manufactured with cleated titanium wheels, s-shape curved spokes, and rocker-bogie suspension systems.

Traxles were the preferred ground vehicle of the radical Christian terrorist group, New Jerusalem. These vehicles were much cheaper than military-grade assault tanks and could easily be modified with armored plating and dorsal gun mounts. And because every traxle was made with a carriage differential, its crude gun mounts would remain relatively steady, and its passenger/cargo compartment would journey comfortably, even over the roughest of Martian terrains. (Unfortunately, comfortable was hardly the ride for Hewst, Kiiswood, and Alex; their traxle's differential was broken.)

Hewst could see nothing for the opaque hood that covered her head. Yet she knew that she lay between Kiiswood and Alex, for they were being tossed into each other with every rebound of the traxle carriage. She also knew that the two paladins were close, for she could hear them talking, but apparently not to each other. They were clearly not speaking in a shared conversation, and they frequently spoke over each other.

"Hey, Chief," whispered Hewst. She spoke ever so softly, trying not to draw the attention of their captors. "Can you hear me?"

"I can hear you," Kiiswood whispered back. "Are you okay?"

"I'm okay," she replied in a whisper, even though the side of her face was sore from being struck earlier. "I *am* getting tired of being flung around on this floorboard."

"I'm fine, by the way," Alex interjected quietly, "just in case anyone was wondering."

Although she was pleased to hear of her artificial friend's welfare, she opted not to respond. Instead, she made a covert suggestion. "Listen, Chief," she surreptitiously proposed, "there are three of us and only two of them. Perhaps there's a way we can overtake them. I've been listening to them, and I think they're distracted with other matters."

In a slightly louder whisper, Alex balked, "Are you out of your mind? You *do* realize that they're armed, and we're not." Satirically, he added, "We're prisoners because of that simple disparity. Remember?"

"I'm trying to focus on our advantages," she replied, "and not on theirs."

"So you believe that distracted, yet armed paladins are our advantage?" asked Kiiswood. "I don't know whether you're being brave or foolish, Commander."

"Neither," Hewst replied with a smirk behind her hood. "I'm afraid of what awaits us at our destination."

"Well, ma'am, I agree with you," the chief whispered confidently. "They *are* distracted. They're both on their c-nexes, engrossed in their own respective conversations."

"You can see them?" she asked. "Aren't you still hooded?"

"These hoods block visible light," Kiiswood answered, "not infrared." He continued, "I could probably neutralize both of them single-handedly, but I'd rather lie back and let *them* do the driving."

Hewst immediately realized that the chief was not a mere victim of circumstances; he had a plan. "You intended for us to be captured," she observed. "I was wondering why you just surrendered without a fight."

"Wait, you *wanted* to get captured?" the meta-droid asked.

"I saw the automated logs in the control room," the chief explained. "There was a coup at the station; it left them unprepared to fend off a terrorist attack." Kiiswood paused, checking to see that the two paladins were still preoccupied. "If any of the station's personnel were taken prisoner, we may be their only hope of rescue."

"It's noble of you to want to rescue our captured team members," Alex commended, "if there are any. But you're taking a huge risk getting yourself captured. How do you know that they won't just kill us?"

"They might still," Kiiswood admitted, "but not yet. I intercepted one of their c-nex messages from their enclave, and I delayed its receipt until I could get to sickbay and surrender myself. It seems that their bishop is interested in meeting the commander."

"Meeting *me*?" puzzled Hewst. "Why?"

"I don't know," the chief answered. "But I'm confident that they won't kill us, at least not until after the meeting."

With a touch of sarcasm, Alex retorted, "As much as I've grown to trust your instincts, Chief, wouldn't it have been wiser to call Camp Lundgren and have *them* deploy a rescue party?"

"Camp Lundgren has gone silent," Kiiswood answered. "I don't know why. But even if they were receiving our hails, they wouldn't respond."

Hewst inquired, "Why not?"

Kiiswood looked again at the paladins talking on their c-nexes. He then elucidated, "I discovered that Aerospace Intelligence has disavowed the very existence of *Project Belshazzar*, by order of the Minister of Defense. It seems that the government is willing to sacrifice all of us just to keep their secret."

"How do you know this?" the meta-droid asked.

The chief replied, "I used Captain Petrenko's c-nex and accessed her command files."

"She's dead," Hewst inferred, "isn't she?"

"Aye, ma'am," he answered. "I found her body in the control room, as well as the bodies of Fuentes and Riddari."

Alex wondered, "A c-nex is formatted to each person's own neural network. How could you use the captain's?"

"Stratogens apparently have a way around that," Hewst answered. She then noticed that the two loquacious paladins had suddenly gone silent; they had ended their c-nex conversations and were now focused on their arrival. "Alex, don't let them know you're an android," she whispered.

The traxle perceptibly began to decelerate as it pulled into a Terran-normal pressurized and gravitized chamber. Soon, it came to a complete stop and powered down inside an underground parking bay. Within seconds, the traxle's side-hatch was opened, and the still-hooded captives were brusquely dragged out of the vehicle by at least seven awaiting paladins. Their hands still bound behind their backs with cannula tubing, the three of them were curtly hustled through a maze of winding stairwells and hallways. Several minutes later, they were ushered into a room and were forcibly prodded down into three side-by-side chairs. The paladins standing directly behind the chairs unceremoniously yanked the burlap hoods from their prisoners' heads.

Suddenly, Hewst, Kiiswood, and Alex found themselves face to face with a weathered and grizzled old man, whose rugged, surly form seemed out of place sitting there in a plush leather chair. He sat behind a beautiful neo-deco desk, the most conspicuous piece of furniture in a rather spacious office. In front of him, on the desktop, lay Alex's carabiner and wedding bands, Hewst's necklace, and their three c-nexes. Behind him was a large beveled window whose view of a subterranean township was now obstructed by the militant flag of New Jerusalem—a white flag prominently sporting a bright red Jerusalem cross. Clutched in the old man's hands was a ragged and worn book; written on its tatty cover were the inverted words "Holy Bible." Its once-gold-trimmed pages had long since lost their luster. Standing around the old man were nearly a dozen well-armed (although not uniformly armed) paladins. Some had rail-rifles, either cradled in their arms or slung over their shoulders. Some had pistols, either brandished in hand or shoddily holstered. And some had only improvised machetes or blades tucked in their bandoliers. All of them were wearing unkempt civvies; and no two were dressed alike or uniformed in any way. Every one of them, however, did bear the same black and red armband, the notorious emblem of the Hesperia enclave.

Ambling about in the midst of this mob of militants were two vandalized androids that were handing out coffee and prepackaged field rations from a service cart. These androids were defaced of much of their artificial dermal integument. They may have once resembled human beings, but now they were little more than automatous metal skeletons. A few scraps of threadbare clothing were all that covered their exposed mechanical subframes. Having worked closely with the engineers of the Whitaker Institute, Alex recognized these disfigured androids as decades-earlier models—archaic forerunners of his own meta-droid neural network.

As the paladins stood around, consuming the spoils of their conquest, Kiiswood did not hesitate to impress himself upon this roomful of Christian terrorists. "I see you've made yourself right at home in the mayor's office," the chief said.

"You've been here before?" asked the old man.

"Not at all," Kiiswood answered. "But it's obvious that this is—or was—a town hall office, and the only township within a short traxle drive from the station is Sterling Point."

"I'm genuinely impressed," the old man complimented. "Perhaps I should extend my thanks to your government for evacuating Sterling Point for us. By leaving these androids as the town's only custodians, the Terrestrial Assembly made it easy for us to take it over." He carefully set his bible on the desk and began to unwrap a processed bar of seasoned salmon. "And perhaps I should also thank your government for such tasty field rations. The Salmon Clavius is my favorite." Taking a bite of the bar, he then spoke with a mouthful of salmon. "I'd offer the three of you something to eat, but because your hands are tied, it would be pointless." As an afterthought, he said, "Let me introduce myself."

"You're Joshua Bleum," the chief interjected, "the sectarian bishop who commands the Hesperia enclave of New Jerusalem."

"You're well-informed," Bleum acknowledged.

"I know my terrorists," the chief replied.

"Oh, you cut me deeply," the bishop said, feigning offense. "But, in point of fact, we're not terrorists at all; we're crusaders—Christian soldiers for the kingdom of God." Picking up his bible, Bleum stood from his seat and stepped from around the desk. "As one soldier to another, Chief Kiiswood—if that backwards writing on your suit is indeed your name and rank—you know that we're only a terror to those who have reason to fear the wrath of Christ. As the New Jerusalem, we will descend from the sky upon the Earth and reclaim it for the Lord from the hands of the wicked." Bleum stood directly in front of the chief and continued, "We ran facial recognition scans on you—on all three of you. And I can say most assuredly, you and your cohorts are *not* with the Interplanetary Health Agency." Leaning in toward Kiiswood's face, the bishop said, "On you, the program says 'Axial Symmetry Error.' Maybe there's something wrong with our equipment. I've never seen that particular error notice before; I don't even know what it means. But it *does* say that there's an eighty-seven percent probability that you are Chief Petty Officer Níyol Kiiswood, special warfare operator. It also says that you were assigned to a

273

sorteer team during the war nine years ago. There's no other data on you since then." He then asked, "Why nothing more recent?"

With an almost imperceptible grin, Kiiswood answered, "They don't let me out much."

"I guess I should be grateful for that," the bishop commented. "You sorteers killed a lot of my fellow paladins during the war."

Kiiswood's grin became more evident. "As one soldier to another . . ." he said.

Bleum then stepped in front of Alex and looked squarely into the meta-droid's eyes. Yet, even upon such close examination, the bishop did not realize that he was staring at an artificial face. "On you, there's no data at all. Why is that?"

Coyly, Alex answered, "As you said yourself, there must be something wrong with your equipment."

Bleum grew suspicious with Alex's response. "Why is there no name on your compression suit, just these backwards numbers and letters?" he asked.

"I'm not military; I'm a civilian scientist," Alex answered truthfully. "This is just the suit they gave me." Then, for his own sake, he maintained the lie that Hewst had initiated back at Belshazzar Station. "I'm Dr. Francis Hewst, astrobiologist."

"Yes," Bleum acknowledged. "According to some old database records, you're a professor at Inverness University of Arts and Sciences. But that seems to be the last entry in the database, and that was nine years ago."

Before the bishop could probe any further into Alex's history, Hewst distracted him by interjecting herself into the interrogation. "That's because nine years ago, New Jerusalem wiped out the university and all of Nova Scotia with it. My brother was fortunate that he was visiting Polis Aristarchus when the attack happened."

The distraction seemed to work—for the moment. Bleum stepped away from Alex and tried to assume an intimidating stance in front of Hewst. "And on you, woman," he said, "the facial recognition program also says 'Axial Symmetry Error.' But it *does* say that you're likely Veronica Catherine Hewst, professor of religious studies at the Terrestrial Assembly Defense Force Academy." Looking at the inverted rank insignia on her compression suit, he derisively remarked, "So you're both a professor *and* a commander."

"I'm a teacher," she contended. "The rank is incidental."

"Oh no," Bleum protested. "There's nothing incidental about being an anathema before Christ. It doesn't matter whether you're a professor or a commander; both are holy abominations to the will of God. 'I suffer not a woman to teach, nor to usurp authority over the man, but to be in silence.'"

"First Timothy," Hewst stated, "chapter two, the twelfth verse."

"I'm amazed," Bleum confessed. "A woman who knows the Word of God. Have you been washed in the blood of the Lamb?" he asked.

"I'm a Christian, if that's what you're asking," Hewst replied. With a vaguely blithe attitude, she added, "But I really don't use hematology theology to describe my faith."

"Do you have a husband, woman?" the bishop asked. "Do you have a man who speaks to God on your behalf?"

"If and when I so choose, I'm quite capable of speaking to God on my own behalf," she answered indignantly. "It says in the New Testament that there is no male or female in Christ."

"Women cannot speak to God," Bleum said with clear condescension in his voice. "Women are the image and reflection of men. Women must consult their husbands about spiritual matters, for men are the image and reflection of God."

Hewst smiled and unequivocally responded, "You're conflating and distorting verses from First Corinthians."

The bishop tightened his grip on his bible so firmly that his fingernails were digging into its cover. He raised his bible in the air and raised his voice in pomposity, "Don't you presume to teach *us* the holy scriptures, woman!" At the elevation of both his bible and his voice, all of the paladins in the room blessed themselves with the sign of the cross. "Even the devil can quote scripture!" he exclaimed.

Hewst tried to ignore his quip about the devil. "The apostle Paul says that teaching is a spiritual gift," she said. "Now, I ask you, why would God give women a gift and then forbid them to use it?"

"Women who teach aren't gifted by God," Bleum avowed, "they're inspired by the devil. Eve was the first to forsake the divine law because Adam was too strong to be tempted. Women have been agents of Satan ever since."

Inexorably, Hewst realized that reasoning and debating with the bishop were pointless. "If you believe that I'm so demonic," she asked, "why are we having this conversation? Why not just execute me outright?"

"I might yet," Bleum replied. "But this tribunal hasn't reached a verdict." He took a few steps back and addressed all three of his prisoners at once. "When your engineers first showed up, digging holes in the ground, we really thought you guys were IPHA, looking for some Martian germs that caused the pandemic we've all been hearing about. But when we found out that a Defense Force interrogator was on her way from Venus to work with IPHA, we quickly realized that you guys weren't really a humanitarian organization out here on the plains of Hellas. So we sent out Amos Sharl and his wife on a sacred mission in Tyrrhenus to pass summary judgment on your team." Bleum then looked straight at Hewst and said, "But when our holy martyrs failed, you, woman, risked your own life to protect the Sharl child. For that act of charity, I decided that you at least deserved a hearing before judgment."

"How do you know about me?" she asked. "How did you know that I came here from Venus?"

Flatly, Bleum replied, "We have our sources."

"The browless man works for you," Kiiswood supposed. "You're the one who sent him to kill Silas Dorch."

"Yes, I did. Dorch was an apostate, and he earned his fate," the bishop piously admitted. "But his apostasy is encouraging news, in a way. It's a divine portent that the end of days is nigh, that Christ will soon return, that the wicked will be vanquished, and his saints will inherit the earth. As scripture says, 'In the latter times some shall depart from the faith, giving heed to seducing spirits, and doctrines of devils.'"

"You seem to have a predilection for quoting First Timothy," Hewst observed.

"It's not my fault that the Word of God happens to be relevant," Bleum replied.

The chief said to Hewst, "The browless assassin evidently saw you in Dorch's cellblock, Commander. He must have reported that information to this enclave. That's how the bishop knows about you."

"It's also how I know about you too, Chief," Bleum confided. "The way you were able to chase him down—I know that you're more than just a sorteer. The Terrestrial Assembly won't admit that perversions of nature like you exist, but I know that *you*, Chief, are a stratogen."

"We had always presumed that three stratogens were killed in action nine years ago," the chief acknowledged. "But at least one of them apparently turned traitor and became your enclave's personal assassin. And that's why we couldn't identify him; his ID records didn't appear in the regular databases because he was listed as killed in action." In a light-hearted, yet mocking manner, Kiiswood asked, "So how is my fellow perversion? He obviously survived his high-altitude dive through the Venusian atmosphere. If he has a moment, I'd very much like to say hello."

"I'm sure he'd like to say hello to you as well," replied Bleum. "But he's currently on another mission."

"I'm assuming you've sent him out to lead other terrorist cells," Hewst surmised. "You've sent out your assassin to spread the pandemic with your biological weapons and to murder whomever you deem unholy."

"That's all Terrestrial Assembly propaganda! We're holy warriors, not murderers!" the bishop protested. "The enemies of Christ are sinners, and the wages of sin is death. We just pay them what they've earned." He elaborated, "The Assembly and the Confederation are simply trying to veil their own iniquities by blaming New Jerusalem. And I suspect that the Alliance is in on it too. But they're all like the great whore of Babylon, trying to make us drink the wine of the wrath of her fornication." Then Bleum began to pontificate like an apocalyptic preacher, weaving bits of disjointed verses into his oration. "And as much as New Jerusalem might want to take the glory for the pandemic that's

277

unleashed upon the worlds, the glory belongs to God. In his righteousness, He has judged the worlds. For the heavens have opened up, and the Almighty has sent forth His angels to pour out the last plagues full of the wrath of God. But those of us who have gotten the victory over the beast, we sing the song of the Lamb, saying: 'Great and marvelous are Thy works, Lord God Almighty; just and true are Thy ways, Thou King of saints.'"

All throughout the bishop's sermonizing, his fellow paladins accentuated his message with crescendos of "Amen!"

Bleum noted the subdued expressions on the faces of his three captives. "Your enthusiasm for the Word of God is noticeably lacking," the bishop observed. Addressing Kiiswood, he asked, "Are you an enemy of Christ, or is your name written in the Lamb's book of life?"

"Oh, Jesus and I are good friends. We go a long way back," the chief replied humorously, yet honestly. "I'm sure my name is on his nice list."

Bleum then turned toward Alex and asked, "And you, Mr. Hewst? Have you been born again?"

Alex did indeed feel as though he had been born again. As he pondered the bishop's question, he realized that he had been startlingly reborn when he awoke in the Whitaker Institute. He had been wondrously reborn in his encounter with the Aeon. And he had been painfully reborn with the death of Earnan Cobisson. "Yes," Alex answered emphatically. "I have definitely been born again." He nodded his head toward his two friends and continued to answer the bishop's question. "But if you're asking whether I believe in God—I'm much more inclined to believe in *their* God than in yours."

"Very well," said Bleum. "I think you've told us what we need to know. This tribunal will begin its solemn deliberation and will pray for holy discernment. We'll summon you when we've reached our verdict." The bishop then directed several of the paladins in the room to pull Hewst, Kiiswood, and Alex from their seats and onto their feet. "Take them to the sublevel holding cell," he ordered. As the paladins were steering the three prisoners from the room, Bleum gestured toward Kiiswood and warned, "Keep your weapons trained on that one; he's a guileful sort. You can remove their bonds once they're in holding." He then instructed one of the accompanying paladins to take three prepackaged meals for the prisoners. "And just so they may know the mercy of Christ," the bishop said, "give them these rations."

Although it pained her to speak subserviently to a terrorist, Hewst knew that she was at the mercy of her captor for his favor. "Bishop Bleum, may we also have our personal items?" she meekly pleaded. "Please?"

Bleum did not immediately reply. Instead, he pretended to ponder Hewst's request simply to overdramatize his power, including the power to bestow even the smallest of mercies. "Very well," the bishop finally acquiesced. He picked up the items from his desk and approached his captives. Intruding well into Hewst's personal space, he reached over her and leisurely slipped the necklace over her head and around her neck. Bleum then turned to Alex and said, "If you want me to return your rings, Mr. Hewst, you'll have to ask me nicely, like your sister just did."

Alex did not immediately reply. He too pondered, but not as a pretense. In all that he had been through during the past five weeks, he truly felt as though he were born anew. He was not Earnan Cobisson, and he was not a mere machine. Alex was his own person, his own soul. Despite being a captive of New Jerusalem, despite having his hands bound behind his back, he felt strangely liberated from his past. He suddenly had no desire to be attached to Cobisson's wedding bands. To possess them seemed only to bind him to a history that no longer defined him. "You can keep the rings," Alex said. "I don't think I'll need them anymore."

Bleum said nothing. He slipped the carabiner and its rings into his pocket and directed the paladins to usher the prisoners to the holding cell.

After weaving through another confusing maze of stairwells and hallways, Hewst, Kiiswood, and Alex were finally led to the sublevel of an adjacent building—a building that was once the constable's station. There, the three of them were brutally shoved into a large, austere holding cell.

The cell was filthy, poorly lit, and not furnished for comfort or ease. On its far wall was a tiny steel sink. Beside it, was a petite steel toilet, which lacked the amenities of a door or partitions for privacy. (There was at least a roll of paper on the floor beside it.) Also along the far wall were several narrow benches that ostensibly doubled as sleeping racks; they were really nothing more than low-hanging, wall-mounted shelves. On one of the benches lay a man who was evidently suffering from serious physical trauma. And standing over him was a woman who was trying in vain to tend to his injuries and to comfort him.

Just as the accompanying paladins were shutting the cell door, they tossed the three packages of field rations on the cell floor at the prisoners' feet. Hewst shouted to the paladins as they were locking the door, "Hey, aren't you supposed to remove our bonds?"

One of the paladins shouted with insidious amusement, "Get your friends to do it!"

Kiiswood watched as the paladins walked out of sight. He then contorted his shoulders and arms behind his back. Hewst and Alex would not have otherwise believed that such bodily distortions were humanly possible were they not witnessing it for themselves. Kiiswood pulled his elbows together, straightened his forearms, rolled the sides of one hand nearly together, while elongating his thumb and fingers. Within seconds, the chief had made his hand narrower than his wrist, and he slipped free of the cannula tubing that was binding him.

"I'm impressed, Chief," Alex remarked as Kiiswood began to untie the meta-droid's fettered wrists. "But I wish I could unsee your contortions; they were ghastly to watch."

The chief smirked. "I'm sure that's something that your android body can't do."

Satirically, Alex replied, "I hope you're right." In short order, his hands were freed from their bonds.

"That's a handy skill, Chief," said Hewst as she too turned to have Kiiswood untie her bonds. "You'll have to teach me that trick sometime."

"Are you planning to be tied up by terrorists more often, Commander?" the chief joked as he quickly removed the tubing from her wrists.

"Catherine?" uttered a familiar voice from the far end of the holding cell. "Is that you?"

Hewst quickly recognized the owner of that familiar voice—Dr. Střelec, the research team's mathematician. "Tereza?" replied Hewst, with resolute joy in her own voice.

"Oh my God!" exclaimed Střelec. "We thought the three of you were dead when the cavern vanished!" She literally ran to Hewst from across the cell and hugged her tightly, as though clinging to her for dear life. After an interminably long embrace, Střelec stepped back to look Hewst in the face. "What happened to you?" she asked.

Hewst reached up and touched her bruised cheek. "One of the paladins struck me," she answered. "I'm okay."

"No, you look different," the mathematician witnessed. "All three of you look like yourselves, but different." Then, with an astonished countenance, Střelec noticed their inverted compression suits. "Hold out your right hands," she directed, "all of you." Hewst, Kiiswood, and Alex put forward their right hands—or, what was right for them. But, for Střelec, they had put forward their left hands. With a certain scientific giddiness in her voice, she asked, "You passed through a four-dimensional manifold, didn't you? You were drawn into a higher spatial dimension by some kind of hyperbeings. But all three of you were axially turned around when they returned you to three-dimensional space." Střelec noted their confused looks and realized that she needed to use a more relatable example. "It's like what happens if we peel a scalene triangle from its two-dimensional page. If we flip it while it's in our three-dimensional space and then stick it back on the page, it's still a scalene triangle. But now it's inverted from its original orientation."

"So," pondered Alex, "how do we fix it? How do we revert back to the way we were?"

Střelec answered woefully, "You can't. It's geometrically impossible in three-dimensional space." She added, "You may have to get used to reading backwards."

Hewst took Střelec by the hand and asked sympathetically, "How did you end up here?"

With a tremble in her voice, Střelec answered, "After the cavern vanished—with you three in it—Captain Petrenko sequestered everyone and threatened to kill the entire team just to conceal our work as a government secret. We learned that she had even injected every person in the station with nanites to interrupt our autonomic functions—to kill us instantly if she needed to. She ordered Dr. Ammon to infect all of us, even himself, when we first reported aboard. Well, not you, Alex." Her tremble became more apparent. "When her sorteers killed Dr. Cobisson, several Defense Force personnel mutinied. Lieutenant Jalloh and a few others tried to escape in an areopter, and that's when all hell broke loose. Petty Officer Sudha tried to rescue us, but the captain activated the nanites in her body and killed her. She did the same to Jalloh, crashing the areopter. In the middle of all that internal chaos, the station was attacked by terrorists. They got inside the station and started killing people indiscriminately. The sorteers fought back, but they were outnumbered." She paused to take a slow, deep breath and then continued. "Dr. Ammon and I survived by hiding for almost two days in the water reclamation module. When the terrorists finally found us, they put us aboard the cargo areopter and flew us here."

"Is that Dr. Ammon?" asked Hewst as she gestured toward the man lying on the bench.

"No, that's Mas'ud Al-Jabiri," Střelec replied. "Thankfully, he's sleeping for the moment, but he's in really bad shape." Kiiswood promptly tended to Al-Jabiri as Střelec continued her story. "The terrorists scavenged the areopter wreckage, and they found him as its single survivor. He desperately needs medical attention, but our captors are refusing to help him because he's a Muslim."

Alex pondered, "I thought that New Jerusalem made it their practice to summarily execute persons of non-Christian faiths?"

"They usually do," answered Hewst. "But some enclaves have been known to let their wounded prisoners suffer as they slowly die from their injuries."

"How is that Christ-like?" the meta-droid asked.

With sure and passionate indignation toward her captors, Hewst responded, "It's not!"

Returning from Al-Jabiri's improvised bedside, Kiiswood assessed, "His abdomen is swollen and purple; he's slowly bleeding internally. It's my guess that he suffered blunt force trauma of his liver or spleen, but I'm not a physician. I can't do anything else for him, except try to make him comfortable." The chief looked around the holding cell and asked, "Where's Dr. Ammon?"

Střelec's eyes started tearing. "He's dead," she barely answered. "Our captors learned about the nanites that Dr. Ammon put inside all of us. So yesterday, they made him turn over the nanite access codes." A tear quickly ran down the side of her face. "They confirmed his information by testing the access codes on him."

While gently squeezing Střelec's hand, Hewst commented, "So Bishop Bleum can execute any of us at the mere press of a button."

"How's that much different than the mere pull of a trigger?" the chief rhetorically posed.

Again, Střelec embraced Hewst and confided, "Catherine, I'm scared."

Chapter 23 – The Heavenly Court

Sterling Point, Hellas Province, Mars

(Areographic Co-ordinates: S 35.436, E 94.259)

Sunday, 23 December 2429 CE

Time: 0930 Zulu

During the dark hours of early morning, Petty Officer Mas'ud Al-Jabiri succumbed to his internal injuries. Quietly, peacefully, he passed away, breathing his last breath while blessedly unconscious. His four cellmates covered his still body with the lesser filthy of two blankets in the holding cell. Hewst could not remember the appropriate words for an Islamic funeral, so she simply uttered the takbir instead.

And now, a few hours later, the shadow of death also loomed over Hewst, Kiiswood, Alex, and Střelec. The four of them had been restrained with magnetically bound handcuffs, removed from the holding cell, and escorted to Sterling Point's community natatorium.

The four well-armed paladins who escorted the prisoners were strangely masked: one mask was a featureless face-covering, one roughly resembled an ox, one resembled a lion, and one resembled an eagle. Upon arriving at the natatorium, the masked paladins seated their prisoners in four rigid armchairs that were bolted to the floor at one end of a large swimming pool. Using his c-nex, the paladin behind the featureless mask redirected the magnetic force such that the prisoners' handcuffs suddenly uncoupled and bound them separately to the armrests of their chairs. The prisoners of the New Jerusalem sect were now inexorably confined to their seats.

Hewst, Kiiswood, Alex, and Střelec sat just a few meters in front of a 10-by-25 meter swimming pool. Its water was calm and unrippled, its surface as smooth as glass. At the far end of the pool was a large, opulent chair whose ornate design was obviously intended to resemble a throne. Several of the overhead lights in the natatorium were purposefully angled to highlight the far-end chair in ostensibly throne-like majesty. Seven evenly spaced halogen lanterns decoratively lined the far edge of the pool just in front of the throne. Along the left and right sides of the pool were twenty-four smaller chairs—twelve on either side. And standing like spectators around the four walls of the natatorium were well over a hundred variously armed paladins.

Staring out at the bizarre scene before her, Střelec asked, "Why have these fanatics brought us to a swimming pool?"

Kiiswood speculated, "Perhaps it's trial by ordeal."

"Possibly, but I doubt it," Hewst assessed.

Alex was unfamiliar with the chief's historical reference, so he asked, "What's trial by ordeal?"

"It's an ancient superstitious practice," answered Hewst. "If the guilt or innocence of the accused couldn't be determined by human means, then medieval jurors would appeal to God as judge. Sometimes the accused were thrown in the river. If they sank, they were deemed innocent; if they floated, then God declared them guilty." She then drew the obvious inference, "It's a lose-lose proposition."

Střelec looked at her fellow captives and, with apprehension in her voice, remarked, "It seems ironic that Alex could be the only one among us found innocent; his android body could sink and still function."

"These paladins think Alex is human," Hewst confided in a soft tone. "Please don't tell them otherwise."

"Well, Commander," asked Kiiswood, "if they don't intend to drown us in the pool, why do you think they brought us here?"

"They don't want the water disturbed," she answered. "They want it to be calm and glassy. They're replicating the heavenly court in the book of Revelation." She sarcastically added, "They're playing Bible."

Suddenly, a procession of twenty-five paladins dressed in flowing white robes entered the natatorium from an adjacent locker room. Leading the procession was Bishop Joshua Bleum, who carried a regal-looking shepherd's crook in one hand and his tattered, leather-bound Bible in the other. With pageantry and flamboyance, Bleum took a seat in the throne at the far end while the other twenty-four paladins filed along the sides of the pool, taking a stand before their respective chairs.

In unison, the four masked paladins exclaimed, "Holy! Holy! Holy! Sovereign Bishop of Hesperia and Hellas, who was, and is, and is to come!"

After the masked paladins had finished shouting their praises, the twenty-four who stood before the chairs dropped to their knees and fell prostrate. In one accord, they extolled their bishop, saying, "Thou art worthy, O Bishop, to receive glory and honor and power!" Bleum then pounded the base of his crook three times on the floor, whereupon the adulating paladins arose from their prostrations and took their seats.

The bishop slowly stood from his throne and addressed his prisoners with a memorized passage from the Christian scriptures. "'All shall know that I am he which searcheth the minds and hearts!'" he declared. "'I will give unto every one of you according to your works!'"

Hewst shouted out at the sanctimonious bishop. "Is this why you've brought us before this biblical charade?" she indignantly asked. "You're sentencing us as though you speak for God Himself?"

Bleum replied to his four captives, not with a simple yes or no, but with what seemed like incoherent blather. He replied with another memorized quote from scripture, as though it endowed him with the righteous will of God. "'The law is not made for a righteous man,'" the bishop proclaimed, "'but for the lawless and disobedient, for the ungodly and for sinners, for unholy and profane, for murderers of fathers and murderers of mothers, for manslayers, for whoremongers, for them that defile themselves with mankind, for men-stealers, for liars, for perjured persons, and if there be any other thing that is contrary to sound doctrine.'"

"You know how to quote the Word of God," Hewst challenged, "but you don't comprehend its life. You see it as judgment, as a conviction of your enemies. But its true power is self-conviction—the power to strip away your own pretentious merits, so all that's left to define you is unmerited grace. You read it, but you don't embody it. You recite it, but you don't give it flesh. You wield the Word of God as though it were a weapon, but you don't know how to live it as the incarnate Word."

"You're a woman," Bleum sniped. "Your words mean nothing before the throne of Christ."

"You should listen to her," Kiiswood proclaimed. "Her words would be no truer if uttered by men or by angels."

"We're obviously wasting our breath trying to reason with you, Bishop Bleum," Hewst remarked. "The piercing edge of theological discourse is being blunted by the thick wall of your zealous dogmatism."

Bleum pretended not to hear their protestations; rather, he proceeded to address each prisoner in turn and to pronounce their sentence. "Of the Střelec woman," he said, "I have this against thee: thou hast given thyself over to fornication, and hast gone after strange flesh. Henceforth, thou must suffer the vengeance of eternal fire in like manner even as Sodom and Gomorrah."

His words were archaic and unfamiliar, yet Střelec quickly inferred that the bishop was expressing his personal indignation with her lifestyle. She was incensed, yet said nothing.

"Of the Hewst woman," he resumed, "I have this against thee: thou art the woman Jezebel, which calleth herself a prophetess, to teach and to seduce my servants to commit fornication. Henceforth, He Who ruleth thee with a rod of iron, as the vessels of a potter shalt thou be broken to shivers."

Like Střelec, Hewst said nothing. To protest at this juncture seemed pointless.

The bishop continued with his sentencing. "Francis Hewst, I have this against thee: thou art wretched, and miserable, and poor, and blind, and naked and knowest it not. Henceforth, because thou art lukewarm, and neither cold nor hot, I will spew thee out of my mouth."

Alex greeted the bishop's statement with incredulity. "If there really is a Christ in heaven," he said, "then you and every one of your terrorist friends will have to stand before Him and answer for all this hatred and evil that you do in His name."

Convinced of his own righteousness before God, Bleum snickered at Alex's judgment. The bishop then offered his final pronouncement. "Níyol Kiiswood," he said, "I have this against thee: thou sufferest that woman Jezebel.

Thou art the devil's home; thou art where Satan dwelleth. Henceforth, I will remove thy lampstand out of its place."

With brazenly biting sarcasm, Kiiswood replied, "Oh no, the prince of darkness doesn't live within me. But, he does occasionally stop by—just to chat. He says he's your father," the chief announced, "and that he misses your mother."

Kiiswood saw the look of fury on Bleum's face, just before the eagle-masked paladin clouted the chief sharply in the back of the head with the butt of a rail-rifle. As the chief was struck, Hewst recoiled vicariously in her seat, at least as much as her restraints permitted.

"Are you okay, Chief?" asked Hewst.

Ignoring the pain, Kiiswood lifted up his head and answered candidly, "I've had worse."

Bishop Bleum straightened up from his usual hunched posture, pushed out his chest, and declared, "Your sentence is hereby witnessed by the four living creatures and by the twenty-four elders that surroundeth the throne and the sea of glass like unto crystal. The great day of God's wrath is come. None may hide his face from Him that sitteth on the throne, and from the wrath of the Lamb." He then pounded the base of his crook three times on the floor. At that signal, a large holographic projection of a nondescript traxle parking bay suddenly appeared to hover over the still water of the swimming pool. At that same moment, the four masked paladins (that is, the so-called living creatures) released their prisoners from their armrest restraints, pulled them up from their seats, and re-engaged the bonds of their magnetic handcuffs. "Take them to the horsemen," ordered Bleum.

Piously obedient to their bishop, the masked paladins whisked away the prisoners. Minutes later, they arrived at the eastside parking bay—the same parking bay through which Hewst, Kiiswood, and Alex had initially entered the township of Sterling Point. There, parked at one end of the bay in their respective charging ports were eleven crudely battle-modified traxles and two commandeered armored assault vehicles. At the other end of the bay were the so-called horsemen: four (horseless) paladins outfitted in bulky, mismatched, and ominously labeled compression suits. Each wore a compression suit that was a different color and had a different label. The one in white was labeled "Conquest"; red, "War"; black, "Famine"; and pale green, "Death." With rail-rifles strapped over their shoulders, these four stood like sentries at an enormous, windowed hatch that led into the bay's airlock chamber. This spacious airlock served essentially as a vehicle access tube, allowing entry to and exit from the Martian roadways on the surface above. But today it would serve as an execution chamber.

Upon arriving at the airlock hatch, the masked paladins unceremoniously delivered their prisoners to the charge of the four horsemen. Staring grimly into the eyes of the condemned, the horseman called Conquest sadistically asked, "I see the four of you are dressed for the occasion. Who wants to go first?"

Initially, Hewst, Kiiswood, Alex, and Střelec, stood in grave, phobic silence. They felt subdued by the imminent and inescapable demise that seized their souls. Finally, with a pronounced tremor in her voice, Střelec exclaimed, "You can't put us in there! We're not wearing helmets!"

"But that's the point, isn't it?" Kiiswood queried rhetorically. "It's supposed to be death by ebullism, isn't it?"

Conquest did not know what ebullism meant, so he did not answer. Rather, he continued to press for a volunteer. "The one who goes first won't have to watch your friends suffer," he proposed.

"Let Francis go first," Kiiswood quickly suggested. His proposal drew expressions of astonishment from his three team members. They knew that Alex would not be harmed by the dangers of the airlock, nor by the thin, frigid Martian atmosphere just beyond the outer hatch of the chamber. Yet Kiiswood greeted their astonishment with an ever so subtle wink.

Just then, Hewst realized that the chief had a plan, but she knew not what. If ever there was a time to risk an escape, she thought, now was the time. So, trusting her friend, she decided to play along. "Yes, Francis," she said to Alex. "I know that you wouldn't want your life's last memory to be the sight of your sister suffocating in an airlock."

Alex had no idea what the chief had in mind, but he, too, trusted his friends. He looked to Hewst, then to Kiiswood and asked, "What should I do?"

The chief answered with a grin. "Just be yourself."

Alex knew that the airlock itself posed no direct threat to him. But he also knew that his ruse would be exposed and that his identity as a meta-droid would be revealed, resulting in these terrorists summarily demolishing him and scavenging him for parts. Stepping into that airlock would be an inexorable risk to his very being. Yet, in an act that could only be described as a leap of faith, Alex volunteered to be the first.

Conquest promptly opened the enormous hatch with his c-nex while his fellow horsemen (War, Famine, and Death) grabbed Alex by his arms and escorted him into the airlock chamber. Once they were inside the chamber, Conquest sealed the hatch. He fastidiously turned toward a small ceiling-mounted hologram camera, bowed for the audience watching in the natatorium, and recited a passage from the book of Revelation. "'Fear God, and give glory to him!'" he shouted, "'for the hour of his judgment is come!'" After his recitation, he peered through the large window in the hatch to confirm that his fellow horsemen inside had indeed secured their helmets. Conquest then pressed the activation key on the adjacent control panel. Immediately, the relief ports in the airlock chamber opened, and the rumbling sound of sudden decompression echoed throughout the parking bay.

Hewst, Kiiswood, and Střelec watched intently through the window of the hatch, as did Conquest and the masked paladins. But they quickly lost sight of everyone inside the airlock as soon as the depressurization was initiated. A heavy fog filled the chamber as its temperature and relative humidity rapidly changed, and a thin veneer of frost formed over the window and other surfaces inside the airlock.

Seconds later, as the fog cleared and the frost sublimated away, War, Famine, and Death expected to see their asphyxiated and cyanotic victim lying unconscious on the floor. Instead, they were astounded by what they witnessed—Alex was still standing, he was very conscious, and he appeared to be quite impervious to the virtual vacuum of the airlock.

Unwilling to believe what he was seeing, Famine reached up to his visor and, with his glove, tried to wipe away any residual frost obstructing his view. "He's still alive!" he yelled in utter panic.

Shocked and bewildered, every paladin in the parking bay fixed their attention on Alex. As they were now keenly focused upon the spectacle on the other side of the hatch, they were, for all intents and purposes, distracted from what was happening with the other prisoners, which Kiiswood surreptitiously exploited. Having already contorted one hand free of his magnetic restraints, the chief shoved Hewst and Strelec to the floor and bolted for Conquest. With inconceivable speed, agility, and strength, Kiiswood twisted Conquest's arm behind his back in such an aberrant position that the horseman was forced to hold himself upright just to avoid excruciating pain. Employing Conquest's incapacitated body as a human shield, the chief took control of the horseman's rail-rifle, wielding it while it was still slung over the terrorist's shoulder.

The four masked paladins were caught off guard by Kiiswood's offensive. While three of them were still trying to unsling their weapons, only one—the ox-masked paladin—had managed to train his rifle toward Kiiswood. But, in that instant, the chief preemptively shot a single round squarely between the eyes of the ox-mask, killing its wearer before he could fire off a round of his own. And as the dead paladin was falling to the floor, Kiiswood shouted out to the other three, "On the ground! Face down! Now!" The masked paladins readily complied and immediately lay down on the bay floor. "If you even hint at raising a muzzle," the chief added, "I'll likely kill you as not." He then released his debilitating grip on Conquest and forced him to the floor, immediately relieving the horseman of his rifle and c-nex.

Meanwhile, as Kiiswood was launching a one-man assault on the paladins in the parking bay, Alex stood inside the airlock chamber, wondering what he should do next. He was surrounded by three astonished horsemen who stood startled in disbelief that their victim was still very much alive. These religious extremists were so indoctrinated to see demons and evil spirits everywhere that they quickly attributed Alex's survival to malevolent forces.

In wide-eyed terror, the horseman Death cried, "He's possessed by the devil!"

So frightened that his own soul might be seized by demons, the horseman Famine raised his rifle and rashly, impetuously shot Alex.

The meta-droid lurched sharply backward as his chest absorbed the full impact of the bullet. He instinctively stepped back to maintain his balance. With jaw-dropped surprise, he looked down at the bullet hole in his compression suit. He saw no blood pouring from his wound; he felt no pain. But strangely, he *could* feel the terrorist's bullet still lodged between his titanium sternum and his synthetic skin. Once he realized that he was not dying, his mortal fear turned to resolute fury. Alex screamed in rage and, with his magnetically cuffed hands, grabbed Famine's rifle by its barrel. He ripped the weapon from the horseman's arms and began to swing it at him like a club. Dodging the meta-droid's awkward and furious swings, Famine lost his balance and fell to the floor. Alex then tossed the rifle aside, pounced on the terrorist, and began frantically whaling away.

Convinced that Satan himself had just unleashed an unholy wrath upon them, the other two horsemen in the airlock panicked. Death dropped his rifle and ran for the hatch to the parking bay. Pounding violently, desperately on the hatch's window, he shouted, "The Antichrist is come! Let me out of here!"

War, on the other hand, did not run for the hatch. Instead, he stood momentarily frozen in place, seized by fear of Alex's unbridled indignation and inhuman abilities. Then, driven by desperation to help his fellow horseman who was being pummeled mercilessly, War haphazardly pointed his rifle toward the meta-droid and aimlessly fired.

Alex's head recoiled abruptly as the bullet struck the side of his face. The round ricocheted from Alex's titanium skull, but not before it tore through much of the synthetic dermal tissue that was his face. Alex suddenly ceased thrashing Famine once he noticed that his own handcuffed gloves were red with the horseman's blood. Alex saw that the ricochet had pierced Famine's chest.

The meta-droid slowly turned his bullet-torn face toward War. Ribbons of frayed synthetic flesh dangled from Alex's face, exposing kinesiopolymeric tissue, optical filaments, and his alloyed zygomatic subframe. Still, his disfigured face betrayed a stunned countenance. "Did *you* just shoot me too?" shouted Alex.

War steadily realized that Alex was neither a human nor a demon. "You're a damned android," he uttered barely audibly.

Suddenly, the horsemen heard the voice of Kiiswood speaking to them through their helmets' headsets. "Yes, he is! And he's also our friend!" the chief shouted, using Conquest's c-nex to communicate with War and Death. "When I open this hatch, you two better be lying on the floor, face down with your hands behind your back! If not, I will put your fanatical asses down definitively!"

As a stratogen, the chief's genetic enhancements, along with a highly classified cerebral implant, enabled him to access other c-nexes as though they were his own. Kiiswood had placed the terrorist's confiscated c-nex on his temple and immediately accessed all of the information, including security codes, stored in its nexus memory. With it, he disabled all other c-nexes, cameras, and sensors in the bay; he repressurized the airlock; and he deactivated the magnetic bonds of all their handcuffs. He was even able to use it to mimic Conquest's neurometrics and, hence, to circumvent many of the enclave's security systems.

Within seconds, the airlock chamber had completely repressurized to Terran Indigenous. Kiiswood opened the hatch and, armed with Conquest's rifle, stormed the airlock chamber. There, he found that War and Death had indeed complied and were lying prone on the chamber floor. He also found a facially disfigured Alex standing beside Famine's lifeless body.

"I think I killed him, Chief," said Alex.

Kiiswood could not discern from Alex's voice whether he was expressing remorse or stating a simple fact. And he certainly could not discern such from the meta-droid's damaged face. Whatever Alex meant, Kiiswood had neither the time nor the inclination to be a coroner or a counselor. The chief was too busy trying to be a soldier. "Alex, give me your cuffs," Kiiswood ordered. Taking the handcuffs, the chief immediately bound one of Death's wrists to one of War's ankles. He also removed the power cells from the horsemen's surrendered rail-rifles, effectively disabling their weapons. Kiiswood and Alex then left the chamber to rendezvous with Hewst and Střelec.

293

In the parking bay, Střelec was standing as a reluctant sentry, guarding the captured and prone-lying paladins with one of their own rail-rifles. Hewst was cuffing the captured paladins to each other like links in a chain—ankle to wrist to ankle to wrist—just as Kiiswood had directed.

Once Hewst noticed the strips of synthetic tissue hanging from the meta-droid's face, she cried, "Alex, are you alright?"

"I think so," answered Alex. "I think the damage is mostly cosmetic."

"It's nothing that a little duct tape can't fix," Kiiswood quipped. No one laughed at the chief's jest.

Střelec felt extremely uneasy holding a weapon on the terrorists. She was a mathematician, and as such, she had never before had a reason to hold anyone at gunpoint—that is, until now. With angst in her voice, she asked, "What do we do now?"

"Right now, we each grab a rifle and take cover," Kiiswood answered.

Sensing that Kiiswood was posturing for a firefight, Hewst cautioned, "We can't take on the entire enclave, Chief."

"We don't need to take on the entire enclave, Commander," Kiiswood explained. "We only need to fend off a few of them just long enough to escape." Pointing to the confiscated c-nex on his temple, he continued, "With this, I'm able to track the movements of every terrorist in the township. At this very moment, there are sixteen heavily armed paladins taking up tactical positions in the adjacent hallway," he revealed. "I've bolted the doors into the parking bay, but they're about to break through by blowing the seals." He then added, "We need to get out of the open, now."

The chief quickly guided his colleagues to take cover among the traxles, steering them between two of the battle-modified vehicles parked in their charging ports. As the four of them crouched quietly behind a traxle, a smartly placed explosive charge violently blew the hallway door off its frame. Before the dust from the blast could settle, a platoon of armed paladins rushed into the parking bay, taking cover behind walls, partitions, and traxles—anything that might shield them from rifle fire. Two of the paladins took up tactical positions behind one of the partitioned charging ports very near Hewst, Kiiswood, Alex, and Střelec.

Just then, the voice of Bishop Bleum broadcasted over the PA system throughout the parking bay. "I must say, Chief Niyol Kiiswood, I admire your particular skillsets. Our enclave could use another stratogen like you." Bleum began to apply his skill as a keen psychological manipulator—the very skill that made him an effective leader of the enclave. "I know how the Terrestrial Assembly has treated you and your fellow stratogens. As long as you were fighting their battles for them, they treated you like nobility. But once you vanquished all their enemies for them, they had no use for you anymore, did they? You and your kind were a perversity that had no place in their civilized worlds. The Terrestrial Assembly discarded you like refuse, didn't they?" The bishop then proposed, "But it doesn't have to be that way. You have a choice. If you will bend a knee to me, reaffirm your faith in the Lord Jesus Christ and pledge your allegiance to the New Jerusalem, I give you my word: you will have a home among us. You will be welcomed and embraced in our Christian brotherhood. I'll even let the women live. That soulless, mechanical abomination, however—that thing we'll strip down for parts." Bleum paused. "So what's your choice, Chief?"

Kiiswood stared into Hewst's face for what seemed to be an eternity. His own face appeared stoical. Then an ever so subtle grin emerged.

Intently, piercingly, Hewst stared right back. "Chief?" she posed.

Finally, Kiiswood broke his silence. "Choices are about sacrifice," he whispered. The chief peered around the edge of the traxle and leveled his weapon on the heat signatures emanating from behind the adjacent partition. In rapid succession, he fired two shots through the partition, instantly killing the two paladins on the other side.

"I'll take that as a no!" said the voice of the bishop. "I now condemn you and your cohorts to the purifying flames of hell."

Within seconds, Bishop Bleum activated the injected nanites that were designed to disrupt their brainstem functions. Dr. Tereza Střelec instantly fell to the floor unconscious. Moments later, the mathematician was dead.

"Tereza!" shouted Hewst, horrified at the sudden death of her colleague.

Kiiswood placed his finger over his lips, gesturing to Hewst and Alex to say nothing. Once more, he peered around the edge of the traxle and fired several more shots, killing two paladins and wounding three others who had prematurely broken cover. The chief looked back at Hewst and Alex. "They were genuinely caught off guard," the chief whispered. "Bleum believes that he had killed all of us with the nanites."

"If that's true," Alex asked, "why are you two still alive?"

"Now's not the time to ponder; it's not the time to mourn," said Kiiswood. "Now's the time to act." The chief glanced at the airlock chamber and saw the two awkwardly bound horsemen trying desperately to stand. He then glanced back at his two friends and asked, "Do you trust me?"

"What are you about to do?" asked Hewst.

Kiiswood pointed to a particular traxle in the parking bay. "Do you see that traxle? That's the one we arrived in. Our helmets and EV packets are still inside. I need the two of you to climb inside and stay there. Commander, you need to put on your helmet and packet as soon as you climb in."

Hewst protested, "We'll be exposing ourselves, Chief," protested Hewst. "We'll be mowed down before we can get there."

"I'm about to create a distraction," Kiiswood countered. "Promise me that whatever happens, you'll do exactly as I've said." The chief then uncharacteristically said, "Please."

Hewst and Alex were apprehensive, but they agreed.

Kiiswood once again glanced at the two horsemen in the airlock. "On three, run for the traxle as fast as you can." The chief counted down, "One . . . two . . . three!"

True to their promise, Hewst and Alex ran hard for the specified traxle. They brandished their commandeered rifles haphazardly as they ran, for neither was familiar with how to use firearms. Even though they were keenly focused on reaching the traxle safely, Hewst kept a peripheral glimpse on Kiiswood, who was sprinting with stratogenic speed for the airlock. As he ran, the chief was firing his rail-rifle like a semi-automatic weapon, trying to strafe back the few paladins who were shooting at him, and possibly at his two friends. Bolting past the open hatch and into the airlock chamber, Kiiswood tackled the two tangle-cuffed horsemen who were still staggering to stand.

As Hewst and Alex were about to round the forward edge of the traxle, the commander could see from the corner of her eye that a paladin had run up behind the airlock hatch. She witnessed the paladin slamming the hatch shut, and immediately pressing the airlock activation key on the adjacent control panel. "NO!" screamed Hewst, as she was foolishly distracted. She was horrorstruck at the notion that Kiiswood was now suffering and dying from rapid decompression inside that chamber. She knew that the chief had no helmet or EV packet; she knew that he was not an invulnerable android. And, despite all of his genetically enhanced advantages, Hewst knew that her stratogen friend was quite mortal.

The sound of a metallic ping roused her back to her perilous surroundings; a bullet had zipped about a centimeter or two past her and struck the armor plating on the traxle. Hewst and Alex quickly darted behind the shielded safety of the vehicle before the next bullet could find its target. But there, awaiting them as they raced around the forward edge, was a pistol-wielding paladin who had managed to take up a tactical position beside the traxle's side-hatch. The paladin fired a single round at the two of them as they ran furiously at him. The bullet struck Alex and lodged into the kinesionomic hardware of his shoulder. But he hardly slowed down, and neither did Hewst. With the added momentum of her sprint, Hewst clouted the paladin in the face with her fist before he could fire off a second round. She hit him with such force that he fell to the floor unconscious.

"Alex, are you alright?" asked Hewst, opening the side-hatch with one hand while shaking her other hand from the pain of punching out a terrorist.

"My shoulder coupling is messed up," the meta-droid replied as he clumsily but hastily climbed into the traxle with his rifle. "I'm having trouble moving my arm."

Hewst tossed her rifle into the traxle and then jumped in herself. She closed and locked the side-hatch behind them just as the clanging sound of exterior bullet-strikes echoed throughout the traxle's cabin.

Even though his face was torn and distorted, Alex's countenance was still able to express consternation. "Wait," he protested as Hewst sealed the hatch. "What about the chief?"

Hewst said nothing as she began to don her EV packet and helmet. Instead, she answered Alex with a modest, forlorn nod of her head.

While Hewst and Alex sat on the floorboard of the traxle, its engine unexpectedly powered up. The unpiloted traxle suddenly lurched forward as it detached from its charging port and accelerated through the parking bay toward the airlock chamber. Against all established safety protocols, both internal and external chamber hatches opened simultaneously as the traxle quickly approached the airlock. The entire eastside parking bay and its connecting hallways explosively decompressed as they were now directly exposed to the deadly Martian environment. All manners of unsecured equipment, as well as several unsuited paladins, were violently, even fatally, blown out onto the planet's surface. Amid all this chaos, the speeding traxle continued on course, racing through the open airlock chamber, out into the night and onto the Martian terrain, indiscriminately rolling over everything, and everyone, in its way.

Hewst and Alex felt helpless. They were unwitting passengers in a traxle that seemingly had a mind of its own. As they rode through the airlock chamber, then out onto the Martian surface, they experienced an abrupt shift from augmented gravity to the planet's normal gravity. For a brief moment during the transition, the two of them felt as though they were in freefall. But the feeling soon passed as they adjusted to the weaker gravity of Mars.

The traxle raced along the dusty terrain for about a minute. Then it slowed to a complete stop several hundred meters away from the terrorist-seized township. Suddenly, the traxle's cabin depressurized. Hewst and Alex heard a knock on the side-hatch, followed promptly by the rattle of someone trying to open it. The two of them quickly grabbed their rail-rifles and readied themselves to combat whoever was trying to break in. As soon as the side-hatch flew open, Alex nervously, aimlessly fired off a round from his rifle into the Martian night, easily missing the intruder.

"Whoa! Whoa! Whoa!" shouted Kiiswood. Despite his voice being muffled by his newly acquired helmet and the thin Martian atmosphere, his two friends could hear his shouts clearly. "Hold your fire, Alex!" the chief yelled. "It's me!"

Hewst quickly helped the chief into the traxle while Alex put their rifles aside. Both of them were surprised, relieved, and overjoyed to see their friend.

"I'm so sorry, Chief," Alex profusely apologized. "I thought you were a terrorist."

Kiiswood responded while grimacing. "Terrorists don't bother knocking."

Hewst immediately noticed that Kiiswood had sustained a leg wound. "Chief, you're bleeding!" she stated. Surveying the cabin, Hewst soon discovered a casualty response kit. It was woefully undersupplied, and all of its contents were seemingly labeled backwards, but she was able to find some sterile dressings and pressure bandages in the kit. "This is a bullet wound," she commented as she applied pressure to his injury. "It looks like your suit's compression webbing has helped minimize the bleeding. Still, I'm amazed that you were even able to walk on this leg."

"Yeah," Kiiswood acknowledged, "I caught a stray round. Thankfully, it passed clean through, and it missed the femoral artery."

In a tone that revealed both her anger and her relief, Hewst remarked, "Chief, when they sealed you inside that airlock, we thought you were dead."

"I actually felt the saliva on the back of my tongue begin to boil," Kiiswood replied. "I knew I'd have only a few seconds in that airlock." Tapping his stolen helmet, he continued, "But that was enough time to appropriate a helmet and EV packet, and to fasten them to my own suit." The chief then dispassionately commented, "Their previous owner no longer had need of them."

Alex found an antiseptic unguent in the response kit. He handed it to Hewst as she tended to Kiiswood's wound. "The traxle?" the meta-droid asked the chief. "Was that *you*, driving it remotely?"

"Yes, it was," the chief answered. "I also overrode the safety protocols. Apparently, that paladin Conquest had extensive security access to the enclave's assets—equipment inventory, automated systems, defense codes. And much of it is stored right here in this nexus memory," said Kiiswood, pointing to the commandeered c-nex on his temple. "It even contains files on his fellow paladins—their particular duties, skill sets, and c-nex accessibilities."

As Hewst applied the unguent to the wound, Kiiswood winced from its slight antiseptic sting. "Baby!" she chided, scolding the chief. With a note of disapproval, she then asked, "I know that you needed to create a distraction for our escape, but wasn't there a better option than running out into the open through a hailstorm of bullets? Why did you have to run for the airlock?"

"To get this," Kiiswood answered. He reached into a small utility pouch on his sleeve and pulled out another c-nex. "This belonged to the one named Death. By acquiring this, our chances of escape are greatly improved."

"But we've already escaped," observed Alex.

"Not yet," the chief assessed. "Bishop Bleum will send his assault teams after us, in very short order. We need to get moving."

Chapter 24 – Camp Lundgren

Hellas Province, Mars

(Areographic Co-ordinates: S 34.917, E 93.780)

Sunday, 23 December 2429 CE

Time: 1153 Zulu

In a hijacked traxle, Hewst, Kiiswood, and Alex had escaped an enclave of radical Christian terrorists. The traxle had left the Martian highways shortly after fleeing Sterling Point and was now speeding under a starlit sky across the frigid desert plains of Hellas. Undeterred by pits and rocks, it raced covertly toward Niger Vallis without the aid of headlights or navigation lamps.

But it was not alone. About three minutes behind it, a platoon of five radar-tracking, armored traxles gave chase across the Martian desert. Unlike their target, the chasing traxles conspicuously lit their way with bright headlights and dorsal-mounted flood-lamps.

Bishop Joshua Bleum had dispatched an assault platoon with orders to run down the hijacked traxle and to execute its occupants. The bishop would have deployed combat air support, but the enclave's only pilot (Death) had been killed during the escape. Still, the assault platoon had assumed a wedge formation and was closing fast on its target.

Arch-deacon Enoch Joith, platoon leader and driver of the lead traxle, coordinated with the other traxle drivers via c-nex. "Maintain formation," Joith directed. "Continue to monitor radar for any change in direction. They might try to use the darkness to flank us."

Yet the hijacked traxle did not veer from its current course. It continued to race ahead at full throttle. Even so, the assault platoon gradually closed the distance. In a matter of minutes, the 50-millimeter rail-cannons mounted on the chasing traxles were finally within effective range.

Using his c-nex interface, the gunner in the lead traxle linked the radar-targeting scope directly into his visual cortex. "I have crosshairs on the target, sir," the gunner announced to Joith.

"All units," Joith ordered, "open fire!" Immediately, the cannons on all five pursuing traxles unleashed a flurry of armor-piercing rounds upon the fleeing target. Each fifth round was a pyrotechnic tracer, which lit up the target (and the night) with blazing streaks of fire. The fierce hail of large-caliber bullets shredded the hijacked traxle such that fragments of metal plating and hull composites copiously peeled away from the runaway vehicle. But even as one of its six cleated wheels was blown off, the hijacked traxle continued on its course. Confident that Hewst and Kiiswood had been killed in the barrage of cannon fire, and that the meta-droid also had been destroyed, Joith ordered all platoon gunners to cease fire. But even though it was now only a rolling frame, the hijacked traxle continued to speed ahead, and the assault platoon continued to pursue, plowing over the wake of strewn traxle parts.

Suddenly, every driver and every gunner in the five assault traxles received an interlinked c-nex call from their adversary. "Is that the best you can do?" The voice of Chief Kiiswood was clearly taunting Joith and the paladins under his command. "Are you trying to kill us, or are you just shooting blindly, hoping that you'll hit something?"

Joith was bewildered by the chief's message. The platoon leader was genuinely mystified that anyone could have survived such a salvo of artillery, even a stratogen. He suspected that some devilry was at work and that the chief was trying to goad the assault platoon into a trap. "All traxles, reduce speed and maintain relative distance," a very suspicious Joith ordered. Accordingly, the assault traxles complied and reduced speed.

"I knew it!" said the voice of Kiiswood. "The New Jerusalem is nothing but a brotherhood of cowards!" Continuing his verbal baiting, the chief added, "Jesus would be ashamed of you!" Kiiswood's provocation apparently struck a nerve, for one of the assault traxles left its wing position and accelerated toward the hijacked vehicle.

"Traxle Three," Joith commanded, "stay in formation!" But it did not comply; instead, it passed the platoon's lead traxle and began firing its rail-cannon once again. The arch-deacon turned to his gunner and remarked,

"When we get back to Sterling Point, I'm putting that driver and gunner in hack."

Kiiswood took note of the rogue traxle's breach of protocol and encouraged its insubordinate pursuit. "Finally," said the voice of Kiiswood, "a couple of courageous paladins who know how to serve their bishop."

The rogue traxle's driver bore down on his target at full speed and was finally close enough with his flood-lamps to make visual contact. His gunner zealously strafed the hijacked traxle with several more rail-rounds. So much wreckage now dangled from the bullet-riddled vehicle that the traxle became veiled in the clouds of rusty dust raked up in its wake. Still, Traxle Three madly plowed through the wafting banks of Martian dust as it gave chase.

Further behind, the rest of the traxles in the assault platoon stopped abruptly, for their drivers were not blinded by the cloud of dust. They could see the imminent threat on the horizon; indeed, they saw that they were running out of horizon.

"Traxle Three," Joith shouted, "stop now!" But his imperative came too late.

Without even slowing down, the hijacked traxle heedlessly soared over the cliff of Niger Vallis. Seconds later, Traxle Three blindly followed its target through the shrouding dust and over the edge. In low Martian gravity, the two freefalling vehicles plummeted in a wide parabolic arc as they both hurtled downward through 900 meters of darkness, fatally plunging into the floor of an ancient outflow channel.

Kiiswood suddenly lost his c-nex connection with the hijacked traxle. His link to its remote controls was abruptly severed when the vehicle slammed into the valley floor. He turned to his friends, who sat beside him in the unlit areopter cockpit, and said, "Frankly, I'm amazed that even one of them actually followed the traxle over the edge."

Hewst, Kiiswood, and Alex did not perish in the crash; they were not even in the traxle when it careened over the cliff. They had exited the hijacked traxle under the cover of night shortly after driving out onto the planet's surface from the parking bay. The three of them then hiked a few hundred meters to the township's areopter pad and commandeered the impounded sky-crane.

Although the terrorist enclave had reprogrammed the areopter for its own insidious purposes, Kiiswood was able to take control of it with the horseman Death's c-nex.

"Your ruse almost worked, Chief," Alex acknowledged. "Only one of them took the bait."

"No, the ruse worked perfectly," Hewst assessed. "The goal was never to terminate the assault platoon. It was to keep their eyes on the traxle and off the areopter."

"So what do we do now?" the meta-droid asked.

"Now, we keep low to the ground, in order to avoid detection," answered Kiiswood as he piloted the areopter, keeping his eyes keenly focused on the blackness outside the forward window. Yet the three of them sat in about as much darkness as was outside. The chief had turned off the cockpit lights, as well as most of the panel lights on the flight instruments; he was trying to make the sky-crane as invisible as possible. Hewst and Alex, unable to see anything outside the forward window, were nervous passengers. Kiiswood, however, was flying by infrared sight. But even he had some difficulty seeing the contours of the Martian terrain; the temperature variations between the surface and the atmosphere were very slight. "We also need to fly a more circuitous, less predictable course," Kiiswood added.

Alex asked, "A less predictable course? Where?"

"Camp Lundgren at Tyrrhenus," Hewst guessed.

"Aye," the chief agreed. "Tyrrhenus is the nearest population center, and Camp Lundgren is the nearest Defense Force installation for a thousand kilometers."

"Have you tried again to communicate with Lundgren?" asked Hewst.

"Aye, ma'am," answered Kiiswood. "They're still silent, and so is the entire town of Tyrrhenus. They're not even acknowledging the areopter's transponder signal."

"Aerospace Intelligence has disavowed Project Belshazzar," Alex remarked. "Do you think that's why they're ignoring our hails?"

Kiiswood was slow to reply. "I have no idea what kind of welcome we'll receive when we get there," he responded. "I'm picking up no communication traffic on any Martian channel whatsoever—neither Assembly nor Alliance channels."

Hewst allowed her imagination to entertain the disconcerting possibility that what had happened at HAS *Sagan*, at New Guinea, at Vitruvius Crater, and at northern Arizona had now happened at Tyrrhenus. "I don't think they're ignoring us," she surmised. "I think they're unable to respond."

"Why?" Alex puzzled.

Kiiswood answered, "We'll find out soon enough."

"So," the meta-droid wondered, "what do we do when we get there?"

Hewst grinned and answered, somewhat humorously, somewhat seriously, "I plan to find a cup of coffee."

The three of them sat quietly for a while as the chief cautiously navigated the areopter through the darkness. He quickly relearned how to fly with an inverted flight control panel.

After some moments of spiritual introspection, Alex said, "I feel so grateful to have escaped with my life, but at the same time, I feel guilty for surviving." The meta-droid continued, "I'm genuinely grief-stricken that Mas'ud and Tereza didn't make it; yet I feel ashamed because I'm so grateful that it wasn't me who died."

Hewst felt an affinity with Alex and with his sense of guilt. "So many of my crewmates died during the war," she said. "I, too, felt guilty that I survived and they didn't. I contemplated all sorts of theological explanations to assuage my guilt. I tried telling myself that God let me live because I was favored, or because God had some special purpose for my life. But in the end, all of these explanations were just frail props."

Alex asked her, "Why is that?"

"If I believed that I was favored," she replied, "then I also had to believe that others are disfavored. If I believed that I was saved for a special purpose, then I also had to believe that others are dispensable at God's whim.

I just can't live in a universe that's populated by disposable people or that's governed by a capricious God."

"So how do you make sense of it all?" the meta-droid wondered.

"I have to believe that there's some divine purpose that transcends all sense and reason," Hewst answered. "But of late, I've accepted that, on this side of heaven, there is no sense in why some live and some die. I simply accept that I survived, and that there's no sin in feeling grateful."

For the next few hours, the three of them said little as they rode into the night, their areopter precariously skimming just a few meters above the planet's surface.

As the predawn light began to illuminate the Hesperian plateau, but before the sun had peeked above the horizon, the sky-crane clandestinely approached the dark and inert aerodrome at Camp Lundgren. Kiiswood tried to hail Lundgren Control; he squawked the areopter's transponder code but received no response. He then tried using the Unicom frequency to activate the pilot-controlled lighting on the areopter pads. Again, no response.

Kiiswood observed, "I don't see any runway or pad lights. I'm not detecting any station activity whatsoever." The chief then commented, "We'll have to land without ground support."

The areopter was now in clear visual range of Tyrrhenus. Looking out at the city's topside structures, Hewst remarked, "I don't see any lights, either. The entire town is dark."

"Look," said Alex. "The sun is rising over Tyrrhenus Mons."

In the light of dawn, Kiiswood spotted a landing pad that was relatively clear of drifting sand. He aligned the areopter's landing gear for a shallow approach and a roll-on landing. Although he had not received a response to any of his previous hails, the chief nonetheless declared his intentions, on the off chance that someone was listening. "Lundgren Control, this is Phobos-Niner-Golf-Romeo on final approach for Pad Seven," he announced while gazing at what appeared to him as an inverted "7" on the areopter pad. He pitched the rotors for a four-degree glide angle and touched down gently on the landing pad. The taxiway to the areopter hangar was impassable—blocked by several abandoned gunships, troop carriers, a delta-wing fighter, and a Martian long-shuttle. So the chief simply rolled the sky-crane to a stop on Landing Pad Seven.

Kiiswood powered down the areopter rotors, but not before the rotor-wash blasted away much of the wind-blown Martian dust that had settled on and around the landing pad. But as the shifting and drifting dust was blown away, the three passengers beheld a dreadful revelation.

"Catherine," Alex asked as he peered wide-eyed through the side window of the cockpit, "are those bodies lying on the ground?"

Hewst was in awe at the sight of at least eight bodies littering the grounds around the areopter. "Yes, they are," she quietly replied. One of the dead was in a compression suit with an open helmet. The rest were in their regular service uniforms. But all of them were pristine, frozen, and tinged in brownish-orange dust—well preserved in the frigid, carbon-dioxide atmosphere.

"This is probably why no one has heard anything from either Tyrrhenus or from Camp Lundgren," Kiiswood proposed.

"Are you suggesting that the entire town is dead?" asked Alex. "How did they all die?"

Hewst made sure that hers and Kiiswood's helmets were sealed and secured, then reached over and opened the cockpit door. "Let's go find out," she said as she led the way out of the sky-crane.

Hewst, Kiiswood, and Alex headed directly toward the ground-crew airlock, passing near a couple of dead crewswains lying partially shrouded in the Martian sands. Kiiswood and Alex reached the airlock and discovered that its hatch had been blown off its frame. Hewst, however, had stopped short of the airlock, pausing to take a closer look at two decedents sprawled on the ground. Once Kiiswood and Alex realized that their friend had not kept up with them, they turned to see what had captured her attention.

"Catherine, what is it?" asked Alex.

Studying the two bodies before her, she answered, "I'm trying to understand what happened here."

"The aerodrome wasn't attacked," Kiiswood observed. "There's no indication of mortar hits, laser scorching, or bullet strikes."

Alex pointed back at the damaged hatch and offered his theory. "It's my guess that they were accidentally blown out of the airlock," he surmised.

"That seems likely," Hewst concurred. "But something doesn't look right."

"What do you mean?" Alex wondered. "Their skin is cyanotic and broken, which is characteristic of hypoxia and ebullism."

"Yes, I see that," she agreed with her meta-droid friend. "But I'm mystified by what I *don't* see." She pointed at the two frozen bodies and remarked, "Look at their comportment. There's no grimaced expressions, no sign of clutching at their faces or throats for breath." She then pointed specifically to the one decedent in a compression suit. "And look at *this* guy whose helmet is opened."

With his damaged arm, Alex awkwardly gestured toward the open helmet. "There's the reason that his helmet is open," he observed. "There's a small rock lodged in its spindle mechanism."

Hewst again agreed. "Yes, I see that too." She knelt down and dislodged the small rock; the helmet immediately closed and sealed tight. "But why wasn't he trying to remove the obstruction? Why wasn't he struggling to close his helmet? He looks strangely placid, as if he peacefully accepted his suffocation."

"Aye, they *all* look peaceful," Kiiswood concurred with bewilderment as he scanned the scene, surveying all the corpses in the area. He then gestured to his two friends and said, "Let's find a way inside."

The three of them spent the next hour trying unsuccessfully to enter the camp's subsurface compound through a number of ground-crew airlocks and even a couple of hangar airlocks. In a few cases, the airlocks were inoperative and could not be opened without specialized equipment, which they did not have. Other pressure hatches could be opened manually, but they dared not open them and depressurize adjacent compartments, putting at risk people who might be on the other side of the airlock.

Eventually, they discovered a way inside Camp Lundgren by crawling through a very narrow utility access tunnel—so narrow that they had to crawl in single file. Tediously, they climbed into one dark and cramped compartment after another, sealing a sequence of utility hatches every few meters behind them. Finally, at the end of the tunnel, they reached a large mechanical room that housed much of Camp Lundgren's life-support equipment.

The mechanical room was dark, cold, and unpressurized—no lights, no heat, no oxygen. The only light in the room came from Hewst's helmet torch. (Alex was not wearing a helmet, and Kiiswood's commandeered helmet was not equipped with a light source.) The room was a maze of mechanisms that were either shut down or broken down: waste management systems, artificial gravity generators, helium-3 reactors, water and oxygen reclamators.

The three of them weaved their way around the cold, inert machinery until they emerged from the mechanical room and into the main compound of Camp Lundgren. There, they found that the Defense Force installation was frigid and lifeless, sparsely illuminated by intermittent emergency lighting. Everywhere they wandered, they discovered dozens and dozens of dead, frozen bodies.

Alex queried, "What the hell happened here?"

Neither of his friends answered. They simply kept moving through the compound, stepping gently and reverently over and around the vast number of deceased. Soon, they came upon Camp Lundgren's Action Information Center (AIC).

"Alex, you asked what happened," Kiiswood commented. "Perhaps we can get some answers here?"

The three of them entered the cold darkness, side-stepping another two bodies on the deck. Kiiswood and Alex followed closely behind Hewst; her helmet torch was the only illumination in the dark compartment. Upon reaching the main information access station, Hewst tried pressing a few keys on the console, but to no avail. The keyboard did not light up, the monitors remained dark, no holos were projected. The workstation had no power. Kiiswood reached up to an overhead storage slot and pulled out a small helium-3 reactor drum. He then knelt down, reached under the console, opened a service panel, and connected the drum to the console's hardware in an improvised and rudimentary manner. After he repositioned some helion fusion components behind the service panel, the workstation powered up. The monitor before them began flashing a warning in bright red, inverted letters: GLOBAL QUARANTINE. Also flashing on the monitor, just below the warning, was the inverted logo of the Interplanetary Health Agency.

"Am I reading this correctly," Hewst asked unnervingly, "that the entire planet is under quarantine?" She began typing slowly, meticulously on the console's keyboard since the keyboard that was inverted; the alphanumeric characters were inscribed backwards.

"May I, Commander?" gestured Kiiswood. Hewst graciously stepped aside and yielded the console to the chief.

One of the benefits of Kiiswood's genetic enhancements is that they allowed him to adapt quickly to his situation, certainly quicker than most people. Although he too started out pressing the keys slowly, he was soon typing on the inverted keyboard as if by instinct. In less than two minutes, the chief had bypassed the Defense Force security protocols and had successfully hacked into Camp Lundgren's computer mainframe. To expedite their search for information, Kiiswood activated three forward monitors and adjacent keyboards, one for each of them. Hewst and Alex followed the chief's example and began searching the database for answers. What had happened to the inhabitants of Camp Lundgren and Tyrrhenus?

Alex struggled to use his keyboard since he did not have full mobility of his damaged android arm. Slowly, though, he made some progress. "Chief, you're the only one among us wearing a c-nex," the meta-droid remarked. "Couldn't you access the installation's mainframe faster if you use that?"

"I'm wearing a terrorist's c-nex," Kiiswood replied. "I can't access a Defense Force mainframe with it."

Alex thought for a moment, and then offered a helpful suggestion. "Perhaps we can pressurize this compartment, so that you can open your helmet and use any one of these crewswains' c-nexes? As a stratogen, you can do that, right?"

Kiiswood grinned as he answered, "It's not a matter of whether I can do it; it's a matter of whether it's safe to do so."

Alex's mangled meta-droid face looked perplexed. He quickly assumed that the chief had come across some distressing data on his monitor.

"Whether it's safe?" he asked. "Do you suspect some kind of nerve agent in the ventilation system?"

"No, the installation's hazard management team didn't detect any chemical agents in the life-support system," Hewst replied. "But I think the chief's cautions are justified," she said as her gaze was fixed on her monitor. "I'm looking at the sickbay records—at the chief medical officer's logs, specifically. She reports some kind of fast-spreading pathogen that overran the town of Tyrrhenus and was rapidly spreading through this military installation. Her last log entry ended abruptly."

Alex shook his head in disagreement. "No, that can't be correct. No pathogen spreads so rapidly." The meta-droid began scrolling through a montage of public video recordings on his monitor—recordings of daily ongoings throughout the town and the installation. "Look at all these videos from about a week ago. People are busy at their daily routines: active at their workstations, walking and dashing to and fro, eating in the mess hall, conversing and socializing with each other. Then, suddenly they all just seem to disengage from life." Alex began pointing at particular images to demonstrate his point. "Some of them just stop right where they are. Some sit down, some lie down, some just stand in place, and some seem to roam aimlessly. They stop eating, they stop talking, they stop interacting."

"They obviously stopped maintaining their life-support systems," Kiiswood observed as he continued to scan the video recordings. "Some of them calmly walked off elevated pedways and tram platforms. A few of them casually walked into airlocks and opened the hatches. But most of them slowly suffocated or froze to death. Of course, given that they weren't eating and drinking, they would have all eventually died from dehydration or . . ." The chief stopped in mid-sentence as one particular video recording caught his attention. With a tone of surprise in his voice, he continued, "Of all the astonishing things that I've seen in the course of my life—I never thought I'd ever see anything that could astound me like *this* does."

Hewst and Alex both turned their focus to the video recording that had captured Kiiswood's attention. On the monitor, the three of them watched a civilian contract welder at work. One moment, he was welding some components to Camp Lundgren's auxiliary carbon-dioxide scrubber. The next moment, the worker dropped his welding torch and just wandered away, but not before the welding torch set his tunic sleeve on fire. Within seconds, the wandering welder was completely engulfed in flames. Yet he did not scream, he did not panic, he did not writhe in pain. He simply meandered about like a walking funeral pyre. He strolled ablaze among his disengaged coworkers, none of whom did anything to help him. He roamed around on fire, as though nothing were wrong, until his cremating body could move no more. The burning man toppled to the floor like felled timber.

The three of them stood momentarily in awe and silence at the sight of that horrific video recording. Finally, Hewst said, "No response to pain, no danger avoidance. He showed no sense of self-preservation. He just let himself burn to death."

"They're all like that," Kiiswood added. "It's as if their survival instincts were instantaneously shut off—like someone throwing a switch."

"That's just not possible," Alex protested. "As an astrobiologist, I can tell you that pathogens may spread quickly—through the air, through food or water, through insects, though human contact. But no pathogen exists that can spread like this—not instantaneously."

"Unless we're facing something new," Hewst responded. Pointing to some classified medical data that she had displayed on her monitor, she continued, "Before her last entry, the CMO referenced an old autopsy file from twenty years ago. The file mentions a remote Martian settlement in the Casius Province that was wiped out in 2408 by a neuropathogen. It says here that the Interplanetary Health Agency deployed a forensic pathology team whose members all died shortly after arriving on scene, despite their precautions. IPHA then deployed medical androids that autopsied the bodies and identified a new pathogen of Martian origin." Then, with slight frustration in her voice, Hewst added, "That's all I can read; the rest is redacted."

As Alex was trying to read the inverted pathology file on Hewst's monitor for more details, Kiiswood made yet another interesting discovery. "Well, this is curious," the chief commented. Hewst and Alex once again turned their attention to the image on Kiiswood's monitor—an image of a sickbay ward with several lethargic in-patients lying in medical beds.

"When was this video recorded?" asked Hewst.

"This isn't a recording," Kiiswood answered. He pressed a function tab on his keyboard, and the video image on his monitor suddenly appeared as a small holographic projection hovering over the workstation console. "This is a live feed," he said.

Hewst's eyes widened with hope. "Do you mean to say that those in-patients are still alive?" she optimistically asked. "How?"

"Apparently, sickbay is under emergency power," Kiiswood answered. He honed his attention on inverted data readouts that scrolled across the lower part of his monitor. "And it's one of the few compartments that never lost air pressure."

Alex puzzled, "But if these in-patients are like all the others—not taking in food or water—they too should have died of dehydration by now."

Hewst was also trying to interpret the inverted data that scrolled across the screen. "No. These particular in-patients are hooked up to sickbay's automated intravenous system," she observed. "Since the onset of this mysterious pathogen, they've been receiving a steady line of IV fluids. That's why they're still alive."

"Aye, they're still alive," the chief acknowledged. "But not for long. Their bodies will inevitably starve to death."

Alex wondered, "Can we do anything for them?"

Hewst also wondered whether they could help these chance survivors. Could they help them without risking exposure to infection? "Chief, can we adjust their intravenous solution from this workstation?" she asked. "Can we adjust the solution to supply them with a daily caloric intake?"

"Aye, ma'am," replied Kiiswood. Indeed, anticipating Hewst's request, the chief had already accessed sickbay's automated medical system and was supplementing the intravenous lines with hyperalimentation fluids. "Be aware, Commander, this will only delay the inevitable," Kiiswood alerted. "They're still infected."

Alex then uttered an ominous concern. "How do we know that *we're* not infected?"

Alex's concern had already crossed Hewst's mind. "Since we don't know how the pathogen spreads, we don't know that we're not infected," she candidly responded. "But we haven't jumped off a roof or set ourselves on fire yet. So I take that as a good sign."

Kiiswood was puzzled at the way Alex expressed his concern. "What do you mean by 'we'?" he asked his synthetic friend. "You're a machine. You can't be affected by contagions."

"My neural network is artificial," the meta-droid confided, "but it's patterned after human neural templates. Perhaps I'm just as prone to a neuropathogen as any human being."

"Well, if we're not infected yet," Hewst proposed, "I suggest we leave before we are."

"Leave? Leave where?" Alex puzzled. "The Hesperian highways are closed, the maglev rail system is shutdown, the g-trains are offline. The entire planet is under quarantine."

Glancing at Kiiswood, she answered, "Off-world."

With an affirming nod, the chief concurred.

Chapter 25 – Ascent to Orbit

Camp Lundgren, Hesperia Province, Mars

(Areographic Co-ordinates: S 21.628, E 105.872)

Sunday, 23 December 2429 CE

Time: 1744 Zulu

Catherine Hewst's coffee craving would have to go unsatisfied, at least for the present. For the moment, she, Kiiswood, and Alex were working diligently to get away from Camp Lundgren, the town of Tyrrhenus, and the planet of Mars.

The Federal Aerospace Intelligence Agency had disavowed them. The Interplanetary Health Agency had abandoned them. The entire planet was under quarantine and communication blackout. No one was coming to rescue them—not the Martian Alliance and not the Terrestrial Assembly—and they could not call for help. If Hewst, Kiiswood, and Alex had any hope of survival, they needed to go off-world.

They had opened several ground-crew airlock hatches between the aerodrome on the planet's surface and Camp Lundgren's subsurface compound in order to create a clear and easy access between a long-shuttle above and the provisions they would need below. They had opened these hatches without endangering any living soul, for all of the installation's personnel who would otherwise be exposed to the deadly Martian atmosphere were already dead.

Kiiswood was topside, on the planet's surface, prepping the long-shuttle for its forthcoming take-off and subsequent orbital rendezvous. The shuttle was a *Tÿr*-class aerospace vehicle with a variable-sweep-wing configuration. It was a short-range craft and was clearly not designed for interplanetary transits. Its primary purpose was to shuttle eight passengers, and two pilots, from the planet's surface, into Martian orbit, and back. During take-offs and landings, its expansive wings would fully extend to produce the required lift at subsonic speeds. But when its wings were swept back in a delta configuration, the long-shuttle could soar at hypersonic speeds through the thin Martian atmosphere with negligible drag.

Kiiswood had already removed the shuttle's gust locks, wheel chocks, cowling plugs, and inlet covers; now he was trying to replenish its fusion fuel. Of all the helium-3 fuel lines that serviced the installation's aerodrome, the chief was able to find only one that was still functioning, and that line was nearly 200 meters from the long-shuttle. Eventually, he managed to link several lines together and to reach the shuttle's ventral charging port. As the shuttle's depleted helion power cells were recharging, Kiiswood conducted a preflight walk-around to inspect the aerosurfaces, including the elevator, rudder, flaps, and ailerons.

Meanwhile, Hewst and Alex were at work in the subsurface compound of Camp Lundgren, gathering supplies for their flight and for a possibly prolonged stay in Martian orbit. Hewst had raided the galley's pantry and had gathered up as many bottles of potable water and prepackaged field rations as she could pack into a culinary service cart. Likewise, Alex had loaded an overhead mag-lift pallet with dozens of helium-3 power cylinders from the fuel hold in the reactor room.

Before the two of them began to haul their supplies topside to the long-shuttle, Alex turned to Hewst and sought her assistance. "Catherine, would you help me with something?" he asked while holding a small, thumb-sized power cylinder in his hands. "I need to replace my power cell. I can probably do this by myself, but with my arm not working properly, I'd feel better knowing someone was with me—should I need help."

Hewst felt apprehensive; she feared that, despite her well-meant intentions, she might inadvertently make matters worse for Alex. After all, she was not an engineer, and she certainly was not a cyberneticist. But she decided that if her meta-droid friend needed her, she would do her best to help him. "Of course, Alex," replied Hewst. With a feigned confidence, she added, "Tell me what you need me to do."

Alex handed the power cell to Hewst to free up his hands. "I usually change out my power cells on my own," the meta-droid responded as he toggled the memory-alloy actuator at the top of his collar module, "but I've never done this without someone else nearby, just in case something goes wrong." He unfastened the front of his compression suit and rolled it down to his mid-torso, revealing his t-shirt. "If I don't have enough reserve power to complete the cell connection myself, I'll need you to complete it for me."

Hewst soon became aware that her assistance was less important to Alex than was her simple presence. The meta-droid was concerned that, in the worst-case scenario, his mechanical functions might cease—that he might die. And he did not want to die alone.

With his damaged arm, Alex awkwardly lifted up his t-shirt, baring his meta-droid abdomen. Except for a nearly imperceptible seam where his appendix would otherwise be (if he had an appendix), Alex's abdomen appeared quite human. Suddenly, the seam opened up like a multi-leafed iris, creating a seven-centimeter aperture in Alex's side and exposing the integrated microcomponents just inside his artificial gut: quantum transistors, superconducting couplers, electron interference devices, magnetic memory elements, *etcetera*. A small power cell receptacle then slid out through the aperture like a desk drawer opening. Reaching into the receptacle with his good arm, Alex extracted a small, near-spent helium-3 power cylinder and handed it to Hewst. The empty receptacle immediately emitted a rapid clicking sound, indicating that it was awaiting a replacement cylinder. The clicking continued as Alex took the fresh cylinder from Hewst and inserted it in the place of the old one. The receptacle suddenly ceased its clicking and retracted back into the meta-droid's abdomen.

As the aperture in Alex's side closed up, Hewst asked, "How long will that cell last you?"

Alex pulled down his t-shirt and adjusted it to a straight fit. "It depends on my level of activity," he answered, "but, on average, about a week." He put his compression suit back on and said, "Thank you, Catherine."

From behind the visor of her helmet, Hewst smiled and nodded at Alex.

As the two of them began hauling their supplies up to the surface, Kiiswood stepped from around the corner and met Hewst and Alex in the corridor. In his hands, the chief was carrying two duffle bags that he had filled with spare components for their suits—helmets, EV packets, and other life-support elements that they might need for their flight. "The long-shuttle is prepped and ready to go," Kiiswood announced to his two friends. "Do you two have your provisions ready to load?"

Hewst nodded and said, "Let's get off this rock!"

Within forty-five minutes, they had carted their provisions up to the planet's surface and stowed them aboard the prepped long-shuttle. The three of them finally boarded the shuttle through its rear ventral hatchway and retracted the access ladder. Soon thereafter, they "dogged down" the hatch (that is, they manually secured it), they powered up the passenger cabin and pressurized it with Terran-normal atmosphere.

Hewst slowly opened her helmet, removed it from her collar module, and drew in a deep breath of cabin air. Kiiswood and Alex watched her intently to see whether she bore any of the symptoms that they had earlier witnessed on the AIC monitors. But even after several minutes of normal breathing, she showed no sign of that insidious contagion that had overrun Tyrrhenus and very likely most of Mars. In turn, Kiiswood removed his commandeered helmet and breathed deeply as his two friends watched. Like Hewst, the chief exhibited no symptoms.

Having been on the run from Christian terrorists and a Martian neuropathogen for the past twenty-four hours, the three of them were grateful to be in the warm safety of the pressurized shuttle cabin. Indeed, the cabin seemed quite peaceful, even luxurious. They each took the opportunity to clean up and freshen themselves in the long-shuttle's lavatory—first Hewst, then Kiiswood, and finally Alex. While the meta-droid was in the lavatory, brushing off the Martian dust and inspecting his torn face in the mirror, Hewst and Kiiswood took the time to eat a meal from among the stowed field rations.

As Hewst was finishing the last morsel of her ration, Kiiswood retrieved a helmet from one of his duffle bags. Unlike the one that he had commandeered from the terrorist at Sterling Point, this helmet was designed specifically for his compression suit and would mount better to his collar module. Before he closed its visor, he removed the c-nex that he had taken from the terrorist and discarded it, along with the terrorist's helmet. They had each served their purpose, but were no longer needed.

Alex soon emerged from the lavatory, and the three of them stood momentarily quiet in the passenger cabin, looking at each other. Kiiswood broke the silence as he said, "Let's put on our helmets and strap in for launch."

Although the long-shuttle was pressurized, wearing fully equipped compression suits was a standard precaution for transits into and out of orbit. So Hewst complied and once again donned her helmet. Alex also took a helmet from the duffle bag and put it on, even though his android body did not need it for life support. Rather, he put it on because neither he nor Hewst nor Kiiswood were wearing their c-nexes, as the paladin terrorists of New Jerusalem had taken them. The helmet's headset would allow Alex to communicate with his two friends.

Kiiswood sat down in the pilot's seat in the cockpit and asked Hewst to take the co-pilot's position beside him. She, of course, did not know how to fly a long-shuttle, but she would be able to assist the chief with the instrument readouts on her side of the cockpit. Alex, for his part, was quite content to sit in the passenger cabin. As soon as all three had strapped themselves in, their EV packets automatically plugged into access ports adjacent to their seats. The shuttle's life-support system was now supplying oxygen directly to their helmets and, at the same time, recharging their EV packets.

With his headset, Alex hailed his friends in the cockpit and asked, "So where are we headed?"

Kiiswood pointed vaguely in a random direction and drolly answered, "Up."

"Could you be a bit more precise?" the meta-droid asked while rolling his eyes. "Is there a specific space vessel that you plan to rendezvous with?"

The chief powered up the engine and slowly began to taxi the shuttle to aerodrome runway three-six. "We're under a global communications blackout down here on the surface," Kiiswood replied as he maneuvered toward the runway. "So we have no idea what ships might be in orbit above us, or whether any are in orbit. Because of the global quarantine, the entire planet might be under an orbital ban. We won't know until we fly above the Martian mesosphere and access our orbital navigation sensors."

"Space is vast," Alex noted, "and we're just a speck by comparison. The chances of being on the right trajectory to rendezvous with a ship would literally be astronomical. We can't just fly off into space without a destination."

Hewst thought for a moment about Alex's concern. She then realized that a fixed position does indeed exist in Martian orbit. "Schiaparelli Terminus?" she asked the chief.

"Aye, ma'am," Kiiswood replied. He ignored the hold markers on the taxiway and drove the shuttle directly onto the runway. "Schiaparelli Terminus is in an areostationary orbit," he said as he lined up the shuttle for take-off and extended its massive wings to their maximum span. "If there are any military or commercial vessels in orbit, they will likely be docked there." Without any other notice than a wily grin on his face, the chief pressed a button on the forward console that turned on some very loud, upbeat, preprogrammed music. He then throttled up the aft engine, and the long-shuttle shot forward.

Hewst and Alex were caught off guard. Their bodies unexpectedly thrust back into their seats, and their heads jolted back in their helmets as the shuttle furiously accelerated down runway three-six.

"You know, Chief," Hewst shouted over the loud music, "you could have warned us before you took off like a bat out of hell."

Other than his wild laughter, Kiiswood said nothing. He simply bobbed his head to the beat of the music as he steered the hurtling shuttle toward the runway's end.

Alex was momentarily fear-stricken as he gazed out at the Tyrrhenian landscape that streaked by his passenger window. The meta-droid realized that he was at the mercy of an audacious daredevil. His hands latched onto the armrests of his seat like vice-grips. With a touch of sarcasm, he yelled, "Catherine, it's possible that our lives are in the hands of a madman."

Still laughing, Kiiswood replied, "Surely, Alex, I've purged you of all doubt by now."

For the next several seconds, the long-shuttle accelerated down the long runway. Once it reached a speed of 250 meters per second, Kiiswood pulled back on the yoke, and the long-shuttle took off. It continued to accelerate as it raced north toward the Martian equator, rapidly gaining altitude all the while. Within minutes, the shuttle was passing over Cerberus Dorsa and many of the seemingly lifeless townships of Hesperia Province. There, the chief began a very shallow bank to the right. He could not bank any steeper against the shuttle's own inertia without losing lift in the thin atmosphere. After several more minutes, he leveled out the wings over Licus Vallis and lined up the shuttle on an eastward trajectory directly over the equator.

"We're equatorially aligned and ready to transition for ascent to orbit," declared Kiiswood. He slowly pitched the shuttle's nose up while gradually increasing thrust. Soon, the shuttle's airfoils exceeded their critical angle of attack as the craft pitched vertical. All of the shuttle's lift was now being produced by the fierce thrust of the aft engine. Kiiswood then retracted the shuttle's massive wings and drew them into a tight delta-configuration. He turned off the music, cleared the aeroflight instruments from the forward console, and activated the ascent-to-orbit displays. The long-shuttle had transitioned from an aircraft to a spacecraft. "Standby," Kiiswood called out. "ATO in three, two, one." The chief immediately initiated a preprogrammed ascent sequence, and the long-shuttle rocketed skyward. "Sit back and enjoy the ride," announced Kiiswood. "We'll attain orbital insertion in three hours, twenty-two minutes."

Hewst, Kiiswood, and Alex made themselves as comfortable as possible even as they endured the g-forces of powered ascent. They settled in, tried to relax, and spoke very little during the preprogrammed flight.

As the long-shuttle raced toward orbital insertion, its aft engine periodically gimbaled its thrust, making subtle adjustments to the flight path and gradually pitching eastward. About an hour and a half into its journey, the long-shuttle soared from daylight into night as the sun passed behind the western arc of the red planet. Flying ever higher into the darkness of space, Hewst turned off the cockpit's overhead lights. The black sky in the forward window suddenly lit up with sharp, brilliant constellations. For about an hour, she sat in silent wonder of such radiant starlight until the shuttle emerged from the shadow of Mars and the light of dawn flooded into the cockpit.

After hours of monitoring the shuttle's altitude and speed, Kiiswood counted down the final seconds of powered flight. "ASO insertion in four

321

seconds," the chief said, "three, two, one." The shuttle engine abruptly shut off.

Reading the telemetry displayed on the forward console, Hewst said, "Orbital velocity: 1.448 kilometers per second. Altitude: 17,031 kilometers. Inclination: equatorial. Orbital period: synchronous." She looked at Kiiswood and remarked, "Well done, Chief. We're in areostationary orbit over Syrtis Major Planum."

Alex removed his seat restraints and immediately began floating in the cabin's zero-gravity environment. Using the overhead handrails, he slowly pulled himself into the cockpit; with his friends, he glanced out the long-shuttle's forward window. There, he gazed at the sun hovering in the blackness. "Are we there yet?" he asked.

Kiiswood opened a panel on his armrest and accessed the RCS column. "Brace yourself, Alex," the chief advised. The meta-droid complied and held onto the handrail a little more firmly. Kiiswood gripped the control column with his hand and tilted it slightly forward. The long-shuttle promptly responded, slowly pitching nose down about 45 degrees. Through the forward window, the bright red sphere of Mars scrolled into view.

"Ironic, isn't it?" pondered Hewst. "With all the terror and death happening down there, Mars looks so serene from up here."

"It does look peaceful," Alex agreed. "But, I don't see Schiaparelli Terminus."

Kiiswood activated the orbital navigation sensor on the forward console and quickly examined its data. "That's because it's currently 21,000 kilometers behind us," he replied. "Commander, would you please try to hail them?"

Hewst patched her headset into the shuttle's communication system. "Schiaparelli Terminus, this is Long-Shuttle . . . " She realized that she did not know the shuttle's registration number. Kiiswood quickly came to her aid by pointing to the number displayed at the top of the console. "This is Long-Shuttle Juliet-Six-Hotel-Two-India-Seven," she continued. "Please respond." Her receiver was silent. "Schiaparelli Terminus, this is Long-Shuttle Juliet-Six-

Hotel-Two-India-Seven, please respond," she repeated. Again, silence. Hewst wondered, "Are they receiving us, Chief?"

"We're transmitting, ma'am," Kiiswood answered while examining the communication equipment. "But there's no way to know whether they're receiving us."

"Could the terminus have been affected by the contagion?" she ominously considered.

"That's a possibility," the chief responded. "It's also possible that they're just ignoring us for fear that *we're* infected."

"So they're either not hearing us, or they're not talking to us," Alex summarized. "How do we find out which?"

Kiiswood replied, "We rendezvous."

Looking at the navigational data on the console, Alex asked, "So do we just hold here until the terminus catches up to us?"

Hewst tittered. "I'm not a pilot, but I'm pretty sure that it's not as simple as that."

"We need to execute a co-orbital rendezvous," Kiiswood explained as he was reviewing the navigational data for the forthcoming phasing maneuver. "We need to speed up to enter a larger, slower phasing orbit. As Schiaparelli Terminus is catching up to us, we slow down to leave the phasing orbit and return to our original orbit. We'll then be in position to rendezvous."

Alex was a brilliant astrobiologist, but he seemed to have some difficulty understanding the chief's cursory tutorial in astrodynamics. "Wait, are you saying that we have to speed up to slow down?"

"I'll gladly explain it to you later," Kiiswood said as he reviewed how much delta-v would be needed for the maneuver. "But for now, I need you to take your seat and strap in. I'll be initiating Point of Impulse in a few minutes."

Alex was content with not fully understanding the physics of orbital phasing; he had confidence in the chief. The meta-droid returned to his seat, strapped in once again, and sat ready for the forthcoming maneuver.

Using the RCS control column, Kiiswood pitched the nose up so that it was level with the direction of orbit. The long-shuttle was now ready for phasing. "Standby," he said. The chief then initiated the phasing maneuver that he had programed into the navigation computer. "Coming up on POI. Phase burn in three, two, one." The engine fired, and the shuttle began rocketing into a new, higher orbit.

Hewst kept a careful watch of the orbital telemetry on the forward console. "How long will you burn the engine?" she asked.

Looking at the readouts on the flight instruments, Kiiswood replied, "For another two minutes, twenty-eight seconds."

Suddenly, unexpectedly, a forceful voice called out over the shuttle's communication receiver. "Two-India-Seven, this is the TAS *Freyja*: we are monitoring your phase orbit burn on our navigation sensors," the voice announced. "Declare your intentions."

Kiiswood quickly accessed the shuttle's own navigation sensors and scrutinized its data. There, he discovered the ship's position relative to the long-shuttle. He looked at a rather baffled Hewst and said, "The *Freyja* is a *Maxwell*-class destroyer currently proximate to Schiaparelli Terminus. If they've been monitoring us on their sensors, they already know our intentions." Even as he monitored the sensors, Kiiswood continued to watch the engine-burn data. "Engine shut-down in ninety seconds."

Once again, Hewst patched her headset into the shuttle's communication system and replied to the ship's hail. "*Freyja*, Two-India-Seven: our intentions are not hostile. Request permission to rendezvous and dock at Schiaparelli Terminus." She awaited a response. But her request was greeted with protracted silence, keenly accentuated by the roar of the shuttle's engine.

Finally, the *Freyja* responded. "Two-India-Seven: request denied. Repeat, request denied," the forceful voice decreed. "Your vessel is designated as quarantined. You are instructed to break orbit immediately and return to Tyrrhenus."

Still watching the burn data, Kiiswood called out, "Engine shut-down in forty-five seconds."

Hewst persisted, "*Freyja,* Two-India-Seven: we're declaring an emergency. We are the only survivors of a terrorist attack on Belshazzar Station." She paused only fleetingly, then added, "We are not infected!"

Again, after another moment of silence, the *Freyja* ordered, "Two-India-Seven: break orbit and return to Tyrrhenus immediately!" The forceful voice of the destroyer concluded, "No further warnings will be issued!"

Hewst suddenly remembered the Venusian cloud-hopper—how a fighter-craft shot it down as it approached HAS *Landis.* She stared at Kiiswood with a look of cold trepidation. "Chief, that destroyer wouldn't actually fire on us, would it?"

Kiiswood did not make eye contact with the commander. "Even at this distance," he replied, "we're well within range of its pulse lasers." With his eyes still fixed on the engine-burn data, he counted down, "Engine shut-down in three, two, one."

But the long-shuttle's engine did not shut down.

The chief was genuinely alarmed, even though he continued to project composure. Frantically, he began poring over the instruments on the forward console, trying desperately to determine what was happening. "The controls are frozen!" he exclaimed. "We're locked out."

"What?" cried Hewst.

"Shut-down plus twenty-three seconds, twenty-four, twenty-five," Kiiswood called out as he observed the burn data on the instruments. Yet, observing the instruments was tragically his only course of action; the chief could not regain control of the shuttle. "The engine is applying too much delta-v for rendezvous," he said. "The shuttle is still accelerating."

"What happened?" she asked.

Then Kiiswood noticed that the shuttle's navigation protocols were being superseded by a new transponder code. The long-shuttle was now operating as a drone—as a remote-controlled extension of the destroyer. "The *Freyja* has overridden the long-shuttle's flight controls," the chief determined. "We can't shut down the engine."

Hewst was also genuinely alarmed; she, too, projected composure, but not as convincingly as the chief did. "If we can't shut the engine down," she inferred, "it'll consume all of our fuel."

The chief quickly reviewed the telemetry for both fuel consumption and acceleration. "If we can't shut down the engine," he said, "the shuttle will exceed escape velocity." He then turned to Hewst and confided, "Commander, we're flying out into deep space."

Chapter 26 – Schrödinger's Cat

Týr-Class Long-Shuttle, on Extra-Mars Trajectory (EMT)

(Heliocentric Co-ordinates: / 212.908, *b* –0.048, *r* 236,065,440 km)

Tuesday, 25 December 2429 CE

Time: 1807 Zulu

"Mayday, mayday, mayday," Alex signaled. The meta-droid sat alone in an underlit cockpit, belted to his seat so that he would not drift about in the zero-gravity environment. He had removed his helmet to make himself more comfortable and had turned off the overhead lights to conserve power. The cockpit's only sources of illumination were the shafts of sunlight that streamed through the shuttle's windows and the soft glow of instrument lights on the forward console. Alex was referencing the instrument's data as he repeatedly transmitted a distress signal. "Long-Shuttle Two-India-Seven. Fuel is depleted; heliocentric longitude 212.908 degrees, latitude minus 0.048 degrees, distance 1.578 AU; on extra-Mars trajectory."

The long-shuttle was adrift; it had indeed exhausted all of its propulsion fuel thirty-seven hours ago. The TAS *Freyja* had remotely accessed the shuttle's navigation computer during a short-term engine burn and prevented that engine from shutting down. So for six and a half hours, the shuttle continued to accelerate beyond intentions, finally acquiring too much speed to remain within Mars' gravitational hold. After hours of nonstop acceleration, the shuttle was now hurtling out into deep space, having spent its entire helium-3 reactor supply. Although the shuttle's engine was effectively dead in space, the cabin's life-support system still had enough power to maintain heat, light, and breathable air—at least for the time being.

For comfort's sake, Hewst and Kiiswood had also removed their helmets. They had spent several hours in the aft section of the passenger cabin, meticulously inventorying their supplies and prioritizing the cabin's power allocations.

Alex, meanwhile, had spent the past few hours trying to distract himself from his own melancholy. He was well aware that their chance of rescue was remote. Still, he sat in the cockpit, trying to hail a response to his persistent distress signals.

"Mayday, mayday, mayday," Alex repeated. "Long-Shuttle Two-India-Seven. Fuel is depleted . . . "

"You've been trying to send a mayday for almost two hours now, Alex," Hewst interrupted. "Why don't you take a break?"

Alex decided that he would welcome a respite; he had grown disheartened at the silence that greeted his calls for help. He unstrapped himself from the cockpit seat, pulled himself along the zero-gravity handrails, and joined his friends floating in the forward end of the passenger cabin. "I know that a rescue is unlikely," Alex responded. "As I said earlier, space is vast, and we're just a speck by comparison. I just want to try every option."

"The crew of the *Freyja* knows exactly where this speck is, Alex," replied Kiiswood. "They launched us out here. They don't want to rescue us; they're trying to rescue themselves *from* us."

"Maybe we should try hailing the *Freyja* directly," Alex suggested, exploring yet another option. "Maybe there's a way we can convince them that we're not infected—that we're not a threat."

Kiiswood did not wish to crush the meta-droid's optimism, but he also wanted to be tactically realistic. "As long as we're way out here, drifting helplessly," the chief noted, "they *know* we're not a threat."

The three of them hovered in silence, anxious and dispirited, each of them tried to take solace in the company of one another. Finally, Alex said, "We're going to die, aren't we."

Kiiswood laughed as he waxed philosophically. "Of course we're going to die someday." Then, upon reflection, he added, "Well, the commander and I will die; we're mortal. But you, Alex—you might suffer a system failure someday, but technically you can't die."

"Chief, I'm a living organism—of a sort," Alex reminded. "And all living things finally die."

Hewst pondered what Alex had just said. She wondered whether her android friend was feeling a need to talk about his mortal fears. "Do they, Alex?" she asked. "Is death so final?"

The meta-droid thought her query was a bit odd; he wondered why she would question something as self-evident as death. "Of course it is," Alex answered. "Surely, you're not suggesting that human beings might be immortal, are you?" he asked rhetorically. Alex then began to respond like a dedicated astrobiologist. "Natural selection abhors the immortality of an individual organism. Genes stand a better chance of long-term survival by diversification through a population of organisms. That diversity is threatened if an individual organism participates in the gene pool for too long. So evolution plays the favorable odds; it prefers the inevitable death of an individual over immortality. Death is an inexorable evolutionary trait."

"I agree with you, Alex," Hewst concurred. "From a scientific standpoint, life serves gene propagation, and death is final. But as factual as evolutionary science is, you yourself are a living example that life and death must be more than a matter of biology. As a machine, you have no genome to propagate; yet, you're an individual organism—of a sort. You're a self-aware living being."

"Aye," Kiiswood said humorously, "maybe you're the first of a new species—*homo mechanicus*." The chief continued, "As an android, your lifespan will far exceed mine or the commander's."

"Perhaps," conceded Alex, "but longevity is not immortality. Biological evolution might not account for *my* final outcome; but certainly the second law of thermodynamics does. A closed system inevitably degenerates into a more disordered state. So, whether biological or mechanical, the death of a living system is an inexorable trait of the laws of physics."

"Again, I agree," Hewst continued. "But my point is this: life must certainly be more than an object of genetics, or memetics, or clever engineering. Life is self-awareness. It's paradoxically aware of itself as an object of genetics, or of memetics, or (in your case) engineering. Life is awareness of the universe and of one's self in the universe, of others and of one's self in others. You're more than an individual organism, Alex. You *are* life. We all are. And if life is more than biology or physics, then perhaps death is also."

329

"Are you proposing a religious doctrine that death is an illusion," Alex asked, "that human beings are actually immortal?"

"Not at all," she answered. "Most religions acknowledge the reality of death." Hewst continued, "No, I don't doubt its reality; I just question its finality."

Alex appreciated Hewst's spiritual and pastoral counsel, as well as her scientific literacy, but he now wondered whether she fully grasped the unassailable laws of physics. He commented, "Catherine, you can't reverse entropy."

"Oh, I know," she acknowledged. "Death is the evolutionary or entropic fate of an organism, but I question whether it's the ultimate fate of life—of consciousness—of soul."

"So what do *you* think death is?" the meta-droid asked her.

Hewst grinned in momentary silence. She gripped the overhead handrail to steady herself as she was drifting slightly in zero gravity. "In truth, Alex," she finally replied, "I don't know what death is." Her thoughts quickly turned more metaphysical. "We talk about death—we have a word for it—but we don't know its referent. We don't know what the word really means. Certainly, we know that death is the cessation of biological functions, and so we extrapolate—we speculate that death is the cessation of consciousness, of soul. But in the end, that's all we're doing: speculating. We're trying to understand death from the outside; we're trying to know death from the perspective of living. It's like the space-time boundary of a black hole. Death is an event horizon beyond which consciousness cannot see. Try as we might to imagine the death of our consciousness, we're confronted with an incontrovertible truth: it's our own consciousness that's doing the imagining. The cessation of consciousness—the death of the soul—is unimaginable. Any awareness of death is, in that same moment, an awareness of self, of soul, of being alive. Death curiously fades away in that paradox."

"As a scientist, I constantly face the unknown," Alex remarked. "Yet, I find solace in the scientific premise that the universe is eventually knowable, even that which is currently unknown. The entire scientific endeavor succeeds on this reasonable premise. But if what you propose is correct, then death is not only unknown, it's also ultimately unknowable, at least on this side of life's horizon. How do you find solace in such nescience?"

Hewst responded, "I believe that all things are knowable, if not by the scientific mind of humankind, then certainly by the omniscient mind of the divine."

"Even death?" the meta-droid asked.

"We Christians make the rather audacious claim that God Himself dies in the crucifixion of Christ," she answered. "So whatever death is, I believe that God knows it—God is already there. I take solace in that belief."

Alex tried contemplating what his friend was saying, but he was soon distracted by his own concerns. "Whatever might be beyond that event horizon, I'm not ready to find out," he said. "I don't want to die."

With a reassuring smile for her meta-droid friend, Hewst responded, "Neither do I."

"I wish you two would find a more cheerful subject to talk about," Kiiswood complained. "After all, it *is* Christmas."

Hewst activated the holographic chronometer display on the sleeve of her compression suit. The chronometer lit up with bright uplifted holographic characters: TUESDAY, 25 DECEMBER 2429. "You're right, Chief," she said, "I'd lost track of the days." Hewst looked about the bare passenger cabin and at the sharp streaks of sunlight that teemed through the port windows. She noted the dead calm of the still engine. She then looked at Kiiswood and Alex and said, "Here we are—beaten, wounded, torn up; on the run from terrorists; evading a pandemic contagion; disavowed by our own government; marooned by our own military; helplessly hurtling through deep space. Admittedly, our providences seem bleak. This is not how I thought I'd be spending Christmas."

Kiiswood gripped the overhead handrails and pulled his weightless form to the aft end of the cabin. There, he retrieved a small art project that he had crafted while cataloging the shuttle's supplies. He returned forward with a collage of field ration containers that he had crudely fastened together in the rough shape of a little Christmas tree. "I know it's not very attractive,"

Kiiswood admitted, "but I thought we needed something to mark the occasion."

Hewst smiled widely at the inelegant tree; she was sincerely touched by the chief's thoughtful gesture. Her gratitude plainly showed on her face.

"Do you like it?" the chief asked.

Hewst could no longer hold back her laughter. "It's the ugliest tree I've ever seen," she answered. "And yes, Chief, I love it." She added, "I'm truly fortunate to call you both my friends."

"Our providences may be bleak, Catherine," said Alex, "but at least we're not alone."

Kiiswood secured his handmade tree to the overhead handrails. In most other circumstances, his tree might be regarded as hanging upside-down. But in their current zero-gravity environment, any direction could be regarded as upright. As he looked upon his handiwork, the chief commented, "Disavowed, marooned, helplessly hurtling through space—ironically, this is perhaps my best Christmas in many years." He then chortled and cynically posed, "How sad is that?"

"Not at all, Chief," Hewst consoled. "It's not sad at all."

The three of them hovered in silence, staring at the ugly Christmas tree. Then, quite unexpectedly, Kiiswood started singing:

> *"O Word of life, be Thou my soul;*
>
> *I have no life apart from Thee.*
>
> *Live Thou my life and make me whole;*
>
> *Live Thou my life, my God, for Thee."*

Hewst and Alex stared at the chief in genuine amazement. They had never heard him sing, and they had no idea that such a dulcet sound could come from the stratogen's combat-hardened soul.

Kiiswood suddenly stopped once he realized that Hewst and Alex were fixedly watching him. "What?" he asked. "I know it's not a Christmas carol, but it's the only hymn I know."

"Please, Chief," Hewst implored. "Please, continue."

Kiiswood complied and began singing the second verse:

"O Word of love, be Thou my heart;

I cannot love apart from Thee.

Make known to all the love Thou art,

And be Thou loved, my God, through me."

Hewst joined in, harmonizing *acapella* with the chief as the two of them sang the chorus together:

"O Christ, true God of God above,

True mortal of mortality,

O Thou, Who art incarnate love,

Be Thou my true humanity."

Alex softly clapped his hands, complimenting their duet with his one-person applause. "That was wonderful," he declared. "Thank you."

Hewst was noticeably lost in thought as she pondered the lines of the hymn.

"What is it, Commander?" the chief wondered.

"'True humanity,'" she uttered in response. "That's the issue at stake, isn't it? What is the *true* humanity?"

Kiiswood and Alex were puzzled. Their friend was a theologian—an expert in religious philosophy—so surely she understood the meaning of the hymn. Kiiswood answered, "Christ is the *true* humanity because the rest of us messed up human nature. That's what the song's about. But you know that."

"I'm not talking about the hymn," replied Hewst, "at least not directly." She continued, "No, I'm referring to the message from the presence in the cavern. The Aeon said that we are children of the One, but that we also disavow our childhood. They called it humankind's duality—humankind's two states of being. And that duality is our extinction."

"Yes, I remember," Alex acknowledged. "And by some mysterious choices that we're supposed to make, we'll save humanity from extinction."

"No, there's more to their message than that," countered Hewst. "It's not enough that we save humanity from extinction. They want us to determine which humanity we truly are."

"What are you talking about?" the chief asked. "We are who we are. There can only be one humanity."

"That's right, there can only be one humanity, but that humanity exists in two states simultaneously," she again countered. "Remember? The Aeon said that there's the humanity that acknowledges the One, and there's the humanity that dares to be the One for itself."

"What are you saying?" the meta-droid queried. "Are you saying that humanity is like Schrödinger's cat—both alive and dead—until we look inside the box?"

"I think that's what their message means," Hewst answered. "That's exactly the choice that the Aeon wants us to make. They've placed it in our hands to look inside the box, to decide whether or not we are the humanity that's worth saving."

"What do you mean, 'the humanity that's worth saving'?" wondered Alex. "Worthy of what?"

"Worthy of communion with other children of the One," answered Hewst. "That's what the religious statements in the fractals and stelae were all about. They're statements from other sentients—the souls that live on the worlds of many stars. The entire cavern is an announcement that we live among other self-conscious beings in the universe. It's also a reminder of humanity's own devotion to divine love and compassion—a compassion that makes communion with other children of the One possible."

"In other words," the chief rephrased, "the Aeon wants the three of us to decide whether human beings are worthy to join the family of aliens that believe in God?"

"I don't understand," Alex admitted. "Why wouldn't we be worthy?"

With a sense of remorse for his own humanity, Kiiswood responded, "Because we human beings have historically been poor examples of the love and compassion that our religions profess. We lie to each other, we steal from each other, we kill each other. We justify our sins in the name of God, as though God Himself were as apathetic and as selfish as we are. And if we treat one another like this, imagine how we would treat sentients elsewhere in the universe." He then paraphrased the message from the Aeon, "If humanity disavows its own childhood, then it also disavows the childhood of other children."

"Regrettable, but true," Hewst concurred. "But we human beings have also demonstrated great benevolence and selflessness. We have borne the pains of one another, we have shown mercy to those who would otherwise destroy us, we have even saved others through self-sacrifice. Humanity can be wondrously compassionate."

"So why are we three the ones who have to choose which is the true humanity?" the meta-droid asked with reluctance in his voice. "Why are *we* the ones who have to determine whether the cat is alive or dead?"

"We're the confluence of space and time," Hewst answered. "That's what they told us when I asked that question."

"That seems more like a riddle than an answer," Alex noted.

"Perhaps it means that the three of us will be in the right place at the right time to decide humanity's fate," she conjectured.

Kiiswood offered, "Or maybe it means that we were in the cavern at the right moment to encounter the Aeon."

Alex considered the chief's suggestion unlikely. "The three of us had been in the cavern together many times before that moment."

Hewst was suddenly taken by a thought. Her mind replayed all of her treks into the tetrahedral cavern. "My necklace," she said as she gestured where her necklace would otherwise be hanging were it not under her compression suit. "That was the first occasion that I wore my necklace into the cavern."

Kiiswood expressed skepticism. "Is that significant?"

"I don't see how," Alex replied. "I examined the pendant myself. It's just meaningless strands of DNA, a polynucleotide with no genetic function."

"Perhaps you're right," she conceded. "It's probably just a coincidence."

The meta-droid hovered momentarily in quiet contemplation, reflecting on their current plight and recalling their transcendent encounter with the Aeon. He then commented, "Here we are—helplessly hurtling through deep space. How can the three of us possibly affect the fate of humanity in this untenable situation?"

The chief softly, yet resolutely answered, "That's why we're not going to die here."

Alex grinned. "So you believe the Aeon?"

"I can't deny what's happened to me," Kiiswood confessed. "I have been transfigured by the experience—physically, emotionally, spiritually. So if the Aeon says that our choices might avert humanity's extinction, I believe them."

"So do I," Hewst eagerly acknowledged.

"And there's another reason I can emphatically state that we're not going to die here," Kiiswood stressed. Perhaps he was trying to console himself in the face of uncertainty. Perhaps he was trying to inject some humor into an otherwise somber situation. Perhaps he was trying to do a little of both. "The commander hasn't had a cup of coffee in several days," the chief quipped. "She can't meet her Maker without some caffeine in her."

Hewst responded merely with a nod and a smirk.

Alex's grin became a smile. "Merry Christmas, Catherine," he bade. "Merry Christmas, Chief."

The three of them hovered together in the stillness of the sunlit cabin. Soon the silence felt awkward, so Hewst began to sing again—singing the only hymn that her friend claimed to know. Hewst and Kiiswood sang the verses so many times that Alex soon learned the lyrics and began to sing with them.

Without forewarning, the smile on the meta-droid's disfigured face vanished. His form became as rigid as a mannequin, his eyes as lifeless as a doll's. His still body drifted unsecured in the cabin; he no longer steadied himself with the overhead handrails. Alex had suddenly turned off.

"Alex," Hewst called out. "Alex, can you hear me?"

Alex did not answer.

The sunlight that had shone so brightly through the shuttle's window mysteriously vanished. The cabin was abruptly palled in near darkness. The faint glow of the cockpit instruments offered some light in the darkness, but very little.

Hewst quickly grew uneasy. "What happened to the sun?" she asked.

Kiiswood sought answers. He climbed into the cockpit, trying to see what had blackened the sun; but he saw nothing. Quite abruptly, a piton nozzle speared the long-shuttle's hull and pierced the fuselage. The cabin and cockpit were flooded with an incapacitation agent—a colorless, odorless gas that quickly saturated the compartment's air. Within seconds, Hewst and Kiiswood fell unconscious.

Chapter 27 – JCS *Oberon*

Jovian Confederation Ship *Oberon*

(Heliocentric Co-ordinates: *l* 212.997, *b* −0.044, *r* 236,071,487 km)

Wednesday, 26 December 2429 CE

Time: 0804 Lima

Catherine Hewst awoke. She heard no chatter, no stirrings, just the steady purr of a ship's zero-point quantum engines in the background. She opened her eyes to a modestly lit cubicle, lined with automated medical equipment and telemetry monitors. To her bewilderment, she found that she was wearing a med-sensor unitard and lying in a hospital bed.

"Ah, Commander," Kiiswood announced from his chair. "It's good to see you're still with us." The chief sat stalwart beside Hewst's bed, having been keeping watch over his friend as she lay unconscious. He too was wearing a med-sensor unitard.

Hewst shot up in bed. She looked over Kiiswood as though inspecting his well-being. "Chief, are you okay?" she asked.

Kiiswood laughed. "I'm fine," he answered. "They treated me for the bullet wound in my leg. They did an excellent job on collagen regeneration; there's not even a hint of scarring from the entry or exit wounds. The question is, are *you* okay? You're the one who's been asleep for several hours."

Swinging her legs from under the covers, Hewst set her feet upon the floor and sat up on the edge of the bed. Ignoring the chief's question about her welfare, she posed one of her own. "How's Alex?"

"I haven't seen him since the long-shuttle," the chief replied, "but they've assured me that he's just fine. They have him in the engineering department for an overhaul and upgrades."

"They? Who are *they*?" she pressed. "Where are we, Chief?"

Before Kiiswood could respond, the voice of an unseen medical officer answered. "You're aboard the Confederation spacecraft carrier *Oberon*." From around a partition emerged a woman wearing a medical officer's lab coat over her khaki uniform, followed by a visibly apprehensive corpswain carrying a meal tray. "Specifically, you're in the *Oberon's* sickbay," the medical officer continued. "I'm glad to see you up and about, Commander Hewst. You've been out for several hours now. You didn't recover from the incapacitation agent as quickly as Chief Kiiswood; he's been here at your bedside since he came to a few hours ago." Because the corpswain clearly preferred to be anywhere else but in that cubicle, the medical officer took the meal tray and dismissed him. She then set the meal tray on the overbed table beside Hewst and said to her, "I'm sure you must be hungry."

While still sitting on the edge of the bed, Hewst lifted the cover from the meal tray. Among the steamed carrots, apple slices, and grilled chicken breast, she delightedly spied what she had been craving for days. "Coffee!" she exclaimed. Hewst immediately grabbed the cup from the tray and lifted it to her lips. But just as she was about to taste its hot, brewed contents, she paused to ask the medical officer, "Perchance, would you happen to have some amaretto?" She sampled the unflavored beverage without waiting for a reply.

With a half-hearted response, the medical officer answered, "If it's not on the tray, we don't have it." She then returned to her purpose. "My name is Dr. Ikumi DeVaul. I'm the xenopathologist assigned to your case."

"Our case?" queried Hewst, as she flavored the rest of her coffee with some of the cream and sugar on her meal tray. "And what case are we?"

DeVaul replied rhetorically, "Well, where should I begin?" She reached into the pocket of her lab coat and pulled out a tiny, transparent vial that she then handed to Hewst. "For one thing, we transcutaneously removed these from you and the chief a few hours ago."

Hewst intently studied the contents of the vial; she could just barely see the minute metallic strands inside. "What is it?" she asked as she handed the vial to Kiiswood.

"They are nanites," DeVaul explained. "Nanometer-sized machines. Once they were inside your body, they linked together to form tendrils around your brainstems—yours and Kiiswood's. Nasty little bugs, they are. They were designed to disrupt your autonomic functions. These particular nanites were designed and manufactured by the cybernetics engineers of your own government's Defense Ministry. And they didn't get into your bodies by accident." DeVaul turned to Kiiswood; of her two patients, she assumed that he was the one more apt to answer her question. "So why would the Terrestrial Assembly infect its own Defense Force personnel with a cybernetic weapon?"

"The project's physician injected all of the team members with what he called an immunization booster," the chief answered. "Apparently, we were deemed expendable to protect our government's secrets," he said as he inspected the contents of the vial. His genetically enhanced vision allowed him to examine the nanite strands more clearly and distinctly than Hewst could with her unaided eyes. "These must be what killed Dr. Střelec," the chief surmised.

"Those nanites should have killed us too," presumed Hewst. "I wonder why they didn't."

"Because these nanites couldn't receive a signal to activate," DeVaul expounded. "They're symmetrically inverted. Their nano-receivers are misaligned." She continued, "And this brings me to my next concern. Our medical scans indicate that both of you exhibit a condition known as *situs inversus*; your internal organs are reversed. But we don't believe that your condition is congenital. What are the chances that the only two survivors of *Project Belshazzar* would both have this condition?"

As Hewst ate slices of apple between sips of coffee, she pondered whether to ignore DeVaul's question or to venture an extraordinary answer. Should she recount the encounter with a four-dimensional, incorporeal intelligence? Should she embellish her account with allusions to angelic intervention? Any answer that she could offer seemed incredible; even the truth was incredible. She simply replied, "By my count, there are three survivors."

"Three? Are you referring to the android that we retrieved from the long-shuttle?" asked DeVaul. "That's yet another reason that we're trying to understand what happened to you. Our ship's engineers have been repairing and refitting the android, and they've discovered that its internal structure doesn't match the schematics from the Whitaker Institute. All of its components are backwards, just like the nanites—just like you two." DeVaul continued, "We have access to all of Project Belshazzar's records: scientific research, intelligence operations, language translations, even your medical records. We know all about your team's research at Hellas Planitia. What we don't know is what happened to you after the cavern vanished. "So, what happened?"

Kiiswood handed the vial of inverted nanites back to the xenopathologist and said, "You wouldn't believe us if we told you."

Placing the vial back into her lab coat pocket, DeVaul remarked, "I regard your medical scans as unbelievable, but I can't deny the facts at hand. Since I can't explain it, I'm willing to consider the inexplicable."

"From *our* perspective," Kiiswood replied, "it's the rest of the universe that's inverted—the digits on a chronometer, the words on a page, the maps on a monitor. The constellations appear backwards to us; the planets rotate in the opposite direction. Left is right; right is left. Even the name and rank on your lab coat are inverted."

After a moment's pause and another sip of coffee, Hewst finally acquiesced to DeVaul's question. "Our team's mathematician, Dr. Tereza Střelec, speculated that the three of us were pulled into a higher spatial dimension. Our three-dimensional forms were turned around in the extra space of a fourth dimension."

"That's a remarkable theory," DeVaul responded, "and yet the two of you are clearly here, and your condition is demonstrably real."

Hewst felt gratitude for DeVaul's medical care and hospitality. "We're here only because you and the ship's crew graciously rescued us from a derelict long-shuttle," Hewst said. "Thank you."

"It's Commodore Esteban you need to thank," the xenopathologist confided. "I sincerely mean you and Chief Kiiswood absolutely no ill will. But I should be candid with you; if it were up to me and most of the crew, we would have left you drifting out in space." DeVaul elaborated, "We knew your long-shuttle's point of origin. We knew that you flew out of Tyrrhenus—from a quarantined area. I advised the commodore not to bring you two aboard.

341

Your presence—your very proximity—presented too great a threat to our crew and too great a risk to our mission."

Hewst suddenly felt like a pariah. Now she understood why the corpswain was so eager to take his leave. "I appreciate your candor," Hewst noted sincerely, yet grudgingly. "But we're not infected."

"Oh, but you *are*, you both are," DeVaul declared. "We all are. The entire human race is infected."

"What are you talking about?" asked Kiiswood. "We saw the effects of the pathogen that infected the town of Tyrrhenus. We're not exhibiting any of the symptoms that we observed."

"That's because you're still in pathogenic latency," DeVaul replied, "and that fact alone is astonishing in itself. Whenever any infected person exhibits pathogenic vivacity, that person is immediately contagious, and everyone within a few kilometers is instantly affected by the contagion. How the pathogen remains dormant in the two of you is truly mystifying."

Kiiswood conjectured, "Perhaps we're unaffected because we don't carry the pathogen."

DeVaul grinned and nodded. "We executed a very thorough cerebral scan when you two came aboard. Most of your neurons are compromised." She reiterated, "Like I said, the entire human race is infected."

"Compromised neurons?" pondered Hewst. "We saw a report about a neuropathogen from the CMO at Camp Lundgren. But the report was heavily redacted. We didn't learn much, except that it wiped out a Martian settlement more than twenty years ago."

"You're probably referring to the Casius settlement," DeVaul commented. "I was on the original IPHA team that isolated and classified the Casius pathogen. Our team assigned its classified nomenclature: the Casius organelle—Casius, for short.

"This pathogen," asked Hewst, "is it viral or bacterial?"

"Neither," DeVaul answered. "This pathogen is of Martian origin. And as such, it didn't co-evolve with Terran-based life forms; Terran and Martian biologies evolved independently. That's how it has gone undetected for so long. Our human physiology never developed an immuno-defense mechanism against it, so this alien pathogen has managed to evade detection for decades—perhaps even longer."

"Longer?" the chief wondered. "Are you saying that humankind crossed paths with this pathogen before the Casius settlement?"

Dr. DeVaul paused for a moment to consider her answer. "The Interplanetary Heath Agency first became aware of the pathogen when the Casius settlement went dark twenty years ago. That's when IPHA assembled a team of xenopathologists from both the Jovian Confederation and the Terrestrial Assembly. Once we learned how to identify its subtle organellic footprint, we began covertly accessing the medical records of billions of people from across the solar system. Specifically, we looked at the certain neurometabolic factors in cerebral scans—factors that might appear to the uninitiated as extraneous and would otherwise go unnoticed. But in every scan, without exception, we saw the telltale neurochemistry that's indicative of the Casius organelle. Statistically, the infection is ubiquitous; there's not a single unaffected human being." She continued, "We ran hundreds of infection-rate simulations, and there's no way this pathogen could have infected all of humanity in just twenty years. We believe that humans may have first encountered this organelle more than a century ago—perhaps as early as the first Martian colonists of the twenty-second century."

Having now eaten nearly all of her meal, Hewst returned the cover to the tray. She then asked, "What do you know about this Martian pathogen?"

"It's a cell-like microbe," DeVaul responded. "It stores its genetic information through XNA—xenonucleic acids. It uses an exotic enzyme to copy its genes into DNA and then recopies those genes back into a new XNA molecule. With each copy, with each generation, there's a slight change in the gene sequence, so it replicates and evolves in this roundabout way. It replicates rapidly and spreads through every imaginable medium—air, food, water, physical contact, and sexual contact. It even spreads from mother to fetus *in utero*. For all intents and purposes, it's as inert inside an organism as it is inside Martian soil. But it seems to have a predilection for mammalian neurology. Once it encounters a mammalian neuron, the pathogen enters the nerve cell

343

through a nongated ion channel. And there it sits, like an innocuous neural organelle, until it starts talking to other Casius organelles."

"Talking?" the chief queried. "Are you saying that the pathogen can communicate among the neurons of an organism?"

"Would that the host organism were the only one affected," DeVaul replied with a muffled chuckle. "No, the pathogen communicates among all compromised neurons over a few kilometers. Each organelle works like a microscopic transceiver. As soon as one organelle activates, it transmits electromagnetic signals to all other organelles in range. All compromised neurons suddenly coordinate to block neuroanatomic responses to pain. These neurons then no longer work for the infected persons but against them, impeding their natural danger-avoidance mechanisms."

"That would explain what we saw on the AIC monitors at Camp Lundgren," Kiiswood commented. "The entire population just disengaged, and it seemed to happen instantaneously."

"Yes, but it doesn't explain *us*," Hewst conjectured. "If what you say is true, Dr. DeVaul, then the chief and I shouldn't be in pathogenic latency. If we're infected, then why haven't we succumbed to the pathogen? We were certainly within range of active Casius organelles at Hesperia Province."

"As I said earlier," DeVaul reminded, "the two of you are truly a mystery. I may have originally opposed your presence aboard the *Oberon*, but now that you're here, I plan to take advantage of your latency and to study your organellic infection for anomalies."

Hewst still felt like a pariah, but now she also felt like a laboratory experiment. At first, she was speechless. Finally, she said, "Well, if you can't explain why our infection wasn't triggered, can you tell us what initially triggers the first Casius organelle to begin transmitting its signal to other organelles?"

"We just don't know," the xenopathologist admitted. "Initial activation of any single organelle appears random. Since each organelle is a mutation, we speculate that vivacity is triggered by certain permutations of organelles in proximity. Yet there are nearly an infinite number of permutations. After more than twenty years of research, we haven't been able to discern a causative pattern." DeVaul continued, "But if we look at the organelles collectively, the

344

pathogen follows quantum probability theory, and from that, we can discern a propagation pattern. After calculating even the most conservative propagation rate, we estimate that the human race will be extinct in less than a century."

Was humanity's extinction imminent, as the Aeon had declared? The message of the angel-like presence was seemingly more and more prophetic, Hewst thought. She glanced at Kiiswood, looking for some clue from her friend as to how she should respond, but the chief simply shook his head. After some introspection, Hewst responded to DeVaul's ill-omened prediction by asking, "Has IPHA found a vaccine to immunize against the infection? Or perhaps there's a medical procedure to remove the organelles?"

"The organelles are neither bacterial nor viral," DeVaul grimly answered, "so antibiotics and virucides are useless. Our cyberneticists were able to engineer a neuro-vector delivery system to implant intra-neuronal nanites—mechanical microsurgeons to remove the organelles. Unfortunately, at the first sign that any single organelle is being removed, the entire organellic collective activates. We can't remove them fast enough because they communicate with each other at light-speed."

With wide-eyed amazement, Kiiswood remarked, "That's one hell of a defense mechanism."

Anxious to hear some hopeful words, Hewst asked, "So are you telling us that nothing can be done to preclude our extinction?"

DeVaul cryptically replied, "Our two governments are working together on something."

Hewst was encouraged by the xenopathologist's terse answer, but only vaguely. The commander paused intently, listening for more details. Alas, DeVaul did not explain her answer.

Finally, Kiiswood broke the pause in the conversation. "If we were too much of a risk to the safety and mission of your ship, why did your CO go out of his way to bring our long-shuttle aboard and rescue us?"

"Rescuing the two of you wasn't part of our mission," answered DeVaul. "The commodore hauled your long-shuttle into our hangar deck because he was under orders to retrieve the android."

How ironic, Hewst thought. Alex was once concerned that he was expendable—that his mechanical life was of lesser worth than human life. But it seemed that those values were now reversed. Indeed, Hewst's life and the life of Chief Kiiswood were now expendable, and Alex's life was paradoxically of greater worth than the lives of his two human friends. Hewst found an ironic pleasure in this reversal of fortunes.

"If I may ask, ma'am," the chief probed, "what's the *Oberon's* current mission?"

"That, I'm not at liberty to say," DeVaul said. "Mission information is at the commodore's discretion. You are, of course, most welcome to ask him yourselves when you see him. He plans to debrief the two of you at some point while we're underway."

"And how long will we be underway?" wondered Hewst.

"On our current trajectory," DeVaul answered, "about three months."

Knowing that their rescue had been only at the commodore's mercy, Hewst was grateful. During the past several days of crossing a Martian plane, escaping Christian terrorists, evading a neuropathogen, and being marooned in space, she had had little time to think about anything else but surviving. But now that she and her friends were safe, she was thinking about her colleagues at the Defense Academy who must surely be concerned about her welfare. She very much wanted to contact Vice Admiral Trendle to let him and the faculty know that she was alive and well. So Hewst asked, "Dr. DeVaul, I'd like to send a message to Earth, to the Defense Academy. Can you help me with that?"

"I'm sorry, Commander," DeVaul replied as she picked up the finished meal tray from the table. "The Jovian Confederation has ordered all of its ships to operate under EMCON conditions."

Kiiswood realized that Hewst did not understand the military acronym. "EMCON—Emission Control," the chief explained.

As DeVaul turned to leave the cubicle with the tray, she clarified, "It means we're running under communication silence. Absolutely no messages are to be transmitted—commodore's orders."

Just before DeVaul left the cubicle, Kiiswood asked, "Excuse me, ma'am, can you tell us—what's our heading?"

"Saturn," she said.

Chapter 28 – The *Dove*

The Jovian Confederation was an allied government with the Terrestrial Assembly. It was originally founded in the late twenty-third century as a union of Europa, Ganymede, Callisto, and Io–the four Galilean moons of Jupiter. The Jovian moons were initially colonized by employees of several corporations–specifically, fusion energy corporations from the five worlds of the Terrestrial Assembly. These colonists came to the Jovian system seeking their fortunes by harvesting the very lucrative isotope helium-3 from Jupiter's atmosphere. But during the devastating economic upheaval of 2256, the Jovian worlds were essentially cut off from the rest of human civilization in the inner solar system. For their own survival, these isolated colonists confederated their worlds and declared their independence from the Terrestrial Assembly. Eventually, the Jovian Confederation established additional settlements of its own in the Saturnian system–Enceladus, Tethys, Dione, Iapetus, Rhea, and, of course, Titan.

Saturn proved to be an economic boon for the Confederation. With less gravity and much weaker radiation belts than Jupiter, Saturn offered the Confederation an easily accessible and virtually limitless supply of fusion reactor fuel. The Jovians found that they could more easily fly their harvesting drones through Saturn's upper atmosphere, scooping up copious supplies of helium-3. And with their gas separation facilities on Rhea and Titan, the Jovians conveniently processed thousands of megatons of reactor fuel every year. After processing its coveted fuel, the Confederation shipped it throughout the solar system to trading partners, including the United Prefectures of Ceres, the Trojan Provincial Independents, and, of course, the Terrestrial Assembly.

The helium-3 industry had transformed the Jovian Confederation from despairing colonists (whose resources barely sustained their homesteads) into one of the solar system's economic and military superpowers, second only to the Terrestrial Assembly. The helium-3 industry also transformed humanity's energy consumption habits, making every world dependent upon the Confederation's product. The solar system's dependence on helium-3 was so critical that the Confederation's interplanetary tankers became strategic targets during the Martian War.

Although the Jovian Confederation had hoped to remain neutral during the war, the realities of interplanetary trade made neutrality impossible. When Mars proclaimed itself the New Jerusalem and implemented a Christocratic government, it seceded from the Terrestrial Assembly, declared war on the other terrestrial worlds, and blockaded the Jovian tankers from entering the inner solar system. The red planet even commandeered several Jovian tankers, effectively declaring war on the Confederation. Thus, for its own economic interests, the Jovian Confederation allied itself with the Terrestrial Assembly against the Christocracy of the New Jerusalem. The Confederation and the Assembly had been allies ever since. They were allies in trade; in interplanetary defense; and, of late, in a clandestine mission, the same mission that now had the JCS *Oberon* on a trans-Saturn trajectory.

For nearly three weeks since their rescue on Christmas day, Hewst and Kiiswood had been incidental guests aboard the *Oberon*. At first, the two of them were restricted to sickbay, where they were subjected to one medical test after another, as Dr. DeVaul tried to learn why the pathogen within them lay dormant. After several days of medical scans, blood work, and tissue sampling, they were deemed noncontagious and were assigned to temporary berthing quarters in a converted utility compartment. The commodore eventually permitted Hewst and Kiiswood to discard their med-sensor unitards, to don their Defense Force uniforms, and to move about the ship in designated areas. But their presence on the ship was very grudgingly accepted by the crew, who preferred instead to eat at distant tables in the mess hall or to work out at the far end of the gym compartment. Gradually, Hewst and Kiiswood became more accepted (or, perhaps, less shunned), once the crew realized that their incidental guests were not contagious with a mind-altering pathogen.

349

However, during the nearly three weeks they had been on board, they had not seen their meta-droid friend even once, nor had they spoken with the *Oberon's* commanding officer. But that was about to change. Just as Hewst and Kiiswood had finished dinner and were leaving the mess hall, Petty Officer Parker Adena, the commanding officer's yeoswain, met them in the passageway. "Excuse me, Commander, Chief," said Adena, "Commodore Esteban has directed me to escort the two of you to his stateroom for debriefing."

News of the debriefing came as a surprise to Hewst and Kiiswood not because the commodore wanted to debrief them, but because he wanted to debrief them now. Hewst glanced at Kiiswood to see whether he knew of a scheduled meeting with the commodore that she might have otherwise forgotten. But the chief knew nothing of this meeting until now.

"The commodore wants to meet with us now?" she asked the yeoswain.

"Aye, ma'am," Adena promptly answered. "Please, follow me," he said politely with a gesture to follow.

Hewst and Kiiswood followed the petty officer through the brightly lit, bustling passageways and ladderwells of the spacecraft carrier. Other than having a different color scheme, the passageways were quite similar to those of Defense Force vessels of the Terrestrial Assembly. After passing through winding halls, multiple decks, and crowds of crewswains rushing about, they finally arrived at the entrance to the commodore's stateroom. Adena did not announce their arrival with his c-nex. Instead, he notified the commodore with a centuries-old tradition—the yeoswain knocked on the door.

From behind the door, the commodore's voice ordered simply, "Enter!"

Adena opened the door and, with sharp military bearing, formally ushered in the ship's guests. "Excuse me, Commodore," the petty officer reported, "Commander Catherine Hewst and Chief Níyol Kiiswood are here as ordered."

"Thank you, Yeoswain," the commodore acknowledged from behind his desk. "Carry on."

"Aye aye, sir," Adena replied as he took his leave, closing the stateroom door behind him as he left.

True to its designation, the commodore's stateroom was indeed stately. Although the compartment was not very large, it was significantly larger than any other line officers' personal space. Around the room were three aniline leather sofas: two full-length matching pieces and a shorter settee. The sofas encircled an oval wool rug that bore the intricately woven seal of the ship's name and nomenclature: JCS OBERON—CS-844. Although dignified and colorful to behold, the ship's seal was partially obscured by the polished teakwood coffee table at the center of the compartment. At the far end of the stateroom was the commodore's desk; it too was made of polished teakwood. Three of the four bulkheads were generously adorned with framed photographs of various Confederation space vessels; the most prominent photograph was of the *Oberon*. Hanging on the bulkhead behind the commodore's desk was the Jovian Confederation flag, smartly displayed between two large portholes that arguably yielded one of the best dorsal views of the ship's bow—second only to the vista seen from the ship's bridge.

Dr. Ikumi DeVaul was seated on one of the larger sofas; she was drinking some coffee that she had prepared for herself from the coffeeware set on the center table. Standing beside the commodore's desk was the ship's executive officer. And, seated behind his desk, combing through the holographic data that hovered just over his desktop, was the commanding officer of the *Oberon*, who was fastidiously studying the military personnel files of his two guests.

The commodore looked up from his files only long enough to acknowledge the new arrivals. "Commander, Chief, have a seat," he directed. "We need to get some new c-nexes for you two. It would be so much easier to call you than to send my yeoswain looking for you."

"Our cybernetics team is working on it, sir," DeVaul volunteered. "We've run recent neural scans and are formatting new c-nexes for both of them. They should be ready in another day or two."

The commanding officer curtly offered introductions and extended some obligatory niceties. "I'm Commodore Sebastián Esteban." He gestured toward the other officers in the stateroom. "This is my XO, Captain Leighton

Toulon. You've already met Dr. DeVaul." Returning his attention to the holographic files, he added, "Help yourselves to some coffee."

At the commodore's direction, Hewst and Kiiswood took their seats on the settee. While Kiiswood sat at attention, Hewst availed herself of the commodore's hospitality and poured herself a cup of coffee.

Shuttling his attention between his guests and their service records, Esteban said, "Chief Níyol Kiiswood, special warfare operations, Terrestrial Assembly Defense Force. Current assignment: SOC, Sorteer Unit Four. Current status: MIA." The commodore paused for a moment to assure himself that he was correctly reading the holographic information, or, rather, the lack of information. "No date of birth, no family listed. No fingerprints, no voice-prints. No retinal scans, no cerebral scans. No DNA profile." He then inferred, "You're either a ghost, Chief, or you're one of the Assembly's genetically engineered weapons—a leftover from the Martian War." With consoling words that did not seem to fit his impassive expression, the commodore added, "I know who you are, Chief. My sympathies on the way your government has treated your kind."

Kiiswood said nothing; he merely gave an affirming nod.

Esteban continued, "Commander Veronica Catherine Hewst, former chaplain, Terrestrial Assembly Defense Force. PhD in religious paleography. Temporarily recommissioned from the Defense Force Academy, where you were teaching courses in religious studies. Current assignment: TAD, Federal Aerospace Intelligence Agency. Current status: MIA. Only family listed: an adoptive father, deceased."

"Obviously, sir, we're not missing in action," Hewst noted. "That being the case, there are people who would probably like to hear that we're alive and well. Is there any way that you can get a message out that we're okay?"

"To whom would you send a message?" the commodore asked. "Your records show no immediate family."

"I have friends and colleagues at the academy," she answered. "They're probably concerned about my welfare."

With his still impassive expression, Esteban replied, "Be that as it may, I can't help you, Commander. For security reasons, we've been ordered not to transmit any signals that might give away our heading; we're operating under EMCON conditions. We can't even squawk our transponder code." Without a word, he glanced at Kiiswood, indicating that the chief could not message anyone either.

"Oh, I'm good with that, sir," Kiiswood responded drolly. "If my government wanted me to have friends, they would have been issued in my duffle bag."

Taking his cue from his commanding officer, Captain Toulon began to debrief Hewst. "Commander," the executive officer asked, "why would FAIA need the services of a paleographer?"

"You obviously have access to Belshazzar's project reports," she responded. "I assume you've read them."

Esteban interrupted, "Indulge my XO, if you would, please; answer his questions."

Hewst felt uncertain as to whom she should be speaking, so she addressed both Esteban and Toulon. "Respectfully, I have a few questions of my own."

"First things first, Commander," Toulon replied.

Hewst realized that Esteban and Toulon were not obliged to answer any of her questions. She supposed that she stood a better chance of getting her own questions answered if she cooperated. "Aerospace Intelligence discovered an ancient scroll in a subsurface cavern on Mars," she said. "As a paleographer and an expert in religions, I was called in to investigate, to find out what it was doing there."

"And did you?" asked Toulon. "Did you find out what it was doing there?"

"Aye, sir," Hewst answered. "It was one among hundreds of scrolls. We saw a large collection of manuscripts that apparently comprised a sort of religious archive."

"Our review of Belshazzar's records shows that your team discovered only two manuscripts," challenged Toulon. "There was an ancient Levant scroll that was recovered soon after the cavern was discovered, and there was a birch-bark scroll that you were in the process of retrieving when the—when the phenomenon happened." He then asked, "Where did you see these hundreds of scrolls?"

Hewst wondered whether she could answer the executive officer's question intelligibly, so she resolved to describe what she had seen as best as she could. "During that phenomenon, as you so call it, we saw these scrolls stored in multiple caverns—caverns that seemed to be inside each other." She tried to read Toulon's expressions, wondering whether he believed her. "That tetrahedral cavern was a kind of religious archive—a repository to serve as a reminder to humankind."

"A reminder?" Toulon queried. "A reminder of what?"

"A reminder of our own religious history," Hewst answered. "The purpose of this archive is to remind us that we have an innate obligation to be kind and compassionate to each other—to all self-conscious beings. That seemed to be the prevailing message of all the inscriptions in the cavern."

Toulon pressed, "And you discovered this purpose through paleographic investigation?"

"Not exactly, sir," Hewst answered reluctantly. "We were told as such." She glanced at Kiiswood, who nodded in agreement.

"Told?" the executive officer asked. "Told by whom?"

"An alien presence," she said with even greater reluctance. "A hyper-dimensional intelligence." Hewst expected Toulon to greet her response with incredulity, but she was surprised that he seemed accepting of her answer, as though he were expecting it.

"Aye," Toulon acknowledged with a furrowed brow, "Dr. DeVaul told us that you two had some kind of encounter with a higher dimension. Your inverted bodies are evidence of a hyperspace interaction." He then used his c-nex to activate the stateroom's projection system. A holographic projection suddenly appeared in the center of the room above the coffee table. The projection was of a rotating image of the tetrahedral cavern overlaying a transparent image of the Martian subsurface. Gesturing toward the projection, Toulon continued, "Our theoretical physicists reviewed your project team's research, and they concur with the supposition of Dr. Tereza Střelec, your team's mathematician. They believe that the entire tetrahedral cavern and the equivalent volume of subsurface basalt overlapped each other through four-dimensional space. They theorize that the basalt and the cavern were both occupying the same three-dimensional space simultaneously. So the cavern vanished, not because the cavity suddenly filled up with rock; the indigenous basalt was always there. The cavern simply moved out of the way through hyperspace."

Amazed at Toulon's presentation and its implications, Kiiswood generalized, "So every time we were walking around inside that cavern, we were also walking through solid rock?" The chief smiled and added, "That's amazing."

Returning to his questioning, Toulon asked, "This intelligence that you mentioned—did it say anything else?"

"Aye, sir," Hewst's reply was pointed. "The presence said that the extinction of the human race is imminent."

The executive officer then implored Hewst for a more pointed reply. "Did this presence happen to mention a cure?"

"A cure?" she queried.

"A cure for Casius," Toulon specified.

"No, sir, they said nothing about a pathogen." Hewst elaborated, "They implied that humanity's imminent extinction is our own doing. They said that we're estranged from our source of being and compassion."

"Well, that's maddeningly vague," judged Toulon. "What the hell does that mean?"

Hewst thoughtfully paused, then answered, "I take it to mean that our lack of compassion for others is a threat to our own existence."

Like a skilled military tactician, the commanding officer sat back as his executive officer conducted his interrogation. Esteban listened to Hewst's responses as he assessed her candor and credibility. "Compassion is quaint sentimentality," the commodore interjected, "but hardly relevant to our present concerns."

Hewst responded almost stoically, "What concerns could be more relevant than humanity's compassion for one another?"

"My primary mission is the very survival of the human race," Esteban replied without hesitation. "Survival takes precedence. What's the point of compassion if there's no one around to be compassionate?"

"Respectfully, sir," retorted Hewst, "what are we saving if we lose our humanity? What's the point in surviving if not for compassion?"

Esteban smirked. He then gestured to his executive officer to continue.

"Commander," Toulon resumed, "I see here in your project reports that you were the one who provided your team member, a Dr. Jonathan Driggers, with the needed key to translate some of the mystery languages in your Martian cavern."

"I discovered a pattern," Hewst confirmed. "Each fractal contained its own unique religious pronouncement inscribed in numerous languages."

"And in your reports," he added, "you say that you were working on a hypothesis concerning the origin of these mystery languages—where they come from. Is that correct?"

"No, sir," she countered, "Dr. Driggers was the team's linguist. You'll need to consult his research for that information. My hypothesis concerned the specific origin of the particular religious pronouncements."

Captain Toulon looked at Esteban for authorization to proceed with the next line of questioning. After an affirming nod from the commodore, Toulon asked, "What do you know about the Thaller star system?"

Hewst wondered why the captain would ask her such a question. "I'm not a stellar astronomer, sir," she responded. "But I know that our team's astrophysicist, Dr. Glendon Ferris, interpreted a series of mathematical symbols as denoting the location of five stellar systems. And if I recall correctly, one of those was the Thaller system."

"Since Dr. Ferris isn't here, speculate for me, if you will," Toulon solicited. "Is it possible that some of the mystery languages might have originated from the Thaller system?"

Hewst felt all eyes in the stateroom fixed on her, all ears keenly focused to hear her response. "Some of the languages clearly originated from Earth, sir," she said, "and one of those five stellar systems that Dr. Ferris identified is our own. So, by extension, it's my opinion that some of the unknown languages in the cavern possibly originated from other stellar systems, including the Thaller system."

"Thank you for your candid insights," Toulon said graciously. He then entreated, "Is there anything else that you know about the Thaller star system?"

Kiiswood, noting the executive officer's persistence on the topic of the Thaller system, interjected himself into the interrogation. "It's apparent to me, Captain, that you've spoken with Alex, and you're already aware that we know more about it."

"Who's Alex?" asked Esteban.

Dr. DeVaul answered, "That's the nickname that the Belshazzar team members gave to ALX-63, the project's meta-droid."

"Alex said something about it to me and the chief," Hewst admitted. "He said that Thaller system was the name of a subdirectory in some of his lab equipment at Belshazzar Station. He inadvertently discovered that Aerospace Intelligence redirected that equipment from a research project called Columba Noachi." Esteban and Toulon were notably disquieted as they contemplated the commander's admission. "I can see that I struck a nerve," she observed. "I presume that the chief and I aren't supposed to know that name. At the risk of pressing the envelope, what's Columba Noachi, beyond its obvious biblical reference?"

The silence in the stateroom seemed interminable. Finally, the commodore addressed his executive officer and said, "Captain, have Yeoswain Adena escort Dr. Madina to the stateroom. And have him bring his android with him." As Toulon was contacting the yeoswain via c-nex, Esteban looked at the former chaplain and asked, "Do you believe in miracles, Commander?"

"Aye, sir, I do," she thoughtfully answered. "I believe in miracles; I just don't expect them."

"Why not?" Esteban asked.

"If it's expected," she replied, "then it's not a miracle."

After a moment's pause, Esteban began to wax philosophical. "Scientists tell us that Venus and Mars each suffered at least one mass extinction event, and Earth has suffered several. They tell us that each extinction event tended to wipe out the dominant species at that geological period. Here, in the Interplanetary Age, it's humankind's turn in the barrel; we're the dominant species this time. The only way for us to survive system-wide extinction is to scatter our genes through more than one star system. We have to become an interstellar species. Project Columba Noachi is our Hail Mary effort for a miracle. It's a joint, clandestine mission of the Jovian Confederation and the Terrestrial Assembly to secure the future of the human race. For the past eight years, our two governments have been constructing a massive interstellar spacecraft near Saturn. And in about another three months from now, it'll be ready to launch on a trans-Thallerian injection."

Kiiswood interjected, "How massive?"

With a couple of keystrokes on a small control panel at his desk, the commodore changed the holographic image at the center of the stateroom. The projection now displayed a rotating schematic of an enormous interstellar craft, surrounded by space-dock scaffolding and orbiting above the Saturnian moon, Titan. "Columba Noachi, aka the *Dove*," he answered as he pointed to the schematic. "It's 4.5 kilometers long, and over a half billion metric tons. With advancements in zero-point technology and improved EM engines, it should theoretically be able to achieve forty-five percent of light-speed. It'll reach its destination in about three thousand years—that's just the blink of an eye in a cosmological time-frame."

Studying the schematic, Hewst noted the scale of a spacecraft carrier beside the interstellar ship. She was awed at the enormity of the *Dove*. "That ship," she asked, "its destination is the Thaller system?"

"Aye, it's a G-type stellar system in the constellation Columba," responded Esteban. "Based on their best astrophysical observations, our scientists believe that a planet in the Thaller system is the most Earth-like of all known exoplanets in its atmosphere, water, landmass, gravity, rotation, and magnetosphere. There's even clear evidence of a plant-based biosphere. The Thaller system looks like humanity's best chance at a fresh start."

Hewst began to consider the ethical consequences of such a brave and daring endeavor. "What about sentient life?" she pondered. "Don't we have a moral obligation to respect their autonomy?"

"Our mission specialists have already considered that possibility," the commodore replied, "but there's no evidence whatsoever of technological development on that planet."

"The absence of technology is not the same thing as the absence of sentience," she commented, stating the obvious.

"Aye," acknowledged Esteban, "but there's no evidence that the planet supports any sentient inhabitants."

"Perhaps there is, sir," proposed Hewst. "I believe that's why you and your XO were asking questions about languages associated with the Thaller system. If there are inhabitants who are language users—who have a religious conscience—then they are self-aware, sentient beings. If there are indeed sentients inhabiting that planet, then we can't avoid the moral quandary of intruding into their world, can we?"

The commodore responded, "Don't we have a moral obligation to the human race? To have the means to save humankind and then not act—that would be morally irresponsible."

"Excuse me, sir," Kiiswood interjected. "I know that I'm no engineer, but as I'm looking over the specs in this schematic, it seems to me that your interstellar lifeboat lacks sufficient volume to ferry the entire human population to the stars."

"That's correct, Chief," Esteban admitted, "and it isn't intended to."

"Of course, this debate in survival ethics is merely academic," observed Hewst. "Despite the obvious moral dilemma of deciding who gets to go and who stays behind, Project Columba Noachi is a futile mission at its outset. If you're planning to send human beings away to escape the plague, we're all already infected. Whomever you send will inevitably succumb to the pathogen. Sooner or later, your lifeboat would turn into an interstellar mortuary while underway."

"You're absolutely right, Commander," the commodore agreed, "and that's why there won't be a single living soul aboard." As confusion settled on the faces of his two guests, Esteban explained, "The ship is designed to carry cryo-preserved embryos." With another keystroke, he highlighted certain parts of the holographic schematic, indicating the location of the ship's cryogenic chambers. "Humankind has been freezing embryos for centuries—long before we encountered the Casius organelle. Our two governments have acquired hundreds of thousands of uninfected human embryos that will be gestated in ectogenetic chambers once they arrive in a new world three thousand years from now."

Hewst quickly realized the significance of the commodore's revelation. "Do I understand you correctly, sir?" she asked. "The Assembly and the Confederation are writing off every human being in the solar system as a hopeless cause and are opting instead to start afresh with a new humanity in another star system."

"Human life in this system *is* a hopeless cause," Esteban declared unapologetically. "No one lives forever, but if we as a species are worth saving, this might be the only way to do it."

"That makes sense to me," quipped Kiiswood.

Hewst wondered, "Commodore, how do you know that the embryos will remain viable for three thousand years?"

"We've been able to gestate three-hundred-year-old embryos to full term with no increased incidents of developmental abnormalities or birth defects." Esteban then confessed, "Of course, we have no three-thousand-year-old frozen embryos to test, but we see no reason that they won't remain viable for the duration of the journey."

Esteban's answers did little to placate Hewst's curiosity; instead, they seemed to prompt more questions. "Centuries ago, when we colonized the terrestrial planets and the Jovian moons," she said, "we had to establish parts of a Terran ecosystem just to survive. We did that because humans evolved in symbiosis with other organisms. So how will a new human race survive without that ecosystem?"

"The ship's payload includes everything that a new human colony will need to survive: embryos and seeds from farms, zoos, arboreta, and wildlife preserves throughout the solar system. But we're not just securing the future of the human gene pool; we're securing the future of our meme pool as well." Esteban highlighted a large portion of the schematic's payload section. "The bulk of the payload comprises humanity's greatest works of art, literature, philosophy, science, and technology."

With a caustic smirk, Kiiswood remarked, "So all those news reports about terrorist assaults on museums and archives were a ruse. The artifacts weren't stolen, they were actually confiscated for Columba Noachi."

"There's nothing to be gained by letting human culture die with a doomed humanity," the commodore noted.

"I'm curious, sir," Hewst asked, "once the *Dove* reaches its destination, and its automated systems grow a population of human infants in ectogenetic chambers, what happens then? Human beings are social creatures. Those infants will be utterly dependent on human contact and interaction. They will need to be socialized, nurtured, and educated; they won't survive otherwise. How will you teach them what it means to be human?"

"That's where your artificial colleague comes in," Esteban replied. "Part of your government's contribution to this mission is 125 androids, each programed with its own particular personality and scientific specialty. These meta-droids, as the Whitaker Institute calls them, are designed to simulate self-awareness and personhood. As androids, they will be able to endure the three-thousand-year transit through interstellar space. And once they reach the Thaller system, they will be able to facilitate colonization with their scientific expertise. With their ability to mimic human empathy, they'll provide the nurture and socialization that the new colonists will need to survive. In effect, these meta-droids will show the new generation how to be human." He highlighted the android storage compartments on the schematic and continued, "The Federal Space Administration has already delivered 124 meta-droids for the mission. But one of them—the one your team calls Alex—was temporarily assigned to Project Belshazzar, to be delivered later. When Belshazzar Station went silent, we assumed that we lost that asset. Thankfully, the Whitaker Institute installed tracking beacons in all their meta-droids. So when your long-shuttle attained orbital insertion, our sensors picked up the tracking beacon. Apparently, the project administrators wanted to give the mission every chance of success, so they ordered me to risk the *Oberon's* crew to retrieve the remaining meta-droid." Esteban gestured toward Dr. DeVaul and said, "We were frankly amazed to find you two still alive. Against the counsel of our xenopathologist, I decided to bring the two of you aboard. I guess I was genuinely curious; I wanted to know how you two survived a quarantined area."

"Incidentally, sir," DeVaul offered, "I still haven't been able to determine how the commander and the chief evaded contagion. I first thought their inversion might have been a factor, but even their inverted organelles have electromagnetic receptors."

"I wish I could explain it, sir," Hewst confided. "The chief and I are simply grateful to be here."

Kiiswood added, "Perhaps it's one of those miracles you mentioned, Commodore."

"I need to ask, sir," Hewst probed, "did Alex know about the tracking beacon? Did he know that he was manufactured for Columba Noachi? In the weeks that we worked together, he mentioned none of this."

"He?" laughed Esteban. "*It* very likely was unaware of its mission. The meta-droids know only what their respective network donors know. Due to the secrecy of the project, none of the donors were informed of the final mission objective." He then said, "But with the launch date fast approaching, I'm sure that Dr. Madina's team has brought it up to speed."

"Commodore, I just realized that I misspoke earlier," admitted Kiiswood. Pointing at the schematic, he said, "This isn't a lifeboat. A lifeboat rescues souls in distress, but the *Dove* isn't rescuing anyone."

"The chief is right," Hewst agreed. "The *Dove* isn't a lifeboat. It's an interstellar ark." She continued, "The flood narrative in the book of Genesis is not a story about God rescuing humankind; it's about God starting over again. That's the mission of this interstellar ark—to start over again in the constellation Columba."

Esteban concurred, "That's why we call it Columba Noachi—Noah's dove."

"But there's a problem with the Noah analogy," Kiiswood countered. "The ark in the Bible didn't have sails or a rudder; it didn't go anywhere. It just floated above the earth until the danger receded." The chief then asked, "Why do you need to send your interstellar ark to a distant planet? If humankind is going extinct, why not just park the *Dove* in Terran orbit until the danger recedes? Then your meta-droids can restart the human race on the vacated Earth."

"Alas, I wish it were as simple as that," the commodore replied. "Casius doesn't infect only humans; every mammal in the solar system is infected. But in all other mammals, the pathogen inexplicably remains dormant—at least it has so far. So even after human beings have gone extinct, the pathogen will still inhabit this solar system." Esteban turned off the holographic projection and added, "No, Chief, if the human race is to start over, it will have to do so around a new star. Humanity is destined to be an interstellar species."

"Destined, sir?" asked Kiiswood. "Are you saying that humankind has a manifest destiny? Historically, manifest destiny has never favored the indigenous populations."

Esteban responded, "As the commander herself has referenced, the human race has colonized the inner planets of the solar system, as well as its outer moons. It's our history to colonize, and it's our future. It's in our nature to reach out and establish new homes for ourselves."

Hewst retorted with a courteous and reverential tone, but with contentious words. "I understand that our two governments are trying to make a new home for the human race. But, respectfully, sir, it's not colonizing when it's someone else's home. It's invasion."

"Your ethical qualms are duly noted," the commodore replied. "But indigenous populations or no, colonizing the Thaller system is the right thing to do for the sake of humanity's survival. What other choice do we have?"

"Choices are not about righteousness, sir," answered Hewst. "Choices are about sacrifice."

Suddenly, everyone's attention was drawn to the stateroom door as someone knocked from the other side.

"Enter!" the commodore ordered.

Yeoswain Adena opened the door and ushered in two new faces. The two newcomers were rather conspicuous, for they were the only ones in the room not wearing military uniforms. Instead, they were dressed in civilian attire. "Excuse me, Commodore," the yeoswain reported, "Dr. Sarito Madina is here as ordered."

"Thank you, Yeoswain," acknowledged Esteban. "Carry on."

"Aye aye, sir." Adena closed the stateroom door behind him as he left.

Gesturing to the two newcomers, Esteban once again made introductions. "Commander Hewst, Chief Kiiswood," he presented, "this is Dr. Sarito Madina, a neurocartographer with the Whitaker Institute." As his guests were exchanging handshakes, Esteban continued, "And, of course, you already know your colleague."

Yet, they did not know this unnamed newcomer. The chief did not recognize the face, but he instantly knew that the unnamed civilian was an android. Kiiswood's enhanced senses allowed him to see the silhouette of the android's automatous subframe. And although Hewst did not have the benefit of Kiiswood's genetic enhancements, she sensed something eerily familiar in the unnamed newcomer. His comportment, his mannerisms, his hair, even the subtle contours of his face, vaguely reminded Hewst of her father.

"Catherine!" the stranger announced with a familiar voice. "It's me, Alex!" The meta-droid embraced Hewst with a grateful hug. "I'm so happy to see that you're safe."

Hewst easily recognized the voice of her friend. "Alex?!" she replied, as she hugged him in return. "I was so worried about you."

"Chief, I'm happy to see you too," the meta-droid said as he then embraced Kiiswood. "They wouldn't let me out of the cybernetics lab for weeks. Sarito assured me that the two of you were alright, but his assurances aren't as good as seeing you two with my own eyes."

Kiiswood's reaction was less affectionate than Hewst's; he returned Alex's hug with a mere one-armed pat on the back. Still, he was genuinely glad to see his friend or, rather, a new version of his friend. "So, Alex," the chief asked, "what's new with you?"

Alex chuckled. "I know it's a little strange to see me with this new look," he acknowledged. "While they were repairing my damages, I asked them to modify my structure and visage to look more like Francis Hewst, the man who inspired me to become an astrobiologist. I hope you don't mind, Catherine."

"Not at all," she answered. "I imagine he'd be honored."

Alex continued, "They replaced all of my kinesionomic joints and my polymeric sub-tissue; they even reshaped my synthetic dermal casing." Alex added, "No more bullet holes, no more facial disfiguration."

Madina reached out and once again shook Hewst's hand. "Commander, I want to thank you and Chief Kiiswood for retrieving our property. The meta-droid told me how you escaped capture and execution by religious terrorists. You two could have easily left it behind, but you risked your lives to bring it with you. Your heroism has increased the chances of the *Dove*'s success."

As she continued to shake his hand, Hewst responded, "Dr. Madina, I'm glad that Alex will be an asset to the *Dove*'s mission, and I appreciate your expressions of thanks. But I fear your gratitude is misplaced. We didn't retrieve your property; we rescued our friend."

"Actually," the chief interjected, "Alex risked himself to rescue us."

"To be clear," Madina chortled, "you two do know that your so-called friend is just a machine." In a slightly more solemn tone, he continued, "Whatever your motives were, I'm grateful to both of you for returning our meta-droid. And as an expression of that gratitude, you two are most welcome to socialize with our property for the remainder of our journey to Titan."

"Well, not the entire journey," Esteban interjected. Addressing Hewst and Kiiswood directly, the commodore remarked, "The two of you will not be going to Titan with the rest of us."

"Sir?" the chief queried.

"You two might indeed be in pathogenic latency, but the project administrators have decided not to take any chances. Before EMCON conditions were initiated, they directed me not to bring you two anywhere near the space-dock prior to the *Dove*'s launch."

"If I may ask, sir," Hewst apprehensively inquired, "what do you plan to do with us?"

"I plan to drop you off before we reach space-dock," he answered, "at an old facility called Porco Station."

Chapter 29 – Porco Station

Jovian Confederation Ship *Oberon,* on Titan Approach Phase (TAP)

(Heliocentric Co-ordinates: l 270.415, b +1.307, r 1,487,601,011 km)

Sunday, 07 April 2430 CE

Time: 0018 Lima

After several months on its trans-Saturn trajectory, the JCS *Oberon* had entered the Saturnian system. It was decelerating for a low-orbital insertion around the ringed planet's largest moon, Titan. There, the *Oberon* would rendezvous with the joint-forces armada—the orbital fleet of ships that were providing military support and defense for the interstellar craft, the *Dove.*

The spacecraft carrier had assumed a wider-than-usual approach angle so that it could insert one of its shuttlepods into High Titanian Orbit (HTO). That shuttlepod was being launched in order to deliver Commander Hewst and Chief Kiiswood for their rendezvous with Porco Station, which was orbiting about 2,300 kilometers over the Titanian surface.

During their time aboard the *Oberon,* Hewst and Kiiswood had been effectively shunned by most of the ship's hands. When the two of them first walked through the passageways, the crew would give them a wide berth. But as the months passed, and the crew gradually accepted the notion that their unwelcomed guests were not spreading the feared contagion, the attitude aboard the ship seemed more relaxed. But the crew members still avoided interacting with Hewst and Kiiswood, and would do so reluctantly only if their duties required it.

For the past three months, Hewst and Kiiswood had kept mainly to themselves. The only other person who was regularly included in their shipboard circle of friends was Alex, whose newly constructed face they gradually came to accept. Together, the three of them spent much of the journey to Saturn entertaining many profound and musing questions. What is the destiny of humankind? How imminent is the demise of the human race in this solar system? Can our species find a home around a new star? What, or who, will the children of humanity find on a new world? Will they greet the children of another star as enemies or friends—or perchance as family? Is there a divine purpose at play in all of this? Do Hewst, Kiiswood, and Alex have a part in that purpose, as the Aeon had declared?

On occasion, Hewst and Kiiswood expressed hope and encouragement for their mechanistic friend, who would soon embark on a long, perilous journey for the sake of humanity's future. And on more than one occasion, Alex lamented for his two human friends whom he was soon leaving behind in a condemned solar system.

The *Oberon* was now about ninety minutes away from its rendezvous with the armada, and the shuttlepod bound for Porco Station would be launching in a few minutes. The shuttle pilot was already on board, completing her preflight checklist. Having donned their Kronian-rated compression suits, Hewst and Kiiswood reported to the shuttle's boarding compartment and stood ready to access the pod. Alex joined them in the compartment to bid an affectionate farewell to his friends, whom he would surely never see again. As the close-out crew readied the pod for boarding, the crew leader conducted a final integrity check of Hewst's and Kiiswood's suits.

After inspecting the fittings and life-support equipment on Hewst's suit, the crew leader declared, "Bravo Zulu, Commander, your EV packet is fully charged and you're good to go."

As the crew leader turned to inspect Kiiswood's compression suit, Hewst turned her attention to her meta-droid friend. "You're about to leave everything and everyone you know, Alex. You're about to spend several lifetimes hurtling through interstellar space. I don't know whether you're brave or foolish."

"I'd like to weigh in on that," Kiiswood interjected.

Replying to Hewst, Alex said, "The chief thinks I'm rushing in where angels fear to tread." He continued, "But I think I'm rushing in where angels have long since trodden."

Hewst apprehensively asked the meta-droid, "Are you sure you want to spend the next thirty centuries racing toward a completely alien world, to an unknown and uncertain future?" The air of uneasiness in her voice was unmistakable.

Alex smirked and countered, "Since when has the future ever been certain?"

"Three thousand years will seem like an eternity," she responded. "How will you fight the interminable boredom?"

"For those of you who stay behind, it'll be about three thousand years," he answered. "But for those of us who make the trip, we'll shave about three hundred years off that time—a quirk of special relativity." Alex continued, "Besides, I won't be alone. I'll have 124 of my fellow meta-droids with me—the souls of 124 network donors. Also, Dr. Madina tells me that we'll spend ninety-five percent of the journey turned off. We'll periodically be wakened on a rotation schedule to inspect and maintain the ship's systems."

"Well, at least for most of the journey, you won't be aware of passing time," imagined Hewst.

"Won't I?" wondered Alex. "I'm sure I'll dream while I'm turned off; I always have before. In fact, I've been having the same dream of late. In it, I'm standing on a cliff edge at sunrise, looking out on the ocean. But the sun seems strangely different." He then remarked, "Well, if I'm going to have a recurring dream, at least it's a pleasant one."

"To dream for thousands of years . . ." she mused without completing her sentence. Hewst then added, "Just don't lose your grip on what's real."

"Look at me, Catherine," the meta-droid laughed. "I was once a human being. Now I'm a ghost in a machine. Look at me, and tell me what's real."

"The machine doesn't make you any less a human being, Alex," she replied. "As long as you have your compassion, you have your humanity."

Surrounded by the bustle of the close-out crew, in the awkward and congested space of the boarding compartment, Alex abruptly hugged Hewst. "I'm going to miss you," he said as he pondered her fate. Would Hewst and Kiiswood live out their normal span of life, he wondered? Or would they succumb to a premature death at the whims of the Casius pathogen that now

369

plagued humankind? In either case, he knew that his friends would surely have been dead for millennia by the time he awoke around a strange and distant star. "I love you, Catherine," he uttered softly as their embrace continued.

Likewise, Hewst pondered Alex's fate. Would he and the ship's cargo survive the trek, she wondered? Would he and the new humanity be able to live among what, or whom, they might encounter in an unfamiliar world? "I love you too, Alex," she returned.

"Bravo Zulu, Chief," the crew leader said to Kiiswood. "Your compression suit is secure, and your EV packet is fully charged. In fact, your suit is Titan-rated, and you've bundled your EV packet with redundant equipment. You really don't need that thruster and deployment gear; Porco Station orbits about 1,000 kilometers above the atmosphere."

"It won't impede suit effectiveness," Kiiswood asserted.

"No," the crew leader replied, "it just makes your suit heavier than it needs to be."

Hewst commented with a grin, "The chief believes in being prepared for any contingency."

Alex then effusively embraced Kiiswood and charged, "Take care of Catherine." He knew that his next words would likely make Kiiswood feel ill at ease, but the meta-droid did not want to live with the regret of saying nothing. "I love you, Chief."

Kiiswood reciprocated by briefly hugging Alex with both arms. He patted the meta-droid on the back to express, in part, his sincere affection for his friend, but, more so, to signal that he had welcomed the embrace long enough. "Go, save the human race," the chief declared.

"Okay, Commander, Chief," the crew leader interrupted, "we're fast approaching our launch window. We need to get you two on board so we can secure the hatch." He then addressed the meta-droid, "Alex, is it? You need to exit the boarding compartment at this time."

As the meta-droid left the room, waving as he departed, Hewst and Kiiswood closed their helmets. The two then climbed through the exterior hatch of the boarding compartment, through the interior hatch, and into the cramped space of the shuttlepod. There, the close-out crew strapped them securely to their seats, egressed the pod, and sealed them inside.

Once they had secured the exterior hatch, the close-out crew exited the boarding compartment. As they stood in the shuttle bay passageway looking at an external view of the pod on a large video monitor, the crew leader called the ship's primary flight control on his c-nex. "Tower, this is the close-out crew-leader," he said. "Pilot and passengers are strapped in, pod is secured, power and oxygen umbilicals are detached, and close-out crew has evacuated the compartment."

A voice on the c-nex returned, "Close-out crew, Tower; acknowledged."

Aboard the shuttlepod, Hewst and Kiiswood immediately felt the effects of an unplugged power umbilical; the pod's artificial gravity, as well as its inertial dampening effects, suddenly vanished. The pod's occupants were immediately thrust back into their seats as their bodies now bore the full g-forces of the *Oberon*'s deceleration.

The shuttle pilot finished her preflight checklist and announced to the tower that the pod was ready to launch. She kept her eyes focused on the flight controls in front of her, even as she addressed Hewst and Kiiswood, whose seats were behind her. "I'm Lieutenant Olsen; I'll be shuttling you to Porco Station today. We'll be launching in two minutes—mark!" she informed them as she activated a countdown display on the forward panel. "Once we undock, intrashuttle communications will still be possible with our helmet headsets and c-nexes, but we'll no longer be able to communicate with the *Oberon*, at least while EMCON conditions are in effect. And once we've cleared the docking bay, we'll still be carrying a lot of relative velocity, so we'll be pulling a few g-forces during orbital phasing. Try to make yourselves comfortable."

Olsen's invitation to seek comfort was tinged with irony, for this particular class of shuttlepod (a *Dactyl*-class) was notoriously uncomfortable. Unlike Terrestrial Assembly shuttlecraft, Jovian Confederation shuttles were designed for Spartan efficiency, with only a passing consideration for passenger comfort. Indeed, about eighty-five percent of each *Dactyl*-class shuttle was essentially an enormous ascent/descent engine. It was a roughly spheroid-shaped vehicle that was occasionally used to shuttle as many as four people

371

from a ship to an orbital station. But its primary function was to ferry personnel to and from the surface of Saturnian moons—except for Titan. (The *Dactyl*-class was not designed for atmospheric flight.) Appended atop the engine was a very cramped crew cabin equipped with only four seats. Tucked within the engine housing were four retractable landing struts that would extend just before touchdown. Each landing strut was armed with a piton launcher, which, if needed, could anchor the shuttle to low-gravity surfaces.

As Hewst and Kiiswood lay back in their seats, they watched the countdown on the forward display. Because their helmets' headsets were automatically patched into the intrashuttle communication system, they could not avoid overhearing the flight control's incoming message for the pilot. "Dactyl-four-victor-seven, Tower Actual," the voice said. "Be advised, Low Titanian Orbit is restricted until EMCON conditions are lifted. We'll contact you then."

"Tower Actual, Dactyl-four-victor-seven; acknowledged—LTO restricted," the lieutenant replied. "L-minus thirty."

Ten seconds before launch, the *Oberon*'s main engines suddenly shut down so that the pod could neatly undock, clear the shuttle bay, and maneuver away from the ship's ventral hull. For that brief moment of shutdown, Hewst and Kiiswood felt as though they were in freefall; they were quite grateful for the restraints that now held them to their seats in the zero-gravity environment. They felt as though the pod had already undocked from the spacecraft carrier, but, in fact, it had not—not yet.

Olsen knew that she had only a few seconds before the *Oberon* would be required to reignite its main engines for its decelerating approach to Titan and orbital insertion. "Detach in three, two, one," the lieutenant counted down as she undocked the pod from the shuttle bay. She then fired the RCS thrusters and translated the shuttle several meters away from the carrier.

Hewst was fortunate to be seated near a small porthole in the shuttle's hatch. Beside the porthole, she noticed a small red lever inscribed with luminescent letters that, to her, appeared inverted: *Emergency Egress*. Being careful not to touch that lever, she leaned close to gain a view. Through the porthole, she could see the retreating hull of the JCS *Oberon*. The ship, she thought, was remarkably illuminated—remarkable, given that it was being lit by the diminished light of a distant sun—a sun now a billion and half kilometers away. Hewst stared in swelling awe at the sight. As the distance between the shuttle and the ship increased, more and more of the enormous spacecraft carrier came into view. Even so, Hewst could not behold the ship in its entirety; both bow and stern spread beyond her field of view. But then, the massive *Oberon* suddenly raced away from sight as the carrier's main engines reignited.

The shuttle pilot once again fired the thrusters to realign the pod for orbital phasing. "We're approaching Point of Impulse," she announced. "POI in three, two, one." Once again, the pod's occupants were immediately thrust back into their seats as the shuttle engine ignited. "We'll be pulling almost three Gs for twenty-three seconds," Olsen informed.

As she strained to tolerate the g-forces, Hewst asked Olsen, "How long before we rendezvous with the station?"

"If we burn the engine too long," answered the lieutenant, "we'll never reach our rendezvous point. We'll hit the atmosphere and burn up." She counted down the remaining seconds, then shut down the engine. The g-forces immediately abated. "I'll initiate one more engine burn in about seventeen minutes, when we reach POA."

"Phase Orbit Apoapsis," Kiiswood explained. "It's the final stage of our high orbital insertion."

"Aye," Olsen acknowledged. "We should rendezvous with the station in about twenty-four minutes."

"If we're under EMCON conditions, how will the personnel at Porco Station know when to expect our arrival?" asked Hewst.

"There *are* no personnel at Porco; the entire station is automated." Olsen replied. "Once we dock there, the three of us will be the station's only residents."

"So," Hewst soberly commented, "Commodore Esteban is marooning us in an automated detention center."

"Aye," she answered, "at least until EMCON conditions are lifted, and that won't happen until the *Dove* is well on its way to the Thaller system."

Kiiswood wondered what had happened to the thousands of Jovian citizens who called Porco Station home. He knew Porco as a thriving way station for the gas separation facilities on and around Titan. "Why was the station abandoned?" the chief inquired.

"All HTO stations were evacuated seven years ago," the lieutenant answered. "All of the facilities on Rhea were evacuated as well. Their workers and residents were all relocated to various Titan stations either in low orbit or on the surface—stations refitted and refashioned to service the construction of the *Dove*. Porco is still a nominally habitable station, but, for all intents and purposes, it's a high-orbit ghost station."

The chief wondered, "Why is the Jovian Confederation maintaining a ghost station?"

Although she was trying to be cordial to her passengers, the pilot did not allow her courtesy to impede her responsibilities. "POA in four minutes— mark!" she confirmed as she primed the shuttle for high-orbit insertion. She then responded to Kiiswood's question. "The Confederation maintains Porco Station, as well as the Rhean facilities, as future settlements for all of us who are involved with Project Columba Noachi—workers, contractors, government officials, and our families. After the *Dove* is launched, the stations on Rhea and Titan will become our new homes. Each station is isolated and independent from the others; there aren't any highways or g-trains that connect them. So when the Casius pandemic begins to spread, and civilization falls into anarchy, we'll be taking refuge in our respective stations—our own little fortresses of safety."

"Since everyone is already infected," Kiiswood reminded, "you're just postponing the inevitable."

Rather than responding to the chief, Lieutenant Olsen said, "POA in forty-five seconds."

"Where are you from, Lieutenant?" asked Hewst.

"Geinos," she answered, "on Ganymede."

"The chief and I might be detainees at Porco for the time being," observed Hewst, "but it seems to me that you and your family will also become unintentional detainees within your little fortresses of safety." The commander continued, "You'll never be able to go home again."

Olsen considered that Hewst might be correct, but the lieutenant preferred the safety of future confinement to the risks of going home. "POA in three, two, one," she said as she fired up the pod's engine for the final insertion maneuver. After burning the engine for the prescribed duration, the lieutenant shut it down and announced, "We're now in a high circular orbit." Reading the data on her flight instruments, she continued, "We're currently at a mean orbital altitude of 2,291 kilometers above the surface of Titan and 1,021 kilometers above the thermopause. Our orbital velocity is 1,358 meters per second."

Hewst looked up through the porthole in the shuttle's hatch and beheld the crisp, brilliant beauty of the sixth planet from the sun. Its rings shimmered bright in the sunlight like bands of freshly fallen snow. Their brightness would otherwise surround the planet, but the rings seemed to end abruptly as they looped around into the black of Saturn's shadow. Still, even the darkness of the planet's shadow was not so black; tiny specks, like fireflies, lit up the Saturnian clouds as distant lightning flashed on the planet's night side.

She angled herself, as best she could against her seat restraints, to see around the pilot's seat and to catch a glimpse of the scene through the forward window. There, she saw only the deep dark of space. But when she stretched herself slightly upward, the orange, hazy arc of Titan's atmosphere, capped by thin layers of bluish hues, came into view in the lower foreground.

As she strained to look through the forward window, Hewst asked the lieutenant, "Where's Porco Station?"

Olsen slowly pitched the shuttle around 180 degrees; the forward window was now facing the direction of orbit. "There," she answered, pointing at a shiny point in the distance. "That's Porco Station, about 15 kilometers downrange."

Porco was a very antiquated orbital station, one of the solar system's oldest orbital facilities still in use. Constructed in the early twenty-fourth century, it was originally commissioned as an astrophysical research facility, but over the decades, it had been transitioned into a way station for Titan's gas separation facilities. It was similar in structure to the ring-shaped orbital platforms of Venus, but larger—much larger, and much wider—with six large spokes radiating from the hub to the habitat ring. The station was 1,789 meters in diameter and was clearly visible even from 15 kilometers downrange. Since its christening about a century ago, Porco had undergone three overhauls, including the addition of two co-circumferential rings, effectively tripling both the station's width on the outside and its habitable space on the inside. Yet, despite its many renovations and refurbishments, Porco Station still lacked graviton generators; its artificial gravity was centrifugally induced. The entire station could generate a 1.0g acceleration along its circumference by spinning on its axis about one rotation per minute. Currently, however, the station hung motionless in space, like a stopped clock drifting high above the Titanian haze.

With a series of minute pulses from the RCS thrusters, Lieutenant Olsen gradually closed the distance between the shuttlepod and its destination. Slowly, meticulously she maneuvered the pod through the mooring hub and gently docked with Porco Station. After she secured the hard dock, Olsen powered down the shuttle and opened the pod's forward docking hatch. The pilot and her two passengers then entered the station.

The nonrotating station was apparently operating with minimal power—maintaining basic life support, but with no artificial gravity. The air quality smelled fresh, and the temperature was a comfortable 22 degrees Celsius. Yet the station's passageways were dark, the gangway carriages were not in service, and the mainframe data suite was offline. The station's three new inhabitants located a small control panel in one of the spoke's service tunnels and turned on the tunnel's auxiliary lighting. The lights were sparsely spaced, scarcely lighting the 890-meter tunnel; some of the old lights were flickering, obviously teetering on failure. Although the service tunnel was narrow, its pathway was clear. So, using the zero-gravity handrails that ran the length of the spoke, the three of them gracefully pulled their weightless forms toward the habitat ring at the other end.

After fifteen minutes of drifting through the service tunnel, they finally traversed the distance from the station's hub to its circumference. Upon arriving at the habitat ring, they entered the main control center and spooled up the station's helium-3 reactors to full power. The faint auxiliary lighting was immediately replaced by the station's much brighter primary lights. Bracing for artificial gravity startup, Hewst, Kiiswood, and Olsen secured their feet in the floor-mounted footholds and held firmly to the handrails. They then activated the outboard thrusters of the rotation control system, initiating a very slow and gradual spin of Porco Station. Within minutes, the station achieved a once-per-minute rotation rate, inducing an acceleration rate of 9.81 m/s² all throughout the habitat ring. Having established Terran-normal gravity, the outboard thrusters automatically shut off. Hewst, Kiiswood, and Olsen were now able to stand upright on the floor.

Olsen walked over to the internal-systems console in the control center and tried to project a holographic schematic of Porco Station. At first, the projection faltered as the image of a wheel and four dots of green light rapidly flickered in and out. After the lieutenant made some adjustments on the console, the holographic projection of Porco Station stabilized. Inside the transparent image of the ringed station were three small, tightly-grouped points of green light, representing Hewst, Kiiswood, and Olsen. "We have the entire station to ourselves," the lieutenant said, referring to the points of light, "at least for the time being." As she spoke, certain areas on the schematic were automatically highlighted, corresponding to the parts of the station that she was referencing. "All extra-station communication systems have been disabled. Life support, water reclamation, and waste management are automated systems and are all online. The medical treatment center is also fully automated. The cafeterias use a self-service system and are completely stocked. You have been granted unrestricted access to the gym, the recreation facilities, and the mainframe data suite. The only parts of the station where you're prohibited from going are the communication kiosks and the shuttle docking bay. I'm the only one with authorized access to those areas." Olsen then pointed to a certain section of the habitat ring on the schematic and added, "You have your choice of guest cabins. I recommend that you go, change out of those compression suits, put on some civvies, and make yourselves at home."

Hewst and Kiiswood took their leave of Olsen's service and courtesy, and began to explore their new residence. They resolved that if Porco Station would be their home (at least for the immediate future), then they would make it *feel* like home. For Hewst, this meant finding the closest source for coffee. Kiiswood accompanied his caffeine-craving friend to the nearest cafeteria.

There, the chief helped himself to a simple snack of an apple and some club soda, while Hewst prepared herself a cup of coffee.

This cafeteria seemed to be none too extraordinary—a rather conventional self-service eatery. But it did have one unique feature: a prominent bay window that looked out into space. This window imparted a kinetic and beautiful interplay of light and shadows in the cafeteria. Because of the station's slow rotation rate and its current position in Titan's orbit, the distant sun seemed to revolve leisurely across the window's panoramic view. Accordingly, the tables and chairs cast gentle, rolling shadows all around the sunlit cafeteria.

With her cup in hand, Hewst rummaged through the cafeteria's store of coffee flavorings. "Completely stocked?!" she exclaimed. The look of disillusion on her face was apparent. "The lieutenant said the cafeterias were completely stocked. There's no amaretto! How is this completely stocked?"

Kiiswood said nothing. He simply grinned and consolingly shook his head at his friend's discontent. The chief then took a bite of his apple and gazed out the cafeteria's bay window. With the half-eaten fruit still in hand, he pointed toward the revolving sun and bantered, "Hey, Commander, I can see your home from here." With his genetically enhanced vision, Kiiswood was indeed able to see an insignificant speck of light—a glint of the far-off planet Earth.

Hewst, of course, was unable to see the Earth with her unaided eyes; its glimmer was washed out by the much brighter sunlight. Still, she tried in vain to catch a glimpse of her Terran home. She smiled at the chief's feigned humor and soon forgot about the petty vanities of amaretto. She was grateful not to be alone.

Her body was now so very far from home that she suddenly felt her very soul so desolately far from God. Still gazing through the window, Hewst sipped some of her coffee. She then confided to her friend, "You know, Chief, I've never been so far from Earth."

Or so she thought.

Chapter 30 – Hewst

Porco Station, in High Titanian Orbit (HTO)

(Titanographic Co-ordinates: N 4.4, E 11.3, Altitude: 2,291 km)

Sunday, 14 April 2430 CE

Time: 0637 Zulu

A week had passed since Veronica Catherine Hewst had become a reluctant resident of Porco Station in orbit around Titan. In that time, she had set up quarters for herself in one of the guest cabins and had already established a daily routine. Every morning, she worked out in the gym with Chief Kiiswood— a workout that would culminate in a 5.6-kilometer run around the circumference of the station's habitat ring. Some days, they would double their distance and run a second lap around the ring. Hewst would then meet with Lieutenant Olsen for breakfast. (Kiiswood tended to take breakfast by himself. Despite his improved tolerance for the company of others, the chief still coveted his solitude.) Afterward, Hewst would spend her morning assisting Kiiswood and Olsen with simple maintenance and upkeep of the station— replacing faulty lighting elements, flushing the carbon-dioxide scrubbers, sterilizing the water reclamation filters, recalibrating the radiation screens, *etcetera*.

But this morning, Hewst deviated from her routine; she arranged with Kiiswood to run their laps while wearing compression suits. Although the chief regarded her choice of workout attire as curious, he indulged her, and the two of them began their Sunday morning run in their suits. As always, jogging through the habitat ring of Porco Station seemed like a prank on the senses— the slope of the deck looked like a persistent uphill run, but each step felt like striding on level ground. About 3.4 kilometers through their first lap, they came upon one of the station's six airlock compartments. Hewst abruptly stopped at the airlock entrance. "Hey Chief," she said, gesturing for Kiiswood to follow, "let me show you a detour."

Kiiswood laughed; he quickly realized why Hewst had asked him to don his compression suit. "I don't think this is a shortcut, Commander."

"No," she acknowledged, "but it's most definitely more scenic than running inside this giant gerbil wheel."

The two of them stepped inside the airlock compartment, secured their helmets, and closed the hatch. Once they had sealed themselves inside, the warm, breathable air around them was swiftly evacuated from the airlock. The airlock status indicator, which initially read *Terran Indigenous*, soon displayed *Vacuum*. Hewst then climbed the compartment's ladderwell to an overhead hatch, opened it, stepped outside, and tethered herself to the outer hull of Porco Station. Kiiswood promptly followed. There they stood on the roof of the habitat ring, held down by simulated gravity—by a centrifugal-induced force generated by the station's steady rotation.

Their view was stunning, even humbling. Although Porco Station was racing eastward in its orbit and emerging from the night side, the sun had not yet broken over the edge of Titan. Still, the features of the station were vivid to behold, brightly lit by the reflective light from Saturn and its rings. Hewst and Kiiswood stood on the inner rim of an enormous wheel that encircled them, reaching nearly two kilometers above their zenith. From their vantage point, they could see only two of the station's six spokes. Each spoke was immense, extending nearly a full kilometer and culminating overhead at the central docking hub, where the shuttlepod had been moored for the past week. The panorama on one side of the station was adorned by the backlit arc of Titan's methane atmosphere—a hazy blue and orange slivery crescent. On the other side, the brilliant sphere of Saturn and its encompassing icy rings dominated the panorama. Indeed, these overwhelming vistas only seemed to rotate leisurely along the axis of Porco Station; what was actually rotating, of course, was Hewst's and Kiiswood's standpoint. Their souls were consumed in awe of the space-scape. They felt insignificant compared to the universe that surrounded them.

The only words that came to Hewst were a few verses from the Hebrew scriptures. "'When I look at Your heavens,'" she quoted, "'the work of Your fingers, the moon and the stars that You have established, what are human beings that You are mindful of them? What are mortals that You care for them?'"

Kiiswood stood wordless for a while, silenced by the grandeur. "Psalm 8," the chief finally responded. "I was thinking the same thing." After another silent pause, he added, "I feel so small, Commander."

"Humility before such splendor," Hewst commented. "Isn't that what a soul is supposed to feel in the presence of such magnificence?" She continued, "And that's the paradox, isn't it? Only something as majestic as a soul can be awed at the vastness of creation. Perhaps the universe itself should be awed at the souls that behold it."

The chief grinned; the commander's words reminded him of the psalm's next verse. "'Yet You have made them a little lower than God,'" Kiiswood said, "'and You crowned them with glory and honor.'"

"A little lower than God," Hewst echoed. "Despite our pettiness, perhaps we really are children of God, as the Aeon suggests." As the small, distant sun dawned over Titan, she looked at Kiiswood with a full smile and said, "Happy Easter, Chief."

The two of them stood taciturn for a time, spending their Easter morning literally staring into space. After several minutes, Kiiswood glanced at the chronometer display on the foresleeve of his compression suit and said, "You're late for your breakfast with Lieutenant Olsen."

"I tried to c-nex her earlier," Hewst replied. "She didn't answer, so I left her a message that I'd be a little late. But I guess I should go catch up with her. After breakfast, she wants me to help her inspect the air quality system near the service tunnels of Spoke-Five. She's concerned that the carbon dioxide count is higher than normal."

Hewst was reluctant to leave such inspiring scenery, but she had promises to keep. She stepped down through the hatch and began to make her way into the airlock. But as she started to climb back down the ladderwell, she lost her grip and her foot slipped from one of the rungs. She would have otherwise fallen to the airlock floor, but Kiiswood, with his genetically heightened reflexes and enhanced strength, caught her by her arm. He held her up and steadied her so that she could regain her grip and safely climb down to the floor.

"Thank you, Chief," she acknowledged gratefully.

"Be careful, Commander," the chief replied. "I can't always be there to catch you."

As Hewst continued down the ladderwell, she noticed that Kiiswood was not following. "Aren't you coming?" she asked.

"I think I'll enjoy the view a little longer," Kiiswood answered. "I'll continue my run here outside the station. Go, have breakfast with the lieutenant, and I'll catch up with the two of you at Spoke Five."

"Okay, Chief," acknowledged Hewst. If anyone else had told her that he would be running on the outer hull of a rotating space station, she would be sure he was joking. But, because Kiiswood often pressed his workouts beyond human limitations, she took him at his word. "I'll see you later," she said. Hewst then sealed the overhead hatch, repressurized the airlock, opened her helmet, and returned to the habitat ring.

As she jogged to the cafeteria, where she and Olsen usually met for breakfast, Hewst tried once again to call the lieutenant with her c-nex; once again, there was no answer. She checked for a message from Olsen but found none.

Hewst soon arrived at the cafeteria, but, inexplicably, Olsen was not there. She was genuinely puzzled, so she decided to run a diagnostic of her own c-nex. Almost immediately, it accessed her visual cortex with a cerebral form of a text message: INTRASTATION COMMUNICATION SYSTEM IS CURRENTLY OFFLINE.

Since Hewst was late for her breakfast meeting, she supposed that Olsen might have already eaten without her and then proceeded directly to the service tunnel in Spoke Five. So Hewst decided to forego her morning coffee and to look for the lieutenant at the service tunnel.

After jogging a little further, Hewst reached the carriage bay at Spoke Five. The adjacent service tunnels were strangely idle, quiet, and dark, with no sign that the lieutenant was nearby. However, she found the gangway carriage, parked and powered up on the habitat level, ready for ascent to the shuttle docking bay. How strange, she thought. For station protocol, Olsen always kept the carriage secured at the docking bay, which was at the other end of the gangway. Perhaps the lieutenant was working in the docking bay; perhaps she awaited Hewst's assistance and so had parked the carriage on the habitat level for her. Of course, Hewst knew that the docking bay was off limits, but she decided nonetheless to break protocol and to ride the carriage up the spoke's gangway.

Hewst took a seat, belted herself in, engaged the lift, and began to ride the carriage up Spoke Five. She felt the weight of her body steadily ebb as the carriage ascended through the gangway. In about two minutes, the carriage traversed the 890-meter spoke and came to rest at the docking bay in the station's hub. The centrifugal force at this level was so nominal as to be effectively nonexistent.

Indeed, Hewst was fairly certain that Lieutenant Olsen was in the area. All of the lights in the docking bay's boarding compartment were turned on. Surely, she thought, these lights would not be on were Olsen not here. "Lieutenant!" called Hewst. But she heard no response. "Lieutenant!" Again, Olsen did not answer.

Suddenly, Hewst heard something—an indistinct noise. She opted to investigate, so she unbuckled herself from her seat and began to float about the docking bay. With the slightest effort, she pulled her near-weightless form into the brightly lit boarding compartment. There, she discovered that the passageway hatch to the shuttlepod was open. And, peering through the passageway, she saw that the shuttle's hatch was also open and that the pod's cabin lights were on.

"Lieutenant," Hewst called out through the passageway, "are you in there?" Once again, her call was met with silence.

Cautiously, warily, Hewst drifted through the passageway and into the cramped cabin of the shuttlepod. Immediately, she noticed that the entire forward control panel was lit up, as though the shuttle had been readied for launch. Even the L-minus chronometer on the forward panel was counting down. Hewst noticed patches of dried blood staining parts of a rear seat and aft bulkhead. Just then, in an aft section at the far end of the pod, she saw Olsen, twisted and contorted in an otherwise untenable position, as if stuffed aside like a discarded duffle bag.

Hewst was shaken; her heart raced in horror. "Lieutenant?!" she shouted, but she saw no movement—no reaction. She reached over to Olsen's still form, easily shifting the lieutenant's cold, lifeless body in the microgravity. Just above the blood-stained back of Olsen's khaki uniform, Hewst saw the hilt of a blade protruding from the nape of the lieutenant's neck.

Hewst suddenly felt seized by a fear of confinement. She tried calling Chief Kiiswood on her c-nex but was quickly prompted that the comm-systems were still offline. In a panic, Hewst scrambled to crawl out of the constricted space and to egress the pod as fast as she could. But, just as she began to pull herself through the hatch and into the passageway, the powerful hand of a stratogen—Olsen's killer—grabbed Hewst by the arm.

This stratogen, donned in an Alliance-surplus compression suit, restrained her arm against the hinge of the hatch. He pinned Hewst's forearm at such an angle that, with a single, forceful thrust from his other hand, he broke both her ulna and radius. As she screamed out in pain, he grabbed her by the neck; with stone-cold focus, this browless man stared Hewst in the eyes and tried to throttle her. But, despite his enhanced strength, he was unable to apply enough force to deprive her of breath or blood flow; the collar module on Hewst's compression suit was too rigid. So he ferociously pummeled her instead; he punched her repeatedly in the face. With several blows of his fist, he broke her cheekbone, her maxilla, and her nose. Blood spewed profusely from her mouth and nostrils. Hewst lost consciousness.

The countdown was nearly complete, and the browless man had already wasted too much of his time dealing with Hewst, whose unexpected presence was impeding his mission. Instead of wasting more time hauling her broken body out of the pod and out of his way, he removed her c-nex and kicked her to the far end of the pod's aft section, alongside Olsen's corpse. He then sealed the shuttlepod's hatch, climbed into the pilot's seat, and quickly belted himself in.

He had no sooner released the shuttle from hard-dock when the countdown display on the forward panel reached zero. Immediately, he fired the engine, and the shuttle rocketed away from Porco Station, having barely cleared the docking hub when the engine engaged. The browless man was thrust back into his seat and spent the next several minutes monitoring the instruments on the forward panel. He verified that the flight-control sensors were compensating for the additional mass inside the pod and that the shuttle was indeed applying its preset delta-v and following its preset intercept-course.

Once the shuttlepod was on its specified trajectory, the browless man shut down the engine. No longer accelerating, all of the shuttle's occupants were now subject to zero gravity. The browless man was safely secured in the pilot's seat, but the unrestrained bodies of Hewst and Olsen freely drifted in the aft section. Of course, in such a confined space, they did not drift about much.

Hewst began to spit and cough out blood as she gradually regained consciousness. The first and most prominent sensation that seized her emerging awareness was unassailable pain. She found each breath effortful, for she was bleeding into her throat and her nasal cavity. With every breath, every swallow, she could smell and taste her own blood. She slowly opened her eyes only to a murky blur. With her unbroken arm, she reached up to her swelling face and wiped away the small globules of coughed blood that had floated into her contused eyes in zero gravity. As her focus soon returned, she could see the instruments on the forward panel and much of the shuttle's flight telemetry. She could see a corner of the shuttle's forward window and an ever-increasing image of Titan therein. She watched as Titan's terminator passed by, as the shuttle's trajectory took it over the night side of the Saturnian moon. She watched the cabin grow darker, no longer brightened by the reflective Titanian cloud tops. And she could see, protruding from his open helmet, the dark silhouette of her assailant's head, backlit by the dim lights of the instruments on the forward panel. He seemed clearly intent on his clandestine mission, making subtle RCS adjustments to the shuttlepod's course.

Aching and throbbing too much to fight, or even to move about and speak, Hewst still labored to form a question. "How did you get aboard Porco Station without any of us finding out?" she asked.

The browless man laughed haughtily. "Woman, you are so blissfully naive, aren't you?" he answered in condescension. "I was already aboard the station when you and your company arrived. I had been for a couple of weeks. The better question is, how is it that you and your stratogen friend didn't notice my presence? Keeping out of sight was easy enough—the station is huge. I was able to reprogram the mainframe data suite to mask my presence on the station's schematics, but I couldn't avoid consuming food and water; I couldn't

385

hold my breath. I was sure you'd notice the increased water consumption or the elevated carbon dioxide levels. Yet you never connected these anomalies to an extra person on board."

Hewst spat a little more blood and said, "There were no other shuttles docked at the station. How did you get there?"

"I secured passage with the skipper of a bypassing commercial freighter," he replied, "a skipper who, for the right price, asked no questions. I jettisoned with my equipment inside one of the freighter's life-pods, parked outside the station's hull, entered through an unsecured airlock, and went to work."

Hewst looked with anguish at Olsen's body and at the blade still protruding from the lieutenant's lifeless form. "Yeah, I recognize your *work*," she scorned. "Why didn't you just kill me too, like you did Dorch and Pratiss back on Venus? Like you killed Olsen over here?"

"Killing that woman—Olsen—wasn't part of the original mission," he confided. "You weren't even supposed to be here. Your arrival interrupted New Jerusalem's mission to fight the corrupt inclinations of your heart."

"What the hell are you talking about!?" she cried out. "What mission?"

"The mission to destroy that abomination that the Assembly and the Confederation built," he piously declared. "That sacrilege—your so-called space ark. For weeks, I was scavenging parts from Porco Station, modifying the life-pod, turning it into a kinetic impact missile. Then I was going to deliver it down into low Titan orbit to end that abomination with my version of an FOG—a Finger of God. I was also able to equip it with a helium-3 fusion weapon that I fashioned from redundant systems, just in case the missile failed to make direct impact. Unfortunately, I couldn't make the propulsion system work. So I prayed to God, and, in His righteousness, He delivered this shuttle to me—a much bigger Finger of God. With this shuttle, I'll truly be the right hand of God's mighty wrath. This shuttle will be the fist of God. While the three of you were making yourselves comfortable in the habitat ring, I was making several EVAs outside the docking hub, retrofitting my fusion weapon to the shuttle's hull."

Hewst struggled to articulate her words through her busted mouth. "Surely you must know that space-dock is heavily defended by a fleet of Jovian Confederation ships." She coughed as she continued. "They'll likely blow you out of orbit long before you get anywhere near it."

"That's possible," he doubtingly admitted, "but not likely. I know their tactics; they'd surely shoot down a bogey, but they'll hesitate to fire on one of their own, especially while under EMCON conditions."

"They don't need to fire," she retorted. "They'll simply access the navigation computer and take control of the shuttle."

"Of course they would," he conceded, "if I had programed the navigation computer to execute an automated flight plan. But that's why I'm here—to pilot the shuttle manually. I disabled the navigation computer so that it can't be hijacked or flown remotely. That's what that woman pilot caught me doing yesterday when she showed up in the docking bay unexpectedly. I had no choice but to execute summary judgment for her unrighteous life. I had to neutralize her."

"Was I not deserving of your self-righteous judgment?" she quipped sarcastically. "After all, I'm a woman with both rank and education." Her sarcasm continued. "Why didn't you kill me—you know, the way Jesus killed all those who got in his way?"

The browless man was unaware of any stories about Jesus the killer; he did not know whether Hewst was being serious or simply flouting his biblical illiteracy. "Keep taunting me, woman," he threatened. "I still might. The only reason I didn't kill you earlier is that I didn't have the time. I had a very narrow launch window to intercept that space ark in low Titan orbit. Of course, killing you wasn't originally part of the plan. The docking bay was supposed to be off limits; you were supposed to stay in the habitat ring. But then you suddenly showed up here and got in my way; you forced me to improvise." As he spoke, he noticed that the course telemetry, although not on right down the middle, was still within an acceptable approach corridor. "But be assured, you'll die soon enough; we both will. I've linked the thermonuclear device to my c-nex. This is a one-way mission."

While spitting more blood, Hewst asked, "Why in God's name do you want to destroy Columba Noachi?"

"Because that ark of yours has nothing to do with the name of God," he replied. "God had only one ark—Noah's ark—an ark that saved the righteous few from God's wrath upon the wicked. But *your* ark was built to save the ungodly; yours is the ark of Satan."

"I see it as a sign of God's grace," she responded. "Perhaps it's a gift from God—a gift of hope for a doomed humanity. An extinction-level pathogen will end the human race unless we start anew on another world."

"The plague is God's judgment upon the wicked," he proclaimed, "like the purifying flood in the days of Noah."

"Then how does your faith explain that a few of New Jerusalem's own enclaves have already been wiped out by that plague?" she challenged.

Before he could answer, a panel alarm sounded; with it, a group of warning indicators lit up among the flight instruments. After inspecting the indicators, the browless man determined that the piton launcher on the starboard landing strut was offline. "It looks like part of our landing gear is inoperative," he commented. "No problem—we won't need it." As he turned off the alarm, he responded to the commander's question. "If any of our enclaves were beset by plague, they must have been apostates, like Dorch. They weren't truly among the righteous. The human eye might be fooled by false piety, but God alone knows the evil intentions of the human heart."

"That isn't faith," Hewst surmised. "That's a self-reinforcing delusion."

"Woman, your very words are as sacrilegious as that space ark!" exclaimed the browless stratogen. "You're talking about creating a new earth and a new humanity. Creation is the sole purview of God, not human beings. God created us in His own image—He gave us a soul. But you're talking about going to another world to create beings in humanity's sinful image. You're talking about creating soulless humans and raising them by soulless androids. Your ark is an abomination because it dares to depose God and enthrone humankind in His place."

"You're so noble in your self-righteousness, aren't you?" she derisively remarked. "You're willing to sacrifice yourself, to murder me, Lieutenant

Olsen, and tens of thousands of space-dock workers, as well as every soul who might be on board that ark, because you think it threatens the sovereignty of God."

"It *is* a threat!" he retorted; "an unholy threat to the righteousness of Christ Himself. One day, New Jerusalem will rise up from Mars; we will descend from heaven upon the Earth like a bride adorned for Christ, and we will restore God's fallen creation to its intended glory. But that ark of yours—it threatens God's glory. That ark is Satan's design to flee beyond the reach of God's righteous judgment. And its soulless offspring might one day return, bringing with them all manner of false theologies that they learned from whatever soulless alien beings they encounter. They might return like false shepherds, leading Christ's sheep astray, making war with the righteous citizens of New Jerusalem. As Christ's dutiful paladin, I cannot allow the ungodly to evade God's wrath. So if Christ can die on the cross for the righteous, I can certainly sacrifice for His righteousness. I can be the fist of God."

The agony of her broken bones and the obsession of her zealous assailant tested her spirit and her faith. She wanted to surrender to her hopelessness but, by sheer will, she refused to despair. "You and I read the same scriptures," she professed, "but we clearly do not hear the same *Word*. There's nothing soulless in those who differ from you, there's nothing sacrificial in killing others, and there's nothing Christ-like in what you're doing." Hewst then declared, "Christ didn't die for the righteous; He died for the ungodly."

He did not initially respond; instead, he turned his attention to the anomalous course telemetry. He noticed that the shuttle was no longer within an acceptable approach corridor. "It appears that we're shallowing up on our approach angle," he observed. "Apparently, the flight-control sensors didn't apply the correct delta-v for the additional mass." He then conjectured, "Woman, you must weigh more than the sensors estimated. I'll have to initiate another engine burn to compensate." As he was calculating the amount of power and time he would need to burn the engine for course correction, another alarm abruptly sounded. Dozens of warning indicators now lit up the forward panel. "What the hell?!" he cursed.

As the browless man meticulously studied the indicators, Hewst took advantage of the distraction and of the darkness. Discreetly, she withdrew the blade from Olsen's body and tried to conceal it behind her uninjured forearm as she palmed the hilt backwards in her hand.

As the browless man fastidiously worked the flight controls, his bearing seemed less confident and more harried. "The magnetic confinement system has failed!" he exclaimed. "The reactor is offline! There's not enough power to fire the engines. There's not even enough power to fire the thrusters."

Despite her own debilitating pain, Hewst could not help but fear for her friend Alex, who most certainly was now aboard the *Dove*. Indeed, she feared for all the meta-droid souls that were now aboard that interstellar ark, for all the souls working at the space-dock, and for the success of Project Columba Noachi. So she took the shuttle's engine failure as good news, and she took pleasure in her assailant's frustration. "I guess you're not the fist of God after all," she gloated.

Infuriation began to hamper his reason. "Woman, did you have anything to do with this?" he distraughtly asked.

Hewst smirked—although it was not quite apparent through the blood, bruises, and broken bones of her face. "You've beaten me mercilessly, and you have my c-nex," she replied. "You're the one at the helm. What the hell can I do from the back seat?"

"Nothing at all," he concurred. "No matter. We may be approaching too shallow to make a direct impact, but we'll pass within half a kilometer. That's certainly close enough for a fusion explosion to have a terminal effect on the target. All I need to do now is calculate the point of periapsis, where I'll trigger the detonation for optimal effect."

Her hopes of stopping the browless man seemed much darker than the shadow of Titan that now shrouded the shuttlepod. She was now too broken to contend with this stratogen, and she was always too slow and weak to be his match. Even so, his death, or the removal of his c-nex, would merely trigger the thermonuclear detonation automatically. Her spirit did not want to surrender hope, but if the browless man was the dark exemplar of human depravity, then perhaps the human race itself was too dark and depraved to deserve a place among the children of other stars. No matter what she considered doing, there was no right choice.

But in the midst of that darkness, a lifetime of faith raced through her soul in an instant. Hewst remembered her faith—in God, in humanity, and in herself. Yes, humankind *was* dark and depraved. But if this God that she remembered, the God of her faith, would dare to sacrifice for this depraved race of beings, then perhaps there was something redeemable about this ungodly species—a species that included one so wretched as this browless man but also included one so compassionate as her own father. Perhaps there was hope for humanity's future.

Through her pain, and under her breath, she prayed to God for the first time in nearly a decade. She prayed for mercy and forgiveness; she sought pardon for being distant, silent, and resentful for far too long, and she sought pardon for what she was about to do. Indeed, there was no right choice. But then, as the Aeon said, choices were not about righteousness; choices were about sacrifice.

As the browless man was distracted with his calculations, Hewst stealthily edged up behind the pilot's seat with the blade in hand. She reached around the seat and thrust the blade at the stratogen's head. Despite her intense pain, her grip on the hilt was relentless. But, for lack of gravity and leverage, her lunge was awkward. For lack of martial skills, her aim was clumsy. The browless stratogen easily dodged her assault; his heightened awareness was too sharp, and his enhanced reflexes were too swift. Hewst did not draw his blood; instead, her blade wedged into the spindle mechanism of his open helmet.

The browless man retaliated instantly; with the immense strength of just one hand, he reached over, clouted Hewst in her already-battered face, and shoved her back from his seat. But even as she screamed out in pain, her grip on the hilt remained resolute. The wedged blade snapped off in the spindle, as Hewst's momentum carried her shoved body into the back seat.

The browless man began to laugh. "I give you credit, woman; your effort is commendable. But, like all the enemies of Christ, you're destined to fail. God's love clearly favors me," he declared boisterously. He reached up and tapped his c-nex in Hewst's sight, showing her that, at the right time, and with a mere thought, he would set off his thermonuclear device.

"Love?" she questioned. "You know nothing about love. You think God loves you because you smite the unrighteous? You confuse God's love with anger, self-righteousness, and fear. And because of that, I truly pity you."

Feeling provoked to indignation, he exclaimed, "Woman, you don't get to preach to me about the love of God! You just tried to kill me!"

"You're right, I am just like you," she admitted. "I agree with you that the human race is wretched and undeserving of divine mercy. But, unlike you, I don't feel God's love in the conquest of my enemies. I feel that love in the compassion I have for my friend aboard that ark that you're about to destroy. And yes, I feel that love in my compassion for the wretched and undeserving human race."

"You can preach about pity and compassion all you want, woman," he countered, impassive to her words. "Those are merely the wiles of the ungodly to beguile the weak-minded, like the wiles of the serpent that beguiled Eve. Your sentiments of compassion do nothing but allow the ungodly to flourish in their wickedness—to spread their wickedness throughout God's creation with impunity. But if you were truly motivated by your love for God, you wouldn't allow God to suffer the ungodly."

"No, sir," she disputed. She suddenly thought about the words that she had encountered in that mysterious cavern months ago and worlds away. "There is no love without compassion, and there's no compassion without sacrifice." Throwing aside the broken hilt that snapped free from the wedged blade, she reached up, gripped the emergency egress lever on the shuttle's hatch, and slid it to its armed position.

The shuttle's cabin lights flashed red, and an alarm sounded. "Warning!" announced an automated voice. "Emergency egress system is now armed. To fire pyrotechnic bolts, pull the lever down. To disarm, slide the lever back."

The browless man smiled smugly. He accessed his c-nex; he signaled the thermonuclear device to detonate and piously embraced his imminent martyrdom. A few seconds passed. Then several seconds passed. The browless man sat bewildered; his smile faded.

Hewst did not know why his device had failed, but she would not allow the browless man a second chance. She pulled down on the lever, the pyrotechnic charges ignited, and the shuttle's hatch was abruptly blown out. All of the air in the cabin explosively evacuated.

By design, the stratogen's helmet pivoted to close at the instant of decompression. But it did not completely close; indeed, it could not. His visor jammed against the broken blade that was still wedged into the helmet's spindle. In a panicked scramble, he was quickly able to extricate the blade; still, the spindle was too twisted and wrenched for his helmet to close.

All of the cabin's air exploded through the hatchway, taking with it everything that was not strapped in or secured down, including Hewst and the lifeless body of Lieutenant Olsen. Hewst's helmet automatically closed shut as she was blown out into the vacuum of space. She was propelled with such force that she fractured her tibia against the hatchway's edge as she was launched out and away from the shuttlepod.

Alone and untethered, Hewst drifted helplessly through the quiet vastness of space, plummeting toward the thick, frigid atmosphere of Titan. Her body slowly tumbled end over end, carrying the rotational momentum of being blown from the derelict shuttle. She lost sight of the shuttle as the gap between her and the *Dactyl*-class craft quickly widened—not that she would otherwise be able to see it. Indeed, Hewst, the shuttlepod, even the massive *Dove* in its space-dock (wherever it was) were all shrouded in Titan's shadow. Were it not for her helmet torch, she would not even be able to see her own hand before her face. Her only visual frames of reference were the bright planet Saturn and the broadening daybreak-edge of Titan's atmosphere, which regularly came into view with each tumble.

For several minutes, she drifted in the dark silence, hearing nothing but the sound of her own breathing. She eventually activated the heads-up display on her helmet's visor to learn which systems of her compression suit were still functioning. Her visor suddenly lit up with an abundance of data, all of which appeared inverted to her. Some of the telemetry was faintly blurred by specks of her own blood that dappled the inside of her visor, but Hewst was still able to read its data. Her suit integrity was uncompromised, but her radiation dosimetry system was inoperative, as was her communication system. Her carbon-dioxide scrubbers were still functioning, and the power cells in her EV packet were amply charged, as were her oxygen canisters. And although she had at least twelve hours of oxygen, she soon realized that she did not have twelve hours of breath. According to her orbital dynamics telemetry, she was racing furiously toward Titan at nearly five kilometers per second. Though her compression suit was protecting her from deadly radiation and from the vacuum of space, it would not save her from the intense aerodynamic heat of slamming through the Titanian atmosphere.

With only moments left, Hewst prayed. "Gracious God, Source of my being and my compassion: I have been angry with You for far too long, and I have been a poor envoy of Your grace. I have no merit to entreat You on my behalf; I have no right to beg for pardon. But, here at the end of all that I am, I ask that You deliver the destiny of humankind from its brokenness. Make it a new creation in the image of Your compassion. May it find a home and a kinship with all your children among the stars. I ask that You watch over all the souls, both friend and foe, that You have placed along my life's trek, especially my friends Níyol and Alex. Forgive them their vanities, and keep them safe, I pray. May Níyol find You in his compassion for others, and may Alex find You in his love for himself. Of my own vanities, I dare not ask for deliverance; I do not ask for salvation. For I have been more resentful at my father's death than grateful for the gift of his life and his love. I ask only, do not let me die in my resentment, and do not let me die estranged from You. For I have been away for far too long, and I have missed You."

The telemetry on Hewst's HUD began to flash with bright red characters: INTERFACE ALTITUDE: 1270 km. She then felt the subtle drag of Titan's thin thermosphere. At first, the friction was barely perceptible, but it was enough to stay Hewst from tumbling. She arched her back and used aero-resistance to level herself. Soon she felt the warmth of frictional heat as her body collided with the steadily thickening atmosphere of Titan.

As her compression suit was quickly enveloped by the rising heat of atmospheric entry, a pair of arms seized Hewst from behind.

Chapter 31 – Kiiswood

Before she discovered the lifeless body of Lieutenant Olsen, Hewst had been standing outside Porco Station with Chief Kiiswood, standing in awe at the panoramic space-scape. And, before she was beaten, broken, and taken captive by the browless man, she had left Kiiswood, her security guard, her friend, to continue his run on the roof of the station's habitat ring.

During the course of his military career, Kiiswood had carried out his PT regimen in many exotic venues, but perhaps none so exotic as the topside of a space station's habitat ring. He did not want to waste this opportunity. So, boldly, daringly, he detached his EVA tether from the hull, tucked it into the thigh pouch of his compression suit, and began to sprint unsecured along the roof of the habitat ring. To keep himself secured to the deck, he depended solely on the centrifugal force of the rotating station and his own inertia.

As he ran a mostly unobstructed course around the rooftop circumference, he still needed to skirt the occasional airlock hatches and RCS thruster housings that were situated along the station's hull. The only major obstacles he encountered were the enormous spokes that connected the habitat ring to the central docking hub. But even the spokes were no real hindrance; the chief had enough running space between the side of each spoke and the edge of the ring—*enough* space, but not a lot. Just a few good strides in the wrong direction, and the chief could step off the edge and be hurled by his own inertia out into space. The very possibility that he might accidentally run over the edge and fall into oblivion, he found perilously exhilarating. Of all his PT regimens, none was as beautiful and as precarious as this one. Kiiswood felt alive.

He had run about three-fifths of the circumference when he came upon something that appeared odd—something not a part of Porco Station's hull. It was of such a curious and unusual nature that Kiiswood stopped to take a closer look. There, tethered to one of the station's RCS clusters was the rummaged hulk of a commercial-grade life-pod. As he examined this shell of a pod, he quickly assessed that it could no longer function as a deep-space lifeboat; it was being refashioned to serve another purpose. Its laid-bare insulation, which was not usually exposed to the ambient radiation of space, had not yet begun to fade or decay, so it could not have been on the station's hull for very long. Its thruster array had been reconfigured and now resembled a small plasma-propulsion system; its battery-well had been altered to accommodate a much larger helium-3 power cartridge. And its life-support equipment had been stripped out in order to create a provisional payload compartment. Kiiswood almost immediately realized that someone was converting a commercial life-pod into a small tactical missile. Someone was building a weapon.

He wondered who would be making a tactical weapon, and for what purpose. He was certain that constructing such a device was not in Hewst's character, nor was it among her particular skill sets as a paleographer or a chaplain. Of course, he did not know Lieutenant Olsen so well, but he had not seen her donning her compression suit since their arrival at Porco Station. If the lieutenant had been conducting EVAs, he would have likely noticed. The only person on board who had the requisite skills was the chief himself, and he certainly knew this was not his doing. Was it possible that the three of them were not alone on the station?

As he pondered the notion of a stowaway aboard, Kiiswood's c-nex began to signal an incoming call. "This is Kiiswood," he said as he answered the call.

"Chief, this is Alex," said the meta-droid. "Is Catherine with you?"

"Alex?" the chief grilled. "Where are you? Are you on Porco Station?"

"No!" he replied tersely, his one-word answer curt and brusque. "I'm aboard the *Dove*, and we're about to launch in a matter of hours."

Kiiswood cautioned his friend, "You're breaking EMCON protocol!"

"This is more important," countered Alex. "I tried calling Catherine, but I can't get through to her." He then charged, "Don't let her out of your sight. She's the key to the Casius pathogen; don't let anything happ . . . "

The c-nex connection was abruptly broken.

Kiiswood was quite troubled. He did not believe that his meta-droid friend was prone to hyperbole, nor was he inclined to disregard security protocols capriciously. The chief decided to take Alex's message seriously.

He tried to call Hewst on her c-nex, but she did not answer. Instead, his c-nex accessed his cortex with a text message: INTRASTATION COMMUNICATION SYSTEM IS CURRENTLY OFFLINE. Kiiswood then connected to the station's mainframe data suite and said, "Schematic: show me the locations of Commander Hewst and Lieutenant Olsen."

The data suite immediately uploaded the requested information directly into Kiiswood's cortex. A schematic of Porco Station appeared, showing a flashing icon of Hewst riding the Spoke Five carriage up to the docking bay. The schematic was accompanied by an audio message, "Lieutenant Olsen cannot currently be located."

Why was Olsen's presence not indicated in the station schematic? How had she disappeared? Kiiswood considered a number of scenarios. Perhaps she was no longer on the station. Perhaps her icon indicator had been deleted from the data suite. Of course, the chief also considered the worst-case scenario: Lieutenant Olsen might be dead. But, wherever Olsen was—whatever had happened to her—Kiiswood was determined not to let Hewst disappear as well.

He looked overhead to the central docking hub, where he knew his friend was heading. There, nearly a kilometer above, he saw the shuttlepod moored in its place. With his ability to see light in the infrared range, he noticed that a particular heat signature was emanating from the shuttle's main fusion reactor—its engine was being primed for ignition.

Then, as he surveyed the shuttle more intently, he saw someone stirring around a strange ovoid device mounted to the shuttle's starboard beam. This *someone* was wearing an Alliance-surplus compression suit, characteristic of the allegiants of New Jerusalem. Whatever this mysterious *someone* was doing to the shuttle, he or she had apparently finished and was now returning through an airlock hatch to the docking bay.

The chief quickly sprinted to the nearest spoke to climb his way up to the docking hub. He decided that he could reach the hub faster from outside the station, rather than re-pressurizing in a habitat airlock and then waiting for a ride at a carriage bay. As he was climbing hand-over-hand on the spoke's exterior service rungs, he accessed the mainframe data suite once again and said," Schematic: augment reality." The cortical schematic of Porco Station immediately expanded and overlaid Kiiswood's own visual perception, augmenting his view of the climb. His ascent was swift, but perilous, for he scaled the 890-meter spoke untethered, securing himself only by the strength of his grip on each consecutive rung. With almost inhuman speed, the chief scampered up the spoke, his weight abating the higher he climbed. All the while, he kept his focus on Hewst's icon indicator so that he knew where he was in relation to his friend.

Soon, the chief was close enough to detect a faint but familiar heat signature emanating from the strange ovoid object mounted to the side of the shuttle. He recognized it as the decay heat from a thermonuclear device—a device with a fission trigger.

Kiiswood was just meters away from the docking hub when the icon indicator vanished from the schematic. Apparently, Hewst had moved through the boarding compartment and was now beyond the range of the station's sensors. The chief presumed that his friend was now aboard the shuttlepod and at the mercy of a New Jerusalem allegiant.

As he reached the hub, the shuttle suddenly detached from hard-dock, and its primary propulsion flaps shifted to their launch configurations. Without hesitation, Kiiswood reacted; he pushed himself away from the docking hub and grabbed onto one of the shuttle's landing struts. He pulled the tether from his thigh pouch and secured himself to part of the strut's truss assembly, just as the shuttle engine fired.

As the shuttle rocketed away from Porco Station, and as the slack was abruptly taken up in his tether, Kiiswood was jerked violently in tow. Despite his stratogenic strength, Kiiswood could not easily scale the shuttle's hull against the g-forces; the acceleration was so great that the chief could do little more than suffer the ride. He dangled dangerously close to the engine skirt and to its propulsive particle stream.

For several minutes, he endured the shuttle's acceleration in this daring position, until the engine suddenly shut off. Porco Station was now a mere speck in the distance—a small point of light nearly indistinguishable among the thousands of stars that dotted the black firmament.

Kiiswood peered at the steadily shrinking arc of Titan's western horizon as the shuttle passed into the shadow of the Saturnian moon. He quickly surmised that the shuttle had performed some sort of orbital phasing maneuver, possibly for a Low Titan Orbit insertion. But Kiiswood suspected that orbital *insertion* was not the intent, but rather orbital *interception*. The shuttlepod had been commandeered as a weapon—a substitute for the small tactical missile that lay unfinished on Porco Station. And the likely target of this improvised missile was the interstellar craft in Low Titan Orbit—the *Dove*.

No longer encumbered by accelerative forces, Kiiswood was now free to move about the shuttle's hull, at least within the limits of his tether's reach. He turned on his helmet torch so that he might see in the darkness of Titan's shadow, and he soon located the thermonuclear weapon mounted to the side of the shuttle. This weapon, he determined, was the most immediate threat, for it was very likely on a dead-man trigger connected to the assailant's c-nex, similar to Miriam Sharl, the suicide bomber back at Tyrrhenus.

Using any recess or protrusion in the hull that he could grip, he crawled his way to the ovoid device. After a cursory examination of its casing, Kiiswood quickly assessed that it was a crudely constructed device, made from scavenged parts of Porco Station. He first considered removing it from the shuttle's hull. But to what end? He could not realistically heave it to a safe distance. He then decided that his only practical option was to disarm it.

Its casing was easy enough to penetrate with the compact tools that the chief had on himself—emergency tools normally used for impromptu repairs to faulty EV packets, leaking helmets, or torn compression suits. He pulled several small micro-tethered tools from the utility pouch on his upper sleeve; with them, he unfastened part of the casing and tossed it adrift in space. He then studied its components: fission trigger (or primary device), plutonium core, explosive lens, detonation leads, and helium-3 implosive charge (or

399

secondary device). He decided that removing the fission trigger was not the best option, for although it would lessen the explosive yield, he would still be left with a primary device that was a functioning atomic bomb. Instead, Kiiswood chose the more time-consuming option. Working fastidiously for several minutes, he delicately removed the plutonium core and threw it away. The chief had disarmed the thermonuclear device.

But now Kiiswood found himself in a moral quandary. The welfare of his friend was of foremost concern in his soul, but he also felt a moral imperative to regard the thousands of others whose lives were in harm's way. He felt compelled to prevent the shuttle from becoming a kinetic impact weapon—from threatening the *Dove* or the space-dock in Low Titan Orbit. He considered trying to break into the cabin section, neutralize the pilot, and take control of the shuttle. But he promptly rejected this idea; while undocked, the shuttle's hatch could not be opened from the outside, not without specialized equipment. An undocked hatch could only be opened from inside—only by the shuttle's occupants. His only other option was to deprive the engine of power, to prevent it from making further course adjustments. And although this option might save thousands, it meant that the shuttle would slam into Titan's atmosphere, killing his friend.

No matter what he considered doing, there was no right choice. But then, as the Aeon said, choices were not about righteousness; choices were about sacrifice.

Disabling the shuttle's power source was a daunting task, more daunting than disarming a nuclear payload. Whereas the explosive device was improvised from scavenged equipment, the shuttle's reactor housing was well-designed, well-built, and would not be easily breached with the little tools in his emergency kit. But then the chief thought of a tool that might work.

He crawled along the shuttle's hull to the foot of the starboard landing strut and wrenched off its piton launcher, taking great care to keep the unit intact. With the launcher in hand, Kiiswood pulled himself to an adjacent service panel and opened it. After ripping out several layers of micrometeoroid shielding, he exposed some of the reactor's auxiliary electrical components. He wedged the piton launcher under some of the components, aiming its muzzle so that it was plumb with the reactor's insulated housing. The chief pulled another small tool from his utility pouch and, with its sharp edge, carefully cut a tiny incision in the foresleeve of his compression suit. He took great care not to compromise the integrity of his suit, but only to expose the electrical wiring of his sleeve's chronometer display. Cutting the wires, he connected them to the electrical leads on the piton launcher. Then, by simply activating his chronometer display, he ignited the launcher and fired its piton into the shuttle's helium-3 reactor. The hole that the projectile made in the reactor housing was small, but it was significant enough to create a substantial rupture in the magnetic confinement system. The reactor could no longer power the engine; the shuttle was now destined to burn up in Titan's atmosphere.

Kiiswood's hopes of helping his friend seemed dark, so much darker than the shadow of Titan that now shrouded the shuttlepod. Even so, his spirit did not want to surrender hope. He crawled along the hull toward the shuttle's hatch to peer through its porthole and to see how Hewst was faring, but the hatch was just beyond his tether's reach. So that he might reach the porthole, he followed his tether back to the truss assembly and disconnected his clip from the strut. Now the only thing that secured Kiiswood to the shuttle's hull was his grip.

With even greater care, the chief slowly pulled his untethered body toward the hatch. As he drew steadily closer, Kiiswood saw, in the darkness, a flashing emergency light emanating from the shuttle's cabin. He was a mere meter or two away when the hatch suddenly exploded from its frame. Kiiswood witnessed as Hewst was abruptly blown through the hatchway like a limp ragdoll jettisoned out into space. The suitless, lifeless body of Lieutenant Olsen immediately followed. Was Hewst protected within her compression suit? Was she conscious? Was she injured? Or, like Olsen, was she no longer alive? The chief did not know.

Without pause, Kiiswood grabbed the edge of the hatchway for leverage, surveyed the cabin in a single glance, and then launched himself after his friend with every bit of leg strength that he could summon. Off in the distance, the chief could see Hewst by the light of her helmet torch, as she tumbled end over end toward Titan. He tried hailing Hewst through her helmet's headset, but he had no indication that his headset was transmitting under EMCON conditions. And even if he were transmitting, Kiiswood saw no indication that his friend was receiving it.

He activated the orbital dynamics telemetry on his visor's heads-up display and programmed it to track Hewst by her tumbling torchlight. From the telemetry, he could see that his friend was carrying much more velocity than he was; he would not be able to catch up to her with the mere force of his leap from the shuttle.

His EV packet was equipped with a thruster bundle, but it was designed for EVA maneuvering only, not for jetting about in deep space. Kiiswood did not have enough thruster propellant to overtake his friend. Indeed, while trying, he expended all of his propellant, but succeeded only in closely matching her velocity. However, he did have another option—a very dangerous option. His thruster bundle had an emergency feature that would allow him to allocate some of his oxygen as an auxiliary propellant. The risk was obvious; he might use up his breathable oxygen. But for Kiiswood, the risk to himself bore no weight in his deliberation. Without even a moment's reluctance, the chief would go after Hewst; he would rescue her, or he would die trying. He activated the emergency feature, accessed his oxygen supply, and raced after his friend.

Their distance soon began to close as Kiiswood's speed increased. He was not far from Hewst when the telemetry on his HUD suddenly flashed with bright red characters: TARGET AT INTERFACE ALTITUDE: 1270 km. The telemetry indicated that she was decelerating slightly as she now entered Titan's thin thermosphere. Seconds later, Kiiswood felt the subtle friction as he too began his plunge into the thin methane atmosphere.

Despite its thinness at this still extremely high altitude, the atmosphere was sufficient to trim Hewst of her tumbling. Then, the chief was elated and grateful when he saw the very first indication of life in his friend. Hewst had arched her back and was using aero-resistance to level herself. She was evidently trying to control her descent attitude—a clear sign that she was alive and indeed conscious, but she would not be so for much longer. Her compression suit was not Titan-rated, and she was carrying too much momentum to survive the frictional heat of atmospheric entry.

With very little oxygen remaining in his EV packet, Kiiswood shut down his thrusters, for he was now able to exploit the upper atmosphere, thin as it was, to maneuver after his friend. Using his body as a streamlined airfoil, the chief pulled his arms back and extended his legs, reducing his drag and diving rapidly toward Hewst. Using his hands and feet like ailerons and rudders, he kept himself stable and on course as he quickly came up behind his friend. And just as the distant sun was breaking over the eastern rim of Titan, Kiiswood reached out, grabbed Hewst from behind, and deftly fastened his tether to a harness ring on her compression suit.

Believing against all reason that the browless man had inexplicably survived, tracked her down, and seized her, Hewst initially fought and flailed to free herself. Despite her struggle, the stratogen's grip was resilient; she could not break free.

"Catherine! It's me!" the chief shouted, but again she was not receiving his transmission. He turned Hewst to face him and fastened the main-lift web of his compression suit to hers, so that he would not lose her in the dense, and fast-approaching, Titanian clouds. Whatever would happen to them in the next several minutes, their fates were now bound together.

The two faced each other as they tumbled through the steadily thickening thermosphere. Taking a sharp look into the face of the one who held her, Hewst suddenly recognized her friend. "Oh my God! Níyol!" she yelled. "What are you doing here?" Struggling to endure the agony of her broken arm, Hewst bravely pressed through the pain to embrace her friend as tightly as she could.

Even though Hewst's voice did not carry beyond her visor, Kiiswood was still able to see her words on her moving lips. He saw the gratitude in her smiling eyes, coupled with the grimace of pain that she plainly wore on her bludgeoned face. He pressed his helmet's face plate against hers, so that they might hear each other through the subtle audio vibrations of their visors. "I realized that I hadn't wished you a happy Easter," the chief quipped loudly so that his voice might be heard through their visors. "I told you to be careful, Catherine!" Despite his strong, assertive tone, the voice of this tough stratogen faintly quivered in empathy, for the very sight of what his friend had suffered was tearing at his soul. "You know that I can't always be there to catch you."

"Apparently, you can," she replied. She then added, "I don't mean to sound ungrateful, but you shouldn't be here. Now we'll *both* burn to death in the atmosphere."

Kiiswood watched the telemetry on his HUD intently, specifically monitoring the steadily increasing atmospheric pressure. He knew that Hewst's compression suit would soon exceed its thermal tolerances. "You're not dying today," declared Kiiswood. He assumed a stable arched position and said, "Hold on tight; this is probably going to knock the wind out of you." His head-up display suddenly flashed the warning: PARACHUTE DEPLOYMENT ALTITUDE. Immediately, a special hypersonic parachute exploded from an upper compartment of Kiiswood's EV packet. As designed, the parachute unfurled in stages, so that its concussive force would not be fatal. Even so, the initial deployment jolted them so hard that Hewst could not breathe for several seconds.

Eventually, she caught her breath, but the decelerating force was so intense that she found it difficult to speak. After several minutes, the g-forces gradually subsided, until the two of them were drifting gently under the parachute's canopy into the opaque methane haze of Titan's atmosphere.

Soon, the orange haze that engulfed them was so thick that Hewst could hardly see the canopy hovering over them, but she could plainly see the chief's unconscious face. "Níyol!" She shouted his name again, but the chief did not answer. She then noticed the oxygen display on Kiiswood's HUD—it was flashing red, indicating that the chief had depleted all of his oxygen.

Exhausted and broken, she strained against her own pain to help her friend. Clumsily, she reached behind Kiiswood and fumbled about his EV packet, trying to find his retractable oxygen umbilical. After much effort, she found it, extended it around to her own EV packet, and tried to plug it into her own oxygen supply. After dropping the umbilical connector twice, she succeeded finally in attaching it to her charging port.

"Oh God!" she prayed. "Don't take him. Please!"

Chapter 32 – Alex

The *Dove*, in Low Titanian Orbit (LTO)

(Titanographic Co-ordinates: S 2.7, W 127.5, Altitude: 1,407 km)

Sunday, 14 April 2430 CE

Time: 0722 Zulu

To date, Project Columba Noachi was arguably humanity's most ambitious endeavor, and perhaps its most dire. A clandestine project, it united the Terrestrial Assembly and the Jovian Confederation (the two most prominent governments in the solar system) in a common cause to establish a new human civilization in the Thaller star system, 1,300 light years away, in the constellation Columba—far away from the extinction-threatening Casius pathogen.

The cornerstone of the project was the most massive, most technologically advanced spacecraft ever constructed: the interstellar ark, christened the *Dove*. Cradled within the scaffolding of an enormous space-dock, the *Dove* was a behemoth of an ark—4,5 kilometers long and over a half billion metric tons. Built with a plethora of redundant systems, the ark was over-designed and over-equipped to ensure its mission's success. The *Dove* was replete with multiple propulsion systems, fusion reactors, replicators, cryogenic and ectogenetic chambers, and cultural archives, all uniformly distributed throughout the ark's countless modules—redundancy upon redundancy.

The *Dove* had been under construction for eight years; during that time, the entire interstellar craft had been assembled and maintained by construction-droids and service drones. With few exceptions, this massive ark had been carefully manufactured without the aid of human hands. Indeed, it had been meticulously protected from direct human contact. Its only current connections to humankind were the power and communication umbilicals that hard-linked the *Dove* to the space-dock and to Columba Noachi launch control.

Such extreme construction measures were necessary to safeguard the *Dove* from microbial infection, especially from the Casius organelle. As a part of its construction schedule, this massive craft underwent periodic sterilization protocols from bow to stern, including dry heating, vapor-phasing, and gamma-irradiation. Perhaps these protocols were excessive, but they were implemented to guarantee that the interstellar ark (and all therein) would not carry with it the very threat that humankind was trying to escape.

Among the *Dove*'s cargo that underwent several disinfection procedures were the linchpins of the mission: the 125 meta-droid passengers. Even though the Casius organelle could not compromise these meta-droids, they were still subjected to peroxide vapor-phasing, just in case their synthetic surfaces were harboring any germs.

The meta-droids had completed their mission training, which oriented them to the *Dove*'s various operational systems. They were instructed how to repair the interstellar craft should the need arise while underway. They were also briefed on the operations of the ectogenetic gestation chambers and how to monitor the embryos in cryogenic storage. Of course, all of these responsibilities were merely a means to accomplish the primary mission—to facilitate human colonization in the Thaller system, and to nurture and socialize the colonists as human beings. The meta-droids were to *humanize* the new human race.

With only a few hours left before launch, the meta-droids were finally placed aboard the *Dove*, each billeted to their respective modules. All of them now wore their project uniforms that bore their new identities. Each meta-droid had been assigned a new name—a personal name rather than the impersonal *ALX* number that had been assigned to them when they were originally manufactured by the Whitaker Institute. Most of them now took on the monikers of the scientists who served as their respective neural-network donors. But not Alex. He wanted a new beginning, a fresh start.

There was a time when Alex knew himself as Earnan Cobisson, professor of astrobiology at the University of Aristarchus, husband of Ronnie Sabinas, and father of Catherine Cobisson. But Earnan was gone, and so were his wife and daughter; the only connection that Alex had to his past was his profession. And if he regarded anyone as family now, he thought of his friends: Hewst and Kiiswood. For this reason, he decided that he would take on the name of the scientist who inspired him to become an astrobiologist: Francis Hewst—a new name to complement his new look. Perchance, millennia from now, when the *Dove* would reach the Thaller system, Alex might also prove himself an inspiration to the new humanity, just as Francis was to him.

As part of a pre-ignition procedure, Alex and the other meta-droids were instructed to shut themselves down twenty minutes prior to launch. Of course, before this shutdown was to occur, Alex needed to secure himself inside his assigned cyber-telemetry chamber, where he was to ride out the long journey when not awake. So, for the few hours he had to himself before shutdown, Alex decided to explore his part of the enormous ship.

As the *Dove* did not have the means (nor the need) to generate artificial gravity for its interstellar voyage, Alex was able to drift about weightlessly through the ark's narrow corridors. He casually inspected his billeted area and the contents of its cargo hold—some cryogenic chambers, a fusion reactor, some on-board service drones, and several archival storage compartments. As he made his way to his cyber-telemetry chamber, he came upon an adjacent workstation and began to survey its equipment. Alex activated the station's computer and accessed the ship's mainframe data suite. For curiosity's sake, he opened the archive manifest to see what treasures of history and human culture were stowed aboard. He discovered that the ark was freighted with the best of humanity's arts and achievements: sculptures, stelae, paintings, scrolls, books, music, videos, photos, and holos. Its databases were loaded with a vast array of human wisdom: sciences, philosophies, religions, and languages.

With such a wealth of knowledge at his beck and call, Alex decided to review the data files on the Thaller star system. He opened one file after another, familiarizing himself with what astronomers and astrophysicists had learned about the star and its habitable worlds. As he perused the data, he noticed that some of the files cross-referenced some research material about a subsurface cavern at Hellas Planitia. The Federal Aerospace Intelligence Agency had apparently downloaded all of the unredacted records from Project Belshazzar into the Dove's mainframe data suite.

Among the records, Alex found some of Dr. Jonathan Driggers' translations and morphologies of the cavern's alien languages, one of which was identified as possibly Thallerian. He found Dr. Glendon Ferris' research on the eight binary numbers in the cavern's fractals—numbers that corresponded to the rotation rates of eight known pulsars. He also came across Dr. Tereza Střelec's files on binary systems and base-2 numbers. He even found his own research on the sterile conditions of the cavern. But Alex was surprised to see one particular file among the research material—a file listed as NECKLACE. Apparently, FAIA had inadvertently downloaded and saved a personal file that Alex had created when he ran spectral and DNA analyses on Hewst's necklace.

As he stared at the file name on the computer's monitor, Alex began missing Hewst (and Kiiswood), so he opened the file to reminisce. The monitor displayed images of Hewst's necklace and all of the spectral and DNA data.

Suddenly, Alex was possessed by an epiphany; he saw the data in a way that he had not seen it before. His original analysis of the necklace was merely an unrelated project; it was just a personal favor for a friend. But now, he saw the data in light of Project Belshazzar's discoveries, and he began to think that the necklace and the cavern at Hellas Planitia were strangely connected. Initially, he had examined the pendant only, but now he wondered whether the chain bore any significance. Was it a coincidence that the links in the chain were made from two different metals, like a binary pattern? Was it a coincidence that there were eight interwoven strands in the chain—like the eight binary numbers that corresponded to eight pulsars?

With the data already on file, Alex directed the computer to count the number of links in each strand of the chain and to delineate each link according to its metallic composition. He then compared this information with the binary patterns found in the cavern. Alex's eyes widened in disbelief as the results appeared. The number of links in each strand matched the number of digits in each binary pattern. But what astounded him most was the fact that the sequence of platinum and titanium links in each strand corresponded perfectly with the sequence in each of these binary patterns.

Alex wondered how this was possible. The strands of Hewst's necklace were encoded with the rotation rates of eight pulsars—the same rotation rates identified by Project Belshazzar's research team. The chance that two things would share the same complex binary pattern was too astronomical to be a coincidence. Hewst's gift from her deceased father and a Martian cavern fashioned by an incorporeal intelligence were clearly connected. But how?

Alex then wondered whether other connections existed, so he decided that the pendant warranted a second look. He had previously examined the pendant to determine whether or not the kernel therein was a mustard seed. Once he had concluded that the so-called mustard seed was nothing more than a jumble of noncoding DNA, Alex gave the pendant no further thought. But now he questioned whether this synthesized DNA chain was engineered to convey something other than genetic codes.

He looked again at the unusual DNA strand that comprised five nucleobases, and he soon noticed a pattern: without exception, every ninth base in the DNA sequence was uracil. Indeed, he noticed that uracil occurred nowhere else in the DNA sequence except as every ninth nucleobase. He quickly recognized that the uracil served as boundary markers, demarking the other nucleobases into eight-bit units of adenine-thymine and cytosine-guanine base pairs. The uracil divided the DNA sequence into octets of nucleobases.

He recalled some of the research tools his team members at Belshazzar Station had employed: Dr. Drigger's information theory and Dr. Střelec's binary information systems. On a hunch that this nucleobase sequence was conveying digital information, Alex ran the DNA strand through several character conversion programs. When he ran it through the Terran Character Code converter (TCC), the following text suddenly lit up his computer's monitor:

Alex:

By the time you read this, I will have been dead for ten years. You will surely find what I am about to tell you to be incredible. But, so that you may believe beyond all doubt, let me begin by telling you that I know you. I have always known you. I knew you before you were formed in the laboratories of the Whitaker Institute. I knew you when you were Earnan Cobisson, when you were a husband and father.

I know that the human race faces extinction from the Casius organelle. I know that you have committed yourself to saving humanity from its inevitable extinction, that you will embark on a mission to re-establish the human race on a distant world. I can tell you that you and your fellow meta-droids will indeed be successful, that humankind will thrive in its new home. I can also tell you that the human race will find communion with other self-conscious beings among the stars. How I know this to be true, I cannot tell you now, but later you will understand.

As you have only now deciphered the text that I encoded within this DNA strand, now is the right time and place to declare this truth: humankind and Casius are fellow self-conscious beings. Yet neither recognizes the sentience of the other; each sees the other as a parasitic threat.

But there is hope of symbiosis; there is hope for the human race to find communion with the organelles. This hope of which I speak is your friend, my daughter, Cathy.

At her birth, she was imbued with a divine gift—she was given a bridge that could span the chasm between humankind and Casius. Indeed, she became that bridge when she was transfigured in the Martian cavern—transfigured by the angels of Hellas. Cathy's very presence is a gift to the solar system. She could save both the human race and Casius from extinction.

If you still harbor hope for the humanity that you and the Dove *will soon leave behind, if you believe that compassion might yet define the human race, I beseech you, seek out my daughter. Help her to fulfill her divine purpose.*

"How very good and pleasant it is when kindred live together in unity!" (Psalm 133:1)

Alex was an intelligent scientist and a rational person, but he could not explain this. He could not explain the connection between Hewst's necklace and the Martian cavern. He could not explain how Hewst's father, a man who had been dead for ten years, foreknew the things that he had encoded in a strand of synthesized DNA. How then could he believe what he could not explain?

And yet, Alex did believe. He believed that the human race was still capable of compassion. He believed that the human race could live in unity with its kindred among the stars. And he believed that his friend was a gift—a gift who could save many from extinction. He did not understand how or why; he simply believed. He believed because he chose to believe.

Alex had been thoroughly briefed on the protocol of the *Dove's* communication system. He knew that the system was intended to be used only after the interstellar craft was underway, and then only for mission-critical purposes. Even so, he broke protocol, entered the override codes, and accessed a hailing channel. He tried several times to contact Hewst through her c-nex, but all of his efforts failed—his friend did not answer. Unable to reach Hewst, he then tried calling the chief.

"This is Kiiswood," the chief's voice said, promptly answering the call.

"Chief, this is Alex," said the meta-droid. "Is Catherine with you?"

"Alex?" the chief grilled. "Where are you? Are you on Porco Station?"

"No!" he replied tersely; his one-word answer seemed curt and brusque. "I'm aboard the *Dove*, and we're about to launch in a matter of hours."

Kiiswood cautioned his friend, "You're breaking EMCON protocol!"

"This is more important," countered Alex. "I tried calling Catherine, but I can't get through to her." He then charged, "Don't let her out of your sight. She's the key to the Casius pathogen. Don't let anything happen to her."

Alex then heard three beeps abruptly interrupting the call, followed by the voice of a launch controller on the space-dock. "ALX-63, this is Launch Director Nnamani," the voice said. "Columba Noachi Launch Control has been monitoring your workstation operations. For reasons of mission security, your transmission has been terminated."

Alex was palpably not pleased that Launch Control had interrupted his call, but neither was he surprised. "Director Nnamani, if you've been monitoring my workstation, then you know why I violated EMCON protocol," he responded. "You can see the same information that I see. If you won't let me contact Commander Hewst, then I beg you, find her—look after her."

411

Several awkward seconds of silence passed; the meta-droid heard no reply. "Hello? Director Nnamani, are you there?"

As he awaited a response from the Launch Director, Alex was abruptly turned off—well before he was supposed to shut himself down. His still body was suddenly drifting freely in zero gravity like a lifeless doll. The launch controllers had shut Alex down ahead of schedule to prevent the meta-droid's willfulness from hindering the mission. The controllers then activated a couple of service drones to insert Alex into his cyber-telemetry chamber and to secure him in place.

Unconscious in his chamber, Alex awaited the launch of the *Dove*.

There, Alex dreamt.

Chapter 33 – Angmar Methane Falls

"Oh God!" she prayed. "Don't take him. Please!"

Hewst and Kiiswood were drifting gently, under the canopy of a hypersonic parachute, through the opaque hydrocarbon haze of Titan's atmosphere. The orange haze that engulfed them was so thick that Hewst could hardly see the canopy hovering over them, but she could plainly see the chief's unconscious face.

Exhausted and broken, Hewst strained against her own pain to rescue her friend. After much effort, she managed to connect Kiiswood's oxygen umbilical to her own EV packet so that the two could breathe from the same oxygen supply.

Again, she prayed, "Please God, not again!" Today, Easter Sunday, was the first day in ten years that Hewst had spoken to God—the first day since the death of her father. "Please, don't do this again!"

A couple of minutes passed, and Hewst received her answer—Kiiswood regained consciousness.

The chief took a few seconds to reorient himself to his surroundings. After a couple of deep breaths, he realized that Hewst was feeding him oxygen from her own EV packet. "Catherine, what are you doing?" he protested. "Don't waste your oxygen on me."

With a defiant and perhaps slightly scolding tone, she replied, "The proper response to a gift is to accept it."

"You're going to need that oxygen for yourself," the chief persisted.

Hewst accessed the data on her HUD and surveyed the rate of her oxygen consumption. "I have enough for about five or six hours between us," she responded.

Kiiswood also accessed his HUD and inspected some of the technical features that would allow him to adjust the drag-coefficient of his parachute. "We're more than 180 kilometers from the surface," he said. "If I reduce the canopy size, we could be on the ground in about five hours."

"So we should have enough oxygen to make it to the surface," she surmised.

"Aye, but then what?" the chief asked rhetorically. "Whether you're under a parachute or on the ground, you can't breathe nitrogen. You need to save your oxygen for yourself."

"I'm not going to ride this parachute down to the surface while tethered to a corpse," she adamantly declared. "No, Níyol, you and I will share the same fate, whatever happens."

Kiiswood reduced the size of the canopy to function as a drogue chute, expediting their descent rate while keeping them even and stable. According to the telemetry on his HUD, the chief estimated that they would touch down safely on the Titanian surface in just over five hours. As they descended through the thick, opaque haze, Kiiswood posed no further objections to Hewst, reluctantly accepting her personal risk. "Thank you," he said.

Grateful for the heroic risks that he too had taken on her behalf, Hewst reciprocated, "Thank *you*."

For the next few hours, Hewst slept in the refuge and reassurance of being harnessed to Kiiswood and his parachute. Sleep afforded her a retreat from her pain, if only temporarily. For his part, Kiiswood kept vigil, making sure that the panels and lines of the drogue chute remained secure and true. Periodically, he reached up to the risers and tested the parachute's steering toggles. With each pull on the toggles, he would watch the digital compass of his HUD to determine the turn rate. Other than the canopy above him and his feet below him, Kiiswood had no visual frame of reference. Surrounded by an opaque, disorienting fog, he saw no ground, no sky, no horizon—just a diffused, murky haze.

Just as their descent through the shrouded atmosphere seemed like it would never end, the haze suddenly opened up as Hewst and Kiiswood dropped below the methane cloud base. There, 12 kilometers below their feet, was the frozen terrain of the channel-strewn Adiri Highlands. "Catherine," he called as he gently prodded her awake. "Are you still with me?"

Slowly, Hewst opened her swollen eyes and soon remembered that she was tethered to Kiiswood under his parachute. "Where are we?" she inquired as she quickly surveyed the ground below her.

The atmosphere was now dense enough to carry their voices. Hewst and Kiiswood were able to hear each other without having to press their helmets together. Still, their words were somewhat muffled by their helmet's visors.

"We're over the Angmar Mountain Range," the chief answered. "We're descending at about 8.5 meters per second. We should touch down in about twenty minutes."

Seemingly out of nowhere, an aerial combat drone furiously hurtled past them. Then a second one raced by them, passing within a couple of meters. Hewst and Kiiswood were slowly drifting down into a swarm of aerial drones.

Looking out at the array of firepower that surrounded them, Kiiswood tried to lighten the moment. "It looks like the Jovian Confederation is giving us an official military welcome," he quipped.

With a nervous irony, Hewst responded, "Yeah, we're receiving a real VIP treatment."

"Evidently, we're violating their defense space," he observed. "Those aren't surveillance drones. They're *Aesir*-class aerial combat drones, and each one looks like it's carrying a full ordnance complement."

"Can we hail the Confederation," she wondered, "to let them know that we're not the ones who launched the assault on the space-dock?"

"Unfortunately, no," he replied. "All communication systems are rendered inoperative during EMCON conditions."

"Are they going to shoot us if we land?" she nervously asked.

Despite the portents of their situation, Kiiswood laughed at his friend's question. "Well, it's not as if we can fall up," he remarked. "Parachutes don't have a reverse toggle."

Hewst also laughed, even though it hurt to do so. "Can you put it in neutral?" she humorously asked.

After several minutes, the chief noticed that the drones had not assumed an offensive posture; instead, they were flying in a defensive formation, providing escort. As Hewst and Kiiswood approached the ground, the drones seemed to yield airspace to them, ushering the two of them to a safe touchdown.

Toggles in hand, Kiiswood skillfully piloted the canopy around the steeper contours of the Angmar Mountains and set his sights on the most level place that he could find. With a landing site in view, he pulled down sharply on the toggles, flared the canopy, slowed their descent, and lined up for a soft landing. For the sake of his injured friend, Kiiswood touched down as gently as he could on the frozen surface of Titan.

Hewst and Kiiswood came to rest among the icy mountains of the Adiri Highlands, landing near the breathtaking methane falls of Angmar. The ground they touched down on was rock-hard ice, frozen water as hard as granite. The surface gravity was so weak that the two of them carried only one-eighth of their Terran weight. The atmospheric pressure was sixty percent denser than Earth's, making their movements a bit like walking under water. Their compression suits were not needed to keep their bodies pressurized, but they were certainly needed to insulate them from the frigid nitrogen atmosphere.

The impact on Hewst's broken body was ever so gentle; still, she groaned and grimaced in pain as they landed. Kiiswood carefully reclined his friend on the frigid ground, removed her connection to his main-lift web, and cut the parachute away. He would have also detached his oxygen umbilical from Hewst's EV packet, but she forbade him, and he did not want to argue with her.

Kiiswood immediately performed LSR treatment and quickly assessed the nature and severity of Hewst's injuries. "Catherine, your arm and leg are broken," he said. "Until I can get you to a medical facility, I need to splint them."

Hewst chuckled as she looked around at the barren mountainscape. "Yeah, I'm sure there's a tree branch or something just lying about," she sarcastically replied. Against Kiiswood's protests, Hewst used her unbroken arm to prop herself up, reposing her back against a gentle slope in the mountainside. There she sat, too infirmed to walk, gazing upon the awe and beauty of Angmar Falls. The viscous liquid methane spilled leisurely over the adjacent cliffs, slowly plunging tens of meters to the base of the falls. Hewst was mesmerized by the shimmering translucent fluid as it cascaded down the side of the icy mountain. "We both know that I can't walk out of these mountains on my own," she acknowledged, "and if you try to carry me, we'll use up all the oxygen before we could find help." Hewst then looked at Kiiswood and added, "Niyol, I want you to take my EV packet. Maybe you'll have enough oxygen to make it. I think I'll just sit right here and enjoy this awesome view."

Kiiswood had no retort, no clever scheme, no witty comeback. He said nothing; he simply sat down beside his friend.

As the two of them sat quietly together, watching the hypnotic flow of the methane falls, Kiiswood heard an incoming message on his c-nex. "Attention! Attention, intruders!" a commanding voice ordered. "You are violating the military defense space and the sovereign domain of the Jovian Confederation. Allay any hostile intentions and stand down!"

Before he could alert his friend about the message that he had just received, an *Artemis*-class troop carrier emerged over the nearby ridge of the mountains. (The *Artemis*-class was a similar troop carrier to its areopter-counterpart on Mars, but with smaller rotors.) It quickly assumed a relative position several meters directly overhead, inundating the two of them in its rotor wash. Almost immediately, a special ops team of four well-armed Confederation marines repelled to the ground from the hovering troop carrier. Donned in their camouflage compression suits, these marines promptly surrounded Hewst and Kiiswood with their rail-rifles at the ready.

"Identify yourselves!" ordered Gunnery Sergeant Anthony Lhoma, the special ops team leader, who kept his weapon trained on the two intruders as he spoke.

Kiiswood immediately recognized Lhoma's voice as the one who had ordered them to stand down just moments ago. "At ease, Gunny, we're unarmed," Kiiswood replied as he rose to his knees and raised his hands over his head. "We're allies; we're with the Terrestrial Assembly Defense Force."

Lhoma did not lower his rifle; instead, he repeated his order more vehemently. "Identify yourselves!" he shouted. "Name and rank!"

"I'm SOC Níyol Kiiswood," he shouted in response, "and this is Commander Catherine Hewst." The chief gestured toward his friend and continued, "Please, help her. She needs immediate medical attention."

Using a hand signal, the gunnery sergeant gestured to his team members and ordered, "Stand fast!" Lhoma shouldered his rail-rifle while the rest of the team kept their weapons leveled on Hewst and Kiiswood. He reached into a utility pouch on his waist and pulled out a handheld scanner. After programming it to link with his c-nex, the gunnery sergeant aimed the handheld device toward Kiiswood's visor and scanned his face. "Confirmed!" he announced. "Positive ID for Chief Níyol Kiiswood!" Lhoma then turned his scanner on Hewst's swollen, blood-stained face and said, "ID probability: ninety-seven percent for Commander Veronica Catherine Hewst." He returned the scanner to his utility pouch and declared, "I take that as confirmation."

Upon hearing the team leader's declaration, the rest of the marines shouldered their weapons and immediately transitioned from a tactical unit into a rescue team. The marines harnessed themselves to Hewst and Kiiswood and adeptly hoisted their rescuees up into the hovering rotorcraft. And as the cabin hatch closed behind them, the troop carrier readily sped away, flying its passengers to the safety of a Confederation processing facility.

Once the hatch was secured, the automated airlock system purged the cabin of the indigenous nitrogen atmosphere and repressurized it with warm, breathable air. Everyone onboard the troop carrier opened their helmets and freely breathed in the Terran-normal atmosphere. Lhoma and another marine knelt attentively beside Hewst as she lay on some blankets that were spread out for her on the cabin's treadway. Although Kiiswood yielded space to the marines who were rendering medical aid for Hewst, he still hovered close to his friend.

Lhoma leaned in toward Hewst and introduced himself. "Commander, I'm Gunnery Sergeant Tony Lhoma. I command Special Ops Team Bravo. We're currently en route to a medical treatment facility, ETE twenty-three minutes." He then gestured toward his fellow marine who held an LSR field kit in her hand. "This is Field Medic Lisa Nakitas," he said. "She's going to take good care of you until we get you to the facility." As he placed Hewst in the field medic's care, Lhoma turned toward the cockpit and shouted to the pilot, "Contact McKay Station; inform them that we recovered two survivors—Chief Kiiswood and Commander Hewst."

"Aye aye, Gunnery Sergeant," the pilot replied sharply.

Holding on to the armrest of an adjacent seat, Kiiswood steadied himself as the rotorcraft sped toward its destination. He asked the gunnery sergeant, "Aren't you breaking EMCON protocols?"

"The *Dove* launched about thirty minutes ago," Lhoma answered. "EMCON conditions have been lifted." He then asked, "Chief, I was informed that you two were being sequestered at Porco Station. How the hell did you two end up on Titan? And how did your commander sustain these injuries?"

"Someone wearing an Alliance-surplus compression suit had stolen aboard Porco Station and commandeered the shuttlepod to launch an assault on the *Dove*," the chief explained. "He was probably an allegiant with the New Jerusalem terrorist sect. He apparently tried to kill the commander when she inadvertently got in his way."

"It was the browless man," Hewst interjected, "the assassin from *Landis*." She continued, "He murdered Lieutenant Olsen."

"Please, ma'am," Nakitas pleaded, "just rest, and try not to speak." Using a precision-laser tool, the field medic meticulously cut away portions of Hewst's compression suit to better examine and treat her broken arm and leg and the broken bones of her face. She soon started an IV and assiduously monitored the commander's vital signs.

The gunnery sergeant continued to question Kiiswood, speaking a little more quietly, trying to be respectful of the commander's need to rest. "So, this terrorist," Lhoma asked, "he killed the pilot and then took the two of you as hostages?"

"Not exactly," Kiiswood answered, also speaking quietly. "He took the commander hostage; he tried to maroon me at Porco Station."

"I'm not following you, Chief," Lhoma confided. "If you weren't onboard the shuttle with the commander, how did the two of you end up together on the surface of Titan?"

"The commander was *on*board," the chief replied. "I was *out*board." Most of the marines in the passenger cabin suddenly stared at Kiiswood; they were honestly impressed as he recounted the daring stunt. The chief continued, "I was disabling the shuttle's systems while tethered to the hull. All the while, I was thinking that the armada defending the space-dock would, at any moment, blast us out of the sky."

"Several of the destroyers were tracking the shuttle as it closed on the *Dove*," Lhoma confirmed. "Their pulse laser cannons were locking on and ready to fire, but they held fast, even as the shuttle passed within a few kilometers of the space-dock."

"I don't understand why they didn't fire," said Kiiswood. "Their pulse lasers could have easily obliterated the threat."

"CIC didn't want to take the chance that the two of you were onboard the shuttle." The gunnery sergeant then confessed, "We were dismayed when we tracked the shuttle burning up during atmospheric entry; we feared that you two might have burned up with it. We also tracked what we believed to be shuttle debris entering the atmosphere, but when we detected a parachute deployment, we had renewed hopes."

"Not that I'm ungrateful," Kiiswood divulged, "but that shuttle might have crippled or destroyed the *Dove*. Why risk the hope of the entire human race just to save the two of us?"

"Launch Control was monitoring all pre-launch activities aboard the *Dove*," Lhoma explained, "and it seems that the meta-droid discovered a message encoded inside a necklace. The message implied that, since your purported encounter with angels on Mars, the commander is now carrying a cure inside her. As mysterious as the message was, some of the launch

420

controllers began monitoring newsfeeds out of Mars, specifically, reports about quarantined communities that were infected with active Casius organelles. They were seeing incredible stories about inpatients at Camp Lundgren's sickbay inexplicably recovering. They also saw reports of survivors from Suata, Cerberus Dorsa, Licus Vallis, and other infected townships in Hesperia Province." He paused for a moment, then asked, "Do any of these places sound familiar?"

With wide eyes, Kiiswood quickly replied, "Aye, all of those townships were along our long-shuttle's flight path when we flew out of Camp Lundgren."

"Every contagious area your commander passed by suddenly became pathogenically dormant," Lhoma announced. "The encoded message said that her very presence could save the human race. If that's true, then Commander Hewst just might be the hope of us all. She just might be the most precious cargo aboard." He then added, "Our mission objective is to ensure her safety and well-being; all other objectives are negligible. Every person on this troop carrier is deemed expendable for the sake of that objective."

"How ironic," Kiiswood remarked. He looked at Hewst, who was receiving excellent care at the hands of the marine field medic. He continued, "It was just a week ago that everyone was shunning us like pariahs. Now the commander is being greeted as if she were the second coming of Christ."

Although the gunnery sergeant's face betrayed his remorse at the way Hewst and Kiiswood had been treated, his reply did not. Instead, he commented, "I'm grateful for you, Chief. You were clearly willing to sacrifice much for the commander?"

Without hesitation, Kiiswood avowed, "I was willing before, and I'm willing still. Not because she's precious cargo, but because she's my friend." He then asked, "Where are we heading, Gunny?"

"The medical treatment facility at McKay Station," he replied. "It's a helium-3 processing station in the Zephyrus dune fields."

While Kiiswood and Lhoma were speaking, one of the marines reached up to an overhead storage bin and retrieved a large thermos. "Chief," the marine asked, "would you like a cup of coffee?"

Kiiswood grinned and politely answered, "Thank you, no."

Upon hearing someone mention coffee, Hewst was roused. "I would love to have some, please," she said.

Nakitas felt pity for Hewst; it aggrieved the field medic to deny her patient a pleasure as simple as coffee. "I can't let you have any coffee right now, Commander. The nature of your injuries calls for NPO; I don't want to do anything that might cause you to aspirate. I'm so sorry, ma'am."

"Oh, that's okay," Hewst accepted. "I'll just tell myself that, without some amaretto, it's probably terrible-tasting coffee."

The marine with the thermos then revealed, "We actually have some amaretto in the overhead bin."

Kiiswood leaned in toward his friend, held her hand gently, and gave it a reaffirming squeeze. With a smile and a sympathizing nod, he said to her, "You just don't get a break, do you?"

Chapter 34 – *Terra Nova*

The Second Planet Orbiting Thaller

A Continent in the Northern Hemisphere

Circa: Sixth Millennium of the Common Era

Time: Incongruous

His recurring dream had come true. Francis Hewst stood beside the cliff edge that overlooked a pebble-strewn beach about 200 meters below. There, he listened to the calm ocean waves gently lapping against the shore. Staring out at the horizon, he watched as a bright yellow star rose slowly over the water, dawning as brilliantly as Earth's sun. But this shore was not on Earth, and the bright yellow star was not the sun—it was Thaller.

Francis cherished the serenity of the cliff-side view. It reminded him of when he once stood on the White Cliffs of Dover, mesmerized by the sunlight shimmering on the rippling waters of the Strait of Dover. Of course, that occasion was back on Earth about three thousand years ago, before he was known as Francis Hewst—even before he was known as Alex—when he was Earnan Cobisson.

The solar system Francis came from was now light-years away—so far away that the light of Earth's sun was too dim even to be a visible star in the Thallerian night-sky. Everyone he had left behind had long since died; indeed, the entire human race might have gone extinct millennia ago. All that was left to him now were the distant memories of his wife, his daughter, and his friends. In some ways, his memories of the souls he once knew seemed like the wisp of a distant cloud fading with the wind. Yet, in other ways, they seemed sharp and crisp, as unassailable as the present moment.

He had spent most of his three-thousand-year-old life hurtling through space on board the *Dove*, an interstellar ark that carried the seed of a new human race. Of course, he and 124 of his fellow meta-droids had spent more than ninety-five percent of their respective travel time in cyber-telemetry chambers, turned off. Or had they?

In creating the meta-droids for Project Columba Noachi and its daring mission, humankind had inadvertently created a new race of sentient souls. These meta-droids were more than mere machines; like Francis, they were self-conscious beings. They had done more than turn off for most of their interstellar journey; they had slept. More than sleep, they also had dreamt. Indeed, more than dream, they had also communed with the Aeons. Their artificial neural networks had some unique ability to resonate in tune with the thoughts and affections of these incorporeal souls.

For thousands of years, across hundreds of parsecs, all 125 meta-droids mostly slept. But once the *Dove* had entered the Thaller star system twenty-three years ago, the meta-droids awoke. And, upon their awakening, they realized that their dreams were not just images emerging from some kind of android subconscious. They were, instead, messages from the Aeons—messages about colonizing the new world.

The message had astonished the meta-droids. The Aeons' message revealed that the many worlds orbiting Thaller were already inhabited by several self-conscious species—eight in all, or, as the Aeons called them, "Children of the One."

Two of these species were indigenous to the Thaller system; the other six were colonists, far from their native stars. The Thaller system had become a refuge—a haven, an interstellar sanctuary where all Children lived as the One intended—in symbiosis, in communion with each other and with the One.

Each species was physiologically and morphologically distinct, so each colonized a suitable niche among the Thallerian worlds. One was aquatic, living in the salty ocean waters of Thaller Two. Two were terrestrial, living on Thaller Two's continental masses. One was hypogeal, living in the subterranean regions of Thaller Two's larger moon. One was nocturnal, living on the perpetually dark side of the tidally locked Thaller One. One was an advanced mechanical life form, living in the near vacuum of Thaller Four. (This mechanical species, which had evolved beyond its ancient organic form, graciously shared androidic technology with its newly arrived meta-droid kin. Their technology improved the meta-droids' function, appearance, and

424

longevity.) One species was a microbial collective, a strain of the Casius organelle, living ubiquitously in the nervous systems of most other self-conscious beings in the Thaller system (as well as in other star systems). And one, the Aeons themselves, lived everywhere, and yet nowhere; they lived beyond the boundaries of space and time. Indeed, the Aeons spoke on behalf of all these species; they spoke as their translators, ambassadors, and intermediaries.

All of these disparate species had lived in communion with each other for hundreds of thousands of years. They lived in harmony, not by evolution of biology, nor by coercion of law, nor by bond of covenant, nor even by mutual self-interest. Their want was not for self, but for the common good of all people—of all souls. For within each one of them was the soul of all of them. They were united by their compassion for one another, by their predilection to sacrifice for one another.

It was into this common good of souls that the human species (*homo sapiens* and *homo mechanicus*) had arrived. Here, they had dared to hope for a new home. But how could humankind find its niche within an already occupied star system? How could it live among other self-conscious species? The meta-droids of the *Dove* faced rather bleak options: they could declare Project Columba Noachi a failed mission and accept humanity's extinction, or they could trespass among the inhabitants of Thaller Two as invaders and usurpers.

But the Aeons had presented them with another choice. The inhabiting species of the Thaller system would not spurn the humans as invaders; rather, they would welcome them as family, as fellow Children of the One. They would welcome the humans in the way of all who are Children of the One—with compassion and sacrifice. Indeed, they had expected the inevitable arrival of the new species; the Aeons had foretold it.

The two terrestrial species that already inhabited the land masses of Thaller Two had selflessly abandoned one of the larger island continents in the planet's northern hemisphere. At great personal cost, these two species had left their infrastructures, their edifices, their tetrahedral monuments, their communal centers, their homes—so much of what defined their lives. They

425

had resettled throughout the other continents of the planet, all to make space for the new arrivals—to make a home for humankind.

Since the *Dove*'s arrival to the Thaller system, the meta-droids had been assiduously about their mission. For twenty-three years, they had been colonizing this new land magnanimously given for the human race—a land they had christened: *Terra Nova*. They had cultivated Terran crops, generated Terran livestock, and built an intricate infrastructure: wind turbines, photovoltaic panels, communication systems, transportation hubs, schools, a hospital, thousands of human dwellings, *etcetera*. The meta-droids incorporated many of their human buildings into some of the existing structures graciously abandoned by the other species. They built their infrastructure around the ancient tetrahedral monuments that dotted the island continent—monuments that commemorated the religious unity and diversity of the Children of the One.

And, since their arrival, the meta-droids had been gestating human embryos to full term in ectogenetic chambers. For twenty-three years, they had systematically gestated dozens of human beings in three-month increments. Gradually, they would create a multi-generational human race.

The meta-droids had become the communal parents of this new humanity. They raised and nurtured them. They educated them in humanity's history and culture, in science and philosophy, in politics and religion, in art and literature, and in humanity's origins from a now-distant star system. The meta-droids taught them about their new star system and about the souls with whom they shared it.

In that twenty-three years, this new human colony had suffered only two fatalities among its thousands of colonists: one by accident (a drowning) and one by premeditation (a murder). Despite its hopes to take its place among the compassionate species of the Thaller system, this new humanity apparently had not left its sinfulness behind. Murder—as biblically ancient as Cain and Abel, and as human as death itself—had followed humankind to its new home.

All of the species that inhabited the Thaller system welcomed the humans as fellow Children of the One. But because the humans could not yet wholly see the others beyond themselves, because they could not yet fully see the One beyond their egos, the humans often faltered to take their place among the other children. Still, the self-conscious species of this star system continued to love the humans and to commune with them. They had faith that human beings would ultimately attain the humanity that the One intended.

Francis Hewst also had faith in the future of humankind, not because of what he had witnessed of their merits, but because of what he had come to accept as divine providence. The compassion of so many species for one another, even at the risk of their own self-interest, inspired him to believe in nothing less than the grace of God. Alas, although he had faith in the future of humankind, he would not likely see that future come to fruition, for he was soon to embark on a new mission. For twenty-three years, he and his fellow meta-droids had breathed life into a new humanity, but now the Aeons were calling upon Francis to offer hope to the humanity that he had left behind.

Now he stood alone beside the cliff edge, certain that this was the last time his eyes would behold *Terra Nova*. He listened to the waves below, and watched Thaller rise brightly like the sun over the ocean horizon. He turned to look behind him at the cityscape that he and his fellow meta-droids had meticulously constructed. Gazing into the distance, he marveled at a skyline accented by numerous tetrahedral monuments shining in the morning light. Francis then glanced back at the ocean and at the dawn, and he began to sing:

> "*O Word of life, be Thou my soul;*
>
> *I have no life apart from Thee.*
>
> *Live Thou my life and make me whole;*
>
> *Live Thou my life, my God, for Thee.*"

Suddenly, an incorporeal—but familiar—presence enveloped Francis; its disembodied voice interrupted his singing. "Frank," said the voice of the Aeon, "the time is at hand, my friend."

Francis said nothing in response; he simply acknowledged with a grin. And after taking one last, fleeting glance at the distant cityscape, he turned toward an adjacent trailhead and set out to begin his mission.

The trail was narrow and declined steeply, leading Francis well below the rim of the cliff. It was an ancient trail, blazed by the former inhabitants of this land. A very daring trail, it hugged the cliff-side with no switchbacks and no guardrails. Although it was clearly not intended for humans or meta-droids, Francis had hiked it numerous times. With much practice, great care, and some difficulty, he was able to navigate its precarious course.

The trail ended abruptly about 50 meters above the pebble-strewn beach and gave way to the mouth of a wide cave that opened into the side of the cliff. Francis walked into the cave; within about ten steps, perhaps fewer, he entered an enormous tetrahedral cavern. This cavern was virtually identical to the one that once existed below the Martian desert of Hellas Planitia millennia ago—the cavern in which he and his long-ago friends Hewst and Kiiswood were transfigured. Like the one that he remembered on Mars, this cliff-side cavern was seemingly covered with thousands of inscription-filled fractals and protruding stelae. But, unlike the one on Mars, this cavern exhibited no gravitational anomalies, nor was it as well-lit—most of its vast expanse was concealed in darkness. The only part that was brightly illuminated was just several meters into the cavern entrance, where the brilliant shaft of morning light shone through the mouth of the cave.

Standing (so to speak) just within the entrance of the cavern were several beings who represented the various species of the Thaller system. Some of them donned special life-support equipment because the cave, the atmosphere, and the sunlight deviated from their natural, tenable environments. They huddled together in the sunlight at the cavern's entrance to lend Francis their support, to express their hopes for his success and well-being, to grieve his departure, and to surround him with their love.

"Thank you for being here, my friends," Francis said, as he stood among those who had gathered on his behalf. Both the humans and meta-droids easily understood his words. As for the others who did not use a phoneme-based language, they too understood his expression of gratitude, because all in the cavern at that moment were immersed in the presence of the Aeon, in whose presence they all remained distinguishable, but became inseparable. They could not necessarily understand each other's languages, but, in the presence of the Aeon, they could comprehend each other's thoughts and feelings.

Francis stood among his fellow sentients in an awkward silence that lasted for only a few seconds, but seemed to last much longer. Indeed, the only sounds echoing through the otherwise empty cavern were the ocean waves that lapped against the shore just below the mouth of the cave.

Finally, the silence was broken when the representative of the new human race stepped forward—a twenty-two-year-old woman who was among the first humans born and raised in this new world. In her arms, she was delicately cradling a four-week-old infant girl who was among the most recent newborns of the ectogenetic chambers. With a tear-drenched face, the young woman tenderly kissed Francis on the cheek. "I know I made things difficult for you when I was a teenager," she confessed. "I wasn't the easiest daughter to raise. Thank you for not giving up on me." Her voice quivered with emotion. "No one ever had a better father. I'm sorry that I haven't told you this before now. I love you so much."

Francis' face cried, but without the welling of tears; alas, although his artificial anatomy simulated most biological functions of a normal human body, crying was not among them. "I love you more than life itself," he said as he reached up and wiped her tears from her cheek. "I'm so proud of you."

The young woman looked dotingly at the sleeping infant in her arms. "This little girl is so blessed that you're going to be her father," she said to Francis. "I guess that makes her my little sister." The realization that she would never again see her surrogate father or her adopted sister tore through her soul. "I'm going to miss both of you so much!"

Present also among the beings in the cavern was one of Francis' fellow meta-droids—a fellow parent to the new humanity. As Francis was one of the so-called meta-droid fathers, she was rightly called one of the meta-droid mothers. She stepped forward and helped Francis don a ventral-mounted infant carrier and a large backpack of supplies.

Francis then very gently took the sleeping infant from the arms of the young woman. The tiny child roused only momentarily from her peaceful slumber, but quickly settled back to sleep as Francis carefully placed her in the carrier. And as he meticulously adjusted the carrier for the baby's safety and comfort, his fellow meta-droid reached into her pocket and handed Francis a small, thin object.

"A c-nex," he commented, as he took the little disc-shaped device and affixed it to his temple. "I haven't used a c-nex in a long time."

"Of course, it's been formatted to interface with your neural network, Frank," said his fellow meta-droid. "But this c-nex is special." She explained, "You're going to a place where there won't be any record of your existence, so our engineers designed this c-nex to upload critical data that will allow you to assimilate into that world. As soon as you arrive, it's programmed to interface with every quantum information suite within range. It will automatically upload a digital identity that we've created for you: birth certificate, college transcripts, bank accounts, *etcetera*." As she reached up and affectionately touched the swaddled infant, she added, "In fact, as soon as you decide on a name for this beautiful little girl, your c-nex will even upload adoption records for her."

Francis looked down at the sleeping child nestled in his carrier, and as the two of them were immersed in the presence of the Aeon, he and the infant were one. Speaking to the Aeon, Francis said, "I can feel what she's feeling." With a contented smile, he continued, "She sleeps in perfect peace—no anxieties, no fears, no distrust." He then asked, "Will the journey be stressful for her?"

"The journey will not disturb her calm," the Aeon replied. "Time and space will move unnoticed around the three of you."

Francis warmly caressed the little girl's head. "So Casius is with her?" he asked the Aeon.

"Yes," answered the Aeon. "A strain of Casius abides within her now; Casius is at home in her human neurons. The strain will shelter her from the organelles that humankind meets on Mars. And, at the appropriate time, when she and the strain are transfigured, she will no longer need to be sheltered; Casius and humankind will no longer be estranged. The two might even find communion, if the two so choose."

"Why wait for the so-called appropriate time?" asked Francis. "Why not begin the mission already transfigured, so that humankind won't even have to face the possibility of extinction?"

"All species inevitably face extinction, Frank," the Aeon declared. "It was the fear of extinction that compelled humankind to create you and your kind—to flee to the stars and to colonize Thaller. It was the fear of extinction that brought you and your infant girl to this time and place, to set out on this mission to give hope to the extinguishing humanity that you left behind."

Francis stood briefly silent, contemplating the paradox that had brought him to this moment. And as he was ready to bid farewell to his fellow Children of the One who gathered there in the cavern, one of them stepped forward with a gift. His fellow sentient reached forth with an arm-like appendage and handed Francis a looped chain—a necklace made from eight intricately interwoven strands.

The gift-giving sentient communed in a language that Francis could not comprehend. "This chain represents the way to all our worlds," the Aeon translated. "Wear it when you are far from us and you will always be near. Wear it when you are alone from us and you will always belong."

Francis smiled in gratitude and joy. He recognized the necklace; it was like the one that once belonged to his friend of old—that would belong to her again—that he would later adorn with a special pendant. "Thank you," said Francis, as he placed the gift around his neck.

Suddenly, the cavern erupted into brilliant radiance. Like a silent explosion, a resplendent sphere of pure light burst overhead. It shone with such an extraordinary brightness that nothing within the cavern could cast a shadow, yet its brightness was neither blinding nor painful to behold. Even the sunlight that shone through the mouth of the cave seemed faint by comparison.

All who stood in the cavern stared into the light, as if hypnotized or paralyzed. Of course, they were neither; they were quite free to move if they so desired. But they had no desire to move at all; indeed, they felt an enveloping sense of serenity just to stand where they were, gazing into the brilliance.

Without warning, the gravity strangely shifted. Everyone in the cavern was gently lifted off the floor and started floating toward the sphere of light. Francis felt wondrously at peace—a perfect peace, the same peace in which his infant slept—with no anxieties, no fears, no distrust.

As Francis and the others hovered in the sphere of light, their senses were set free from the confines of space and time. They could see the entire cavern—top and bottom, front and back, yesterday and tomorrow—in a single glance. They could perceive it in a previously imperceptible direction—in a new dimension. Previously unseen times and spaces, of both the Thaller system and beyond—were now clearly visible.

One by one, all of Francis' fellow sentients vanished from the light as the Aeon returned them to their respective worlds. Finally, the Aeon that had enveloped them, and the sphere of light that had engulfed them, imploded into obscurity. All that remained in the still darkness of the cavern were Francis, the infant girl, and the Casius strain within her.

As his artificial eyes adjusted to the darkness, he saw a small glimmer of light at the far side of the cavern. Slowly, he navigated his way through the maze of stelae until he came upon a way out. When he emerged from the cavern, he found himself under an overcast autumn sky, in a forest of white pine, red spruce, and eastern hemlock trees. He activated his c-nex and immediately interfaced with a public data suite. He quickly discovered that he was standing on the New Brunswick trail system in Mount Carleton Provincial Park, Atlantic Canada. The date was Friday, the tenth day of October. The year was 2397 of the Common Era—two years after the great worlds-wide data crash.

Francis inspected the infant carrier and the precious little life therein; the baby girl was still serenely asleep. And as he gazed upon her sweet, cherubic face, he suddenly remembered quite vividly his own family from a previous life—his wife Ronnie, and his daughter Cathy. So Francis Hewst decided to name this beautiful little girl Veronica Catherine.

Chapter 35 – The Rainbow

Geneva, Switzerland, Earth

(Geographic Co-ordinates: N 46.133, E 6.108)

Wednesday, 16 April 2436 CE

Time: 1108 Zulu

The gentle late-morning shower tapered off, and the rain clouds slowly broke, giving way to modest previews of blue sky. But Catherine Hewst and Robertson Trendle remained dry and at ease as they sat under the awning of Café Lac Léman, a sidewalk café. Dressed in civvies, the two former officers sat at a table, savoring some coffee and flan caramel, and enjoying the view of colorful sailboats that dotted Lake Geneva.

Noticing that Hewst's cup was empty, the café waitron asked, "*Voudriez-vous une autre tasse de café, Madame?*"

"*Oui, s'il vous plaît,*" she answered, "*avec un petit amaretto.*"

Taking the empty cup from the table, the waitron said, "*Avec plaisir.*" He then asked Trendle, "*Et pour vous, monsieur?*"

Handing his cup to the waitron, Trendle answered, "*Non, je vais bien, merci.*"

As the waitron left to procure a fresh cup, Hewst turned to her friend and said, "It's so good to see you again, Rob. I'm so glad you gave me a call this morning. What brings you to Geneva?"

"Mars is being reinstated as a member-world of the Terrestrial Assembly today," Trendle answered. "A delegation from the Martian Alliance is here to sign the Declaration of Admission. The prime minister asked me to serve as a delegate for the Terrestrial Assembly during the signing ceremony later this afternoon."

"I was surprised when I heard that you retired from the Defense Force," she said. "The academy won't be the same without you."

"It's time for younger hands to take the helm," he confided. "I'm confident that Admiral Pettit will make an exceptional superintendent."

Hewst thought for a moment and realized that she was acquainted with the admiral's name. "Renée Pettit, of the *Aldebaran*?"

"Formerly, aye," he answered. "You know her?"

Hewst smiled reminiscently. "Yes, I had the pleasure of meeting her six years ago when the *Aldebaran* ferried me and Níyol to Mars."

Trendle continued, "She wants me to ask you to come back and teach for the academy. She said that it would be a great honor to have an interplanetary hero on the faculty."

Hewst laughed awkwardly. "I'm no hero."

"Evidently, there are billions of people who think otherwise," he responded. "They're alive because you committed three and a half years of your life traveling throughout the solar system just to save as many people as possible from the Casius pathogen."

"They weren't saved because of me," she remarked. "They were saved by this special strain of the Casius organelle that I'm carrying around inside my cells."

"I'm not sure I understand how that works," Trendle said as he took a taste of his flan. "I read in my intelligence briefs that the organelles work like microscopic transceivers that trigger the pathogen. But the special strain inside *you* transmits an electromagnetic signal that counteracts the pathogen."

"That's basically how the xenopathologists of IPHA explained it to me," she confirmed.

"Well, if that's the case, why didn't IPHA simply record the signal that that strain inside you is transmitting and broadcast it everywhere?" he inquired. "Why did IPHA take three and a half years of your life flying you from world to world, city to city?"

Hewst gestured toward her necklace and replied, "According to the message that my father encoded in this pendant, Casius is not a pathogen. Its organelles form a single consciousness; Casius is a sentient life form. And IPHA's own subsequent research seems to confirm this. The organelles

434

appear to communicate with a complex language system. They don't just respond to a simple transmission; they actually talk to each other." She continued, "I don't know why I seem to be the only person who has this unique strain of the organelle, but it's the reason that I had to go on a grand tour of the solar system. Casius requires a living host to carry a viable strain that could actually converse with other organelles. A prerecorded signal wouldn't work. It would be like you and me trying to have a conversation with an automated c-nex message."

"And that's why you're a hero to so many," Trendle returned. "You selflessly gave so much of yourself just to save others."

"Traveling the solar system wasn't such a hardship," she confessed. "I had Níyol with me the entire time looking after me." She then added, "Besides, if someone has the means to help others, doesn't that person also have a moral obligation to do so? Compassion is not just ours to dispense capriciously, it is the worlds' right to receive."

Presently, the waitron returned with a fresh cup of coffee in hand and set it before Hewst. "*Café avec un peu d'amaretto.*"

"*Merci beaucoup,*" Hewst replied even as the waitron was moving on to serve other patrons.

After taking another taste of his flan, Trendle commented, "You mentioned the pendant that your father gave you. His posthumous message was also among the items in my intelligence briefs. When I read the text that the meta-droid deciphered from the DNA in your pendant, I was mystified. How the hell did your father know about Casius, or about Columba Noachi? The project wasn't even begun until years after his death. For that matter, how did he know when his own life would end?"

Hewst paused in deep thought. "I've spent years trying to make sense of it all," she finally answered. "And if there is any sense to be made, it eludes me. So I've just decided to call it an act of God."

"There are billions of people who think *you're* an act of God," replied Trendle, "and I'm one who thinks so too. Nineteen cities across the solar system have erected monuments in your honor. I've even heard of a new cult on Ganymede that venerates you as some kind of prophet, or as the second coming of Christ." He humorously added, "They call themselves Hewstians."

"Yes, I've heard that rumor," she acknowledged with feigned grin. "But I guess it all balances out; I've been told that the New Jerusalem cult, or what's left of it, has declared me the Antichrist." She added, "Defense Intelligence informed me that the terrorists have placed a bounty for my head on a platter."

"I don't think you have anything to worry about from New Jerusalem," he snickered. "Most of those religious fanatics were wiped out either by the Martian Global Guard or by their untimely exposure to active Casius organelles. Even their stratogen hitman who attacked you at Porco Station was found dead among the scorched shuttle-wreckage that careened through Titan's atmosphere. The few allegiants who remain may talk tough, but in reality they're too feckless and too afraid to have you killed."

"Afraid?" she wondered. "Why would they be afraid of me?"

Undauntedly, Trendle explained, "They're afraid that if you die, the pathogen might return and wipe the rest of them out."

Hewst chuckled. "I seriously doubt that New Jerusalem, or anyone else, has anything to worry about. Even if something should happen to me, I doubt the threat will return. The strain has already sent its message; humankind and Casius are at peace." She then conceded, "I just pray that humankind will learn Casius' complex language. Then, we might someday communicate with them, and maintain the peace between the species. Perhaps someday we'll even learn how to live in communion with each other. Perhaps we'll learn to live together as God intended."

"I'm sure we'll learn their language," he said confidently. "Human beings are quite intelligent."

"So you think our intelligence will save us?" she skeptically asked.

"Of course," Trendle replied. "It's the one thing we have going for us. Evolution didn't give us claws or fangs. Natural selection didn't make us the strongest or the fastest. But it did make us the most intelligent species ever to exist. That's our competitive advantage. Our intelligence is what makes us the fittest for survival. The dinosaurs were wiped out because they had no natural defenses against a ten-kilometer asteroid that struck the earth. But because of our natural intelligence, we won't ever suffer the fate of the T-Rex; we have the know-how to move worlds. Our ability to comprehend the nature of the universe has made us masters of the universe."

Hewst almost always valued the counsel of her friend, but in this case, she regarded his confidence in human intelligence as hubristic. "Our intellect is indeed a gift," she admitted, "and I'm sincerely grateful for it. But if the human race is to survive, it won't be because we're rational creatures. It won't be because of our ability to reason our way out of extinction. I believe it'll be because of our capacity for compassion—our capacity to see ourselves in each other."

Before Trendle could ask his friend to say more about her convictions, their conversation was suddenly interrupted. Just as a man and his young daughter were walking by the café, the little girl bolted from her father's side and ran to Hewst. "Mommy! Mommy!" the little girl shouted.

"Hey, princess," Hewst greeted as she hugged the little girl. "What are you doing here?"

"I'm sorry for the intrusion," said Kiiswood—the man who was walking with the little girl. "She saw you sitting here at the café, and she just ran right to you."

"Daddy and I are going to play in the park," the little girl announced.

"I promised her that I'd take her to the park if it stopped raining," Kiiswood expounded.

"Níyol, this is my old friend Robertson Trendle," Hewst introduced.

Kiiswood extended his hand and said, "It's an honor to meet you, Admiral."

"I'm retired," Trendle replied as he shook his hand. "You can call me Rob."

"Call me Níyol," Kiiswood invited. "I understand that I have you to thank for getting me out of the brig several years ago."

With typical childlike curiosity, the little girl asked, "What's the brig?"

Hewst usually encouraged her daughter's inquisitiveness, but on this occasion, she decided that her question about the brig would be better answered at a later time. Instead, Hewst opted to use this opportunity to make introductions. "Rob, this is our daughter, Evie."

"Hello, Evie," Trendle greeted with a smile, "you're a very pretty little girl."

"I know," Evie proudly professed. "My daddy tells me that all the time."

Trendle's smile widened. "And how old are you, Evie?" he asked.

"I'm five," she declared.

"No, you *want* to be five," Kiiswood fondly corrected. "How old are you really?"

Reluctantly, Evie admitted, "I'm really four."

"Well, you're a very precocious four," Trendle noted.

"I know," the little girl replied, "my daddy tells me that too."

Suddenly, the clouds parted and the sun emerged. "Come on, princess," said Kiiswood, as he gestured to his daughter to follow him. "Let mommy and Mr. Rob visit, while you and I go play in the park."

"Okay. Bye, Mommy," she said as, again, she hugged Hewst. And just before she turned to leave, Evie said to Trendle, "Mr. Rob, I'm sorry I said I was five. The inside-people say I should not say things unless they're true." She then ran off with Kiiswood for the park.

Trendle was intrigued by the little girl's contrition. In a soft-spoken voice, he asked Hewst, "The inside-people?"

"The inside-people are the people who live inside all of us," Hewst answered with a grin, "or so Evie says." She continued, "It's not uncommon for four-year-olds to have imaginary friends. Still, she's the daughter of parents who were both . . ." Hewst hesitated. ". . . who were both *changed* by an incorporeal presence. So I can't help but wonder what kind of an effect that might have on her. Perhaps she really can perceive things that the rest of us can't."

Trendle had no response for his friend, so he simply sat quiet. Then, eating the last morsel of flan from his dessert dish, he asked, "Are you sure I can't convince you to come back to the academy? Admiral Pettit will be disappointed."

After a sip or two of her coffee, Hewst replied, "I admit, it's a tempting offer. I do miss teaching; and I miss the students. But the director of the Bureau of Archives and Antiquities offered me this wonderful opportunity to study these ancient scrolls—it's a paleographer's dream come true."

Trendle discreetly wiped his mouth with his napkin. "I thought Project Columba Noachi confiscated everything in the Federal Archives Library," he remarked. "I thought they shipped everything out on the interstellar ark, along with all the rest of the antiquities. What scrolls are left to study?"

"When Alex, Níyol, and I set out for Belshazzar Station from that cave at Hellas Planitia, we decided to leave our retrieval case behind. Since then, I had forgotten all about it." Hewst continued, "But about a year and a half ago, a reconnaissance team with the Martian Global Guard came across the case and discovered that it was stuffed full of ancient religious scrolls and manuscripts." She added, "Apparently, when the Aeons vanished with their cavern, they left us a parting gift."

"Why leave us religious scrolls written by our own ancient ancestors?" he pondered with a furrowed brow. "Why not leave us with some profound wisdom from among the stars instead?"

"Perhaps that's precisely what they did." She expounded, "Religion is a means toward our ultimate transcendence; it's the means of moving from what we are to what we ought to be. Perhaps the Aeons are reminding us of something that we've forgotten."

"And what is it that we've forgotten?"

Hewst seemed lost for a moment as she stared out at the Genevan skyline. The rain had given way to the brilliant colors of a rainbow, and she was seized by its resplendence. "We've forgotten that there is no love without compassion," she finally answered. "And there's no compassion without sacrifice."

"You know, Catherine, I don't believe that you're the second coming," he said as he, too, stared out at the rainbow. "But I do believe you have the vision of angels; you always see the best in humanity."

Hewst then glanced down from the rainbow to the city park just down the street and to the playground therein. "That's kind of you to say, Rob," she stated as her eyes singled out Evie from among all the other playing children. "I confess that I don't always see the best in humanity. But when I do, I see her."